OFFLINING

GJ WEINSTEIN

OFFLINING

Copyright © 2023 by GJ Weinstein.

This is a work of fiction. Names, characters, places, and incidents are products of the author's imagination or are used fictitiously and are not to be construed as real. Any resemblance to actual events, locales, organizations, or persons, living or dead, is entirely coincidental.

All rights reserved. No part of this book may be used or reproduced in any manner whatsoever without written permission except in the case of brief quotations embodied in critical articles and reviews. Reproduction requests may be sent to soulsourcepress@gmail.com

ISBN 978-1-960562-01-2

Published by Soul Source Press

Cover Design by Marta Dec Art and Design
Interior ornaments by Marta Dec Art and Design

For Kim, whose laughter while reading *Offlining* told me at least one person would not be completely horrified by this book.

CHAPTER ONE

It took a lot to get Jerusalem Pix out of his parents' condo. He knew he could fixate a little. One time, he'd ignored a bomb threat so he could level up in CyberMinions V: Attack of the Big-Ass Drones. Still, when the girl he'd been crushing on since high school asked him to do her a favor, Jeru felt like one of those characters he loved to roleplay. A knight being sent on a quest, a warrior undertaking a mission. Nobody offline had ever asked anything of him before. No one had needed him.

Kneading his prodigious gut with worry, Jeru slouched in the newly armored railcar as the northern Atlanta suburbs shot past with numbing uniformity. Strip mall, office park, charred ruin, parking garage, strip mall, chain restaurant, twisted wreckage, strip mall. He couldn't avoid his reflection in the blast-proof window, the accusatory look in his dull green eyes that seemed to say, "You fosh, what are you doing? You're no hero."

The twenty-year-old wiped sweat from his forehead and wished his current adventure were only another video game where he could win the day and get the girl. Lots of fun in the GameSphere, but offlining sucked so far.

The world was so different from what he vaguely remembered. When did the air start smelling like smoke and tasting gritty? Colors looked washed out; everything he touched was hard and scuffed and grimy.

That was the beauty of the GameSphere: you could pursue a band of goblins through a castle, everyone firing arrows or swinging axes, and when you did it again, the scenery would be as clean and fresh as the day it was programmed. Plus, styles weren't always changing. Coders picked a theme and stuck with it. Elves weren't sporting leather one day and homespun the next. So here he was, wearing his usual black polo shirt and matching jeans, but white was now the new black. Everybody else on the train wore it, down to their milk-colored tennis shoes.

He'd forgotten how big the outside world was, too, and how long it took to get from one place to another. Life offline was so inconvenient, confusing, and life-threatening. With no save points or undo button.

To boost his courage, he snuck another glance at the Plasmotix screen, palmed in his hand to prevent his fellow passengers from seeing it, and tapped the device with his thumb. After the Plasmotix tagline (*Small has never been so sexy*™) flashed, he watched the 3-D movie of tanned and toned Geneva Bledsoe soaking in a candle-lit bathtub, red hair slick and dark against her forehead and neck. Her low voice tickled his inner ear, where the tiny wireless speaker nestled, as she asked him to "do this one little thing for me. Please." At the end of her speech, she emerged, dripping and glistening and looking into the camera without shame.

Admittedly, Geneva's nakedness had sealed the deal. She must've known knights and warriors needed a little push. Too bad her "one little thing" was stopping her twin brother Cairo—Jeru's childhood best friend—from becoming the next suicide bomber to rock Atlanta.

Feeling no braver and not even aroused after this hundredth viewing, Jeru rolled up the screen and pushed it into his jeans pocket. He returned his gaze outside. Strip mall, office park, smoking pit, flattened high-rise, gaping crater, wrecked condo, strip mall. Must be getting nearer to the city. Fortunately, he'd used the money intended for his college tuition to invest in virtual real estate instead of brick-and-mortar properties. So far, the terrorists didn't care about blowing up pretend discos floating above mythical islands.

When he'd been at the northernmost terminal, he had seen Cairo board a few cars ahead. Maybe he could talk his old buddy into abandoning this insanity even before the train stopped. He rehearsed his pitch: quit the suicide cult and go back to a normal life of undertaking fantasy quests and screwing nubile aliens.

Jeru grunted as he hefted himself off the plastic seat. Across the aisle, a skinny grandmotherly type, all in white, glanced up from her own Plasmotix screen and sneered at him with disgust. He yanked his shirt over his stomach and lurched to the end of the cabin.

The only other person wearing black blocked the passageway: a huge Anti-Terror cop, suited in full tactical gear. His weapons alone would've cost a million credits in Zombie Cotillion III.

Jeru said, "Uh, sorry, but I sort of need to get to the next car."

"You shall not pass."

Jeru laughed with relief. Finally, somebody from his world. "That's totally blazing. I'd love a job where I got to say that all day. Seriously though—"

He tried to sidle by, but the cop put a hand on one of several pistols and echoed Gandalf again without irony.

As Jeru stumbled back, now awash in sweat, a woman's voice from the loudspeakers announced the station they were approaching. He retreated to the double doors in case it was Cairo's stop and wiped his face again. The only good thing about wearing black was that it hid the perspiration that coated his bulk. Maybe he needed to go on that Aiken's Diet, where his body would serve as the host organism to a mutant tapeworm (*Fastest weight loss EVER™*).

As the train coasted to a halt beside a dingy subway platform, the woman's pre-recorded voice sounded from the loudspeakers again. "Welcome to Five Points, for boutiques and bistros, museums and medical care, courthouses and karaoke. And access to Old Town."

"As if they'd let us into the Kingdom anymore," Jeru muttered. However, he suspected Bledsoe's superiors had aimed Cairo like a guided missile at that enclave of the super-rich.

Bledsoe's church, the Real Salvation Army, had fought the überright-wing and left-wing extremists with its own militia and a cult of suicide bombers, but, according to Geneva, the RSA was now targeting the ultra-wealthy too. If radicals on all sides were engaged in a race to see who could reach martyrdom first, these "PentaHostiles" were winning.

Of course, he only had Geneva's word that her twin had gone on a crusade to slaughter the unworthy one percent. It didn't seem like Cairo's style, but Jeru had lost touch with him recently, having spent nearly every hour since high school graduation online, awake and asleep.

The doors parted with a sigh. Jeru shuffled onto the gritty concrete and scanned the passengers departing from the other armored railcars, searching for Geneva's brother.

Cairo Bledsoe emerged two cars ahead. His white clothes blended with everybody else, and his bleached, spiky hair disguised him well. No obvious bomb-trigger in either hand. Only his toned physique and a tan backpack distinguished him.

Jeru pursued his friend through the crowd, cursing his own sticky, lumbering body. Most people around him were at least as overweight as he was, but they carried their heft with the graceful, swaying assuredness of pachyderms, while he drooped like an overheated mastodon.

Despite the close confines, the station smelled piney-fresh. Air scrubbers clung to the high concrete roof like giant spiders. Interspersed between them were smaller, box-shaped sniffers for biological, explosive, and chemical weapons.

Passing under the last of these threat detectors without prompting an alarm, Cairo reached the exit and disappeared in the daylight. Jeru hurried to catch up. Either Geneva was wrong about the bomb, or the RSA had given her brother a way to shield it.

Jeru emerged on the plaza, which sprawled under the always-bleak sky. The trillions of particles fired into the atmosphere to stop global warming had left the sun looking no brighter than a flashlight in a fogbank. Beneath the murky blanket of white, the air was hot and humid, and it tasted like ash.

He stumbled across imitation cobblestones, as slippery as upside-down plastic bowls underfoot. At regular intervals, synthetic trees grew according to their fractal programming, each unfurling the same number of emerald leaves from identical limbs.

The diehards on their way to the stores marched together in their own arithmetic symmetry. Cairo Bledsoe was camouflaged somewhere among them. In response to the latest threat—"suicide sneezers"—some wore retro respirator masks with silk-screened logos and brand names.

Police officers ambled through the army of civilians, while stationary National Guardsmen perspired in full battle gear. Jeru figured that even if he could've convinced them of Cairo's mission, his friend would soon be long gone. And Geneva had contacted him instead of calling the police out of fear they would shoot her twin on sight.

"Do this one little thing for me," she'd said. Did real heroes feel so inept, so incompetent—so scared? Was the secret to just blunder forward?

He caught sight of Cairo stepping onto a crosswalk, then lost him again in the crowd. Wheezing as he ran, he felt like he might pass out from exertion. Running in video games was a helluva lot easier. Meanwhile, Bledsoe loped with ease across Peachtree Street, weaving between much stouter people. Damn, that suicide cult really kept him in shape.

The crosswalk sign counted down the number of seconds remaining before the automated Traffic Grid unleashed cars on either side of the intersection. Six, five, four...

Jeru dashed to the curb, but the counter reached zero and activated a sonic fence from StaySafe (*Like a backhand from God*™) that slapped the front of his body, keeping him from lunging into traffic.

Many of the vehicles passing him looked like rooms on wheels. Their occupants watched TV, continued office work, or napped in their seat while the Grid steered them through the busy downtown. They zipped by Jeru without a sound except for the friction of recycled tires on the road.

Shifting from foot to foot, Jeru caught glimpses of Cairo. The true believer was gliding far up the block, the sidewalk he navigated a rainbow of colors moving at different speeds. Only Bledsoe picked up his feet as he swept past the other pedestrians: a Christian soldier marching onward.

"Come on, come on," Jeru snapped at the Grid hardware mounted on a nearby pole. Finally, it halted traffic again. He scurried across the intersection and leaped onto the plum-colored glidepath, the fastest one. Arms pinwheeling, he staggered but at last regained his balance and started running again. With the speed of the conveyor and his thudding gait, he raced along at ten miles an hour. Now this felt more like a game. If he could forget he was pursuing a brainwashed RSA bomber, it would be totally blazing.

Ahead, the rows of shops, eateries, and offices gave way to the perimeter of a park with genuine trees: the nearest entrance to the Kingdom. Atlanta's Old Town already contained the tallest buildings, and now the wealthiest one percent were annexing the best tourist attractions for themselves and converting them to suit their tastes: a recent undercover recording posted online showed genetically engineered mermaids frolicking with horny dolphins in the Georgia Aquarium.

At the edge of the park, two technicians in jumpsuits worked on a deactivated sonic fence. The closest security guard had turned his back to the street while he engaged in a shouting match with a pushcart vendor selling BBQ sandwiches and sex toys. Half a block down, Cairo waltzed through the decommissioned fence and among the trees beyond, aiming toward the towers of the ultra-rich.

Jeru considered calling out to the rent-a-cop or the workers to stop the guy with the backpack, but some of them could be RSA, too, there to create a means for Cairo to get in. As soon as the traffic cleared, Jeru followed, cursing himself for getting involved in such madness.

His friend reached a skyscraper and rounded its corner, disappearing again. To catch up, Jeru avoided the twisty walking paths and instead cut straight through the woods, but he kept tripping over roots and recoiling from the claw-like branches. Nature sure was a pain. No wonder the government had gotten rid of it. Apparently, though, the residents of the Kingdom had their own ideas about nature—and probably their own government.

Jeru crashed through the final thicket of shrubs. He hurried around the gigantic marble cornerstone of the office tower.

Cairo stood facing him.

Still crisp in his all-white attire, he wasn't even breathing hard. Like Geneva, her twin had a symmetrical, elfin face. The short, bleached hair suited him. He said, "What do you want, Jerusalem?"

The sweat that soaked Jeru's rumpled shirt smelled like onions. He wiped his face with a forearm and said, "I know what's in your backpack."

"You followed me from the burbs so you could steal my lunch?"

Jeru took a few more deep breaths. "Geneva told me about the bomb."

"What bomb?"

"Stop pretending, Cai. Leave the pack here. We'll tip the police, and they'll take care of it."

Cairo said, "Geneva's crazy. She's always been a lobotomo." He shrugged the rucksack higher on his shoulders. "And why did she reach out to *you* anyway? You're an oversized gerbil. You geek-out over the latest operating system."

"Maybe she thought I could help. Put that down, and we'll go shoot some mutants."

"I'll bet she sent you something kinky. Nothing else would get you out of your folks' condo. Did she promise you what you've been praying for since you finally hit puberty?"

"Quit it," Jeru said, voice quavering. "Why do you wanna blow up a bunch of rich kids?"

"I'd never kill children—they're our future." Cairo smiled like a choirboy. "If I did have a bomb, though, how about I detonate it now? Take us out along with a chunk of this building. I bet Geneva will wear something slinky to your funeral." He clicked a button on his wristwatch.

Jeru felt as much as heard a high-pitched tone: the whine of electronics coming to life. Maybe explosives being armed. He stumbled backward and collided with the marble façade.

"Look who's the big hero now." Cairo snorted. "Go home and tell Geneva you stopped me. Collect whatever reward she promised. By the time she learns the truth, she'll be through with you anyway."

He started toward the tree-lined boulevard, which hummed with streamlined cars in unfamiliar styles and delivery trucks that advertised brands Jeru had never heard of. Calling over his shoulder, Cairo said, "God's forgiven me for a bunch of things, Jeru. He'll thank me in person for this one."

"Cai!"

"The blast range is two hundred feet," Cairo warned. "I'd feel bad if I ruined your snappy outfit." He reached a sidewalk alongside the bustling street and headed west.

Stunned by the reality of the bomb, Jeru slumped against the wall. Time to do the smart thing and go crashing back through the underbrush. No . . . he couldn't just let innocent people die, even rich ones. Though he wasn't a hero, he could pretend. It had gotten him this far.

With legs and lungs protesting, he began to jog after his former friend again. The pedestrians who strolled by—not riding glidepaths, but actually walking—looked athletic and fit in their brightly colored clothes. Despite his all-white ensemble, Cairo blended in. Everybody stared at Jeru as he blundered past.

Should he start yelling that Cairo had a bomb? Who would believe him? If anyone looked like a lobotomo, he did. He figured he only had a few more minutes before a security patrol stopped him.

He'd figured wrong. A chunky black van approached in the oncoming traffic. It slowed momentarily, then blue and white lights flashed and strobed all over its surfaces. The driver accelerated toward Jeru.

With nothing left to lose, he ran directly at the threat. Such insanity always surprised his enemies online, so what the hell. As in the GameSphere, he bellowed as he charged.

The driver swerved, and the van shot past Jeru. It screeched to a halt as he barreled back onto the sidewalk and closed the distance with Cairo, who had stopped to witness Jeru's likely arrest.

Now Cairo took off running as well. "I'll blow you to hell," he yelled over his shoulder and held up his hands, index finger poised beside his watch.

The people nearby screamed and ran into the closest buildings. At the end of the block, a crossing guard stopped traffic for a line of schoolgirls in emerald tunics and plaid skirts who held hands as they made their way into the street. The girls all looked identical, like they were appearing in an ad for a cloning clinic. Maybe they were.

Jeru shouted, "No kids, Cai. You promised!"

Cairo glanced back, frowning. The crossing guard had let through a sleek white limousine before halting the rest of the cars. Cairo disappeared behind a large delivery truck parked at the curb and darted into the street, heading for the limo.

As Jeru ran on a tangent to cut him off, he tried not to think about the explosives that would vaporize him in an instant.

The limo skidded sideways, and Cairo thudded against the long front fender. His arms splayed in front of him, and his face bounced off the hood.

Jeru grabbed him by the shoulder straps and pulled him off the car. Blood from Cairo's nose left a long streak across the bright white paintwork.

Sirens wailing now, the van stopped a dozen yards from them.

Cairo reached for his watch.

Jeru spun him in a tight circle, the backpack pressed between them. Cairo's arms flung outward with the centrifugal force. Tiring quickly, Jeru knew as soon as he slowed down, Cairo would be able to detonate the bomb.

"Jeru, let me go!"

In the blur of spinning, Jeru remembered the large delivery truck at the curb. It sat high on massive tires. Lots of clearance under the chassis. Maybe it would absorb some of the blast.

Cairo screamed, "Let me go, you fat fosh."

With a grunt, Jeru released the straps and stumbled to a dizzy halt.

Cairo tumbled across the pavement. Flailing against his momentum, he rolled sideways beneath the truck. Only his hand with the watch stuck out. His other hand closed around it.

With dragon-like roar, Jeru's world turned to fire.

The truck rocketed ten feet into the air as the explosion seared his eyes and knocked him onto his butt. His head banged against the armored side of the limo. Shrapnel zinged around him and something hit his chest like a fist. Looking down, he saw that it was indeed a fist, with Cairo's wristwatch strapped near the end of the bloody stump.

Jeru choked on bile surging up his throat and coughed from the dense, acrid smoke pouring out of the crater where the burning remains of the truck had crash-landed. Deafened as he was from the blast, the sirens and people's screams sounded far away. Oddly, he felt okay otherwise. Sort of dreamy and calm.

Checking himself for wounds, Jeru noticed someone's left arm lying close by. Not Cairo's: it was much too plump. The hand stretched in futility for something. Something just out of reach.

Then he noticed the ragged flesh and bone below his left elbow. So much blood and more coming. Strange that he felt at peace. Happy even. The same feeling he got whenever he leveled up in the GameSphere.

A police officer appeared in a black helmet and a Kevlar one-piece that crinkled like foil as he kneeled beside Jeru. The cop put a plastic bag around the gory wound, and the synthetic tightened, sealing against what was left of Jeru's forearm.

"What brand is that?" Jeru heard himself ask. "There's nothing like it at home."

The policeman said, "PolyHealth: *Better solutions for better people.*" He continued to move his lips, but someone switched his volume to Mute as Jeru felt consciousness sliding away.

Beside him, the back door of the limo opened and two slender ankles above a pair of glass-like spike heels appeared. A slim, blond teenager in a party dress peered down, prettier than a thousand Geneva Bledsoes despite her frown of concern. Her lips moved, forming sensuous O's and beguiling curves, but he couldn't hear anything except the fading sound of his heartbeat.

He wanted to tell the golden-haired angel not to let anyone forget his arm, but she had read his mind. Before Jeru passed out, he could've sworn she scooped it up and cradled it like it was their baby.

CHAPTER TWO

Reverend Ross Gimbel, founder of the Real Salvation Army, sat on a park bench, watching the teenagers at play. He bent over to scratch a mosquito bite on his ankle. In a nod to the latest evangelist fashions, he'd endured a laser-applied tattoo of solid black for each leg, from shin to big toe. According to his image consultant, the look conveyed the message, "I'm so busy and successful working for God, I don't have time to pick out socks."

His lovers—including several of his deacons' wives—had said he looked like a faun, with his mischievous amber eyes, Van Dyke beard, and feet now the color of hooves. Those hell-bound secular humanists in the press used more satanic comparisons for the leader of the group they'd dubbed the "PentaHostiles."

Leaning over farther, Gimbel glanced under the bench and noted the heavy chain and thick bolts that secured it to the concrete. Excellent. He always recruited well in rough boroughs like Buckhead. Those teens would try anything once, and the RSA missions he had in mind required no return engagements.

Nearby, the teenagers at play comprised a dozen boys, dressed in white tee shirts and white jeans, who should've been yawning through their senior high school lessons instead of revving up AI-controlled BattleBoards (*The Killer Ride*™). With one foot on their artificially intelligent skateboards, the minimally intelligent kids faced off on either side of opposing concrete ramps. Their rocket-propelled toys doubled as stereos and blasted out dueling anthems in the latest music fad, a fusion of rap and klezmer that young people called "krap."

Happily devoid of safety gear or common sense, the boys zoomed up the steep slopes. They collided in midair and kick-boxed and karate-chopped each other before tumbling into the gap between the ramps. After picking themselves up, they taunted and gloated, while stealing glances at their bloody scrapes and fresh bruises. Meanwhile, their skateboards continued to skirmish at their feet. Chomping, slashing, and breathing fire in one case, the souped-up machines followed their psychopathic programming and tried to annihilate their opposition. Gimbel loved it as much as the teens appeared to.

One of the BattleBoards finally sawed its AI opponent in half. The boys clicked their remotes to end the melee and tromped off to opposing sides of the ramps again. While they inspected the damage to their rides, the owner of the sole casualty shuffled over to a trashcan and tossed in his bisected board. The lad plopped onto a bench not far from where he and his friends had opened a fire hydrant, creating a horizontal geyser.

The sight of so much wasted water would've shocked Gimbel when he was a boy, but no longer. Water shortages had ceased to exist in Atlanta ever since the governor sent her National Guardsmen, battle-hardened after twenty years in Iran and Syria, across state borders to seize control of the Coosa River in Alabama and the Tennessee River up north. The Second War Between the States had lasted only a week. When terrorist attacks ramped up around the world on 12/26, everyone quickly forgot the crisis. A treaty ratifying the new state boundaries was signed in a quiet, dignified ceremony at Six Flags Over Georgia. To celebrate, Atlantans turned on their taps and left them running.

The BattleBoard loser morosely splashed his white sneakers in the presumably endless supply of drinking water washing down a storm drain while his friends continued to maim each other on the skate ramps. Gimbel knew they'd all be much happier in heaven. With his help, they'd get there ASAP.

Hopefully Cairo Bledsoe was propelling the cause further down the fast lane to Armageddon.

Gimbel slid his FarSighters (*See what happens next*™) from their perch on his forehead until they covered his eyes like oversized sunglasses. The device projected wrap-around, hi-res images while the earpieces relayed "virtual 360" sound. He chewed the insides of his cheeks as the camera encased in Cairo Bledsoe's shirt button transmitted a maddening turn of events: instead of executing his mission, Bledsoe was taunting some fat guy he called "Jerusalem."

On the concrete ramps, the teenagers zoomed toward another devastating collision, but Gimbel couldn't enjoy it. He tasted blood from his gnawed skin while the real disaster unfolded. The FarSighters displayed a queasy blur of spinning as Jerusalem, acting like a deranged dance partner, whirled Bledsoe around.

Furious, Gimbel twisted his compostable sack from Eden's Toyshop in both hands, mangling the RSA action figure purchased that morning for his nephew. He could've gotten the Bible-and-grenade-toting Crusader at cost, of course, but he always did his part to support the local economy.

Through the earpiece speakers, Bledsoe shouted, "Let me go, you fat fosh."

Gimbel sighed. Obviously, his lectures on "martyr dignity" had been forgotten along with his strategies and tactics seminars. And Bledsoe had been the smartest in his class.

The image Gimbel watched suddenly tumbled sideways, rolling over and over—alternating between white sky and black pavement—as Bledsoe grunted. An instant of utter darkness followed, and then the camera refocused on an extreme close-up of smooth macadam inlaid with mica. Then the image went dark for good. A moment later, Gimbel heard a distant explosion from the south, in the direction of Old Town. The boys didn't even flinch. Instead, they turned up their krap and continued to battle.

"Transmission interrupted," the FarSighters reported in a calm voice, the same tone that Bledsoe should've maintained all along. The picture dissolved, leaving Gimbel with a tinted view of the teenagers cheering. The BattleBoard with the flamethrower had malfunctioned and incinerated itself. Even the board's owner applauded the pyrotechnics.

Gimbel slid the FarSighters back up to his forehead where they clung like shades for a second pair of eyes. He sucked the blood from his freshly bleached teeth and wondered what Jesus would do.

"Mr. Grumble?" A chubby boy of eighteen or so, dressed in a dirt-streaked white pullover and corduroys, shifted from sneaker to sneaker, both white and wet, one a high-top, the other a low-rider.

Though tempted to lash out, Gimbel reined in his temper and took a closer look at the teen: it was the one whose board had been sawn in half. The lad wore the soggy basketball shoe on his left foot. Did that signal something? Though Gimbel's congregation included numerous young people, they always seemed to morph their codes of hipness a moment before he caught on. It was maddening. He said, "What can I do for you?"

"I watch your blog all the time and love it when you preach the gospel and talk politics and give dating tips, and my mom likes it when you tie-in celebrity news with scripture and—"

"And you'd like to video a 'hello' from me?"

"Your v-Hi? Yes, sir!" He detached from his hip-holster a grimy, battered All-n-1, told it to start recording, and pointed the communicator/entertainer/BFF in Gimbel's direction. The split-screen camera would also capture his selfie in reaction to the v-Hi.

"You first." Gimbel brought out his own, the latest model, and summoned the Video/Voice Recipient Terms of Usage Agreement to the screen. "State your full name, age, and National ID Number. Then, read the statement there."

The kid's posture and tone turned last-century robotic as he recited, "I'm London Johnson, but everybody calls me Lun, and I'm eighteen though my mom says I don't act my age, which I don't even know what that means really."

He prattled on in that vein for another few minutes before reciting his nine-digit ID and reading the Terms, promising not to use any frame of video or syllable Gimbel uttered for any purpose not expressly stated in the agreement, which included no authorized uses, only prohibitions.

Even playing it back to himself was a violation and grounds for a lawsuit. Lun finished his mechanical-man recitation, and Gimbel logged his statement.

"Now then," Gimbel said, flashing his teeth for Lun's camera, hoping he'd sucked away the last of the blood. "This is Reverend Ross Gimbel, founder of the Real Salvation Army. Hello to Lun and Mr. and Mrs. Johnson and all the other Johnsons, big and small. Pray for our country, go to church, live at the foot of the cross, and boycott the heretic corporations because they're of the Devil and only benefit the wealthiest one percent. See my website for a constantly updated list. God bless!"

"Totally blazing," Lun said, lowering the device. "Are you letting any more folks into your church? Because me and my mom and—"

Ah, the Good Lord always provides. Lose one to the cause, gain another. Or maybe even a double handful of Johnsons. "Lun, how well do you know scripture?"

"Um, not so good, but I could study and take a test and—"

"In Luke 22:36, Jesus advises His disciples, 'If you don't have a sword, sell your cloak and buy one.' What's that mean to you?"

"Someone's having a big sale on swords, and Jesus doesn't want them to miss out?"

"Perhaps," Gimbel allowed, wondering if Lun was touched in the head. The Lord did indeed work in mysterious goddamned ways. He downshifted into lecture mode, index finger raised. "What our Savior meant was, 'Better to be cold than defenseless.' And the best defense is a good offense, right?"

"Wow, did Jesus say that too?"

"Absolutely. Here, take this." He stood and thrust the bag with the mangled RSA action figure into Lun's hands. "It just so happens that I'm looking for a bright and eager young man to help me do the Lord's bidding. Tell me, what are your favorite video games?"

"Well, I love Dragon Dirge and Zombie Brunch and Sniper Sam, which is totally blazing, and—"

The kid would need a lot of training, but his immaturity was a big plus. Watching the other teenagers speed toward eventual concussion, Gimbel told Lun about Biblical prophecy.

As he talked, he fired off silent prayers like mortar rounds, hoping that Bledsoe's bomb had at least rained down justice on that fat interloper named Jerusalem.

CHAPTER THREE

When Jeru opened his eyes, the blond angel from the limo was still looking at him. Everything else though—their surroundings, her clothes, everything—had changed. Only her lovely, perfect face remained the same. Gently arched eyebrows, flawless skin, mauve lips that curved into a sweet smile.

Her eyes shifted in color, first violet then blue, now green, but stayed keenly focused on him, as if he were the most important part of her world. This time, she wore her hair up, revealing a tender throat and the delicate wings of her collarbones. She sat on a wooden stool, dressed in a tight red blouse and turquoise slacks that showed off her athletic figure. Her perfume, a mix of vanilla and ginger, matched her sweet and spicy vibe. Somehow, his sense of smell seemed sharper than before.

Reluctant to shift his gaze away, Jeru managed to take in the scenery behind her, his vision also much improved. Floor-to-ceiling shelves held hundreds of rectangles of varying thickness. What could they be? It took a moment to come up with the word: *books*. He seemed to be on the movie set of some historical drama. Nearby were a desk and chair, apparently made from the same genuine wood as the stool, with a matching full-length mirror in the corner.

Muted sunlight from the ever-white sky seeped in through large windows. At least that hadn't changed.

Instead of his all-black outfit, short-sleeved pajamas in gunmetal blue draped loosely across his shoulders and against his body. A soft sheet covered him up to his chest. Propped upright in the large bed, he felt different, too, as if he'd grown or something, but he really couldn't concentrate for long on anything but the angel.

Her eyes now glowed yellow. She trembled a little and sighed, as if receiving a jolt of pleasure. In a husky voice, she asked, "How do you feel?"

Even his hearing was better—he caught all kinds of subtleties in her question. He swallowed to wet his throat. "I feel like somebody else."

"We'll have to fix your voice next," the angel said. She narrowed her eyes, which had turned to a shade like milk chocolate. "Without hearing it, Doc couldn't be sure how much to adjust the timbre." With a shrug, she added, "You know, like tuning a piano?"

"Huh?"

"Don't worry." She clenched his left wrist. "You'll love it."

He glanced down where she'd touched him and flashed back to Cairo Bledsoe, the bomb, and its bloody aftermath. Oh God, they hadn't been able to reattach his arm—they'd substituted some lifelike prosthetic. The fake limb, bare up to the bicep, looked tanned and sculpted with muscles. In any other circumstances he would've been willing to give his left nut for her; instead, he'd given his left arm. Strange that he could feel her warm, confident fingers.

"My arm—"

"It's yours, only better. Isn't it great?" She ran a dark red fingernail from his elbow to the back of his hand, pressing just hard enough to make a white mark that soon faded. "Don't worry, everything matches." The angel gave him an up-from-under look and a sly grin. "Everything."

Jeru raised his left hand and ran his fingers through the series of wiggles, curls, and stretches he'd do prior to a gaming tournament. If anything, his digits responded faster than before. He watched with fascination as the tendons on the back of his hand twitched. Not an ounce of flab anywhere. He made a fist and flexed, swelling his forearm and bicep until they resembled those of the heroes he embodied in the GameSphere. His unscathed right arm was equally robust.

He held out his hands to her. "You added muscles?"

"Mostly they were there already. Doc just amped them up big time and carved away the, you know, excess stuff."

"The fat."

She wrinkled her nose in agreement. Even her sneer intoxicated him. She said, "Check out the brand new you." The angel grasped the sheet and yanked it down to the foot of the bed.

He followed her gaze and covered his groin, but not quickly enough. In fascination, he watched the transparent material of his pajama bottoms slowly become blue, matching the upper portion that had been exposed to the light.

While uncovered though, he couldn't help but notice—and notice her noticing—the stranger's body to which his head was now attached. As she'd said, everything matched. Somehow, within his bulk, the "Doc" person had uncovered a tanned, toned hunk. A well-hung hunk.

Jeru tented his fingers, still shielding his not-very-privates from the appreciative, now-pewter gaze of the angel, and watched the invisible material turn opaque. Though no longer see-through, the skimpy cloth still revealed plenty of detail. He grabbed the sheet bunched at his feet and yanked it up to his waist, his reflexes blazingly quick.

"Prude," she said. "I'd always heard that burb-boys were more fun."

"What's with these clothes? I've never seen anything that can change like that."

"The Nite-n-Daze? Everyone I know wears them to bed. *You should see what they're missing.*" After she recited the apparent tagline, she gave his pajama top a tug. "Join me in the closet and we can watch everything vanish."

"But if it's dark, we won't see it."

"Well, that's the tease. It's the reason why the Great Surgeon in the Sky gave us two hands and a mouth." She sighed again and quivered. "You're blushing so hard your ears are pink."

"Are they still my ears or did this Doc guy amp them up too?" He felt the ridges and curves but couldn't remember their previous shape. The doctor probably had altered all sorts of things he would never notice. He knew exactly what his favorite GameSphere avatars looked like, but he was fuzzy about his own details.

"See for yourself." She slid off the stool and rolled the full-length mirror bedside.

Jeru touched his hands to his unfamiliar, now bearded cheeks, mouth wide open. He searched his face for anything familiar. His hair on the top of his head was cropped so short, it appeared to be coming back from a full shaving. Chocolate-brown eyes—hadn't they been dull green? The doctor possibly had left the end of his nose intact, and maybe some of his teeth, but everything else looked different.

Better, he had to admit.

The angel peeked around the mirror. "It's all you. Doc simply mined the buried treasure."

"No way this was me."

"Sure it was."

Jeru raised the sheet a few inches and glanced at his new self, once again revealed through the transparent clothes. "Listen, I'm real familiar with at least a few parts of me and—"

"So I asked for some upgrades," she said, pouting. "Mom said I could."

"Your mom was in on this? She's seen me? All of me?"

"Of course. She had some other great ideas, but I thought we'd better ask before giving you accessories. I didn't want to presume."

"*Accessories.*" He wondered if he was trapped in the GameSphere, except now he was the avatar, getting equipped for an adventure in this bizarre world. *Let's see: flamethrower, plasma grenades, ten-inch willy....*

She said, "We can scroll through the parts catalog later."

"I think I'm fine, just the way I am."

Her expression changed as quickly as her eye color, switching from enthusiastic to belligerent. Hands on slender hips, she said, "Since you're living here now, Jerry, you need to be more flexible."

She must've seen his National ID card. He said, "My friends call me Jeru."

"I like Jerry better. I'm Ellipsis."

"Is that a religion?"

"No, it's a name, you libbot."

He snorted. "That insult's so old it comes with a cane. *Fosh* is the new 'idiot.' "

"I meant asshole," she spat. "Numb nuts. Dickhead."

"*Glans*," he murmured, flinching at her sudden outrage. "It's the latest for . . . that."

Her face brightened, and she nodded, perhaps filing away the word in a mental slang folder.

He asked, "Do you mind if I call you Ellie?"

"I guess, but that name's so old it comes with a cane." Ellie executed a very businesslike handshake with him, as if she were a CEO closing a tough deal. Not the kind of formality he expected from someone who'd picked out his pecker. With her mom.

One of her comments looped back through his thoughts. "What did you mean about me living here now?"

"Just what I said. You did that really brave thing and saved my life, so I decided you should stay. To make things simpler, Mom had you declared legally dead."

He tossed up his hands. "Great. My folks think I was killed?"

"I guess. Mom sent them a sympathy zip or something. Maybe some holo-flowers."

Jeru slumped back. "I can't process all this at once." He settled on a safer topic of conversation. "How old are you anyway?"

"I've got a birthday next week. After my Making Eighteen party, Mom says you can start sleeping with me."

Jeru stared at her.

"I threw a fit over having to wait, Jerry. I mean I really fought hard, but Mom said any earlier would just be too weird."

CHAPTER FOUR

Jeru watched as another tremor ran through Ellie, and she smiled blissfully. He said, "You keep doing that."

"What?"

"Acting like you're having an . . . uh . . . a really good time."

Ellie frowned and then said, "Oh, it's my clothes." She brushed her hands down the sides of her red blouse and turquoise pants. "*Sssagers make everything feel better.*"

"Never heard of them. Are you guys living in some kind of parallel world, with brands you keep to yourselves?"

"Maybe Sssagers are so expensive they don't bother trying to sell them to OTPers."

Jeru conceded the point, still too groggy to argue. To these people, "Outside the Perimeter" clearly meant everybody outside the Kingdom, not just beyond the I-285 loop. He asked, "So, what do they do?"

"They use biofeedback to give me pleasure. I never get hot or cold. And, yeah, they make me feel good whenever I want." She grinned. "As soon as I have a sexy thought, I get a tingle in all the right places. Looking at you gives me lots of those thoughts."

Though his body still felt alien, it responded in a very familiar way. Only a lot more so. He shifted self-consciously and asked, "Are my PJs made of the same stuff?"

"No, Mom thought it would be more than you could handle at first."

Jeru shook his head. They surgically enhanced their captives, their eyes were kaleidoscopes, their clothes gave them orgasms . . . Even though he'd lived much of his recent life in fantastical worlds online, it was too much to take in. He just wanted to go home, where things were tame enough to be boring—and sane. But how to escape?

Hoping he'd think better on his feet, he eased up the sheet to shield himself from her view. He waited until the color returned to his pajamas—and until he'd deflated, which took a minute—before scooting to the edge of the bed.

Out of habit, he pushed himself off the mattress. A grunt formed in his throat as he heaved himself up, but his legs easily handled his weight. He stood taller and was much stronger than before. Hey, this wasn't bad, being in a warrior's body.

Ellie asked, "Are you okay?" She glanced at his rear, which must've been exposed by his perverse pajama bottoms.

"I'm fine." He checked in the mirror. The color was just then returning to the material covering his well-muscled rump. She grinned when he caught her still looking. It was disturbing to be treated like a sex object. Insulting and humiliating. Of course, no one had ever wanted him for his mind *or* his body before, but he felt demeaned being ogled like that.

If the tables were turned, though—if he'd fashioned a nubile Bride of Frankenstein to spec—wouldn't she have felt degraded? No doubt, he admitted. Damn, even cherished sex fantasies were now under assault.

Seeking distractions, Jeru wandered the room in bare feet, walking on nubby, ancient-looking rugs and cold wood planks. The flooring in his parents' condo had offered no contours at all. Come to think of it, everything at home was smooth, bland, and almost featureless. Who needed to feel anything? When you spent most of your time in cyberspace, even sleeping there, touching was done via keyboard or haptic gloves or with your fist around a CtrlStick (*Stick it to 'em*™). In the Kingdom, though, the ultra-rich seemed to have rediscovered texture and color.

His hands itched to touch every foreign, fascinating thing in the room. A book he slid at random from a shelf—*Moby-Dick* of all things—had a density that contradicted the airiness of fanning through the hundreds of pages. Amazing.

He walked behind Ellie and glanced out the leaded-glass window.

Spread below him, several stories down, was a broad green space with flowerbeds in undulating curves and a row of massive trees. And birds. Two bright-yellow something-or-others flitted between branches that almost reached the window. He hadn't seen real birds in ages. Maybe they were robots.

Ellie turned to face him. "What do you want to do now? You hungry?" She looked him over and shivered through another private earthquake. He doubted she was talking about food.

He wondered whether giving in would enslave him. If he and Ellie did the things he'd often daydreamed about, and as yet had only performed in the sterile dry-hump of cyberspace, maybe he'd never be allowed to go home, back to normalcy. Still . . . .

She interrupted his deliberations. "Jerry, are you gay? If so, that's totally fine, but Doc can't help me there."

"I'm not gay," he said. Being treated like a piece of ass helped him decide not to give in—not just yet anyway. Gesturing at the bed, he added, "But I'm twenty. Your mom's right about you being too young to sleep with me."

"No, too young for you to live in my bedroom. Literally sleep with me, she means." Ellie lifted her chin. "I've had sex lots of times. Since I was . . . um . . . thirteen."

Thirteen? When he was thirteen, he was hacking through three levels of child-protection software just to glimpse a bare breast. "Was that with other OTPers you kidnapped?"

"No, you glans." She looked down, focusing on her purple, high-heeled shoes. "There are lots of In-Town boys I've done it with."

"So how many did I ace out to get the top spot?"

"Who says you're at the top? Just because you're living here doesn't mean I won't necessarily see other guys."

The comment stung. It was one thing to be picked as a rich girl's stud, but to discover he was only the latest addition to a male harem was definitely not blazing.

He considered demanding an exclusive arrangement—he wouldn't be just another of her playthings. Then he had to slam on the brakes. What happened to wanting to go home?

Pissed off at his confusion as much as at Ellie, he stomped toward the door.

Only there was no door. Bookcases or antique furniture lined every wall. The twelve-foot-high ceiling featured a chandelier but no escape hatch, and the wood floor looked solid.

He'd seen enough haunted house movies to know about secret passageways, but how would he find the trigger in this . . . what did they used to call it? Oh yeah, *library*.

A rapid, full-circle survey of the room brought back awful memories of spinning Cairo around and the explosion that followed. Jeru rubbed his reattached left arm and asked, "How'd you get in here?"

"What'll you give me if I tell you?"

"A promise to come to your Making Eighteen party?"

She snorted. "You don't know anything. Doc won't let you in."

Jeru knew that pursuing her remark would plunge him into another crazy wormhole with all kinds of horrible new realities leaping out at him. If he wanted to escape the Kingdom and reclaim his life, he had to equip himself with information. Develop a strategy. As with any adventure in the GameSphere, you couldn't blunder around. You needed a plan.

Ellie, he realized, was the classic Unreliable Guide, like the White Rabbit, Gollum, or Jenna Bodacious of the 38DD Quests. The way to handle such characters was to give them a little of what they wanted, but not everything and not all at once. He walked up to Ellie and leaned close to her face. "How about we start with a kiss?"

"Where?" she challenged, though she'd begun to wring her hands.

"Uh . . . your mouth?"

"You know," she said, the bravado and finger-twisting still both on display, "the guy you blew up was probably a lot more fun."

"He blew himself up. I saved your life."

"Yeah, I bet I'll never hear the end of that one." Despite this grousing, her pink tongue darted out to wet her lips.

Jeru took that as a "yes" and tilted his head a few degrees and then a few more. He'd kissed plenty, but only in cyberspace. Well, his favorite avatar Bane—a Conan the Barbarian look-alike—really had all the fun, mouthing other electronic entities. And who knew if the recipient had really been a woman or a dude or an AI construct. Best not to think about that.

Touching his mouth to Ellie's startled him at first. Her lipstick tasted like strawberries. Those virtual reality gimmicks had it all wrong—kissing involved so much contour, texture, and movement: soft moistness, the give and flex of his mouth and hers as they eased into a slow, natural rhythm. By comparison, smooching in cyberspace was like kissing a screen.

The tips of their tongues bumped and retreated for an instant before meeting again inside his mouth. Her hands, rigid as claws, scraped against his back and shoulders as if she were unsure of how to touch him. Maybe she'd faked the whole sexpot routine. Maybe she also had never kissed anyone before. Maybe she felt as scared and excited as he did.

Jeru wrapped his arms around her, cradling her head and letting the silky golden hair cascade over his skin. He slid one hand down the ridge of her spine, heading for the waistband of her slacks. She held him tight and sighed, a sound that seemed to express something much deeper than pleasure or lust. He wasn't sure what it meant, but he knew this was important to her—*he* was important to her.

Clearly she wanted more from him. Ellie's rapid breaths felt hot against his scruffy cheek as his fingers slid farther down, slipping between the top of her slacks and her smooth, warm flesh—no panties, what a surprise. He reached for her firm butt.

She grasped the front of his pajama top. He thought she was groping for the buttons, but she was pushing at his chest. Maybe it was a signal for what she wanted him to do to her. Moving his hands around front, he planted them on her breasts.

Just as the nerves in his palms started to tell his brain what a good time they were having, she slapped his face hard. The whack felt like a troll's club mashing his cheekbone.

He spun sideways, tripped, and fell over. She kicked his rump with the toe of her shoe. Smarting from both assaults, he lay there and gaped at her as she tucked in her blouse, stretching the material deliciously.

Noticing his stare, she kicked him again, a bull's eye in the anus. "You glans."

To protect his tender parts, he sat up. "But I thought that's what you wanted."

"I wanted something romantic—I didn't expect to be mauled." She pointed at him, as if her fingertip contained a death ray. It probably did. She snarled, "Don't you dare move. Stay there until I'm gone. I need to figure out what to do with you."

Ellie stomped around the bed and walked straight into—and through—one of the bookcases.

CHAPTER FIVE

The wall was a hologram. Of course. Jeru cursed his stupidity.

He climbed to his feet, hissing at the pain in his backside from her kicks. When did "yes" become "no" for her? How'd he miss those signs?

At least the beating had blown away the lingering cottony feeling in his head.

His pajamas had filled in with color, from transparent to blue. Not a wrinkle showed, and the sweat stains under his arms had already vanished with no lingering odor. Amazing. Everything about the place was remarkable. Everything about his new body.

He considered inspecting his intimate equipment, now that he was alone, but reminded himself that solitude didn't mean privacy. Surely Ellie—and probably her mom and a whole security team—wouldn't leave him unobserved. Cameras could be anywhere in the room, masked by holograms. He wondered if he could go anyplace in the house without falling under somebody's gaze.

Once he got out of the library, it would be helpful to see where he'd be permitted to roam and what areas were forbidden. With his hacker instincts, he especially wanted to know where he wasn't supposed to go.

Jeru followed the route Ellie had taken, walking straight into the bookcase hologram. He couldn't help flinching as his foot penetrated the seemingly solid wood frame and leather column of book spines. His hand swung through next and then his torso and face.

He cracked his chin and nose against something solid, and his momentum soon pancaked his entire front against the barrier.

"Oof!" Jeru rubbed his face—a bearded stranger's face.

He'd walked headlong into what must've been a sliding door, which had opened silently for Ellie but prevented him from exiting. The hologram remained intact around him: covers of books hovered beside his head and around his body. Before him, he only saw the streaks and swirls of wood grain, the rear panel of the bookcase. Trapped.

When he touched the back panel, his fingertips passed through and settled on a smooth, cold surface, a metal plate. Using both hands, eyes closed against the distraction of the illusion, he felt for seams, contours, anything that might indicate a hinge or latch.

The edge of his hands struck wood on either side of him: actual shelves to his left and right. He traced the outline of what felt like a metal door. Stooping, he pressed his fingernails into a tight crevasse along the floor, maybe a track on which the door slid. He rose on tiptoes, following the seams upward, but they continued past his reach.

On the right side, he managed to wedge his fingers between the adjacent shelf and the wall behind it. The wall felt warmer than the metal door, with a texture that suggested a painted material. If he could move aside one of the real bookcases, maybe he could find a way to trip the door lock, or just dig through the wall.

The thought of taking down hundreds of books and pulling aside the shelves gave him another idea. If people were watching him, they might show up if he tried to destroy something, and then he'd bulldoze his way through them and escape from this room at least. Dismantling the bookcase would be a lot of work, while he could accomplish something violently stupid in mere seconds. WWCD: What Would Conan Do? He settled on violently stupid.

He stepped back from the barrier but kept his left arm within the hologram just to see it slowly emerge as he eased his elbow toward his side. Totally blazing! The effect reminded him of the GameSphere. But the missing portion of his limb also brought back the nightmare of the explosion. His arm lying on the street. Cairo's amputated fist—all that was left of his childhood friend. Blood everywhere. He cringed, as if the bomb had detonated once again.

Need to stay busy. Let's see what this body can do.

Deciding on the best bit of mayhem, he lifted a desk chair with delightful ease and moved to the window. His muscles hardly noted the weight of the dense wood in his grip. With a whoop, he swung the legs against the leaded glass.

The chair bounced back and cracked him across the forehead.

Jeru dropped the chair and clutched his face. A knot began to swell above his left eye, and an ache spread throughout his skull. He imagined a cluster of smug people—Ellie, her mom, uniformed guards—laughing at the display of slapstick comedy on a giant wall screen.

Snarling, he snatched up the chair again and slung it at the full-length mirror. Silvered glass and wood splinters erupted from the collision, and the furniture banged into another set of bookcases. At last, a satisfactory impact.

He waited, but no one appeared. Back to Plan A, but do it with feeling.

Jeru raced to the hologram. He stepped into the three-dimensional image and jammed his fingers behind the adjacent shelving unit on his right. The metal door provided an excellent leverage point as he leaned his shoulder into it and heaved. Nothing. Sweat soon soaked his pajamas but was just as quickly wicked away.

With a grunt, he pulled harder. The bookcase edged away from the wall. Top-heavy with books, it tipped a few degrees. Jeru heard the dense volumes cascading onto the floor like bricks. A little more effort and he could bring the whole thing down.

Soundlessly, the metal panel against his shoulder slid aside. Jeru fell into a carpeted hallway. Inside the library, the bookshelf thumped back to the wall.

He lay at the end of a long passage, where faint rectangular seams denoted what were probably doors every twenty feet along either side. Paintings in gold-leaf frames hung at intervals above spindly tables graced with cut flowers in cobalt-blue vases. Discrete pin-spots angled from the ceiling to brighten each picture. Wall sconces lit the hallway with different washes of subtle colors, as if to coax a progression of moods in someone traveling from one end to the other.

Jeru's mood remained stuck in pissed-off mode.

His fingers stung from bending backward, pinned as they'd been between the bookcase and the wall when he'd fallen. He massaged them but stopped when he saw Ellie's purple, high-heeled shoes and turquoise slacks cross his field of vision. They vanished behind him.

Jeru braced himself for another kick in the ass.

"You really are hopeless, Jerry." She nudged his bare feet, gently at first and then harder.

Guessing she wanted him to move them, he drew up his legs. The door whispered shut behind him.

He rolled onto his hands and knees and stood to face her. With his frantic attempts to break out of the room, he'd forgotten the little details that made Ellipses so desirable and so unlike the vixens of cyberspace. No graphic artists paid such scrupulous attention to the curve of cheekbones, the shadow of a cleft in the chin, or the symmetry between the eyes, nose, and mouth. And hair seldom looked right in the GameSphere, lacking the random loops and strands that fell across the forehead and stroked the sides of an angelic face.

Ellie pushed a blond curl away from her now-caramel eyes. "What are you staring at?"

"Sorry." He looked away, stealing a glimpse at the rest of her. Not quite eighteen years old? Impossible.

"Oh, Jerry, you banged up your face." She stepped in close and stood on tiptoes to examine him. Her chest rubbed against his. "You've got a big, ugly bruise."

Jeru edged backward. "Don't pretend you didn't see how I got it. I'm sure you have cameras in there."

"Why are you acting like this? I wouldn't spy on you."

"Then why did you come back here?"

She rolled her eyes. "Because you're my guest. Don't they teach manners OTP?"

"*Manners*—like slapping and kicking me and locking me in that room?"

"I was just upset because you went so fast. I know you want me, but I want you to like me first."

He scrunched his toes against the carpet. "I like you, Ellie."

"You like the way I look," she said. "There's a difference."

She began to march down the hallway. Turning back, she snapped, "Come on, I'll get you doctored up. Seems like that's what I'm always doing for you."

"Along with making sure I look the way you want." He caught himself studying her otherworldly beauty again. "Admit it: so far, we both like the package more than the person."

Ellie hung her head as she rotated 180 degrees and stalked away.

If the colored lights along the hall were designed to improve his mood, they weren't working. He told himself to act nicer. "Cruel" might get him thrown out, but "nice" could get him a chauffeured drive home—where his parents thought he was dead and gone—and maybe a memorable time with Ellie first.

After a few breaths, he felt his spirits lift. Cool blue and violet blended with soft white emanating from the nearest sconces. Hell, maybe the lighting worked after all.

He trotted up so he could walk alongside her, but she turned her face away, obviously angry. This wasn't creating the kind of memory he had in mind.

"Hey," he murmured. "Stop a minute." He touched her shoulder and said, "Look at me. Come on, I'm sorry. This is all new and scary—even my body is new and a little scary—and I don't know what I'm supposed to do." She looked at her shoes, so he ducked to recapture her gaze. "Forgive me? Give me another chance?"

Her eyes flickered from crimson to gold. "Maybe, glans."

A door shushed open at his back. She said, "We're here: the operating room."

CHAPTER SIX

Enrolling London "Lun" Johnson in the RSA's End of Days extracurricular program wasn't as easy as Ross Gimbel had planned. It first required a personal, albeit virtual, visit to the online office of the eighteen-year-old's ad-exec parents. Ross had chosen an avatar that looked like an illustrated, more buff version of himself. The parents were a couple of sky-blue butterflies, for chrissake, but he managed to get their electronic signatures with only a mildly concerned flap of wings and one anxious antenna twitch. In a synthesized voice that sounded like she was sucking helium, Mrs. Johnson peeped, "At least our son will be learning something soulful, instead of all that violent video game stuff."

With the still-yammering Lun finally installed in God's Boot Camp, Gimbel retreated to the basement of his church, which contained his suite of offices and a firing range. Someone was practicing fifteen-round bursts from an automatic weapon, a Brazilian-made machine gun by the sound of it. At last he could think in peace.

He reclined in his favorite bonobo-skin chair and tapped the FarSighters down over his eyes. Using a few voice commands, he summoned the video of Cairo Bledsoe's pathetic failure and watched it again. This time he dictated sidebar notes and lessons learned. Obviously, Bledsoe's twin sister, Geneva, had brought that Jerusalem asshole into the picture and caused the mission to unravel.

A cyber visit with Geneva would be less than satisfying—he needed to deal with her in person.

"*Vengeance is mine*, sayeth the Lord," Gimbel intoned. After summoning a secure search engine, he spoke in a staccato that kept time with the machine-gun clatter as he sought Geneva's potential whereabouts.

In moments, he'd pulled up the Bledsoe family's address, confirmed from an updated resume he found on a job-posting site that she still lived at home (little wonder—the girl wanted a job in marketing, like everybody else in the country), and learned her times of peak online activity from a profile she maintained. There, she kept a list of eight BFFs. Jesus was in the final slot, an afterthought behind five slutty avatars, a celebrity dachshund, and some AI construct named Oprah.

He studied several of the seemingly infinite images Geneva had posted of herself and doubted that the twenty-year-old redhead was really that attractive. She'd probably manipulated every pixel. Nothing was real anymore.

A friend in the Defense Department—which remained a haven for True Believers, praise God—had given him an encryption program that made his searches impossible to trace. If anything untoward should happen to the misguided girl, and the police happened to come to Gimbel's church looking for suspects, they'd find a search history entirely composed of scholarly religious inquiries and an RSA-run bingo site.

High technology and the physics of gunpowder were all the proof of Intelligent Design that Gimbel needed.

Part of his calling was the desire to get his hands dirty out in the field, where souls were reaped. He logged off, removed his FarSighters, and pulled a customized set of earplugs from his desk drawer. They blocked sound so effectively, he felt a little off-balance as he walked down the corridor to the firing range.

In the first shooting booth, a short, olive-skinned Crusader fired the rest of his clip with a jaunty one-handed sweep, arcing the compact machine gun from left to right. Gimbel looked past him at the big smiley-face pattern shot through a line of terrorist targets.

Gimbel waited for the Crusader to notice him and remove his hearing protection before saying, "I think you circumcised the one in the middle."

The gunman laughed bitterly. "I'd like to do even worse to the ones who've ruined the Holy Land forever."

Gimbel read his lips and replied, "Only God and faith are eternal. Radioactivity decays."

As the Crusader reloaded, Gimbel walked over to the arsenal maintained lovingly on the wall behind him. He selected a Mexican assault pistol and stepped to the adjacent booth.

Since he was a boy, he had excelled at lip-reading, studying his parents' whispered exchanges at church so he knew what blasphemies they'd uttered and could ask for very specific forgiveness on their behalf. A terrorist-spread flu pandemic had whisked his parents up to God for one-on-One counseling. He was sure they didn't go to Hell. Their lingering deaths had allowed ample time for them to seek absolution, which had demonstrated to Gimbel that the Good Lord might forgive, but He didn't forget.

Assuming a two-handed shooter's stance, he targeted the caricature of a hoodie-clad tech billionaire at fifty feet. Inspired by the Crusader's bullet-drawing, he fired a top-down vertical pattern, bisecting his paper foe lengthwise, and completed the cruciform with a horizontal sweep across the villain's chest. The bottom two-thirds of the target fluttered to the ground. Gimbel's hands stung from the concussion of rapid firing, which left a lovely stigmata of inflammation on each palm.

According to the digital counter on the gunstock, thirty shots remained. A hundred feet downrange, he spied the paper image of a trust-fund socialite, obscene in a string bikini, hips canted suggestively, mixed drink in one hand and a ginormous diamond in the other. Another denizen of The Kingdom, one of the wealthiest one percent.

Gimbel dismantled her limbs before firing the coup de grace between her smug cat's-eye sunglasses. He left the smoking gun on a nearby table for the staff to strip and clean. Time to talk to Geneva Bledsoe.

Before Gimbel left, he returned to his office and shut the door. He took an aerosol can—another gift from his Defense Department boosters—from a secret desk drawer and went to the opposite corner of the room, far from his All-n-1 and any other electronics. Paying particular attention to his hair, face, and hands, he sprayed himself and his clothes, shoes, and favorite pistol with an electrostatic mist. For the next few hours, no follicle, skin particle, or mote of lint or dust could escape from him.

The only downside to the aerosol was the delivery of a violent shock whenever he touched metal. And, of course, the unsightly static cling. At the exit door to the church parking lot, he forgot about the electricity buildup. A blue bolt arced from the push bar, stabbing his hand.

"Jesus Christ!"

None of his staff dared to peek over their cubicles at him.

Outside, his black sports car recognized him from fifty feet away and blinked its lights once, asking its question: "Can we go for a ride?" He replied, "Yes," in a low voice, but it heard him nonetheless, coasted over, and unlocked itself. The driver door swung open.

Fortunately, the car interior consisted entirely of fabric and plastics, not a bit of metal. The only harm that came to him as he slid onto the seat was a nasty wedgie.

After the door shut itself, the engine revved loudly, as if to say, "Hot damn!" before settling into silent efficiency. Gimbel's All-n-1 relayed Geneva Bledsoe's address and the best route.

He paid an annual Driver in Command fee to the State of Georgia and federal government so he could personally pilot his vehicle on surface streets. He'd heard rumors, though, that the TrafficGrid would soon be the sole king of the road, leaving him and many others DIC-less.

A padded, U-shaped bar attached to the top of the seat swung forward over his head and locked against his chest. Nestled behind the snug restraint, with butterflies of excitement tickling his insides, he felt like a kid at the top of a roller coaster. Rather than zoom into the road, though, he imposed control on his feelings and drove at a stately pace, following directions uttered by the customized feminine voice he'd downloaded.

"In one hundred feet, turn left, Most Reverend . . . Very well executed, sir."

The compliment caused him to sit straighter, and the way she said "executed" made his loins tingle.

Merging onto the highway forced him to turn the controls over to the goddamned TrafficGrid, which accelerated his car to ninety miles per hour to join the brisk flow of afternoon commuters. The Grid maintained a regulated distance between vehicles while running continuous diagnostics on each one to ensure no breakdowns were imminent. It also typically broadcast on every vehicle console an endless loop of ads for the companies that financed the Grid, but Gimbel paid extra each month to block their fatuous videos.

Instead of getting inundated with news of the latest DNA "code patch" from Ugenix (*Your next child deserves only your best*™), he spoke to his staff via satellite video, recorded messages for the RSA website and social media outlets, and guzzled a jalapeño energy drink. No one in his employ had learned yet whether the meddler called Jerusalem was dead or how many unworthy had been sanctified by Cairo Bledsoe's bomb, but news out of the Kingdom was always slow and often manipulated. Whatever happened to the public's right to know?

The computer announced submissively, "Your exit is approaching, Most Reverend. ETA one minute. Control will return to you momentarily." She sounded so apologetic that it had been taken away in the first place, he had to resist patting the top of the dashboard in consolation.

His car shot onto the exit ramp and began to decelerate. The computer voice counted down, breathless with anticipation. With a soft ping, the steering wheel, shifter, and pedals returned to his command. The notion that his autonomy—even in his own driveway, for chrissake—would soon be completely subverted in the name of traffic safety helped him stay focused on ending the world. Just picturing an automobile outfitted with a snooze alarm made *him* want to strap on a bomb.

Geneva Bledsoe and her parents—and Cairo, until a short time ago—lived in a High-Occupancy Dwelling like most suburbanites. The ten stories of recycled aluminum was as smooth as a bullet, with a gentle curve to the architecture that joined four of these "HODs" into a ring around a central parking garage and a core of large rooms where the residents could socialize together.

Gimbel found a parking space and removed a small leather case from a compartment under his seat. Last year's Christmas present from his Defense Department groupies: a device that would disrupt all tracking systems and video and audio recordings of him.

During his stroll past the social areas, he saw that no one was using them. Nobody ever did. They were too busy competing to assemble the blazingest personal profile or achieve the highest video game scores. Others no doubt were having virtual sex . . . possibly with somebody right next door whom they'd never meet in the flesh.

The great thing about HODs was that, despite housing thousands of people under one roof, there would likely be no witnesses.

All the more reason why that Jerusalem fucker never should've found out about Cairo's explosives, and why he had a bone to pick with—and perhaps from—Geneva Bledsoe.

Gimbel double-checked the directory for the quadrant and floor that housed the Bledsoe clan and rode an elevator up three stories. He would've taken the stairs for exercise, but the heavy steel door looked like it would deliver a far worse shock than the brushed aluminum box. During the short trip, he felt the ends of his hair rising like a mushroom cloud. Worse, video screens on all four sides subjected him to ads for terrorism insurance, two new cars that doubled as offices with room for a lithesome secretary, and word of a new breakfast injection.

The grinning model who pressed the air syringe to her arm and spoke about essential vitamins and amino acids looked and sounded identical to his ex. He wondered if she'd chosen the amoral world of corporate advertising after abandoning her noble role as pastor's wife. Harlot! When he'd insisted on so much cosmetic surgery for her, he had no idea he was equipping her for another career. How she'd victimized him.

With a soft beep, the elevator doors opened onto a pristine, silent hallway of convex walls, recessed lighting, and a seamless laminate floor, all done in cream, as if he'd tunneled into a giant yogurt cup. He patted his crackling hair back into place and headed toward the Bledsoes' door. Surprisingly, the HOD still featured deadbolts on every entrance. The other goodies in his little leather case were useless—lock picks had gone the way of pistons and pruning shears.

He prayed for guidance and, as usual, the Lord was right there with an answer for him: *ring the doorbell.* Good ol' God! As he gave thanks, a door farther down the hall opened, and a small boy ran toward him, dressed head-to-toe like the latest robot superhero. The kid aimed a too-realistic gun at Gimbel and pulled the trigger.

As the annoying blaster sound effects jabbed Gimbel's ears, an itchy sensation spread across his chest. He'd been tickle-rayed by the little creep.

"Hey," Gimbel bellowed as he clawed his static-wrinkled shirt, "how dare you shoot innocent people?"

He'd have to tell the Defense Department their gadgets and sprays weren't proof against toys. Judas Priest—what was the point of America being Number One again if it couldn't make quality products?

A woman of thirty or so, who carried herself like she was sixty, closed her condo door and shuffled after the hellion in a white outfit that sported grape juice stains. Her arms and neck showed the red lines of continuous scratching. She said, "Sorry about Ampersand. Amp, quit that right now."

The boy lifted his cyborg goggles and whined, "But, Momma, I'm killing the bad man."

Gimbel took two quick steps forward and disarmed Amp, giving them both an electric shock. Being tickle-rayed was bad enough, but now his static charge was being dissipated, too. Toy gun in hand, he had to resist the urge to jam the barrel down the front of the kid's bionic pants and fire away.

Amp's mother caught up, looking like she might want to do the same. Wisps of her long, dry hair floated toward his static field. Wearily, she grabbed a handful of robot-costume sleeve and said to Gimbel, "Remember when the worst they could do was microwave the cat? I could handle that." Before he could reply, she hauled Amp to the elevator.

"Momma, he's got my gun."

"I'll buy you another."

"Okay, but get me one that shoots out loud, smelly farts."

The mother stepped onto the elevator, dragging Amp behind her. Gimbel took aim and blasted the kid's backside. Amp stumbled on board, crying out and scratching his butt as the doors closed.

Gimbel reminded himself he had just encountered two witnesses. The Good Lord must've wanted him to martyr a number of souls that day. Fortunately, he had consumed that energy drink on the way over.

He pressed the bell. After a brief wait, the Bledsoes' door swung inward, and Geneva stood there. She looked exactly like the latest photo she'd posted, including the same white outfit. Probably uploaded the picture only an hour ago during the incessant tweaking of her profile, just like every other twenty-something. A closer inspection revealed a dusty orange tint to her face and overly dramatic mascara: webcam make-up. Gimbel knew it well. He'd have to scope out her brand preferences after he killed her.

Geneva looked past him, scanning the yogurt-tunnel hall. "Shit, I missed that little fosh again."

"I disarmed him," he said. He brandished the tickle-ray gun.

"Well, we're safe until Mrs. Indulgent and Rat Boy hit a toy store." Geneva gave him a once-over that made him pat his hair again and try to smooth his shirt. She asked, "Haven't I seen you online?"

"I doubt it."

"You live on this floor?"

He said, "Actually I'm looking for a friend of a friend, a guy named Cairo Bledsoe."

She edged back and grasped the door, her make-up now looking like a death mask over a bloodless face.

"Is something wrong?" he asked in his ministering-at-the-bedside voice, which admittedly was very rusty.

"Why do you want Cai?"

Gimbel recalled the martyr's passion for rock operas. "I heard he could get me backstage at that Beatles-kidnapping musical, *Yo Tengo Ringo*."

She said, "I hoped he'd be home by now . . . or would've sent a zip anyway. Sorry, I don't know where he is."

Geneva pushed the door toward him, but he stopped it with the barrel of the toy gun and, using his free hand, forced it open again. He stepped inside. "You're not looking well. Is anyone else home who can help you, maybe get you to a doctor?"

"No."

"That's too bad." He held his arms out, Christ-style. "Well, the Good Lord provides."

Her eyes widened, and he realized that he'd delivered one of his famous taglines from his broadcasts. His heel struck the door low and hard, and it slammed shut behind him.

As she turned to flee, he whacked the back of her head with the thick pommel of the toy. Geneva fell to the floor and lay there, apparently stunned.

Gimbel checked the trademark on the grip. Made in the USA. Maybe we still knew how to manufacture a good product after all.

CHAPTER SEVEN

Jeru relaxed a little. Despite the dramatic name, the "operating room" resembled a doctor's examination area. Except for the walls. Instead of the usual mass of ads for drugs and medical products such as CelluGon—*Kiss Your Butt Goodbye*™—pastoral watercolors and still-life paintings gave a calming touch to the space. Also, no doctor or nurse awaited them.

"Self-serve?" Jeru asked, fingering the throbbing bruise above his left eye, which made his headache worsen.

"Maybe OTP," Ellie sneered. "Here, we get the best." She pointed him to a table covered with shiny film that crinkled when he sat on it.

He sensed the change in air pressure as a door slid open silently behind him. Before turning, he predicted what the doctor would look like: grandfatherly, trim, sporting silvery-white hair and a lab coat. Exactly like the AI constructs in cyberspace and on TV.

He glanced over his shoulder and sighed. Wrong again.

The doctor was definitely female—beautiful, in fact, like the perfect blend of all the races. Jeru couldn't guess her age; she could've been thirty or a very youthful forty-five. If Ellie took good care of her figure and darkened her complexion and hair, she could mature into someone like the elegant woman who smiled at Jeru, hands hidden in the pockets of a tweed jacket.

Jeru said hello and introduced himself.

"I know who you are," the doctor said with hint of an accent, British of all things. She walked around the table to face him. "I operated on you."

Jeru held out his arms. "You did all this?" Then he glanced at his lap. "Everything?"

"Certainly. I wish I'd had more time to perfect my work, but someone was anxious to wake you." She nodded toward Ellie. "The impatience of young love."

"Doc," Ellie whined in protest. Her face shaded to pink, eyes gleaming like sapphires, then emeralds. She walked past Jeru and busied herself, opening drawers and rattling plastic and metal devices, like she was pretending to be an assistant.

The doctor studied Jeru's face and gave him a frown. She said, "I see you've already marred my masterpiece."

From her pocket, she withdrew two elliptical green sheaths. She slipped her hand into one and it conformed to her, sealing at her wrist. The sight brought back the blood-soaked memory of the police officer placing a similar wrap around the stump below Jeru's elbow. He shivered despite the warmth of the room.

With both gloves in place, the doctor touched the tender area above his eye. The rubbery material encasing her hand smelled like wintergreen.

Her lips pursed as she clucked her tongue.

Ellie appeared at her shoulder, staring at Jeru. "Is it bad?"

"Not nearly as serious as a detached forearm. Or all that cellulite I had to eradicate." She held Jeru's gaze. "I hope this isn't an indication of how you'll continue to abuse your body."

"No, ma'am."

"You may call me Dr. Gomez."

"Sorry. I promise to do better, Dr. Gomez."

She reached behind him and poked his lower back. He yelped and sat straighter.

"Bad posture." The doctor shook her head, dislodging a black strand of hair that swung across her forehead. "Already, your mistreatment has begun in earnest."

He felt as guilty as he did during a Sunday morning rant from the virtual pulpit. However, he sensed that redeeming himself with Dr. Gomez wouldn't be as easy as clicking "I Accept" on the stone-tablet image of the Ten Commandments that appeared at the end of his minister's webcast.

The doctor surprised him again, stroking his temple with a gentleness that lulled him. She asked, "Do you have a headache?"

"Yeah, getting bigger by the minute."

"Any vision problems?"

"No." He shrugged. "Other than not recognizing much of anything I see."

"You don't recognize two sterling representatives of the female sex?" She winked at Ellie.

"You two don't look like the girls in the real world."

Ellie said, "First of all, we're women, not girls. Secondly, OTP isn't the real world. It's like a bad dream, with mad bombers and advertising everywhere."

"Hey, I came from there too."

Dr. Gomez patted his stomach. "It showed. I now have your pledge to do better. Don't forget: anything I added, I can take away." She followed the warning with a sharp tap near his groin and walked toward a cabinet with dozens of narrow drawers. Two of them opened toward her, though she didn't touch anything.

Ellie said, "I bet I picked the right ones, Doc." She revealed a small tube in each hand, one translucent blue, the other cocoa-butter yellow.

Dr. Gomez grinned. "My protégé." Apparently, Ellie wasn't just pretending to assist.

The drawers closed again on their own. Jeru asked Ellie, "How did she do that?"

"Thought commands." Ellie touched her forehead.

"She's psychic?"

"No, fosh. She directed the network with a chip in her brain. How do you think we open doors here without touching them?"

"So that's why I can't," Jeru concluded. The Kingdom seemed to be decades ahead of everybody else. He'd heard of some gamers getting silicon wired into their neural circuits to improve their reflexes and stamina, but devastating side effects were common. Stories abounded about ruined brains, which the media had dubbed "siliputty."

He asked, "Will I get these chips?"

"I thought you wanted to go home," Ellie teased.

Either she was the psychic or he was being too obvious. He told himself to throttle back and stop giving away so much. It was far easier to control facial expressions in the GameSphere—"smile" stayed that way until you decided otherwise; you could slaughter whole armies while grinning like an idiot. He needed to concentrate on "noncommittal."

Dr. Gomez took the vials from Ellie, saying, "It will only take an afternoon if you want the neural chips, Jerusalem. I installed the necessary trapdoor already. If you touch the top of your head, you might be able to feel the hinges."

Jeru reached for his stubbly scalp. When he caught the mirth in the woman's eyes, he lowered his hand. Now even the doctor was making fun of him.

"Exhale mightily," she ordered. "Really empty your lungs." He did, and she twisted the blue tube at its base and placed it under his nose. "Now, take a deep breath."

When he inhaled, a blast of ice-cold air shot into his nostrils. His eyes watered, but the nagging headache vanished instantly. The relief brought with it a sense of gratitude that he tried to stifle. Better not fall in love with this place. It would become that much harder to break free when the time was right.

The doctor said, "Better? Now let's take care of that bruise." She rubbed the other tube against the sore spot, sliding the glassy smoothness over his forehead. The area cooled and the surrounding portions of his face grew warm, as if blood were evacuating the damaged spot. Dr. Gomez touched his brow. "How's that?"

"Okay, I guess." Jeru felt the bruised patch. He pressed harder to see if he could summon the slightest stab of pain. Nope, he was completely cured, which was as totally blazing as it was absolutely frustrating. He asked, "Why can't we get this stuff OTP . . . I mean, at home."

Ellie snorted.

Dr. Gomez provided a translation: "It's likely that only a few could afford it."

"And all of those people," Ellie added, "end up moving here."

"So you do accept outsiders?"

"Certainly," the doctor said. "Mostly based on wealth but sometimes on merit." She gave him a 1,000-watt smile. "We're all very proud of you for saving Ellipsis's life."

Feeling his ears redden, he looked away and tried to take stock of his surroundings: drawers and doors that opened with a thought, miracle medicines, luscious women. Too good to be true. Maybe that was the Kingdom's tagline.

To tweak Ellie and stay on the offensive, he said, "I guess I'd do it again. Maybe."

"Yeah," she replied, "and maybe next time I'll kick your arm into the sewer."

"Enough, lovebirds." Dr. Gomez gestured behind him. "Go through that door, Jerusalem, take off your clothes, and wait for me."

"Uh, what are you going to do?"

Ellie giggled, and the doctor said, "Examine the rest of my work. Off with you. Ellipsis and I need to talk about her Making Eighteen operation."

"Operation?" Jeru said, sliding off the table. "I thought it was a party."

The doctor looked him over. "I'm quite certain the party will come afterward."

Ellie smiled coyly as Jeru frowned at her. What kind of fosh would look forward to going under the knife, assuming they still used knives, just to have a birthday party? He headed for the door, but stopped. "Uh, I can't . . ." He tapped his forehead.

Dr. Gomez and Ellie both flicked a glance his way, and the door shushed open. Walking through, he wondered which of them had won the thought race. Then he recalled the properties of his Nite-n-Daze pajamas—sitting on that table would've bared his backside. Were they both checking out his butt?

He entered some kind of operating theater, but most of the machines perched along the edge of a central table looked too small to be used in surgery, and the larger devices arrayed against the walls were too sleek to guess their purpose. In his favorite online games, he was always a character of the times, never anachronistic. Standing in the gadget-filled room, though, he felt like a caveman transported into the world of Star Pirate.

The doctor's joke about hinges in his head still irritated him. Part of feeling like a caveman was that they treated him like one. Of course, after bashing the furniture and tearing apart the bookshelves, maybe they were right. Only his mind, not his great new bod, would put him back in control of the situation. He needed time to strategize.

His scalp itched. Scraping his fingers against the bristly stubble, he wondered if Dr. Gomez had shaved his head so she could remove shrapnel from Cairo's bomb. Or had she been tinkering with his gray matter?

She entered behind him. "Jerusalem," she said when the door slid shut, "do you have some phobia about nudity?"

"I don't feel comfortable enough to strip." He wished the pajamas included pockets for his hands. All he could do was fold his arms.

"I have already handled every inch of you, inside and out."

"Not while I was awake."

Dr. Gomez said, "Are you really that shy? One of those bold warriors who can do or say anything, but only when anonymous on your Internet?"

She'd scored a bull's-eye, but he seized on the new bit of information she'd let slip. "*Your Internet*? Don't you guys have that here?"

"Disrobe this instant." She glared until he unbuttoned his top. "Now slide off your trousers and lie there."

He turned away, pushed down his pants, and climbed onto the table. The crinkly plastic beneath him warmed his bare back and rump. Dr. Gomez looked him over, her expression showing only clinical detachment and lingering annoyance. She glanced at the small machines mounted along the table edge, and they responded with a multi-colored lightshow and the high-pitched keen of machines coming to life, reminding him once again of Cairo and his bomb.

Some of the box-like contraptions slid along the table while others hovered like drones at varying heights, all of them circumnavigating him as their lens-like protrusions pointed his way. Beneath him, the tabletop lit up with a violet fluorescence. He bent his head back as far as he could and saw moving pictures and text hovering in midair, but his viewing angle was too acute to read anything. Instead, he gazed down the length of his body, which had become the body of a god.

Though the doctor's severe expression didn't change, her tone lightened. "I trust my work meets with your approval?"

Shyness had given way to amazement. He asked, "How did you do all this?"

"Nanotechnology, sonic inducers for cell evolution, deft use of lasers. And a little old-fashioned plastic surgery." She allowed herself a smile. "Can't let the robots have all the fun."

"I guess we can't afford any of this stuff OTP?"

"Doubtful, but demand would be low in any case. People out there seem much more intent on abandoning their bodies for cyberspace. They *escape* from themselves, whereas we *enhance* our humanness."

As she watched the holographic output, Dr. Gomez said, "Now then, you'd asked about my Internet comment. We have all the access we desire, though few of us bother with it. Rather, we utilize our own *Intranet* for information sharing and retrieval, quite apart from your so-called world wide web."

"Can I see it?"

"Didn't Ellipsis tell you about the orientation scheduled for this afternoon? The household's Systems Operator will lead you through the necessary exercises."

"Exercises? I'll do it with my body?"

"No, dear, with your brain. You wouldn't want my very best work to go to waste, would you?"

CHAPTER EIGHT

Jeru felt the top of his head, his sense of violation renewed. "So, you did implant chips in here."

Dr. Gomez glanced at the image suspended above him once more and squinted. The rectangle vanished, and the machines shut down with a descending hum. "Standard issue," she said, searching his expression. "Surely you don't expect everyone to become your personal valet, opening doors and summoning machines at your whim for the next hundred years."

"Wait, you mean I'll live another century?"

"At the very least, and many decades longer if you stay fit. Still, the body eventually wears out despite our best efforts." She looked him over again with her candid gaze.

Jeru sat up and swiveled away from her. "Can I put my clothes on?"

"You may."

He jerked up his pajama pants and buttoned his shirt. Turning back to her, he asked, "How long will I look like this?" He flexed his bicep, which created an impressive bulge under the sleeve.

"You might lose some muscle mass as a natural consequence of aging, but, with occasional visits to your doctor," she said with a slight bow, "you should maintain your present physique for much of your lifetime."

"Can I ask how old you are?"

"I'll be seventy-five in a few months." She nodded as he gaped. "That's right. And there's Ellipsis in the next room, just about to turn eighteen. You two will make a gorgeous, happy couple for more years than you can imagine."

All of Jeru's instincts rebelled against the doctor's matchmaking efforts, but he stifled his response. He wanted more answers while she was in a forthcoming mood. Gesturing at the closed door, he asked, "Has she been amped up as much as me?"

"She had a decidedly better genetic makeup going in, with all due respect to your heritage, so she needed less enhancement. But she's long aspired to a certain look, the artist-palette irises, the impertinent nose, a dancer's figure. And next week she'll get her butterfly."

"You mean a tattoo?"

"A surprise and a delight for both of you. Now then, she's waiting to take you down to lunch with her mother. You'll find Victoria to be a charming, though somewhat eccentric, hostess."

Dr. Gomez glanced at the door, which opened and admitted Jeru back into the examination room.

Ellie was lying on the table, arms folded across her chest, eyes closed. Jeru waited for her to stir, but she remained still. He turned to the doctor, who whispered, "Sleeping Beauty. How was it that the prince woke her?"

Apparently, they'd worked out a game to play with him. As kissable as Ellie was, he resented the ongoing manipulations. He wanted to kiss her plenty—and much more—but not in front of the doctor. Instead, he focused on the door leading to the hallway. There should be a simple command he could relay from the chip in his head to the exit: Door Open.

Nothing happened.

Dr. Gomez murmured, "She's waiting for you. Please don't deny her affections; she has so much love to give."

Open Door. *Nada*. Shit.

"Ellipsis sat with you every day, all day, while you healed. She gave up countless friendships for you. You're her hero come to life." The doctor tapped her foot in agitation, like a disgruntled Cupid who was running out of arrows.

Open Sesame? No, of course not, glans.

He shook his head and returned his attention to Ellie. God, she really was beautiful. The door zipped into its wall pocket, revealing the carpeted hall. Jeru wondered how the hell he'd done it. What was the magic command? Ellie?

The door closed. Jeru glanced at Dr. Gomez, who stared at him. She cried, "How did you do that? You haven't even gone through orientation."

He eyed the door again and thought *Ellie*.

The door whisked aside.

Maybe that wasn't the actual command, but somehow he'd accessed the implant by thinking her name, and his control of the door was subconscious. Still, he had something on them. At least Ellie couldn't trap him in a room again.

He caught her peeking at him, failing to suppress a grin as she lay there. "What?" he demanded.

She sat up. "You look so freaking proud of yourself. Is it because you refused me?"

"Yeah, that's it." He nodded. "I've got a lot of self-control."

Beside him, Dr. Gomez gave a mournful sigh.

Ellie hopped off the table as gracefully as she did everything else. She asked, "Too much self-control to eat lunch?"

"Lunch sounds great." Jeru felt like laughing. He'd managed to hack into his own implants. No telling what else he could do when he got time to focus.

"Then let's go." She started toward the door. It closed inches from her nose. Whirling around, she shouted, "Hey!"

Dr. Gomez put up her hands. "It wasn't me."

"Jerry, I don't know how you did that, but open the door."

"I didn't mean to shut it." He leveled his gaze at the panel and thought *Ellie*.

Nothing happened.

He tried again without success.

Clenching his hands, he focused on the door. Dr. Gomez coughed beside him. She covered her mouth, her cheekbones rising high with a half-concealed smile.

They'd conned him again.

Instant shame at being the butt of their joke made Jeru's face tingle.

"Doc," Ellie complained, "we could've had fun with that all day."

"And you would've never left me in peace. Go, lovebirds, so I can have *my* lunch." She gave Jeru a playful shove. "Don't fret, hero. This afternoon, you'll discover all the wonders of your implants, and Ellipsis will have to come up with more creative games."

"I've got lots of ideas." Ellie winked, and the door opened behind her.

"Of that I have no doubt, dear."

Still smarting from their trick, Jeru trailed Ellie into the hall without saying goodbye to the doctor. He walked in silence, watching the hues emitted by the wall sconces morph from cranberry pink to mimosa. Seeing red himself, he stifled the urge to lash out at the Unreliable Guide who hummed ahead of him and wiggled her remarkable backside.

With a glance down at his pajamas, he grumbled, "I can't go to lunch with your mother dressed like this."

"She won't be out of her robe and slippers yet."

"At least she has a robe."

Ellie looked back at him with annoyance. "There won't be anything under it," she said. "So you'll be even."

Her expression said *Don't ask*, so he didn't. The mysteries continued to mount.

They passed a wide single door marked "elevator," but she kept walking down the endless, tastefully decorated hallway, passing the outlines of door after door. Ellie, her mother, Dr. Gomez, and the unseen staff apparently lived in a former hotel.

At last, the hallway ended in a T-intersection, and she turned to the left, where a long flight of polished wood stairs curved down. Maybe the rich lived in huge houses to force themselves to stay in shape.

Jeru noted that their footsteps didn't clatter or echo as they descended. Maybe the rounded walls concealed acoustic dampeners. It was irritating that there wasn't anything irritating about the place.

Ellie turned to him, knuckles white on the mahogany banister. "Do you like me at all?"

Her hurt tone and the question itself tripped him up. He scrambled to stop his descent, nearly bowling her over. Gripping the rail, he said, "Sure I like you. Are you still angry about the stupid thing I said earlier?" He planted his bare feet on the solid wood step and stood tall, to give his words more authority. "I said I was sorry."

"You mauled me before, but you wouldn't even kiss me a minute ago."

"Ew, not in front of Dr. Gomez."

"God, you're strange. Are all you burb boys this repressed?"

Before he could answer, she turned back and continued down the stairs. She appeared to stomp her shoes but only produced faint thuds.

Jeru followed at a slower pace. He'd never thought of himself as having hang-ups. In the GameSphere, and elsewhere in cyberspace, he acted without scruples—and, in the heat of a battle, without mercy. True, during the scant time he'd been forced to dwell offline, he didn't chase girls with any success or have other kinds of fun, except for eating, but . . . repressed?

Cairo's twin sister, Geneva, was the closest he'd come to having a flesh-and-blood girlfriend, if one evening of wandering a decrepit mall together counted. When he'd tried to kiss her, though, she'd turned away. In his new body, he bet she wouldn't be able to resist. Assuming she didn't blame him for not saving her brother's life.

Ellie led Jeru into a marble foyer that was like the hub of a wheel: the nexus of hallways that led off in many directions. The end of one hall terminated in a large, open room with a cloth-covered table, wood and leather armchairs, and place settings. From the portion of the room he could see framed in the doorway, the dining area appeared to be unoccupied.

Tapping her foot like Dr. Gomez, Ellie glanced at a nearby painting. The nocturnal scene of raggedy men rowing some uniformed guy across a river vanished and was replaced by a blank screen within the gold-leaf frame. "Locate Mom," she ordered. As an aside to Jeru, she said, "I can give these commands without talking, but you wouldn't know what was going on, and I don't want to be *rude*." She turned from him again.

A floor plan filled the screen, and a red light blinked in one of the scores of rooms. Then the graphic slid into the upper-left quadrant of the screen and a schematic of the room with the flashing red beacon appeared lower right. The room was labeled Victoria Stewart—Recreation Room #12. According to the layout, it only contained a narrow lap pool, a cylindrical shower stall, and a lounge chair. The red light blinked on the chair icon.

Ellie breathed a resigned, "Crap." On the larger floor plan, blue lights flashed to indicate numerous bathroom locations. "Undo," she barked at the screen, and the blue lights vanished.

"What is it?" Jeru asked.

She whirled on him. "Don't they say *crap* anymore OTP? Am I totally backward? Outdated? Unlovable?"

"Hey, calm down. I only meant, what's wrong?"

"She's still in her chair. Can't have lunch if she's still in her freaking chair."

She seemed to be on the verge of a meltdown. Was her mom not allowed to sit for a while? To distract Ellie, Jeru pointed at the floor plan in the upper corner. He said, "Show me where we are."

She huffed a moment longer. "Locate me," she murmured.

Within the upper floor plan, a pink light winked on, many rooms away from her mom. The lower-left quadrant filled in with a drawing of the foyer, which showed the pinhead of pink near the wall. Jeru scanned the tall plaster ceiling for cameras or other sensors but saw nothing obvious. No surprise there.

Because he hadn't gone through orientation with the SysOp, he figured the network wouldn't recognize his voice pattern yet. To prove his theory and regain some of the confidence he'd lost in the "open sesame" episode, he leaned toward the glossy screen and enunciated, "Locate me."

An emerald light flashed beside the pink one.

"Hey," he said, "How does it know who I am?"

Ellie snapped, "What were you OTP, a monk in a cave? I can't believe I've put so much time and effort into someone who doesn't know about women and never used technology."

His face flushed. "I know all about tech—I made a really good living online. I taught gaming skills and did cyber-realty speculation. I could hack into my school's network by the time I was eight." He slapped his chest. "I'm the geek's geek."

"Could've fooled me. The system's been studying everything about your voice and movements since you woke up. Every boast, every insult, every mean thing you've said and done to me." She waved her hands at the walls, the ceiling, and the floors. Even the floors?

Ellie continued, her voice rising. "Every misstep, everything you broke, every time you touched yourself—the system knows you better than you do. It's learning to anticipate you."

"So it can stay one step ahead of me?"

"No, glans, so it can serve you. That's the point, to make your life better."

Jeru looked at the floor plan, the emerald light the system had assigned to him, and the nearest outside exit. Even after he learned how to open doors via the cerebral chips, he suspected that certain ones would be closed to him forever. And locked tight.

CHAPTER NINE

The red light on the screen representing Victoria Stewart drifted away from the lounge chair that Ellie clearly despised for some reason. At a languid pace, the crimson blip eased into one of the many halls and approached the foyer. Either she had to travel a great distance for her progress to be recorded on the floor plan, or Ellie's mom walked with the dreamy shuffle of someone who'd left Recreation Room #12 in a state of complete relaxation.

Jeru yawned as he watched the red icon. He shifted his bare feet, still feeling awkward about meeting a stranger while in his pajamas. "What should I call your mom? 'Ms. Stewart'?"

"She won't notice if you call her 'Mr. Stewart.' " Ellie snorted. "Even 'Jimmy Stewart.' "

"Who?"

Rolling her eyes, she replied, "Just call her Jimmy and see."

The weave of Ellie's clothes had become knit-like, well-ventilated, and he noted that she hadn't quivered with pleasure for a long while. Apparently, her outfit was having a tough enough time keeping her cool and calm, with no resources left over for anything else. Or perhaps the material sensed she only wanted soothing, not stimulation. Amazing—OTP clothes didn't understand your moods any better than other people did.

The sconces along one corridor brightened by a few lumens and morphed from marmalade-orange to buttery yellow. At last, Ellie's mother appeared. The red light on the screen seemed to move faster than the woman in the leopard-spotted robe, as if it were trying to coax her along.

From the way she wove unsteadily toward them, she was either drunk, high, or exhausted.

Victoria wore her stark-white hair piled up, with ringlets falling on both sides of her tanned face. Purple streaks swirled through her hairdo like blueberry syrup just added to a whirling blender of milk. Her fingernail color matched those highlights, as did the toenails peeking through the mules on her feet. She was voluptuous under her cinched robe, presenting a much more dramatic figure than the athletic physique Ellie had opted for. Also, Victoria's skin glowed with a rich bronze sheen, whereas Ellie had chosen an ivory tone. Wherever Mom zigged, Ellie zagged.

Nevertheless, some similarities were unavoidable. Dr. Gomez had been right about Ellie mining good genes. Victoria's oval face was lovely, but her wide, unfocused gray eyes gave her the look of someone in a blissed-out trance. Jeru had once played a GameSphere adventure based on Greek myths; Ellie's mom reminded him of a lotus blossom eater he'd laid at an orgy.

Victoria smiled at Ellie— really only looked at her, because a smile already curled the corners of her mouth—and said, "Precious one." Her voice rose and fell like a feather in a soft breeze.

"Mom." Ellie blew hard through her nose and relaxed her fists. "This is Jerusalem Pix."

After a down-and-up glance at Jeru, Victoria continued to address her daughter. "He turned out well, hmm?"

"I guess." Ellie shot him a look. "Maybe Dr. Gomez can implant a better attitude."

Victoria didn't react to the comment but pivoted and extended her hand to Jeru. "Welcome to our humble home."

Her limp handshake felt smooth and slightly greasy, like a melted birthday candle. "Thank you," he said. "May I call you Ms. Stewart?"

"If you'd like. Or 'Victoria' if you want to be more intimate, hmm?"

Victoria's comment made Jeru recall the video game orgy again. He wiped his hand on his pant leg.

Her eyes flared even wider. "Oh, I almost forgot. Your name is now

Bethlehem Splyvex. ANGUS reported your new identity to me this morning."

"*Bethlehem Splyvex*?" Jeru said with a groan. "What did this Angus guy do, use a random letter generator?"

Ellie wrinkled her nose. "I'll keep calling you Jerry. Or 'Beth,' if you want to be more intimate, hmm?"

"Who's Angus anyway?" Jeru asked.

Ellie said, "The household system. ANGUS is an acronym." She lowered her voice, though ANGUS could probably hear her. "It's a dumb name—like that Splyvex crap."

To the OTP world, to his parents, maybe to everybody online, he was dead. "Jerusalem Pix" no longer existed—the Kingdom had remodeled and now renamed him. "I don't want to sound ungrateful for all . . . this," he said, indicating his head-to-toe alterations, "but since I survived the bombing, why did I have to officially die?"

Victoria appeared to be staring at Jeru, but when he rocked to his left and then his right, her eyes didn't track him. She said in her sing-song cadence, "It seemed like the best means for you to enter our world, hmm? Fresh slate, new start. Also," she added with a laugh, "it's not as if you'll want to go back to that hellhole."

"But I liked being the old me. I'd built myself into a brand, with a trademark and everything: *Does Your Gaming Need a Fix? Get Jerusalem Pix.*"

Victoria went on, half to herself, "That's charming, Jerusalem . . . Bethlehem. Odd how OTP parents always mimic the rich. We give our children unique names to set them apart, then word leaks out, and a few years later everyone out there—" she waved vaguely toward a wall "—follows suit." She rotated in an unsteady half-pirouette and eased toward the hallway leading to the dining room. "When we named our children to honor the Middle East cities lost on 12/26 and the others shortly thereafter—Paris, Mumbai, Beijing, and so on—I suppose it shouldn't have surprised us that parents such as yours would usurp them, hmm?"

Beside him, Ellie said, "I have an older brother on the West Coast who's twenty-five. His name is Istanbul, but I call him Bull. Or something worse sometimes."

Victoria scuffed along the corridor, forcing him to drag his feet so he wouldn't overtake her. She said, "Just for fun, we decided to name the next batch after punctuation marks, to see if your people would chase after us like lemmings going over a cliff." She stopped and turned, forcing Jeru to sidestep to avoid crashing into her. "Is Quote Burbank still the latest teen sensation OTP?"

"She was before I was blown up anyway."

"Well, much can change in six months, hmm? Maybe it's now someone named Comma or Em Dash or Ampersand." She laughed with an airy trill, like a flute playing scales.

"I've been here for six months?" He whirled on Ellipsis.

She was staring at her mother, chin trembling. Her eyes appeared to have lost all color. "Mom, you never told me my name was a joke."

"No, precious one. The joke is that a whole generation out there copied it without a moment's thought. If only they would ape us in more enlightened respects, hmm?" Victoria resumed her shuffle into the dining room.

Ellie didn't follow. He took her hand. At first she tried to pull away, but he said, "Come on, let's get this over with. I think you have a pretty name." She relaxed her arm but still wouldn't budge. "Hey," he continued, "at least you weren't named after someplace that no longer exists, and then just renamed after another radioactive wasteland. You can find an ellipsis on every keyboard, right?"

"Wrong," she said, allowing him to coax her into the room. "It's made by putting three periods in a row. It shows a sentence trailing off. Something left incomplete."

She dropped into a chair on the right side of Victoria, who sat at the end of the banquet table. He intended to sit next to Ellie, but she let go of his hand and pointed to the seat opposite her, on Victoria's left. The table was arranged for two dozen, with diminutive place settings that reminded Jeru of a child's tea party: the plates, bowls, silverware, and cups and glasses were all too small. Only the napkins had any substantial size. He draped it across his lap, wondering if mud pies were in the offing. The menu really didn't matter. He felt like he hadn't eaten in—

Six months? An eternity online. His bank and zip accounts would've closed after his death was recorded, stopping all the automated payments. Without his monthly dues, every cyber club and gaming guild had long since removed his name from their roles, and his businesses would've imploded. Everything he'd achieved since high school, the half-million he'd made selling high-level characters to executives who didn't have the time or skills to do it themselves, the clever cyber-realty deals, all blown away.

Maybe his wealth had gone to his parents. Maybe they appreciated him now that they were enjoying his net worth. Maybe he could rent his old bedroom from them.

His glum thoughts reminded him that Ellie was dealing with her own shock. He tried to catch her eye and give an encouraging smile, but she still glared at her mother.

Victoria brushed her thumb across the right arm of her chair and the wood veneer vanished: another hologram. A narrow LCD screen was revealed. With flicking eye movements—the only speedy thing she'd done up to that point—Victoria appeared to be making selections.

The table hummed. Jeru felt the top and along the side, discovering that the linen concealed a surprisingly massive structure. They sat at an appliance, not a table. He reached for his bowl-topped plate to look beneath, but Ellie warned, "Don't."

Something clicked twice, and the small bowl filled from the bottom up with pale-green broth and chunks of various vegetables, the colors of a sliced-and-diced rainbow. Somehow the base of the dishes and glasses could become permeable and then re-solidify. Rosemary-scented steam wafted from the soup as it stopped an inch from the top. He eased up the small bowl, which was still cool to the touch, and tested its underside and the surface of the plate. Both as solid as bone china.

The soup contained more layers of flavor than anything he'd ever experienced. New seasonings kept revealing themselves in his mouth. He felt as if he'd never tasted food before—every spoonful provided surprise and delight. Also, eating with the child-sized spoon took as long as finishing an OTP-sized appetizer, making it seem just as filling. Only his ravenous appetite belied that illusion.

While they were consuming their soup, an amber liquid with perfect cubes of ice rose within their slender glasses. A sip of the iced tea gave him new flavors: chocolaty mint, smooth licorice, and a hint of spice, as if the sweetener had been stirred in with a cinnamon stick. As soon as he drained his glass, he set it on the faint circle where it had rested. With a click, the mechanism replenished his drink. He asked Victoria, "Can I have more soup?"

"It's time for the entrée," she replied. With a sigh, she placed the spoon in her emptied bowl. The smile remained on her lips, as if life were one long pleasure cruise. "In any case, you don't want to get fat again, hmm? That's why we keep the portions small, to savor without wallowing in gluttony." She tilted her head in his direction. "You'll soon learn moderation."

Ellie dropped her spoon into her bowl with a sharp clink. "Yeah, Mom, you're the soul of moderation."

Victoria rolled her gaze toward her daughter, neck bending like a stem supporting a heavy flower. Her left thumb grazed the other chair arm, revealing its own screen. She didn't bother looking at the selections—perhaps she had them memorized. A mechanical murmur issued from her chair. The manufacturer had installed something like Magic Fingers. She sighed.

Ellie said, "Do you have to do that at the table?"

"Hmm?" Victoria closed her eyes.

"Crap."

Jeru avoided looking in Victoria's direction. And he felt uncomfortable looking at Ellie, because she was so pissed at her blissed-out mom. As he resorted to a careful study of his plate and bowl, they dropped through the tablecloth and vanished.

He touched the revealed linen. His hand passed into another hologram, disappearing. Below the surface of the table, he felt intense heat, as if his fingers dangled over a flame. Wrenching his hand back, he decided to keep them safe in his lap until more food appeared. In the awkward silence—disturbed only by Victoria's purring and her whole-body vibrator—he asked Ellie, "Is your dad at work?"

"He abandoned us," Ellie stated.

Victoria murmured, "You know better than that, precious. We've talked about this."

"Okay, he's dead," Ellie amended. "Murdered in his sleep."

"Here, in your house?" Jeru caught himself looking around. Quit that, fosh—it isn't like there'd be a body on display or a chalk outline on the floor.

"It happened on a plane six years ago," Ellie said. "He had a problem with sleepwalking, which he wouldn't let Doc treat—"

Victoria snarled, "He had a condition, not a problem. And it was five years and eleven months." For the first time, the smile had left her face. She stared at the armrest. The vibrations increased in tempo. Her head dropped back against the leather padding.

Golden eyes glistening, Ellie said, "Well, it became a *problem* when the others in ultra first-class thought he was a terrorist trying to break into the cockpit. Five people jumped him. One guy smothered him with a courtesy pillow."

"The little ones with the slipcovers?"

"They're bigger in ultra first-class."

Victoria's foot bumped Jeru's ankle. She'd kicked off her mule. Her warm skin twitched against his and transferred a faint but pleasant tremor through her toes. He eased away. Victoria's quivering foot pursued him until he scooted his legs out of reach.

He returned his focus to Ellie, who wiped her eyes, now celery-green. Her voice hardened. "In the lawsuit afterward, we liquidated those people's houses and things and took all their cash."

"Did they go to jail?"

Victoria moaned deep in her throat. After a final shudder, she shut off the vibrations. She blinked a few times and wetted her wide smile with a sip of sweet tea. "There's no jail here. We simply banish the criminal. Having to live OTP is punishment enough."

Ellie said, "But first we sue their asses."

"Language, precious one, hmm? Let's bring our best manners to the table."

With a click, plates rose from the depth of the appliance. They halted their ascent atop the tablecloth. On the small white dishes lay a medley of steamed vegetables, piping hot, and medallions of some kind of pale meat in what smelled like a buttery wine sauce. Presumably, the machine was also in the process of washing the bowls and spoons and whipping up a gourmet dessert. It most likely cost as much as his parents' condo but probably saved a fortune in labor expenses.

Stomach grumbling, he plucked up a sliver of meat with his tiny fork and tasted it. The sauce spread through his mouth: garlic, onions, and something vinegary while the chicken—or whatever it was—melted between his tongue and palette. He devoured the meat and crunched his way through a variety of veggies that surprised him with their subtle flavors, some savory and others sweet. Way better than anything that ever came out of his parents' microwave from FūdSmart (*Better than natural*™).

He asked Victoria, "Do you eat like this all the time?"

"No, only three times a day. Perhaps you have a disorder, hmm?" She nibbled a floret of broccoli with small, perfect teeth as she peered at him. "Dr. Gomez will install an appetite regulator in your brain."

Jeru held out both hands. "Whoa! There's no need to do anything else to my brain."

Ellie said, "He's right, Mom."

Relieved by her aggravated tone, Jeru lowered his hands.

She added, "We might as well run him through his paces first. That way, we can make a list of all the tweaks Doc needs to do."

Jeru snatched the child-size knife and pointed the tip back and forth at the two women. No one was on his side. And his only weapon was from a kiddy play. "No more surgery," he growled. "Is that the way you take care of everything you don't like?"

"Of course," Victoria said, biting off a millimeter of carrot. "The point of being rich is that you don't countenance the slightest dissatisfaction. You'll learn soon enough."

Ellie said, "Let me get a toothpick, Jerry, and we can fight a duel." He continued to grasp the knife as she shook her head. "Jeez, you're really high-strung. Better eat before your food gets cold. TableChef will pop up the dessert soon."

He said, "How many times have you gone under the knife?" He looked at the toy blade and threw it onto the table with an unsatisfactory plink. "Four times? Five? Six?"

She looked off into a corner, and her fingers rose one by one. Pausing, she asked, "Are we counting small things?"

"Forget it. Victoria, what else is on your list for Ellie? What tiny dissatisfaction is in need of correcting?"

"The choices are hers, not mine. Oh, there are some standard procedures that children of all genders opt for, except for the most rebellious."

"And what happens to them?"

"They miss out, and in a few years they regret it and become positively addicted to perfecting themselves."

He demanded, "So what are the standard operations?"

"First you're obsessed with eating all the time, and now you won't eat at all." Her head lolled in Ellie's direction. "Perhaps a thyroid irregularity, hmm?"

"Beats me—Doc will know."

Jeru said, "Stop bringing up Dr. Gomez." He tried to grip the edge of the table, but the appliance was so massive he felt like he was trying to seize a car fender.

"Tantrums too. Oh dear." Victoria peered at his head, as if the many imperfections there were so obvious they bulged like boils.

"No one touches me again."

Ellie said, "We did have your arm reattached, Mr. Ungrateful."

"And you did whatever else you wanted, too, without my say."

"You weren't in a position to make suggestions."

He said, "I would've called a halt after my arm was back on."

Victoria sipped her tea and reactivated the vibrations in her chair. She asked, "Would you really?"

Jeru looked himself over then studied his reflection in a gilt-edged mirror on the wall behind Ellie. The changes weren't all cosmetic. They'd made him more powerful. His heart beat stronger, and his lungs took in more air. From eyesight to smell, all of his senses had improved immeasurably, and he felt more robust in every way. More alive. The way he only used to feel in the illusion of the GameSphere.

Shit.

He went back on the offensive. "So, Victoria, is the butterfly that Ellie's going to get a standard procedure?"

Ellie blushed, and her eyes literally flashed at him.

Victoria replied, "We find that it ensures satisfaction, even with the most incompetent partner. Don't you agree that everyone deserves satisfaction?" As if to demonstrate, she shuddered again and sighed.

"Why not make everyone competent at whatever you're talking about?"

"Science has some secrets left to . . . plumb," she said and tittered, as if she'd made a pun. She went on, "As in sports, you can give everyone the same outstanding equipment, but not all will excel at the game."

Ellie said, "Jerry, this isn't the kind of thing we talk about at the table."

"Quite so," her mother concurred as another jolt of pleasure rocked her. "Besides, that procedure is still days away. Let's allow our precious one to stay a child a little longer, hmm?"

Feeling his world spin ever faster out of control, Jeru raked his fingers through his stubbly hair. He was reminded again of the implants and the fact that Victoria and ANGUS and probably Ellie could control him by granting him access and denying permission. With the strange world of the Kingdom closing in on him, he staggered to his feet.

Ellie whistled and applauded.

Jeru tracked her gaze downward. His napkin had fallen away from his lap. Having covered it for so long, the material had gone transparent. He turned away from them and heard Victoria's appreciative hum. Of course. Being seated would've bared his backside as well.

He returned to his chair, his only option to regain modesty.

Victoria gave him a nod of approval, a hint of lust in her smile. She accelerated her chair vibrations and jolted upright. "Oh my! Who's ready for dessert?"

CHAPTER TEN

Gimbel now knew all about Jerusalem Pix. The harlot Geneva had used "Jeru" to thwart her brother's glorious moment of self-sacrifice. Classic sibling rivalry. Before she succumbed to her wounds, she'd sworn she hadn't told another soul about the RSA operation. And Gimbel believed her—as an accomplished liar, God forgive him, he had a very sensitive BS meter.

So instead of permitting Cairo to die a holy martyr's death, Geneva had murdered him through the agency of his childhood friend. The Good Book required an eye for an eye. He extracted one of hers with a bit of coaxing and dropped it in a formaldehyde-filled olive jar he'd brought for that purpose. The retinal stem made the souvenir look like an exotic cherry bomb, taking Gimbel back to the carefree days of his youth when no creature was safe.

As a lad, he'd named the animals like he was Adam in the Garden, except that he gave each one the moniker of a sinner from the Bible before gleefully dispatching it. When he knew he would devote his life in service to the Almighty, he began to take souvenirs: proof of his commitment to the most noble of causes. They also looked cool on his desk beside the sci-fi toys and army men.

If Jerusalem had managed to survive Cairo's bomb blast, one of his eyes was destined for its own jar. Gimbel couldn't decide whether to eliminate the meddler's family, too, to make a point. From Geneva's desperate info dump, he'd gotten the impression that Jeru had few dealings with his parents or anybody else offline. Gimbel felt frisky, though, firing on all cylinders. The Pixes lived in an adjacent HOD, so a couple additional killings wouldn't inconvenience him in the least.

He glanced at the bodies of dumpy Mr. and Mrs. Bledsoe near the front door, surrounded by their purchases. A ragged star-shaped hole graced each adult's forehead like a subsonic benediction. They were collateral damage—the rules said no souvenirs should be taken from them. Had Mr. Bledsoe stopped at one more electronics outlet or had his wife lingered to try on another few pairs of SexyPlus 3XL jeans (*Make a big impression™*), they would've only found their dead daughter and not her executioner. He rifled through the zero-petroleum shopping bags and sneered at their bourgeois tastes. Shop till you drop? Indeed.

The beleaguered neighbor and her obnoxious son Ampersand hadn't returned from their own mall expedition yet. Gimbel had set a video pin-cam outside the door to alert him when the witnesses walked off the elevator. If he got lucky, Amp's daddy would arrive shortly thereafter and maybe bring his office buddies home for dinner. And perhaps some more friends would come over for an impromptu party.

He imagined their bodies stacked up like cordwood and snickered. True, he could never achieve the Single-Day High Score without the use of explosives, but he would be the all-time small-arms leader and even more of an inspiration to his followers. He could have the achievement silk-screened on t-shirts and sell them in the church gift shop.

Eager for something to do until the pin-cam alerted him to motion in the hall, he started toward the back of the condo to see if the Bledsoes owned anything that wasn't low-end junk. They had some stuff so old that it was stamped "Made in China" and might appeal to collectors, but everything else was of recent vintage from Canadian sweatshops.

The All-n-1 in his hip-holster issued a Gregorian chant. Gimbel lifted the device and said, "Preview." On the screen, a 3-D image of the caller appeared along with his name, phone number, and calling location: balding, mournful Billy Bob in the church office, looking even more penitent than usual. His legs were bouncing, which made his image jittery, a sure sign of big news—maybe good, maybe bad.

Gimbel said, "Wallpaper background; no location." In his transmission, he would appear to be standing on Calvary with the huge crosses behind him, as if he were reporting live from the crucifixion. Billy Bob was a good man, but, as a rule, church secretaries made unreliable accessories-after-the-fact.

"Answer," Gimbel commanded. He viewed his own image as a picture-in-picture box in the upper left corner of the screen. His suitably dour expression pleased him.

To his humble secretary, he said, "How can I help you, Mr. Bob?"

Billy said, "Sir, I'm sorry to interrupt your day, but there's been a disaster of biblical proportions." Such drama. Every incident, bad or good, was described by Billy the same way, from nuclear war to bowel movements.

"Tell me what happened."

"The terrorists, sir, they hit the church a few minutes ago. Blew up the sanctuary and the gift shop."

Gimbel barked, "Give me some video, for fu—goodness—sake!"

Billy uploaded a file to Gimbel, who watched the high-definition 3-D aftermath of the attack. For a few moments, he didn't recognize anything, other than the fact that all smoking ruins, from Tokyo to Toledo, looked pretty much alike.

Gaping holes in the walls and ceilings let in murky late-afternoon daylight. As the shaky cameraman panned 360 unsteady degrees, Gimbel began to identify aspects of his church amid the rubble: an overturned rostrum on what remained of the altar; dusty, upended pews with their custom EasyBottom upholstery (*Let both ends sing "Hallelujah"™*) miraculously intact; shattered RSA action figures from the gift shop strewn across the holy battlefield along with G.I. Jesus dolls and scorched copies of Gimbel's memoir *God's Plan, Part One—What He's Told Me So Far*.

First that SOB Jerusalem ruined his salvo against the Kingdom and now this. Some fucking Plan—God had a lot explaining to do.

Taking a few deep breaths, soothed by the smell of his victims' blood in the condo, he filed the video in his Infidels folder and resumed the conversation. "Mr. Bob, please tell me that our guards annihilated the terrorists."

Billy whimpered, "Most of our guards are dead, sir. The terrorists had decoy escape vehicles loaded with explosives. When our men shot up the trucks and moved in for the kill, the bombs wiped them out." He patted his face with a handkerchief dotted with little crosses. "What do I do? I'm alone in the basement office. Everyone else took the emergency tunnel over to 4P."

The church secretary uploaded a video from the Petey Pepperoni Pizza Palace of soot-covered church employees gulping icy cups of soda and nervous RSA warriors gnawing on pizza crusts while tracking with their submachine guns as furry robots cartwheeled around the room. Strobe lights flashed and colored bubbles floated by. The audio transmitted hypnotic, delirious Petey Pepperoni PunSongs and the manic squeals of over-stimulated children.

Gimbel counted the aluminum pizza pans and the pitchers of cola on his employees' tables, estimating the total bill plus tip. Come expense-report time, he knew who he could trust and who he couldn't. He also made a mental note to send Petey a personalized copy of his memoir, to reinforce his thanks for letting the tunnel come up into the "Petunia Pepperoncini" women's bathroom.

After filing away that video under Finance, he told Billy, "I'm proud that you've stayed at your post, Mr. Bob. God will reward you more than I ever could. Keep manning the phones and, if you have to, be sure to use that sawed-off shotgun I gave you last Christmas." He paused as an image popped into his mind, no doubt sent by the Almighty. "Just don't shoot me when I get there, okay?"

"Yes, sir. I'm locked and loaded and . . . scared."

"Merely a test of faith, Mr. Bob. Say a prayer now to prove your worthiness in His eyes."

Billy put his palms together and lowered his head. Gimbel ended the call, leaving Billy to it. No time to wait for the witnesses. Anyway, he could tell the DNA-constraining static spray had begun to wear off:

his boxer shorts no longer clung so desperately to Mr. Happy and the Begetters.

Gimbel gathered his gear, left the Bledsoe place, and stalked down the tunnel-of-yogurt hallway. God would not abandon him. If he continued to serve Him well, his rewards would multiply.

Sure enough, when the elevator doors opened for him, the little brat named Amp and his bedraggled mother stood inside.

Hallelujah.

CHAPTER ELEVEN

After they had eaten a delicate concoction of mixed berries and sweet cream, Victoria announced her plan to lie down for a nap. Before she ambled away, she once again welcomed Jeru to his new home but said nothing in parting to Ellie.

Jeru stood before the screen in the foyer and watched her red icon's slow, weaving progress toward another cul-de-sac of recreation rooms. He asked Ellie, "Is she like that all the time?"

She snorted and turned her attention to the screen as well.

He tried again: "You ever see yourself becoming like her?"

"Based on how it's going with you, I might have more fun humping the furniture too."

"You're the one who pushed me away." He crossed his arms, feeling anger build again. "You're kicking my ass one minute and then drooling over me the next. I'm not used to someone treating me like an object."

"He said as he stared at my boobs." She sighed—not with her mother's satisfaction but with aggravation. "Come on. If you're done feeling victimized, it's time for you to plug in."

He touched the back of his head, tentatively feeling for a data port.

"That's just an expression. Jeez, you're so literal."

"Too many movies," he agreed, and told himself to calm down. No way was he going to get control of his situation if he kept losing control of his emotions.

He followed her along a white-paneled hall that featured hunting scenes—men in red jackets and black-domed helmets riding horseback amid racing hounds. The spaniels and retrievers captivated Jeru. His parents had never let him have a dog. Of course, if he'd moved out and gotten his own place like he kept threatening to do, then the dog he wanted to get would've starved to death during the past six months, waiting for him to come home. Sometimes unanswered wishes were good things.

Ellie tapped her foot until he pulled his focus away from the paintings and tagged along beside her. His peripheral vision was excellent—he could study her without turning his head. In all the ways he used to fantasize about, she was a wish that had been answered in spades: gorgeous and willing, smart and sharp-witted. So why not give in, cozy up to her, and become a pleasure junkie himself? At least for a few days? Have some fun and then escape and rebuild his real life online, where he knew what to expect.

But what if this were his real life now? The sex would be blazing, but what if that's all she let him do for the next hundred years or more? And if she got bored with him, Victoria might decide to take a turn, as an alternative to her furniture. Jeru shuddered.

He looked at another hunting scene they walked past and considered what the artist hadn't painted: the fox. Something about being pursued made him want to run, not surrender.

She said, "Sorry I didn't tell you about it being six months since you saved me." From her soft tone, he could tell she was trying to make up. "There was so much work to do on you, and Mom and I kept driving Dr. Gomez crazy by adding to the list."

"My folks did the same thing to the contractor who renovated our—their—condo."

"Lucky for you that we didn't ask for skylights." She reached up and patted the side of his head.

He kidded back, "Still, it looks like you got just what you ordered from the doctor. Even if you haven't run me through my *paces* yet."

"That you know of." She waggled her eyebrows and stopped before a door that promptly opened for her. "Lots can be done when the brain's the only thing asleep." From her smile, he couldn't tell if she were joking or reminiscing.

She led him into a very cold and dark room. The walls, floor, and ceiling reflected no light. The door closed behind him; it too was black. Across a distance of twenty feet or twenty yards—impossible to know without any frame of reference—the hologram of a screen suspended in mid-air provided the only illumination. He couldn't even see his feet as he and Ellie proceeded. He felt like he had embarked on a spacewalk.

The screen showed graphical representations of data: chains of colors and shapes that morphed like lava lamps, strange and organic and, he soon recognized, predictable. He relaxed. Funny that it was here in outer space, watching a nebula of data, where he finally felt at home. At least he would get along well with the SysOp.

He walked ahead of Ellie and studied the screen up close, rubbing his pajama-sleeved arms against the chill. The gradual shifts of some shapes and colors contrasted with the binary states of other patterns—wide, narrow, wide, narrow. Like a pulse. That was it. Along one edge, he saw the name Bethlehem Splyvex, his stupid new identity. Jeru was looking at himself, expressed in raw and aggregated data.

The implants in his brain no doubt reported those stats. Jeru glanced into the scant sphere of luminescence radiating from the screen. A young, bearded man sat in the glow on a wheeled, black office chair, studying him. Different hues washed over his body, perfectly reflecting the spectrum on the screen because his skin was as white as the room was dark. Pecs and biceps strained his short-sleeved pullover, and thigh and calf muscles bulged below satiny running shorts. He apparently didn't mind the cold. The man looked past him as Ellie caught up.

Jeru asked him, "Is this how ANGUS sees me?"

"No," the SysOp said in a molasses-smooth voice, the sort of genteel Southern accent Jeru hadn't heard since he was a child listening to his grandparents. "The system only needs data. The graphics are for us—the lower life forms. I'm Kly-buhn," he added.

It took Jeru a moment to translate that into *Kliburn*. "I'm, well, you know who I am." Jeru glanced back at the Splyvex name. "And who ANGUS says I am. Aren't you cold in that outfit?"

Kliburn's gaze shifted to the screen, where a new pattern of graphics pulsed and flowed. His name—just "Kliburn"—was displayed along the edge. "98.6273 degrees Fahrenheit."

"I mean, don't you feel cold?"

"Ah, a feeling. Define the data set. I might ask the same of you."

Jeru glanced down. Naturally, the Nite-n-Daze pajamas had become transparent during his walk across the dark room and were only now beginning to fill in again. A smirk curled Kliburn's lips, and Jeru caught the amused glance he shot in Ellie's direction. More shared jokes at his expense.

Ellie crouched beside the SysOp's chair. She glowed in the reflected radiance, the colors only accentuating her perfection. On the screen, some of the graphics changed rapidly: Kliburn's heart rate quickened, and a red parabola spiked. His attention returned briefly to the screen, which reverted to its Bethlehem readouts. Jeru was gratified to see that his own biorhythms showed much more control.

"Kly, do you need me here?" Ellie's tone sounded friendly, but there was something else that Jeru couldn't name.

"I was hoping you would stay."

She looked at him for a moment. "Okay, let me take a potty break, and I'll come back." She patted his arm, and Jeru envisioned a new high score on Kliburn's red parabola.

Ellie departed in a flash of brilliant light from the hallway, like a star going nova. Jeru blinked away purple spots. Returning his attention to the bearded man at the edge of outer space, he said, "So what do we do?"

"While we wait for Ellipsis to come back?"

"No, what do we do for me? Ellie said something about *plugging in*."

"*Ellie*, is it? Such familiarity already." Kliburn's green eyes narrowed.

Jeru took a step back. "She doesn't mind the nickname."

"The girl's preferences are a mystery, even in this age when we can analyze every thought."

"You read people's minds?"

"Read yes, fathom no. It is GIGO," he said, using geek-speak for Garbage In, Garbage Out. "Most people deceive themselves with their thoughts. They justify, rationalize, cover up. Only the body never lies." He reached behind his back, his arm disappearing into the void, and rolled another black office chair beside him into the faint circle of light. "Sit," he commanded.

Jeru sat.

"First we will run some standard diagnostics," the SysOp said in his fluid drawl, emotions in check again. "I examined you thoroughly while you were in your surgical coma, and this display tells me that all low-level functionality is operational. So, now I will read your mind."

The screen went blank, casting the room into utter darkness. Great, Jeru thought, just what I was always afraid of.

With a burst of new colors and 3-D shapes, the screen came alive again, and a voice spoke in Jeru's head. It was his voice, but with a detached, professorial tone. It said, "Think of the last event you can recall before waking this morning."

Jeru pictured Cairo's severed hand, blood and bits everywhere, his own dismembered forearm lying on the pavement and then Ellie cradling it. On the screen, shapes somersaulted and the kaleidoscopic spectrum swirled. But Jeru detected a second source of light. On Kliburn's left side, another suspended screen showed different graphics and a data table, some kind of a chemical analysis. Salt and other minerals, along with proteins and water. With his acute peripheral vision, Jeru saw Ellie's name along the border.

Kliburn wasn't looking at Jeru's readouts—he was studying the content of Ellie's urine.

"Hey!" Jeru cried. "Isn't that info kind of personal?"

The man rotated in his chair, as if to block Jeru's view, but then swung back slowly, stroking his beard. He said, "There is no such thing as privacy. As a one-time hacker, you should know that." Jeru started to react, but Kliburn held up a pale hand that the colors on both screens painted with broad, overlapping strokes. "I know all about Jerusalem Pix—where he went to school, his grades, the reports in his file before he learned to cover his cyber tracks. I know about his success as a gamer, the high scores logged on the umpteenth level of the most popular online quests."

Kliburn gestured at the display on his left. Ellie's information was replaced by spreadsheets and account balances. "I would have become his client just to learn how to defeat the gorgons in Level 40 of Swordblazer. His virtual real estate investments were inspired and worthy of study. In other realms of cyberspace, he was more . . . pedestrian. With a penchant for blond triplets." His beard twitched in his version of a smile as logon codes, site selections, and pornographic animated videos scrolled behind him. "Nubile, flexible ones," he added.

"Stop," Jeru said. "You proved your point. You know everything about me."

"Not at all. I know everything about Jerusalem Pix, dead these six months. Bethlehem Splyvex is a relatively clean slate. Other than trashing a simulated nineteenth-century library, ogling and kissing *Ellie*, and trading quips and jibes with her, you are a complete unknown. Not enough behavior has been recorded for you to be predictable."

"But I'm still Jerusalem Pix. I'm still me."

He felt as off-balance as he had in Alice in Wonderland: Tea Party Massacre, one of the first video games he'd ever played. Here he was, arguing with the omniscient caterpillar that, yes dammit, this new world *should* be able to predict and control him entirely.

"No," the SysOp said, pursing his lips as if drawing on an invisible hookah pipe, "Jerusalem Pix lived his life—except for the last fifty-seven minutes of it—in another world. Two other worlds, really: online and offline. Here and now, you are an infant who must discover his new environment step by step. Everything is different, including your body, and you will have to unlearn what you know and absorb this world from scratch. As you do, the world will come to know you."

Jeru grumbled, "And you'll be my guide?"

"I prefer the term *master*, but *parent* might suffice." Kliburn glanced at a corner of the left-hand screen where a tiny map displayed a pink icon heading back down the hall.

"Does Ellie know you track her every move? Even what she does in the bathroom?"

Kliburn studied him a moment as colors painted and repainted his features. "This is a case of mutually assured destruction, my friend, just like on 12/26. You tell her about me, I tell her all about Jerusalem's exploits in cyberspace, and the quite explicit zips you had received from a certain real-life Geneva Bledsoe."

Beside him, Ellie's screen went blank and vanished against the black background. Only graphics of Jeru's thought patterns spun and tumbled in the space nearby.

The door opened and, with another nova of light, Ellie strode across the threshold. When the door closed, darkness swallowed her. Apparently unfazed, she continued to walk with confidence toward them, high heels clicking. Her hand settled on his shoulder as she crouched between him and Kliburn. Colors painted her face and delicate collarbones. Was her other hand touching the SysOp?

She asked, "So, Jerry, now you know how to open the doors and surf our Intranet and order stuff?"

"None of that yet."

She looked at Kliburn. "What have you guys been doing—playing video games?"

"Not at all," the man said, moving his face closer to hers. "I have been explaining how our world works, what the rules are. The beginner's tutorial, like we give the little children."

She said, "I'm surprised he hasn't fallen into another coma, out of boredom. Jerry's smart—he picks up things real fast." She patted Jeru's back. "Well, except how the Nite-n-Daze PJs work. Anyway, show him how to use the implants so I don't have to follow him around like his personal slave."

Jeru teased, "That's right, I'm supposed to be *your* personal slave." To Kliburn, he added, "Doesn't sound like I'll need to order a wardrobe, since her plans for me don't include clothes."

The creep could analyze excretions and semen counts all he wanted.

Jeru imagined himself romping in bed with Ellie for a whole century while Kliburn sat isolated on his personal moon, watching impotently. It made the idea of surrendering to her much more appealing. *Look all you want, albino boy, but know that she wants me, not you.*

She snorted. "You should hear yourself—so smug." She switched her focus to Kliburn, but he was studying the screen with such intense concentration that she had to pinch him to get his attention. "What's got you zonked?"

Kliburn turned, stabbing a fierce look at Jeru, who realized he himself had a powerful weapon. Whenever he wanted to tweak the man, all he had to do was think something lusty about Ellie. After he and she made love, he would only have to reminisce to thumb more than his nose at Kliburn.

The man said, "You're right, *Ellie*. Let's get started."

CHAPTER TWELVE

Kliburn asked Ellie to sit behind them, so she wouldn't "distract the pupil." Somehow, she found another chair in the complete darkness. She kicked the bottom of Jeru's seat like the kids used to do in school. Jeru knew it was her way of showing affection—he braced for spitballs.

"No need to still your thoughts," Kliburn told Jeru in his oozing Southern drawl, "though you might learn to direct them more profitably. Since I have control of the system, I will instruct ANGUS to ping the implanted chips. You will be told to respond to each command that appears in your mind, and the screen will report the result. In this way, we will know that you are fully operational, and ANGUS then will acknowledge your commands."

Jeru glanced back at Ellie. "No more *open sesame* games with the doors."

"I said that I have better ones, so don't get cocky, fosh."

Kliburn frowned, the wrinkles on his brow trapping reflected colors. "*Fosh?*"

A kick sounded from under Kliburn's chair, and he jerked upright. She said, "It's the new slang. See what happens when you sit alone in the dark all the time? You miss out."

The man jutted his chin. "After the diagnostics, I will sift through the sundry contents of our pupil's brain so I can get up to date." He winked at Jeru, his eyelid painted blue and red from the screen. "Just kidding. Here we go."

Jeru was rattling through every malicious slang term he could think of—sift that, glans—when the detached, serious voice interrupted his thoughts. It said, "Turn the square into a circle."

He saw in his mind's eye a white square on a black background. Rounding off the corners and morphing the shape into a circle produced the identical result on the screen, exactly as he conceived it.

"Circle into sphere into cube."

The shaded white ball in his mind squeezed in on the top and bottom and sides until it formed a perfect block, which was again reflected on the screen.

"Repeat in your thoughts, 'Open the door.'"

A featureless door in his mind and on the screen slid open at his command. Jeru turned in his seat, and Ellie smiled at him in the reflected light, but he was looking past her. *Open the door.* The exit slid aside, revealing the shock of light and the hallway. To prove that neither Kliburn nor Ellie was messing with him, he told the door to stay open, but it promptly whipped shut.

"Sorry," Kliburn said. "It is vital that this room remains at a constant temperature."

"Yeah, always freezing," she said. Jeru noticed her shirt seemed thicker than before. Even so, gooseflesh peppered her bare arms, and he could see a faint outline of her nipples. She peered around him, toward the screen, and quickly crossed her arms over her chest. "Jeez, Jerry, even I can read your thoughts up there."

Kliburn cleared his throat. "If you could turn your attention back to the test."

"Sorry." Jeru held up a hand. "But wait a sec. Can you always override my thought-commands?"

Kliburn said, "Of course not. In my domain I can, but in your rooms, for example, your word is final, so to speak."

"How about in neutral areas, like the dining room, or a door that leads outside?"

"ANGUS acknowledges the last command submitted. If I think or say, *Close*, and then you order, *Open*, the door opens."

"So we could get into a thought war, with ANGUS sliding the door open and closed over and over forever."

Ellie laughed. "Don't you think we have better things to do with our time?"

"I'm just saying." As a further tweak to Kliburn, he said to her, "And you could lure me into your bedroom and never let me out."

She blushed and glanced at the SysOp. "Hurry up, Kly, before his imagination runs away with him."

Jeru faced forward and settled within his chair. The commands came faster—manipulating menus, making selections, and ordering from the networked screens located throughout the house. He could select clothes online, to be delivered within minutes from a nearby store, or at worst, in a day or two from around what was left of the world. ANGUS already had a record of his measurements. Anything he wanted, from sports equipment to toiletries to a variety of personal—very personal—services were his upon request.

With the vast array of individuals who could pleasure Victoria, Jeru wondered why Ellie's mom chose intimacy with the furniture instead. Had she slept with anyone since an overly vigilant airplane passenger suffocated her husband with a courtesy pillow? He also wondered if Ellie had availed herself of any of the hunky or luscious attendants pictured on the menu.

He stopped himself—how could he be jealous over someone he'd only met that morning?

Kliburn said, "These menus are only a small part of our Intranet, which is similar to your world wide web, but without any of the useless, deceptive, or disgusting content. We will now run through the basic commands, beginning with Search."

The system introduced Jeru to the search function, branded Omni by a company he'd never heard of. As with everything else, thoughts or spoken words produced immediate results. He had to be careful, though. As his mind jumped around, layers of displayed information piled up like overlapping cards in a game of solitaire.

Jeru shook his head at the mess he'd made on the screen. "I guess I have to learn some discipline."

Ellie giggled behind him and said, "That happens to everyone the first time. Keep going."

Sure enough, he then learned the Pause and Resume commands and other ways to manipulate the Net. He tried again. Still curious about the "butterfly" Dr. Gomez said that Ellie was going to get for her Making Eighteen party, he focused on some keywords and gaped at the summaries, animation, and video from the surgery and health sites that appeared. Labial control, thousands of additional nerve endings, muscular enhancements inside and out. Good God, she'd be able to literally flap her sex like a butterfly.

Ellie slapped the back of his head. "Jerry, you perv, stop it! Kly, why can't I wipe the screen?"

"ANGUS is focused on your friend at the moment."

"Well do something. You're supposed to control it."

"Hmm," Kliburn said, leaning an ankle across his knee. "I do not seem to be able to. He has locked me out."

Ellie smacked Jeru's head again.

Jeru knew Kliburn could've seized control—the SysOp was letting him screw up in front of the girl they both wanted to impress. Quickly, Jeru returned his thoughts to the clothes warehouse, though every time he recalled the details of the butterfly surgery, that site overlaid the 3-D pictures of shirts and pants. For a few seconds, undulating sex organs strobed alternately with haberdashery, until Jeru willed himself to focus.

He felt his mind compartmentalizing, his attention segmenting into pure, distinct spectra. Concentrating on one thing suddenly didn't involve warding off thoughts of other things. He thought about a search for pants, and he got nothing but pants. When he finished his selections, he then chose some shirts and underwear, everything bearing the Sssagers trademark. He thought about personal electronics and was rewarded with a host of gear he didn't recognize. Not only didn't he know the brand names, but he couldn't identify the purpose of many of the items that rotated on the screen.

"That's better," Ellie said. "Shopping's safe." The cushions in her chair sighed as she settled back.

Unable to resist, Jeru focused a new search on her. "Ellipsis Stewart" appeared above her picture, an un-posed but extraordinarily beautiful shot that showed her smiling, arms wide, perched on a stool in the library Jeru had trashed. She wore the same clothes as now, so ANGUS had probably recorded the image that morning, when Jeru awakened. A kick from her shoe rebounded off the bottom of his chair and jolted his butt, but he continued to peruse a seemingly endless stream of photos of her saved in the network. Apparently ANGUS stored the most attractive images it had recorded from every day of her life. And Kliburn had probably made all the recent selections.

"Jerry, do you plan on embarrassing me all day?" She kicked his chair again, harder.

He scrolled faster, a time-lapse movie running backward, as she grew younger, flat-chested, and hipless. Her hair changed colors, grew very long, vanished into a pixie cut, and then streamed Rapunzel-like once more around the cherubic face of a little girl. A handsome, wiry man appeared in many of the pre-teen shots, also growing younger, obviously her father. Her dad wrestled with her, read over her shoulder as she studied an antique book, held her upright on a red unicycle.

Behind Jeru, Ellie sounded like she had begun to cry. Regretting that he'd made her sad, he wondered what color her eyes had just turned. They were brown for most of her young life, but they became cobalt blue in her baby pictures. That was the only time she looked chubby, and the only time ANGUS—or whoever the photographer was—captured her in the arms of her mother. Neither of them looked particularly happy.

Jeru rotated his chair to face her. "Sorry, but I wanted to see you as a kid. It makes me feel like I know you better."

She wiped her cheeks and nodded. Her eyes had become mirrors, reflecting the colors on the screen, much as Kliburn's white skin did. She cleared her throat and said, "Seen enough?"

"For now. Thanks for not kicking me to death."

He focused on Kliburn's name, sending it to Omni Search. The screen didn't respond, but the scholarly voice in his mind reported, "I apologize. Access is restricted."

Jeru glanced at the man, who stared back without expression. Then one corner of the trim beard around his mouth turned up.

Ellie yawned and stood, pushing her chair away. "I'm leaving. Coming with me?"

Kliburn replied, "I wish I could."

"I meant Jerry."

Jeru leaned toward Kliburn. "She meant me, *Kly*. Am I done or do I need to come back for more lessons?"

"ANGUS can lead you through some other tutorials."

"Do I need to interface through a screen?"

"No, just address the system in your mind, and it will respond. You can do it anywhere—in the shower or in bed." He arched an eyebrow. "If you want a multi-media experience, a screen is useful, though ANGUS can provide an array of thought pictures."

Jeru said, "So, was my visit here even necessary?"

"I wanted to meet you," the SysOp said in his syrupy accent.

"Okay, you have. See you around."

The screen changed to dozens of live views of Jeru, as if seen through an insect's eyes, except the images were being taken from all sides, top, and bottom. The entire room—maybe the whole house—was one big camera.

Kliburn said, "Indeed."

When Jeru stood, his chair rolled backward into the all-consuming darkness and sounded like it continued to roll without encountering anything to stop it. Where were the walls? He took Ellie's hand and ordered the exit door to open. It slid aside, revealing a bright, carpeted hallway framed by infinite black. Striding with more confidence than he felt, fearful of colliding with some massive obstruction or tumbling into endless space, he led her away.

She whispered, "What's the matter with you?" She wrestled free of his grip.

"I just want to go."

"There's no need to be rude to him."

The light from the hallway seemed to grow brighter the closer Jeru came, until it turned into a physical thing that stabbed his eyes. Tears streamed and rapid pounding reverberated in his skull. Something was shaking his brain like a box of rocks. He staggered and groped around him, no longer convinced that his next step would strike a solid floor.

"Jerry?"

"My head." Half-digested lunch surged up his throat as a giant's hands seemed to clamp onto his skull and wring it like a sponge. He dropped to his hands and knees and vomited.

Ellie clawed at the back of his shirt, shouting, "Kly, what's happening to him? Don't just sit there!"

"It might be a reaction to the interface with ANGUS. Perhaps it's only a migraine."

Jeru collapsed. He groaned as the brow he'd injured earlier struck the smooth, hard floor and squished in the puddle of gooey puke. He stared into absolute darkness.

"Take him offline!"

"You're not authorized to order—"

"If you don't, I'll have Mom fire you."

The pain left Jeru's head instantly. He rolled onto his back, guessing he was looking at the ceiling since Ellie crouched above him. Of course, in this new world, he could very well be upside down. Light from the doorway gave her the angelic look he recalled after the bomb blast.

Ellie leaned down so close she could've kissed him. Instead she said, "You sure are a pain in the ass."

CHAPTER THIRTEEN

Gimbel worked his thumbnail under a dot of white paint—dubbed "Angel's Wing" by the manufacturer—that besmirched the padded bonobo-skin of his office chair. Billy Bob had assured him that Resurrection Renovators (*Holey . . . Wholly . . . Holy*™) would use drop cloths and take deliberate care during the repairs to his church. Six months later, however, Gimbel was still finding random splatters that suggested a pigeon rather than an angel.

Apparently, Resurrection Renovators' only qualification was the fish symbol on their card. References, Mr. Bob, always get verifiable references. Christ Himself had to provide them before getting a carpentry gig. And then, as now, listing "God" didn't cut it.

Despite the crew's incompetence, the church had been reborn. Gimbel even received state and federal grants under the Victims of Terrorism Act to add shielding and additional armaments. Any jihadists or other terrorists would get some nasty surprises if they tried to knock down his spire again.

But one couldn't play defense in the battle for mankind's soul. Gimbel slid his FarSighters over his eyes and reviewed the latest wargames practiced by the God's Boot Camp recruits. That yammering eighteen-year-old named London Johnson continued to be useless, more likely to blow off his own foot than smite a godless Saracen. Still, the machine of war required fuel for its engine, and youngsters like Lun provided the needed juice. Gimbel watched him stumble in body armor through a live-fire exercise, miraculously unscathed by the rounds peppering the earth around him.

Lun paused, helmet covering his eyes, and raised his machine gun.

He nailed a fellow recruit in the back of the head with a rapid burst of orange paintballs. The teenager that Lun had blasted toppled over, rolled to a sitting position, and shot Lun in the groin, leaving a sunburst of tangerine on Lun's doubtful manhood. Both laughed and shot each other again.

The RSA instructor sent a volley of genuine bullets over their heads, cussing in a very un-Christian manner. This didn't stop friendly fire erupting from all sides, turning everyone but the instructor a vivid orange. To restore order, the drill sergeant came down off the ridge and started shooting the kids pointblank with a real pistol. Bullets whapped the thickest parts of their armor, knocking the recruits sideways and backward and onto their suddenly stricken faces.

Utter chaos. Still, the bruises would provide an effective reminder.

Gimbel knew the signs of fighting dogs kept penned too long. It was time to get bloody and send some souls to God for His judgment.

After removing the FarSighters, he consulted a leaked top-secret list of suspected terrorist safehouses in the Atlanta suburbs. The federal government was too busy relearning how to be a world superpower to eradicate every little nest of insurgents, and the police focused their muscle on tax dodgers and others who cheated the state. According to the governor's latest press release, collections had fallen to 97% of estimates, so the boys in blue would be working overtime. Besides, as a registered militia, Gimbel's church got a deduction for every confirmed terrorist killed. Scalps weren't necessary, but they did provide the necessary DNA evidence.

Arranging the data on the screen by map locations, Gimbel noticed that one potential safehouse was in a Stone Mountain neighborhood near his own, where the huge cone of granite still depicted the Confederate legends Robert E. Lee, Stonewall Jackson, and Jefferson Davis on horseback. They had survived political correctness, erosion, and the occasional rocket attack, and the park at the foot of the mountain still boasted the best darn light show east of the Mississippi River. Gimbel figured he could pick up a taquito pizza, collect some scalps, and make it to the "Dixie Lights Spec-tac-u-lar" before his meal got cold.

His All-n-1 chanted. A quick preview showed Billy Bob in the next room. From the shaky image, Gimbel could tell Billy's legs were bouncing.

"Yes, Mr. Bob?"

"I have a caller you'll definitely want to talk to, sir."

"They've tracked down my ex-wife?"

Billy said, "No, sir, not yet. But this man says he has information about a fellow who the authorities told us was dead."

"Were we . . . involved in that soul's journey to the hereafter?"

"No, sir. It seems that the guy was alive all along." His image jolted even more. Maybe he had to go to the bathroom. "Remember the Cairo Bledsoe 'mission work' that was a disappointment about six months ago? This man—some kind of systems operator in the Kingdom—claims that he can give you Jerusalem Pix. Dead or alive."

CHAPTER FOURTEEN

When Jeru opened his eyes in a dimly lit room, a beautiful woman peered down at him. Ellie had grown older, become a brunette, and gotten a laser tan. My God, how long had he been out this time? Decades?

He realized his eyes were unfocused. Peering up, he now recognized Dr. Gomez.

"Either you are preternaturally clumsy," she said in her British accent, "or you have a crush on me and will go to any lengths to return to my operating room."

"The implants—" His voice caught, so he swallowed and tried again. "They made a terrible pain in my head."

"I ran an extensive series of bioelectrical tests, conducted protein and synaptic scans, and even checked for a tumor or evidence of a seizure. Nothing. Your brain is fine, and my previous work is above reproach." The line of her mouth softened. "When you showed up here draped across a HandyBot, like a centurion on his shield, I did have a moment of self-doubt."

"So, what happened to me?" He sounded pleading when he should've been angry. What were these people doing to him? He tried again more forcefully: "Tell me what's going on here."

Ellie appeared at his other side and touched his forehead, which felt pain-free. "Some kind of strange feedback loop from ANGUS. Kly is looking into it."

"Kliburn did it. He hates me."

"Jerry, don't be paranoid. Kly wouldn't have summoned the robovac to carry you here if he wanted to hurt you."

"And you're proud of him for that?"

"Sure."

"Then he won."

Ellie and Dr. Gomez traded a look that suggested they preferred him unconscious.

Jeru said, "I'm not paranoid. He wants you, Ellie, and I'm the competition. Hell, he even analyzes your—" He remembered Kliburn's threat to reveal certain online activities and interests. *Mutually assured destruction.* "—your pictures and voice. He's listening to us now, watching us through ANGUS's cameras."

"Not here," Dr. Gomez said. "My rooms are off-limits. They're shielded, actually. I have a separate, un-networked system that controls the surgical theater and the rest of the suite. That was part of our contract when my husband and I agreed to become the Stewarts' personal physicians."

"Your husband? Is he around?"

"He died shortly before you rescued Ellipsis. I really could've used his help with you." Her lips pressed tight together for a moment, and she blinked hard. "Can you imagine someone dying at eighty? Rafael had half his life ahead of him."

Jeru wanted to point out that people OTP often died well before eighty. From natural causes sometimes. Instead, he asked what had happened to Rafael, bracing for another bizarre suffocation-by-pillow sort of tragedy.

"Brain aneurism. A tiny one, but in the worst place. Somehow, the robots and I missed it when we gave him his annual physical. You'd think that a wife would pay extra-special attention, but we'd been together for so long I always knew when something was amiss. Nothing was—otherwise I'd know, right? How could I not?" She looked at her hands. "How could I?"

Ellie said, "I bet you thought the same thing was happening to Jerry, like it was Dr. Rafe all over again. I'm sorry, Doc, I didn't realize."

"Well, I was wrong—again."

Jeru thought he should comfort the widow, but he knew it would embarrass the professional in her. How sad that all three women in the household were grieving over lost men. A home full of fascinating, gorgeous, lonely females—and Kliburn. No wonder a new man on the scene had caused such a stir. He said, "So what happens with me now?"

"You're free to go," Dr. Gomez said. "Unless there's some tweaking or elective surgery you'd like." She opened her arms and gestured at the walls, as if to invite him to peruse the showroom and choose some customizing details. Maybe tail fins or a hood ornament.

Which reminded him about Ellipsis.

He sat up and said, "Ellie, would you give me a minute with Doc? There's something personal I want to ask her about."

"Uh-oh," Ellie said, "you're feeling shy again. Well, don't expect me to act like Sleeping Beauty in the next room, waiting for a kiss that'll never come." She marched out, and the door slid shut behind her.

Dr. Gomez said, "Still working your charms on her, I see."

"It's just a game we play."

She rolled her eyes. "What do you want to know?"

"Why did it take six months to finish your work on me? On *Trek X*, they could do anything in hours or days."

Dr. Gomez pounded a fist into her open palm. "Oh blast, I knew I should've consulted those screenwriters when planning your surgeries." She took a deep breath and said with renewed calm, "You, my boy, have a gift for saying things that make a woman waspish. The reason it took so long is that Ellie kept changing her mind about the way she wanted you to look, and she kept adding to her wish list."

"About Ellie and, um, that butterfly surgery she wants—"

"I told you before that it's to be a surprise for you."

"When Kliburn was showing me how to search your Intranet, I learned all about it." He made a sour face. "It's disgusting."

Dr. Gomez crossed her arms. "Why?"

"Because it's unnatural."

"Says the man who came in here sixty pounds overweight with one arm blown off, and woke up in the body of a god."

Jeru tapped his thick pectoral muscles. "But *none* of this is *natural* to me."

"I see. Heart attacks, strokes, diabetes, cancer: those are natural."

"Aneurisms—"

"Yes, damn you, those too. Why would you deny Ellipsis any amount of pleasure?"

"Because it's unnecessary. It's over-the-top."

"It's beautiful, and, I'll have you know, the sensations are wonderful." She pushed his shoulders hard enough to tip him backward. He had to catch himself with his hands. "Lie down," she ordered. "Give me just a few minutes, and I'll undo that wonder between your legs. That grotesque mutilation of your natural manhood."

"No!" He covered his groin.

"Ah! The rules are different for a man. You deserve to experience the extra nerve endings, the baton-like erection, the prolonged orgasm—and instant recovery." She nodded in mock revelation. "Surely that marvel you wield should be enough for poor Ellipsis. She shouldn't need anything other than *you* to maximize her pleasure. If she craves more, then obviously she's a slut, a nymphomaniac, a—"

"Stop it. I see what you're saying. It's just . . ." He gestured helplessly at the exit through which Ellie had gone. "She's more than perfect already."

"There's no such thing. And don't you dare try to control Ellipsis. You have no right to dictate to her."

"Doc, all I'm—"

"You think Kliburn might have shaken you up with a little brain zap? You would not believe how cruelly I could destroy you. Hell itself doesn't have the arsenal at my disposal." The door opened, and she jabbed her finger toward it. "Now get out of my surgery."

Jeru slunk into the infirmary. He ordered the door to stay open as a miniscule show of defiance, but it whipped shut as soon as his back foot cleared the threshold.

Ellie wasn't waiting for him. He continued into the hall. His ability to open that exit and keep it open did nothing to cheer him.

Standing on the long carpet runner, he glanced one way and the other at the paintings, small tables, and progression of closed doors. "ANGUS," he asked in his mind, "where is the nearest viewer?"

Ten yards away, a drab portrait of some pale brunette with a faint, inscrutable smile on her lips vanished, revealing a glossy screen mounted within the wood frame. He approached it and mentally commanded, "Locate me."

An emerald blip displayed his location on a large floor plan and on a close-up of the hall.

"Locate my rooms."

The system marked his suite in another wing of the sprawling former hotel. At least he didn't have to return to the library he'd smashed up earlier. He asked ANGUS to map the path he needed to take to get to his bedroom. A green line on the floor plan showed him the shortest route, which consisted of six turns and two flights of stairs.

He asked in his mind, "Will you help me if I get lost?"

"I will," his mental voice replied in its professorial tone.

Jeru began his trek. Whereas Ellie had led him left at the end of the hall and down a flight of stairs to get to the dining room, he went right and traversed another long corridor before coming to a grand marble staircase that took him up. He found himself in a large foyer, the hub of another wheel with spoke-like hallways.

Trying to recall the map and turn-directions, he started down one corridor where petite crystal chandeliers, rather than wall sconces, lit the way.

"Wrong turn," his mental voice said.

He backed up and tried another route.

"No."

He felt like a fosh asking ANGUS to display the map again, so he ventured down a third path.

"Wrong turn."

Shit.

He commanded, "Screen."

A mirror to his left turned opaque. With a sigh, he said, "Locate me." He asked for his route again and counted eight turns and two more flights of stairs. It was like being trapped in a funhouse.

ANGUS was screwing with him. No, not ANGUS. It was Kliburn.

Jeru could picture the smug, snow-white glans leaning back, studying him from the fly-like perspective of dozens of cameras and reading these very thoughts. Asking for Ellie's location and a map to her would no doubt yield more bogus information, because Kliburn wanted to keep them apart. A sheepish return to Dr. Gomez was out of the question because the woman was ready to strap him down and emasculate him. Or worse.

"Ellie!" He cupped his hands into a megaphone and yelled her name again. After trotting back to the marble staircase, he tried it once more. No reply. Running around lost and shouting didn't thrill him either.

Okay, time to dig into a big slice of humble pie. Backtrack to Doc's operating room where she would threaten to lop off his dick again, but maybe then she'd calm down enough to help.

Muttering, he turned to head back down the stairs but stopped short.

Instead of the passage he'd just traipsed through, a black wall confronted him, as infinitely dark as outer space. Or Kliburn's lair. He pivoted right where another wall now stood, inches away. Turning left, he nearly ran into a third black barrier. Behind him, instead of the staircase, he discovered the fourth side of the box that imprisoned him.

The carpet underneath him vanished into the same void. Expecting to plummet, he nevertheless stood firm but all his points of reference had disappeared, except the plaster far above him.

Then, like a lid crashing down, the ceiling ceased to be—and the remaining light went out.

CHAPTER FIFTEEN

Jeru turned in a circle, a circle within a box of blackness, and realized that he didn't even know if he'd gone all the way around. There was no way to get his bearings. He felt like he was the first image in a video game before the rest of the universe was created around him.

"ANGUS, turn on a light."

Nothing.

"Show me a viewer screen."

Nada.

Shit, here he was again, a nonentity to the system. Except this time it was personal.

Kliburn had boxed him into a hologram of deep, starless space.

He took a tentative step forward and then another one, feeling the weave and texture of carpeting underfoot. His bare toes touched cold stone. Marble. The top of the staircase. It was still there, and he'd nearly tumbled down it.

The black box was an illusion. If he could blindly retrace his steps and blunder back to Dr. Gomez's rooms, he'd be safe from Kliburn's influence.

He eased down the chilly stairs. Finally, he was at the bottom, back on carpeting. He put his hands out to save himself from ugly collisions and shuffled forward. Though he moved freely, he couldn't shake a growing feeling of claustrophobia. He hadn't realized until then how much he relied on his eyesight.

Just when he was feeling a little more confident, his knee whacked a table leg and a vase overturned, spilling water and cut flowers. Jeru groped blindly and felt a wet, varnished tabletop and the thorny stems of roses. He lifted a flower and poked his eye with the petals. What the hell, he was blind anyway. Lowering the flower to his nose, he inhaled its cloying perfume, like a moisturizing cream his grandmother had worn. At least Kliburn couldn't take away his other senses.

Very cautious again, he sidestepped the table and moved in the opposite direction of the dripping sounds from the overturned vase. He tossed the rose aside and heard a slight bump, as if the flower head had struck a wall. Too bad he didn't have a cane he could tap around him.

Arms out again like Frankenstein's monster or a zombie in a cheesy video game, he shuffled along the hallway. In another ten steps, he brushed a wall on his left side. Since he would be taking a left turn to reach Dr. Gomez's suite, he decided to keep his left hand on the wall, hunch over, and put his right hand down low to feel any tables or other obstacles in his way.

From Frankenstein's monster to Igor, he thought, as he hobbled along.

A low hum and slight rumble ahead made him pause. The sounds of a motor and turning wheels were accompanied by a faint chime, like the triangle he used to play in the grade-school band. The chime grew louder, as if warning Jeru of its proximity.

Maybe it was actually some kind of tiny vehicle. The hushed symphony of noises passed him. Then he heard the whir of a vacuum and a quick thump. The machine moved farther behind him where it sucked liquid and swallowed more flowers whole. It must've been the sort of robo-vac that apparently had conveyed him to Dr. Gomez not long ago.

He considered making his way over to it, climbing atop, and holding on while it hopefully took him out of the black box. After two steps in what he hoped was that direction, he heard the machine roll away from him, toward the marble steps. Utterly blind, he had a much better chance of cracking his shin on something than leaping aboard a moving HandyBot.

On the other hand, what if he made another mess and stood by, to await the robot's return? No, by thinking this, he alerted Kliburn to his plan; the bastard would order the robot to stay away. Better stick with his first idea. He reached out for the left-hand wall and felt nothing. Flailing with both hands now, he encountered nothing but empty, endless space.

A horror story popped into his panicky mind. He'd read it for middle school on a BetterTech TeachPad (*Goodbye, Mr. Chips*™). In the tale, a man left his mountain cabin during a blizzard and couldn't find his way back. A white-out, the storm was called. The next day, the man's neighbor found him frozen to death two feet from his door.

Jeru lunged to his left and again touched nothing. *Found dead, two feet from his door.*

What he thought was his heart pounding had morphed into approaching footsteps. Whoever it was didn't weigh much but was wearing heels that made a solid rap on the carpeted wood floor.

Jeru called out, "Ellie!"

"Jerry?" She sounded maybe a hundred feet away. On the other hand, with his most-relied-on sense stolen from him, it could've been a hundred yards. How quickly did blind people adapt to their world? He needed to do it in minutes, not months.

He hollered, "Can you see me?"

"No." After a moment, she said, "Come on, quit playing. Where are you hiding?"

Ahead of him, doors slid open and then, after a minute, closed again. Though he was getting better at hearing them—they actually made a very faint shushing sound—he saw nothing but black. As Ellie got closer, he decided to stay put rather than risk passing her. Why didn't she see a big black wall looming ahead?

He said, "I'm not playing. I'm behind some kind of holographic barrier Kliburn put up. There's nothing but darkness all around me."

"That's crazy. I'm looking down an empty hallway with all the lights on. Where are you?"

"Since you can see, follow my voice." A memory made him smile:

splashing and laughing in the HOD's rooftop pool with a bunch of other little kids. He said, "It'll be the opposite of 'Marco Polo.' "

"What are you talking about?" She had drawn nearer. Again a door opened and then closed at her command.

"Didn't you ever play that? Some kid has to close his eyes and the others swim around him. Every time he shouts, 'Marco,' they have to say 'Polo,' so he can try to follow their voices and catch them."

She said, "Jeez, you OTPers are foshes." So close now.

He jutted out his right hand, and she screamed. His fingers had closed on something soft and curved.

She smacked the side of his head.

"Hey!" He clutched his numb, rapidly warming ear. The hollow ringing masked her reply.

He said, "I wasn't groping you or anything. I'm just trying to feel where you are." Reaching out very slowly, he patted her shirt and the smooth hem at the top of her slacks. Her hand closed on his lips and bearded chin, but her touch was gentle, exploring.

"Jerry, what's happening? My wrist's disappearing into thin air. I can't see the hand I'm touching you with."

He grasped her waistband and pulled her closer. "Do you see my hand?"

"Yes," she said, as her fingers rubbed the line of his scruffy lower jaw. "But it's coming out of nowhere."

Like Bledsoe's disembodied fist, he thought.

She fondled his lower face more aggressively, prodding his features until two fingers thrust up his nostrils. They both cried out and backed away. While he sneezed, she said, "Oh, gross." Fingernails scraped rapidly against cloth. Sure, she could pick up a severed arm, but don't get around her with a booger.

He sniffled and said, "Try again, but lower."

The side of her hand brushed his waist. He took hold and gave her fingers a gentle squeeze. "Okay, we've got each other."

"This is so freaky. ANGUS must be having some kind of meltdown."

"It's not the system. It's your buddy *Kly*."

"Why are you always picking on him?" She tried to take back her hand, but he tightened his grip.

"He hates me—he wants you all to himself." Mutually assured destruction, Kliburn had promised, but Jeru didn't care; the man was driving him crazy. "He watches your every move. He analyzes what you flush down the toilet."

"That's sick—let me go, dammit."

"Quit tugging. I saw him doing it. I'm sure he's recording us right now."

The tip of her shoe struck his calf. He flinched, and then she kicked him again. "Hands off, you glans!"

She yanked backward. He held on but allowed himself to be pulled off-balance. Feeling her stumble and fall, he plunged with her into the fully lit hallway. She landed on her rump and cried out as Jeru tumbled on top of her.

"Get off! Get off!" Ellie's fists pounded his shoulders and the back of his head. Her eyes blazed orange.

"Stop that. Ow!" He rolled off her and glanced down along his body. The Nite-n-Daze pajama top had remained opaque despite the lack of light, which meant the holograms were projected in his mind and Ellie's. But his lower half had disappeared entirely. Not naked—gone altogether.

He wriggled his bare toes and felt the carpet under his pajama-covered legs and butt; however, he saw only the hotel-decor hallway. Visually, he ceased to exist below the waist. "God, that's weird."

"I'm not talking to you," she said, scooting away on her perfect backside. Now at a safer distance, she kicked at his arm. "I wish I'd known you were a degenerate. I would've had Doc glue your arm back on and then dump you OTP."

"Why do you keep calling me names?" He rose on his elbows and ran one hand down his chest and stomach. The fingertips vanished when they passed his midsection. He found the illusion mesmerizing.

"ANGUS just told me all the things you used to do in cyberspace. Yuck!"

His face heated up. Damn all those lonely days and nights with no girlfriend and all the possibilities of virtual couplings just a few commands away.

He asked, "With pictures?"

She kicked at him again, but she'd slid too far away to make contact. "You would've had to save a whole limo full of party girls to make you happy."

"I was lonesome. My buddy Caro was getting wrapped up in the RSA, and I wasn't friends with any real women."

She looked as if she were listening to someone else and then snorted. "You're a liar, Jerry. What about that Geneva tramp? Did she ever do that thing she promised with the crème de menthe?"

He sat up, pulling in his legs but they stayed hidden, as if the hologram of the empty corridor had moved with him. Suddenly he found himself looking into deep, starless space again. Endlessly dark. He jerked his head around, but the void was everywhere, as black as tar over his eyes.

She gasped.

He called, "Where are you?"

"Where'd you go?"

"Kliburn's hologram. You moved too far away from me." Jeru thrust his arms in what he hoped was her direction. "He won't put you in this blackout. Can you see my hands?"

"No. Jeez, this is so damn strange. Why do you keep blaming it on Kly?"

She sounded a few yards off to the left. He crawled in that direction. "Why do you keep defend—" His face emerged so close to Ellie's that he felt her warm exhalation and noted the graceful oval of her pink cheek and her bright blue eyes before she screeched.

As she scrambled backward, he followed on his hands and knees, peripherally aware of his arms vanishing whenever they dropped behind the forward progress of his face.

She sobbed, "You're scaring me. You're like a monster, just this head in midair." She backed into one of the delicate tables. The narrow vase upended, and she cried out as water and yellow flowers cascaded onto her. Pushing petals, stems, and streaming hair away from her face, she yelled, "Stay away from me, you freak. Look what you did to me!"

Her shirt and pants became denser, now looking like thick felt as they probably absorbed the water from her skin and wicked it away. A butter-colored petal had lodged in the wet blond hair beside her face. He reached for it. She flinched and banged her head on the table leg, which set the overturned, cylindrical vase rolling. It tumbled off the edge, hit the carpet beside her hand, and broke into three sharp-edged pieces. The crash only increased her panic. As his fingertips closed on the petal, she lodged her head into the corner made by the wall and table. The broken glass blocked her escape route, so she hunkered and shook like a doomed animal.

"Hey," he whispered. "Hey look, it's just a flower. Everything's okay."

She shut her eyes and kept them closed tight. "Just leave me alone."

"I can't." He scooted his legs under him and stayed beside her. Sure enough, all of him came into view now that he kneeled against her.

He added, "As soon as I move away, I'll be in darkness again and invisible to you, so Kliburn wins either way."

She scowled but peered at him through narrow eyes. "What are you babbling about?"

"If I stay this close, he knows I'll drive you crazy, and you'll hate me."

She turned her face farther into the wall. "I already hate you. I had a special day planned for when you woke up, but you've ruined everything."

"It's a gift. Some people can play the piano or draw stuff; I ruin everything."

"You're not funny."

"I'll make the perfect boyfriend: invisible until you want me against you."

"Stop trying to make me laugh, you glans."

"Did I ever show you my disappearing body act?"

She raked her fingers through her hair and then arranged the damp curls. A reluctant smile undermined her efforts to stay grim-faced. Her battle against giving in was surprisingly sexy. She said, "Don't you ever shut up? Too bad Kly can't put you on Mute."

"So you agree he's the one doing this?" From behind him, he heard the whir and chimes of an approaching robo-vac.

"I don't know." She looked him over, and the weave of her shirt loosened and the neckline plunged. Obviously she was feeling better. "I guess I don't really hate you. Much."

"That's progress," he said, moving his face only inches from hers. "I'll remind you of it next time I ruin everything."

"Fosh."

The word left her lips puckered, and he kissed her fast. With her head wedged into the corner, she couldn't back away. Nor did she try. Her mouth moved against his and then slid away. Close to his ear, the one she'd slugged earlier, Ellie said, "Kly is watching us now?"

"Always." He wondered if they'd have to move aside, to make room for the robot.

"I still think you're overreacting to him."

"I see," he said, leaning back on his heels. "Want me to do my floating head trick again?"

"Okay, okay. This whole thing creeps me out." Her eyes were periwinkle as she scanned the hall behind him. "Where's the HandyBot anyway?"

"Dunno." Jeru stood and helped her to her feet. He noted the puddle of water she'd been sitting in without apparent discomfort—those clothes were amazing. Maybe by the time she led him to his room, he'd have some outfits waiting. The peek-a-boo pajama bit was getting old.

Still holding her hand, he led her into the middle of the hall. A glance behind him showed an apparently empty corridor, but the noise of an oncoming machine sounded loud.

A few feet from Jeru, the HandyBot materialized out of the hallway hologram. Racing full tilt with a pair of jointed metal limbs extended like battle lances, it charged him.

CHAPTER SIXTEEN

Ellie yelled some kind of war cry and struck a martial arts pose as Jeru dove to the side, trying to draw the homicidal robot away from her. Two more steel-pronged arms stood at the ready on the back of the machine, if the first couple didn't finish him off. A vacuum hose arched above like a cobra, taking in a never-ending breath, eager to suck up the evidence of his murder.

Jeru hit the carpeted floor and rolled, every bit of him exposed, vulnerable. He braced for the deep punctures, the relentless thrust of steel through skin and tender organs. Getting blown to bits by Cairo would've hurt a whole lot less.

One of the lances aimed underneath his ribs to puncture his heart, while the other appeared to have targeted his groin. And the latter one would strike first, so he'd feel what was happening to him before the other prongs turned his chest into pulp. With a surge of speed, the robot dashed forward.

Lying on his side, Jeru rolled back toward Kliburn's killing machine. The lance tips passed over him. Too late, the HandyBot corrected their angle, and the tubular arms merely pounded his thigh and ribs. It kept coming though. The tank-like treads bit through his clothes as its massive weight rolled on top of him.

Ellie's shout turned into a curse. She tried in vain to pull the robot off him.

Two hundred pounds pressing against his ribs wasn't the worst part. The real pain came from the machine's revolving treads. Every link clawed at him and the gaps between each one snapped shut like jaws against his clothes and skin. His screams managed to drown out the incessant, cheerful ping of the robot's chimes, its happy song of death and dismemberment.

Lying beneath the machine, at least he was clear of its deadly lances. Jeru wrapped his arms around the bulk and held the robot to him, his chin just beneath its curved front edge. Friction between the treads and his clothes and body brought heat, smoke, and raw, scraping agony. It would soon gouge smoldering trenches through him if it didn't crush him first.

Ellie yelled, "What are you doing? I'm trying to get it off you." One of the metal arms in back swatted her away. She hit the wall with a thump and crumpled over.

Jeru kept yelling as the pain burned deeper and the choking smoke billowed. The hose appeared over the front edge, sucking madly, and darted toward his face. He tilted his head just in time. The hollow end struck his right cheekbone. With contact came immediate vacuum and a keening that competed with Jeru's howls as it inhaled his skin, intent on yanking his face through its two-inch mouth.

His cheek distended, pulling upward until he felt a gap widen at the corner of his right eye. If the hose tilted a fraction of an inch, it would inhale his eyeball. Reading his mind, the robot scraped its hose upward. Momentarily free from the vacuum, Jeru twisted his head away and the hose seized his ear.

Greedy suction deafened his right ear, while his left one dutifully took in his pitiful groans. Above him, the four arms had begun to bend at invisible joints. Shorter but still lethal spears would soon plunge into him.

He flung his arms aside, releasing the machine. It shot across his shoulders and clipped his chin as it roared over him. The momentum ripped the hose from his ear. Above him, Jeru only saw the dark, smooth undercarriage of the HandyBot passing by, while the vicious treads churned on either side of his face.

Kliburn's mechanical assassin recovered control, halted just beyond Jeru's head, and jabbed with its back two arms. The steel tips should have turned his face into a kabob, but he felt himself slide feet-first across the carpet.

Having seized his ankles, Ellie yanked him clear as the prongs buried themselves into the floor. The robot's treads revved in place, its body held fast by the two imbedded arms.

She snatched him by the wrists and hauled him onto his knees. Then, with a cry of pain, she helped him to his feet. Jeru couldn't stand, though; the robot's crushing weight and the burning up and down his chest made it hard even to breathe. She slung one of his arms around her shoulder and, grunting through clenched teeth, dragged him back down the hall.

With a pop, the robo-vac's trapped appendages disconnected from the machine's body and the robot scooted around the twin obstacles. Its remaining two lances levered forward, ready to strike. Above the machine, the neck of the hose rose snake-like again.

She shouted, "Stop it, Kly, stop it. I hate you!"

Oh shit. She should've tried to calm Kliburn down, not piss him off even more. Jeru braced himself for the final, deadly charge. At least, he thought, we'll go together.

The robot surged forward but zipped past them, like a knight on horseback having missed his target. It wheeled around as Ellie and Jeru shuffled back a step. Her hold on him tightened, a sideways hug. Ramrod arms glinted before them. The tips opened into three evil-looking prongs. Perfect for plucking out their eyes.

With a whir of mechanical glee, it pounced.

The arms scooped up the pieces of the vase Ellie had knocked over while the hose inhaled the spilled water, flowers, and smaller shards. All the while, its chimes alerted them to its presence and industriousness. Busy robot here—watch your step!

Dumping the remains in a hatch that opened in the top, it backed away solicitously and dipped its front bumper in a low bow. The machine scooted over to the silver arms it had detached earlier and plucked the deadly spears from the floor. Ping, ping, ping, it rolled down the hall, no longer cloaked by a hologram, as if glad to have been of service.

They stared after the machine. He felt like he'd aged a thousand years. With a grunt, he slid down the wall onto his butt, his legs outstretched. All he wanted to do was fall into a coma. Vulnerable to any kind of attack, he wondered why Kliburn didn't try something else. Maybe the SysOp was still smarting over Ellie's words.

"Thanks for saving me," he said.

She joined him on the floor and nestled her face against his torn and aching chest. The top of her blond head fit perfectly beneath his bruised chin. In fact, she felt perfect everywhere she touched him, even though all those places hurt like hell.

"What danger?" she said, her voice catching. One hand covered her ribs, which must've been injured when the HandyBot had knocked her into the wall. "You were totally overreacting."

They laughed with relief, like survivors of an apocalypse.

CHAPTER SEVENTEEN

Over Jeru's protests, Ellie told ANGUS to connect her with Dr. Gomez. He didn't want to utilize anything Kliburn could manipulate or distort. Admittedly, though, Ellie wasn't strong enough to haul him to the operating theater, and he could never manage the trip under his own power. And they couldn't sit there forever. Kliburn eventually would get over his hurt feelings and shatter the current truce with one hellish torture or another.

She called, "Doc, Jerry's hurt bad. He had a run-in with one of the HandyBots."

The doctor's tart voice issued from a hidden speaker, as clear as if she sat beside them: "I told him to leave the help alone." After a pause, she said, "His vitals are all askew. Yours too, Ellipsis." The smart-aleck tone had disappeared. All business now, she stated, "Wait for me there."

After the doctor disconnected, Ellie murmured to him, "I'm scared. I've never been frightened in my own home before."

"No point in whispering," he said. He had to keep his comments short and his breaths shallow—filling his chest with air hurt too much. "He can hear and see everything."

Even though Kliburn could read his thoughts as well, he stuck out his middle finger—about the only thing not in pain—and panned 180 degrees with it. Much more satisfying than just thinking a curse.

She shook her head and gave him a gentle squeeze. "My eloquent hero."

Dr. Gomez soon arrived behind the wheel of a small vehicle, a cross between a golf cart and a pickup truck. The cargo bed appeared to be long enough to carry him without his feet hanging off the tailgate. She bolted from behind the wheel and kneeled beside him. Taking a purple lozenge from her tweed jacket pocket, she told him to put it under his tongue.

At first the pill seared the soft flesh there like something ultra-cold, but numbness soon replaced the dry-ice burn. His throat relaxed and his head and chest ceased to throb. In a half minute, the pain disappeared throughout his body.

Then he lost all sensation. Unlike his out-of-body experience after the bomb blast, though, he didn't feel euphoric. He felt dead. Had Doc just poisoned him, put him out of his misery?

She must've seen his panic, maybe in his eyes since his face felt as slack as a rubber mask. The doctor said, "It's just a nerve depressant that lets your body focus on healing. All unnecessary activities are shutting down." She glanced at the screen of a thin blue device clipped to her belt and announced that his vitals showed some improvement already.

Dr. Gomez said, "Let's do a little triage. Ellipsis, are you feeling up to helping me?"

Ellie prodded her ribs experimentally and hissed in pain. Dr. Gomez gave her a professional once-over and pulled the side of Ellie's blouse up. Peripherally, as he was too paralyzed to even move his head, he saw her inflamed side where the robot had struck her. The doctor touched a pastel yellow vial to the area, saying, "Can't help the patient if you're out of sorts."

Ellie relaxed and moved with less noticeable strain. She said, "I could drive if you want, while you take care of Jerry."

"I've seen you drive—let's limit the number of casualties we're dealing with, shall we?"

"Gee, thanks, Doc." She peered at Jeru, moving her face so close to his that their noses might have collided. Not being able to feel his nose, he wasn't sure. "He's still alert," she reported.

The doctor rummaged in her pockets and removed more vials and some silver bands that looked like shiny duct tape. She said, "That's just the remnants of adrenalin. He'll succumb in a moment or two."

"What do we do first?"

"Your favorite part. We strip him naked."

Ellie checked his eyes again. He could barely keep them open. "Someday," she said, "you're going to be awake when I do this."

His eyelids slammed shut before she undid the second button on his pajamas.

Jeru awoke in a dim room, lying in its center on a raised platform that was too hard to be a bed and too smooth to be an Aztec altar for human sacrifices. He felt as if someone had turned his skin inside out and used his ribs as hockey sticks and his heart as the puck.

Gentle explorations with his fingers revealed slick, foil-like strips over the wounds on his bare chest. He was only naked from the waist up. The material covering his lower half felt like actual trousers, not pajamas, and he wore a belt. Socks and loafers covered his feet. For the first time since he chased Bledsoe into the Kingdom, he was dressed like a grownup. Half of him anyway.

As his eyes adjusted to the faint light coming from the ceiling panels, he glanced around the room and recognized Dr. Gomez's operating theater. The doctor stood in the far corner, arms crossed. She shoved her fists into her pockets and marched to his side.

"Hey, Doc," he rasped and swallowed to wet his throat. "Three visits here in one day. I hope this one's the charm."

"More like three strikes and you're out. Besides—it's a day later than you think." She peeled back a corner of one of the foil strips and, apparently liking what she saw, ripped all twelve inches of it from his chest.

"Ow! What—"

She yanked off another one and then another. The strips parted from his skin without causing much pain, but the violence of her actions shocked him into crying out each time.

"Stop, dammit!"

She said, "I'm done, in fact. And so are you."

"I don't understand." He touched his chest and felt warm, tender skin, like newborn flesh.

"That much is apparent."

"You made me strong, not smart. Give me a hint."

Dr. Gomez leaned into his face, dark hair tumbling in an avalanche around both cheeks. "Do you know what you've done to us? In a span of less than six hours you ruined this place." A spray of spittle struck his cheeks and eyes. "You've ruined it for Ellie—and for me."

She loomed so close that he couldn't avoid her by turning his head. He shut his eyes instead. His slacks began to massage his legs, like a thousand gentle fingers seeking to soothe him, and the area over his groin warmed, as if to distract him from his anxieties. Even his socks gave him a reassuring foot rub. They must have been the Sssagers brand Ellie kept raving about. He did feel a little calmer, less argumentative. Too bad Doc wasn't wearing them also. With a meek glance at her, he said, "It's not my fault. Kliburn attacked us because she likes me instead of him."

" 'Likes'?" She grabbed his throat with one strong hand and dug in her fingernails until he met her furious stare, then she eased off enough for him to breathe. Doc roared, "Ellie loves you, you idiot. After you saved her from the bomber, she stayed with you every day, neglecting her classes and her chums so she could assist me, not eating unless she could do it in here. She even slept on a cot beside you." The doctor closed her free hand around his bicep and crushed the thick muscle. "When you awoke, you were supposed to be her friend and protector, someone she could trust and count on and make a life with. Until then, she was protecting you. Now look at what you've done," she raged.

"I am protecting her, Doc. I saved her. Maybe twice."

"It's not enough. Suddenly you're the cause of her problems; you're no different than the bomber."

"Kliburn is the new bomber." He grabbed her wrist, surprised at how petite her bones were and how easily he pulled her loose from his throat. She'd made him strong indeed.

Dr. Gomez shook free of him. She stomped around the room, massaging her arm.

He asked, "So what'll happen? He'll keep trying to kill me or find some other girl to obsess over or what?"

"He'll never stop. That's obvious now. He's always doted on her, but that protectiveness has become something much darker."

"So Ellie and I will move out. We'll live in my world, or go somewhere else in the Kingdom."

She frowned for a moment and then smiled thinly. "They still call it that, do they? The nickname started in my time. Sorry, but he can get to you anywhere In-Town—in Atlanta or any of the other enclaves. OTP as well. Even without your neural chips, he'll find you."

He touched his scalp. It was freshly shaven and covered with a network of tender places.

"Don't poke," the doctor warned.

"The chips are gone?"

"Yes, but it's not enough. That was merely to keep him from frying your brain once you leave my secure zone. He can track you in your world using your national ID card, security cameras, everything the government put in place to make you safe."

Jeru sat up too quickly. His head rocked with crashing waves, like a goldfish bowl in an earthquake. He waited for his equilibrium to settle and his vision to clear. His pants and socks worked so hard to put him at ease, he wanted to rip the annoying things off his body. He said, "Let's go to the police."

"They can't touch him. By now he's erased anything that would connect him with the HandyBot."

"Why can't Ellie's mom fire him?"

"She's become addicted to the pleasure rooms and devices he's arranged for her, so she literally worships him. As her physician, that's my fault. Regardless, who jails the jailer? Household SysOps control everything—there's been more than one instance like this one. That's society's fault." She gestured toward the walls. "If not for what my husband called my *obsessive need for privacy*, my small domain here would be under Kliburn's rule as well."

He flexed the dense muscles in his arms and torso. "I could beat the snot out of him."

"As if he'd let you get that close again."

Jeru slumped in defeat, exhausted by all of the dead ends she'd presented. His clothes responded with "there, there" thrumming. He asked, "So what do we do?"

She looked away. "There's a physician I know. Someone I trained actually. Strange fellow, decided to continue to live OTP after he had the means to come inside."

"What's so special about him? What can he do that you can't?"

She glanced at him and said, "It's really a matter of access to materials."

"You're avoiding my question."

"Dr. Torres does cryogenic work. Preservation and reanimation."

"You're going to put me in a deep freeze?"

"No, that's not it," the doctor said. "Of course, he did help preserve my husband after the aneurism. Just in case we came up with something."

"Well, what's this guy do then?"

"In OTP lingo, Dr. Torres is—as I used to be—a steiner."

"Oh shit." Jeru held his head. Why couldn't they just leave his brain alone? He'd heard of steiners, men and women on the bleeding edge of transplant surgery. Their specialty was neuro-something-or-other, but the comparison with Dr. Frankenstein was unavoidable: for an instant identity change, just drop your brain into someone else's body.

He asked, "Why not give me plastic surgery or do a face transplant or something?"

"That would take too long—Kliburn will figure out something by then—and, in any case, have you seen an extra face lying around?"

"Your husband won't miss his."

She snarled, "How about I toss you out of my surgery again and let

Kliburn's HandyBots have another go at tearing off your own face? Then I'll have a spare for the next chap who comes through."

"Okay, okay." He put up his hands in surrender, trying to think of other alternatives. Doc did say that this steiner was located OTP. Too bad the only escape from the Kingdom meant waking up in yet another body; he was starting to like this one. Maybe he could get away before Torres got his surgical gloves on him, though it would mean Kliburn could still track him, and never again would he see—

He looked up and asked, "How will this protect Ellie?"

"Every time I think you're totally selfish, you surprise me. Well, hero, she's going with you to Dr. Torres's. He'll remove her neural chips during the procedure."

Procedure, like having a wart removed.

"So she knows she's going to get 'steined' along with me?" He frowned. "She's willing to trade that perfect face and body for something less, maybe a whole lot less?"

Dr. Gomez paced the long room again, head down, face hidden behind her dark hair.

He snapped, "You haven't told her, have you?"

She whisked a shirt from a nearby table. "Put this on and come along. Dr. Torres expects you both in an hour."

"Doc—"

Dr. Gomez turned her back on him. She said, "I'm certain that, deep down, she knows."

CHAPTER EIGHTEEN

Dr. Gomez collected Ellie from the infirmary. Ellie's face looked puffy and splotched, and red rimmed her eyes, as if she'd had a long, hard cry. Jeru wondered if she had wept over *his* fate or what would become of *her*. Maybe she cried for both of them. She took his hand and squeezed hard but wouldn't meet his gaze.

She had changed into a modest aqua-blue tunic that was a little too large for her and a cream-colored skirt. Probably from the doctor's closet—it wouldn't have been safe for Ellie to leave Doc's rooms. She looked great, of course, but the crying and the mayhem of the past day had aged her. No longer a sunny girl in an angel's body, she looked sad but more mature. Of course, she would be looking a whole lot sadder shortly, in another woman's body.

He could understand her grieving, but his thoughts and emotions ricocheted like video pinball. In a few minutes, he was going home, back to a life and people he at least understood, if not loved. All his friends were online and wouldn't care if he'd gone through two body changes or twenty, as long as his avatar led them to glory again. On the other hand, this steiner Dr. Torres could botch the operations and kill him and Ellie, their brains could reject their new bodies, or Ellie could despise her new look, or his, or she just could hate living OTP, with appliances you had to manually turn on and off and clothes and furniture that didn't give you orgasms.

The doctor herded them through the operating theater and down a short hallway with closed doors on either side. One was marked "Storage" and the others bore no labels. Probably her private quarters.

At the end of the hall, a door slid aside to reveal a spacious garage.

OFFLINING

Beside a stubby silver car of an unknown make, a white limo purred, identical to the one Ellie had ridden in when he saved her from Bledsoe's bomb. The back doors opened by themselves as they approached, revealing a black leather interior with two sets of seats facing each other. The driver door swung wide as well and an Asian man with shoulder-length black hair stepped out. He sported a pistol in a shoulder holster over his crinkly black one-piece, which was similar to the policeman's who'd tended to Jeru when the mayhem had begun six months earlier.

The man said in accent-less English, "Doctor, I confirmed the address with Dr. Daniel Torres' office. They're expecting us."

"Godspeed." She ushered Ellie and Jeru into the comfy back and promised to get in touch as soon as Dr. Torres permitted it.

Ellie said, "You're sure I can't tell Mom that I'll be away for a couple of days, until Jerry gets . . . used to things?"

Jeru stared at Dr. Gomez, who looked past him at Ellie. "It's not safe. I don't want Kliburn to know you've left until you're on your way. And I certainly don't want him to know where you're headed." She swung the door to close it.

"Doc," Jeru said, and she halted, quivering with tension. He continued with, "You're sure your rooms and this garage and everything you say and do are all shielded from ANGUS and Kliburn?"

"Absolutely. The car too. Ben here installed a stealth mask, so no one—not even I—can track you."

Silicon chips defeating other silicon chips: welcome to World War IV. The doctor made a move to secure Jeru's door again, so he said, "I think you have something to tell Ellie."

Dr. Gomez glared at him. "Time's short. Ben, be careful OTP." She slammed the door shut.

The limo rolled forward as the garage doors parted sideways and slid back into the walls. Ben sped them down an alley.

Ellie said, "What's she supposed to tell me?"

Jeru glanced back, expecting Dr. Gomez to be watching their departure with an expression of agonized guilt, but the doctor had already returned to her rooms. She'd left it up to him to tell her. No, that wasn't true—Doc expected him to stay quiet as well. Even Ben the Lethal Chauffeur probably knew the plan. Everyone but Ellie.

Clearly she had been crying for him alone, for his terrible fate and the fact that she'd probably have to leave him OTP. She had been crying because, after the steiner transplanted his brain into a new body, she'd planned to return home to somehow fend off Kliburn and either return to her previous life or await the arrival of another hero.

Ben turned onto a large boulevard. The sun had set, but instead of streetlights glaring down, a million LEDs embedded in the sides of the buildings, along the walkways, and sparkling from tree trunks and branches in patterns as varied and intricate as snowflakes, gave off a soft glow everywhere he looked. The omnipresent cloud cover prevented him from seeing the stars, but he felt like he was traveling among them.

He wanted to stay silent, to get lost in the amazing array of glittering pinpoints, but Ellie asked again, "What was Doc supposed to say?"

Jeru took her hand and said, "Did she . . . uh . . . tell you what'll happen now?"

She nodded and her red-streaked eyes teared up again. Taking a deep breath, she sat straighter, which pushed out her chest in a wonderful way. He could imagine her thoughts: *Be brave for him.* She said, "I hate that it has to be this way. If I knew Kliburn was going to go nuts with jealousy, I would've taken you to the other side of the world."

Not exactly an answer to his question. He squeezed her hand, practiced the words that would reveal the horrible truth she needed to hear, and . . . chickened out. Silently cursing his cowardice, he sank deeper into the seat and watched the light show beyond the windows.

He planned to bolt from the car once they arrived OTP. Home, he corrected himself. "Outside the Perimeter" was Kingdom-speak. He'd have to get used to thinking and acting like a regular old suburbanite again: watching for suspicious people who could be terrorists, microwaving tasteless FūdSmart meals, staying up on all the latest ads so he wouldn't sound like a fosh online, watching 3-D videos of pretty girls instead of cozying up next to the perfect one beside him . . . .

Sweat dampened his armpits, but his shirt loosened its weave and dried his skin. His slacks began to gently massage his legs again in soothing waves. The Sssagers would be his only souvenirs from his weird adventure, especially if he couldn't see Ellie again.

Ellie patted his thigh. "Do you want any music or something to drink or eat? That lunch you ate and puked up was a long time ago." She gestured at the back of the chauffeur's seat. "Ben always stocks the car with great treats."

Jeru was hungry, now that he thought about it, but didn't feel that he deserved a treat. Poor Ellie—she gave her hero everything but a brave heart. Avoiding her eyes, he noticed lighted pictograms on the armrest, one of which depicted a seated stick figure holding a steering wheel. Either it was a way to page the chauffeur or it would put him in control of the limo: the ultimate backseat driver.

Maybe chatting with Ben would keep him from thinking about what he should be telling Ellie.

He tapped the pictogram with his index finger, and Ben said, "Yes, sir?"

Jeru said, "So, um, Ben, have you worked for the Stewarts a long time?"

"No, sir, only a dozen years."

With a laugh, Jeru said, "I'm only twenty. Twelve years would be a career."

"If you say so, sir."

"Quit that butler crap and talk to me. And call me Jeru." He glanced at Ellie, who watched him, her now-dark eyes reflecting the pinpoints of light from outside. "Or Jerry."

Ben lowered the glass privacy partition, a two-way mirror that had separated the front seat from the back. His voice no longer came through the speakers. "Yes, sir . . . Jeru."

Ellie said, "You don't have to bother Ben for food—we just pick from the menu and it shows up in that compartment." She indicated a smoked-plastic box set in the base of the seat facing them. "It's like a TableChef on wheels."

"I'm enjoying talking to the man. He's taking me to this steiner who's going to change my life yet again—the least I can do is get to know him."

"You're acting pretty relaxed about all of this."

Jeru glanced at the icons again and pressed the one to lower his window, letting in the cool night air of April and the sweet smell of some kind of flower. Now he had an escape route if Ben locked his door. He shrugged. "Just another strange twist in a wild story."

Maybe he was overdoing the nonchalance. Ellie had a fairly suspicious mind—she'd know if he were plotting something. Better to distract her. He said, "Ben, you've been driving Ellie since she was a little kid?"

"That's right."

"What's the craziest thing she ever did in here?"

"Jerry—" Ellie began.

Ben replied, "Getting out after you took care of that terrorist. There could've been another one or a hundred more for all we knew. That truck was burning, smoke everywhere, and Ms. Stewart says, 'Oh my God, he saved our lives. Is he dead?'"

She squirmed, and Jeru asked, "So you two were safe as long as you stayed in here?"

"Yes, but she hopped out and gave you this look like you were an angel who'd broken his wing for her. She even picked up your arm before the medics could get there. There's blood all over the place and now all over her, but she kept staring at you." He turned right at an intersection and traffic thinned.

Ahead, where no one else was headed, the dazzling LEDs ended abruptly. The exit from the Kingdom. Beyond lay the blue-white blaze of streetlights and cars electronically shackled to the TrafficGrid and holographic billboards and advertisements on the glidepaths and talking displays along the storefronts. And terrorists and PentaHostiles and civilians risking their lives in defense of the newest addition to the Bill of Rights: the freedom to shop.

Plus lights in every window, with millions watching TV or gaming or talking online or zipping messages to people in another part of America or what remained of the world. Or doing all of it at the same time on wall-size screens divided into giant windowpanes, everyone pretending to be connected even though they were all alone.

In other words, home.

Thinking about it this way, part of him wanted to jump out now and take his chances in Kliburn's world, but that would mean never knowing what would happen from one minute to the next. At least life OTP was predictable. Wasn't it?

Jeru said to her, "And you knew right then that I would live with you?"

"That was my plan. I'm sorry it didn't work out that way." The strain in her voice told him that she was sincere. She gave him a long, hungry look.

Ellie told Ben, "We're distracting you, don't mind us." Her gaze flicked toward the front and, responding to a command from her neural chips, the glass privacy partition rose without a sound. She cuddled up to Jeru, pressing her breasts to his arm. The front of the borrowed tunic was loose enough for him to see all the way down it. She murmured, "The seat facing us can slide forward and lay flat, making this one big bed. And there are dispensers for all kinds of oils and a compartment full of toys. What if we—"

"Kind of like a souvenir, something to remember me by?"

He hadn't meant to sound bitter, but Ellie recoiled and huddled against the door on her side of the limo. After a minute of silence, she summoned a menu, displayed on the back of Ben's seat, and scrolled aimlessly through the food and beverage offerings. Each item had a corresponding picture with such vivid detail Jeru could almost hear the mini-burgers sizzle. Ellie didn't seem to notice the choices. She was expressionless, eyes vacant, her mouth a flat line.

He said, "We can't seem to get our timing right."

Not looking at him, she grumbled, "No, it's just that you can't seem to keep your mouth shut. You always ruin a nice moment with some smart-ass remark."

Ben halted at the perimeter. A well-armed, well-armored security guard greeted him beside a pillbox where two other guards stood. With a quick scan of the surrounding OTP badlands, the man canceled the sonic gate. The more-robust security could only mean that attacks had increased in the past six months. Maybe being exiled wasn't such a good idea.

Ellie switched off the menu. She faced the window, arms crossed. The poor girl was heading unknowingly toward a terrible surprise. She would wake up and realize that everyone she loved, including him, had betrayed her with their silence. That, to ensure her own safety from Kliburn, she could never go home. That her new body could never compare to her current perfection. That life and people sucked.

His situation wasn't much better, but at least he knew what was going to happen. And maybe he could escape before they reached Torres. The best thing he could do was make her happy for a while. Before she woke up and wanted to kill him and everybody else she'd trusted.

Through his open window, he heard the guard say to Ben, "Hope you get to come home soon. There's something in the air out there."

"A new chemical attack?" Ben asked.

"Nothing that definite. It just smells like trouble."

"We'll be careful." Ben eased the limo through the checkpoint and up to an intersection. Jeru imagined the TrafficGrid announcing through the dashboard that Ben needed to enter his destination so he would be "guided with the assurance of safety and timeliness" by the central traffic computer. Even cars from In-Town had to connect to the Grid once they left the perimeter.

The chauffeur lifted his hands from the steering wheel as the limo cruised through the intersection and made a right turn onto an avenue bright with headlights, neon, and streetlamps. From every store, white glare flooded shoppers on the glidepaths. The air smelled different from block to block, depending on the scent-ads employed, and music and voice-overs further competed for attention. If anything, the clamor had gotten worse since he'd been away. The air, however, still tasted like ash—that hadn't changed.

He said to Ellie, "I guess I'm really stressed. I didn't mean to snap at you."

"We've been doing the same dance since you woke up yesterday morning. Next time I take in a stray, I'll have Doc do a psych workup before anything else."

"I'm not crazy. I'm just scared."

She glanced his way but then returned to staring out the window.

He tried again. "It's worse than I remembered out here. You guys in the Kingdom could teach us a few things about peace and quiet."

She snorted and said, "You got that right."

"I'm gonna miss that. But I'm really going to miss you." It wasn't mere appeasement—he realized he meant it. Damn, he was falling for her. Just in time to deceive and lose her forever. Cupid was a cruel SOB.

He eased his hand, palm open, across the seat. Close enough for her to take it, but if she didn't he could leave it there without looking stupid. She'd break his heart if she rejected him, but he figured he deserved that.

She stared at his hand and then at him. "What do you want?"

"Forgive me. Please?"

"Crap," she sighed. She twined her fingers around his.

By the time the TrafficGrid guided the limo onto the highway at high speed, rocketing toward the suburbs, she was leaning against his arm again, head on his shoulder.

Despite the cool wind jetting against his face through his open window, he could smell her hair. Sweet and fruity, like the mixed-berry dessert he'd eaten at lunchtime a day ago. His stomach growled and cramped, utterly empty, but maybe he wasn't supposed to eat before the steiner did his thing.

"Hungry?" she asked.

"Yeah." He kissed the top of her head, taking a deep breath, and felt his pent-up lust growl in unison. His Sssagers responded with a stimulating vibration through his groin and thighs. The massage began against his bare arm as well—Ellie's borrowed shirt was purring.

She said, "Your clothes are giving mine ideas."

"Just your clothes?"

"No. I'm hungry, too."

Ellie rubbed her hand across his chest and pressed harder against him. Her face tilted up, neck stretching, her hair blowing back. The moment before she kissed him, her tongue wetted her lips and grazed his own. Moving her mouth against him, she slid around until she straddled his lap.

Her arms locked behind his shaved head and neck. She held him in place, her kiss becoming harder. With trembling hands, he touched her back and bottom. The wind—or something within—made him shiver.

"Hold me tighter," she breathed into his mouth. Rather than a passionate plea, it sounded like a whimper. Indeed, he felt her tears dripping on his face and neck. She said, "I'm so scared for you."

He wanted to tell her the same, to confess what he knew, but he remembered her jab about never knowing when to shut up. Now seemed like a good time to practice. Crossing his arms behind Ellie, he gripped her shoulders and hugged her against him. The only way to get any closer was to be inside her.

Ben's voice came from the speaker, "We're on the exit, a few miles from Dr. Torres's office." While he spoke, the TrafficGrid announced in a confident airplane captain's voice that control was being returned to him.

Behind the limo, headlights grew brighter as a vehicle sped up and then pulled sharply into the right lane, alongside them.

CHAPTER NINETEEN

Sandoval Yen glanced at the white limo as he drew his explosives-packed car parallel with it. His orders had come directly and explicitly from the Most Reverend Gimbel: "Kill Jerusalem Pix." Due to the opaque limo windows, however, he couldn't tell if the guy was in there.

For hours Sandy had been idling in his bomb-on-wheels—what the guys at church called a "bow-wow"—a few blocks from the northeast entrance to the Kingdom. He'd sat there ever since the Most Reverend received a call from the SysOp in the Stewart estate. Apparently there was a strong likelihood that Jerusalem would be fleeing to the burbs. The RSA leader had dispatched Sandy and the others he most trusted, to watch the Kingdom exits and wait for his call.

The SysOp had alerted the church founder again when cameras mounted outside the Stewart place recorded the limo leaving, and word was passed along to Sandy and the others. As instructed, Sandy said a prayer that he would be successful. "Jesus loves a winner," went the RSA mantra. "Losers go to hell."

It was all about love. Sandy loved the Real Salvation Army. He loved the sense of belonging, the fellowship, the trust that others in the congregation and blessed management had bestowed on him. He loved being able to give his son an RSA action figure that sort of looked like him. He loved that he could buy those action figures wholesale. He loved the unlimited ammunition available at the firing range in the church basement. He loved that the Most Rev. Gimbel asked him to autograph a target with particularly tight groupings on the head and chest and that this was framed and hung in the pastor's office, alongside signed celebrity photos and the letters of commendation received for the church's support of charities and other good works.

And he loved hunting down the terrorists on the far-left and far-right who had scorched much of the world and were intent on destroying the Americas, too. According to the pastor, this Jerusalem Pix, or "Bethlehem Splyvex" as he was now known, was in league with the evildoers. Pix had assassinated Sandy's friend, Cairo Bledsoe.

Cairo had recruited Sandy, took him out of a dead-end job designing virtual menswear for online communities and introduced him to a whole new world of meaning and enlightenment, gave him an outlet for his temper and frustration, and took him on his first raid against a terrorist safehouse. Bledsoe had even set him up on the blind date with a woman that had led to marriage and then to the baby boy who looked more like him every day. A future soldier for the Lord's army.

Now that the Grid had returned control of his car, Sandy was ready to strike another blow for God. If he couldn't shoot Pix to death, he'd detonate his car and wave *hasta la vista* to the limo's inhabitants on their way down to the bad place while he ascended, to receive his commendation for yet another good deed.

The limo sped toward the base of the ramp, where the traffic light was still green. Decelerating smoothly, Sandy slid back behind the limo again and followed it through the right-hand turn.

Of course, it wouldn't be a big deal if he shot the occupants of the white car only to discover Pix wasn't among them. The Most Reverend had given all his Crusaders a "Get out of hell free" card.

"Jesus didn't let His apostles make mistakes," the pastor had preached. "Anything they did in His name, by definition, was correct and had His seal of approval. They were infallible because the only Son of God is infallible. Otherwise, that would mean Jesus had made a human resources error when He put His team together—and we all know that Jesus only picks winners. So, as you are all spiritual descendants of those original True Believers, you, too, are infallible. Invisible to lawmen.

Untouchable by judges. Indomitable to our enemies. But to our Lord and Savior, priceless: innocent, pure, and beloved."

Armed with this mantle of Godly approval, along with a Canadian machine pistol and enough Mexican plastique to put a school bus into orbit, Sandy knew he couldn't fail.

However, it'd make a much better story around the dinner table if he could truthfully describe the look of terror and hopelessness on Pix's face the moment before Sandy erased that face and the skull to which it had clung.

With a flare of brake lights, the limo made another right turn ahead, so sudden that Sandy's car responded for him, slowing quickly to avoid a rear-end collision. He dropped way back and told himself to stop daydreaming. As the limo swung through its turn, he noted that instead of streetlights reflecting on mirrored glass, there was a rectangular gap where the rear right window should have been. Someone inside had lowered it.

Sandy prayed that the white car would move into the left-hand lane, and naturally his prayer was answered. What could be a more obvious sign of heavenly approval for his intended actions?

He eased up along the right side and drew even with the limo, far enough ahead of the open window so he could peer back and see the whole rear interior. Having glanced over, he now blinked and took a longer look.

No one was there.

Then a woman's bare left foot slapped the base of the window frame, her toes curling into the wind. The other pale leg rose up, splayed wide, and the right foot—this one still clad in a woman's dress shoe—banged flat against the door post, as if for support.

Sandy recalled watching his wife give birth and, with the exception of the stirrups, the leg positioning was nearly the same. Was a woman delivering a baby in there?

CHAPTER TWENTY

Jerusalem had lost all feeling in his hands. They were pinned under Ellie, who was pinned under him. The seats had converted into a bed, covering the entire back of the limo, and the interior of the cushions-cum-mattress had jellified on command, producing a waterbed effect. Ellie swung her legs up around his hips and gave his butt some vigorous thumps with her heels. One of her shoes fell between his legs.

He couldn't stop kissing her. Obviously she wanted more, and he did too, but with his hands about as useful as a couple of squids attached to his wrists, he was content to keep moving his mouth against hers. Also, he kept reminding himself, the limo would stop soon and this dream would end with Ben, and maybe the steiner Dr. Torres, standing there. Not enough time to make love to Ellie, but endless minutes remaining to keep tasting her wet lips and her flushed face and neck.

Her feet abandoned the drum solo they were playing on his backside and braced against the door. The air rushing in felt cool on Jeru's neck. By contrast, Ellie's hands were hot as one slipped under his shirt to caress his back while the other wedged into his vibrating pants and groped his butt.

Their clothes seemed to be competing to see which outfit could make its wearer climax first. Her mouth broke contact with his, and she put her chin over his shoulder and moaned.

We have a winner, he thought. Maybe no one in the Kingdom had actual sex—their outfits and furniture did the work and then they relaxed with a virtual joint and maybe snacked on a miniature bowl of soup and three lettuce leaves.

"Did you finish?" he asked, his lips grazing her ear.

She gasped, "Finish? Are you kidding? Only a fosh would stop at one."

"I only get one," he pointed out. And he was trying to hold back on that inevitability too. The Sssagers could do many things, but he doubted their features included a wet-dry vac.

She ground her hips against him, shuddering. "That's what you think. I did have you upgraded."

Oh yeah. Dr. Gomez had told him the same. Instead of a one-shot revolver, he was equipped with a machine gun. With ammo to spare. That reminder almost sent him over the edge, but the "upgrade" apparently prevented premature ejaculation. God, he was going to miss this body. What a shame he'd never discover its full potential. Kinda like trading in a James Bond car before using any of the gizmos and launching the ejector seat. His own launch seemed seconds away; even upgraded hardware could postpone things for only so long.

Ben's smooth voice announced, "We might have some trouble. Someone's shadowing us."

The urge to climax evaporated. Nothing like real danger to abort a mission—roll the rocket back to the hangar, fellas.

"Whoa," Ellie grumbled in irritation. "I didn't ask Doc to install an instant shutdown." Her hand slid around front. "Time for a manual override."

"Didn't you hear Ben?"

"He's a professional bodyguard. He'll keep us safe."

The limo braked and then sped up, rolling them forward and back on the seat. Ellie whooped with joy.

Ben said, "Make sure your U-bars are down. We're definitely being tailed."

Jeru sat back. Ellie, now grumbling, pulled her legs from around him. She scooted to her end of the limo again and commanded the opposing seat to return to its original position. The hide-a-bed hid. From the headrest, a U-shaped padded restraint rose and arched over her, then locked into place against her torso. Glancing at him, she looked hurt and disappointed but not surprised—maybe she'd come to expect that this was how things would always be between them. Just when it got good, either he or some other glans would screw it up.

He shook his hands to get blood flowing into his numb fingers again. Cool, springtime air from the open window dried the sudden panic-sweat on his face. Trying to ignore the painful stinging as his hands revived, he looked out the window and met the gaze of a young man driving alongside them. That man's window was down too, and he smiled and waved at Jeru. Southerners were such friendly folks, never met a stranger.

Jeru keyed the mic and said to Ben, "It's just a guy who's never seen a limo before. He probably thinks we're celebrities." He waved back and grinned with relief.

The man raised a machine pistol at him and started shooting.

Ben braked hard and swung the limo into oncoming traffic as bullets thudded against the armored exterior. Jeru, having thrown himself sideways, heard the blare of horns and squeal of tires as he lay across the seat, his head in Ellie's lap. Her Sssagers sent soothing vibrations up through his cheek. His clothes had shut down, probably scared shitless.

Thank God he hadn't been trapped behind a U-bar. He looked up at Ellie's stricken expression. Several rounds had punched through the padding a millimeter in front of her face and scarred the window beside her. As the limo swung hard to the left and more shots peppered the rear, Jeru grabbed a fistful of her tunic to keep from rolling onto the floor. He groped for the controls on her armrest, since she was too shocked to free herself.

He slapped at the buttons, which lowered her window, turned on a stereo that blared krap from hidden speakers, and engaged a whole-seat vibrator and heating elements. Finally, the bullet-riddled U-bar rose and disappeared back into the headrest. Ellie remained frozen, eyes open. She swayed as Ben took two more tight turns, but otherwise she remained manikin-like. No blood showed—had she died of fright?

Gripping the neckline of her blouse, he pulled her down toward him, away from the open windows. She complied rigidly, bending at her waist. Her soft, warm breasts pressed against his mouth and nose, and he felt her rapid heartbeat dance against his lips. Even in his panicked state, he savored the moment.

Ben's voice, still without inflection, asked something through the speakers, and Jeru had to flail at the armrest buttons again until he shut off the stereo. The chauffeur/bodyguard said, "I repeat, is anyone hurt back there?"

Jeru said, "No," but his reply was lost within Ellie's cleavage. Reluctantly wiggling out from under her, he managed to shut off the seat vibrator and the heater that was roasting his skin, and found the mic control. "We're okay. Ellie's in shock, I think, but she's not hit."

More bullets plinked off the rear window.

Distant police sirens failed to hearten Jeru. He asked Ben, "Can't you use laser cannons or death rays on him?"

That finally got a rise from Ben, whose voice rose with indignation. "Hey libbot, just what century do you think this is?"

A shot made a scary ricocheting sound off the window frame on Jeru's side and embedded with a thud somewhere in the interior. Jeru decided not to bother Ben with any more questions, seeing as how the man was trying to save their lives. He maneuvered Ellie onto her side, so that she was cushioned by the leather seat beneath her and against her back, and he lay facing her, hopefully protecting her front from any pinballing rounds while he tried the nearest control panel again. Mercifully, her window rose, but his was still down.

She blinked a few times. He couldn't tell the color of her eyes or if she even focused on him. He put a hand on her shoulder to brace her in the L of the seat as the limo skidded through two more turns. Jeru wondered if Ben was taking them in a big circle so they wouldn't be far from Dr. Torres if they had to bail out.

Ellie blinked once more and said in a flat, cold voice, "If this is your fault and the assassin doesn't kill you, I will."

"Get in line," Jeru said and kissed her. It was probably his last chance to do that. The police sirens sounded closer, but the predominant noise was the hit man's gunfire and scores of rounds striking the armor and the bullet-resistant glass.

She asked, "Did Kliburn send him to shoot you?"

He'd been wondering the same thing, but why not wait to see where the limo was going and kill him in private, without risking police interference? There were only a few groups he could name that would try a brazen run-and-gun killing: the terrorists at both political extremes, who didn't know of or care about him, and the RSA. And if Kliburn knew "everything about Jerusalem Pix," the SysOp understood that the RSA likely wanted Jeru dead for ruining Cairo Bledsoe's mission. So Kly had unleashed the PentaHostiles. And if something happened to Ellie and Ben? Well, it was just another sad example of how chaotic the world had become. Mamas, don't let your babies go outside the perimeter.

Flinching as a bullet skipped inside the car through his open window and plowed into the ceiling, he explained his thinking to Ellie. The limo swerved and more car horns squawked and tires skidded. It was just as well he couldn't see Ben's desperate attempt to outrun the killer.

She said, "They won't leave me and Ben alone?"

"You mean, Ben pulls over and you guys hop out and say, 'We're not with that fosh in the back seat'?"

"Yeah."

"No, these folks get extra points for collateral damage. And no one can carry a grudge like people who preach forgiveness all the time. I'm sorry. Either we all make it or everyone's toast."

Ellie kneed him in the balls and pushed him onto the floor.

All things considered, she'd taken the news pretty well. Jeru lay there between the opposing seats and tried to catch his breath. His Sssagers revived and sent soothing coolness over his groin, like an icepack without the wetness. Note to the manufacturer: install a jock cup.

The police now sounded farther away, as if Ben were shaking their rescuers while he tried to outrun the bad guy. Ellie called, "Ben, what can we do?"

"Pray he runs out of bullets, or that the cops learn how to drive."

The limo made a sudden right turn on two wheels and bounded over something solid, like a concrete curb. "Ay *mierda*," Ben said.

"Not what I wanted to hear," Jeru remarked. He got to his knees and crouched on the floor, his bruised crotch protected from another assault. Holding the edge of the seat for support, he looked at Ellie lying nearby. Poor girl. All she'd wanted was a strong, studly protector and a flapping labia. Instead, she could die in the next few moments or, if some miracle occurred, merely have her brain dumped into a stranger's skull against her will.

For the second time in minutes, he said, "I'm sorry."

She merely nodded and stared at him. More light came in through the windows, and he could see her irises change from blue to green. Nothing altered in her hard expression. Her final thought would be something bad about him.

Ben said, "Hold on, I got us trapped—this parking lot has only one outlet. Torres is in the building here, but that gunman's too close for you to make a run for it."

The car braked hard. Ellie's arm shot out as she planted her fist in Jeru's chest to brace herself. He glanced down at the smooth white knuckles against his breastbone. At least this fist came with a complete, living, beautiful body attached.

More bullets than ever sprayed the limo, and Jeru heard the rev of a second engine. The killer was nearby. With a scream of rubber, the limo whipped around but stopped again and the shooting sounded much louder. Jeru realized that they now faced the RSA assassin, and Ben was firing his own automatic weapon.

Jeru still trusted his gamer instincts. They told him to bail out—making a run directly at the enemy this time would not end well. Bullets from the RSA gunman winged off the side and window closest to Ellie, as if the killer were circling that way.

Giving Dr. Gomez all due credit for his quickness and strength, Jeru shoved one hand underneath Ellie and the other between her clamped thighs and slid her over to his side of the interior. "Get ready," he warned.

Before she could reply, he pushed open his door, and, pulling Ellie with him, fell out backward with her atop him to cushion the impact for her.

He landed on his back against the rough asphalt, head bouncing hard, and lay stunned for a moment. She rolled off and helped him onto his knees.

They were in the vast, well-lit parking lot of a sprawling office complex. There must've been spaces for two thousand cars. After decades of remote work, couples had returned to jobs outside the home in an effort to save their marriages.

Shielded from the assassin, Jeru decided they'd run up the nearby landscaped hill of synthetic pine straw and fake azaleas and down the other side. Then he'd make another plan to get to the office building.

Ben's latest volley apparently scored a hit. From the other side of the limo, the gunman cried out. The guy's car revved loudly. Ben shouted, "Brace yourselves," and opened up again with what sounded like a thousand rounds of ammunition.

Jeru and Ellie staggered to their feet, and they sprinted toward the hill. He'd never run flat out in his new body. It covered ground like a track star. Still, Ellie matched his strides with ease, maybe even holding back a little so he could keep up. The gunfire sounded evermore distant, the hill just a dozen long steps away. They would make it.

Then the dying RSA terrorist ignited his bomb.

CHAPTER TWENTY-ONE

Propped upright on a hard mattress, with a thin pillow trapped between his back and a tubular headboard, Jeru awoke in a room devoid of warmth or texture. Pale light came from oval plastic ceiling panels. Everything was painted or laminated in smooth cream: the walls, the ergonomically maximized and extraordinarily bland furniture, and the floor. Heaven would've had a better design esthetic, and hell wouldn't have been this boring, so he definitely was OTP.

He tried to remember the number of times he'd floated to consciousness lately after some terrible assault, starting with the Bledsoe bombing. Maybe he'd never fall asleep again like a normal person. Maybe he could promote a new sleep aid for insomniacs: *Concussion4U: Get the rest you need*™.

Of course, constant pounding to one's body and brain might not be—

He blinked a few times and tried to focus on a table and chair in the corner. They were the usual Brazilian knockoffs of antique "Swedish modern," but his blurred focus made them even more featureless. Something had happened to his eyesight. And to his body.

To lift his left hand, he had to think about it, like he was commanding a robot to move for him. He rotated it with growing horror. Not only had he lost his miraculous vision, but he'd aged forty years. The hand was mottled pink and tan with a few liver spots and chipped, yellowed nails. Jeru pushed up the gray pajama sleeve. His bicep had lost its sculpted musculature, and he'd gained a waddle under his upper arm, as if the muscles had melted and then congealed beneath the bone. Maybe it was a good thing he couldn't see so well.

In a fit of depression, he raised his arms jerkily to grab two handfuls of his hair, but all he felt was the now-familiar prickle of stubble. However, his fingers also encountered a raised, sensitive ridge that he followed around the entire circumference of his head, just above the barely discernible hairline. A scar. He was definitely OTP—Dr. Gomez wouldn't have left a scar.

The realization struck him. His body. His brain. Now his brain in someone else's body. Someone middle-aged and myopic. What else could have gone wrong?

He groped under the pale coverlet, past his scrawny, birdlike chest, for his pajama-covered groin. Good thing he used two hands—he might never have found the meager offerings with just one. A thin, pitiful cry escaped his dry lips. He'd been agonizing over what would happen when Ellie discovered herself in a new body, but somehow he'd never considered his own fate. This was beyond nightmarish.

Given the choice now, he would've rather hid out forever in Dr. Gomez's quarters. One day, the doctor would've started to like him. Eventually, he might've talked her into a three-way with Ellie. The thought caused a stirring below his waist, but it was like a worm stretching after a nap. Even his original body could've done better than that. Of course, back then he needed to be standing in front of a mirror to verify its fullness because he couldn't see past his stomach, but, hey, at least he could've knocked on a door with it. This thing could've been mistaken for a thumb.

Footsteps shuffled beyond the open doorway. A reedy female voice with a country drawl called, "You up?"

"Yeah," he said and winced. His own voice, gravelly and low-pitched, startled him. Ellie had once mentioned that Doc could alter a voice like tuning a piano. It sounded like his piano had been tuned by dropping a boulder on it.

A hefty woman of about forty with a splash of freckles across her nose and cheeks and a lava flow of red hair entered. Dressed in pink hospital scrubs, she panted from the apparent effort of coming down the hall from the nurse's station or wherever she normally sat. She leaned on the doorjamb and wiped her forehead with a thick wrist. "You feeling okay?"

"Is this what healthcare has come to OTP—asking the patient if he's okay? Aren't there supposed to be monitors or something?" God, his voice could be used as a low-frequency weapon.

The nurse seemed to think so too. She started to cover her ears but apparently remembered her Southern manners and folded beefy arms across her abundant chest. In a screech that made him go through the same hear-no-evil routine, she demanded, "What are you babbling about?"

"Where's Dr. Torres?"

"He's supposed to arrive any minute."

"So this isn't part of his office?"

"No, it's a recovery facility. You've been here for a week."

He muttered, "I've lost another week." Hell, why didn't he just sleep through his whole life? Feeling his beaky nose and sharp cheekbones, he asked, "Can I have a mirror?"

"You look all right."

"I'm skin and bones."

She snorted and said, "What I wouldn't give to be skinny again."

He growled, "Can I have a mirror? Pretty damn please?"

Talking to herself, the woman shuffled to the desk tucked into the corner. She grabbed a hand mirror and a plastic bottle with a straw. Though his new sense of smell wasn't much better than his eyesight, he thought she smelled like she'd bathed in a vat of candy-scented perfume. She offered him the drink first.

He sipped. Yup, the same old chlorine-flavored tap water he remembered.

"Mirror," he ordered.

"Don't you have any questions?"

"Yes, I do. And right now they're all centered on how I can get that mirror out of your hand."

She glared at him and dropped the mirror onto his poor excuse for a lap. With a huff, she flopped into the chair beside the desk, glistening with sweat from the apparent effort. Why couldn't he get a playful, sexy nurse?

He told his right hand to close around the mirror handle. For an instant, he flashed onto a memory of being six in a grocery store: trying to manipulate, through a Plexiglas window, a mechanical arm with a claw at the end that was suspended over a four-legged spaceman he'd wanted. Never did get the damn toy, wasted all the money on his Kidz Credit Card (*Zero interest so they don't lose their interest in spending*™), and drove him to focus exclusively on video games.

At least this claw, four gnarled fingers and a yellow-nailed thumb, found its mark the first time. He gripped the smooth plastic and hinged his elbow to draw the mirror toward his face.

The fifty-something man staring back at him bore an eerie resemblance to his father. Small, angular features, all slits and corners, vaguely hawk-like. He resembled the guy who was always cast as the accountant with a perverse secret or Slasher Victim #2. He gave the mirror back to the nurse, who tossed it carelessly on the desktop.

From geek to god to geezer. Somehow he had to prepare himself for Ellie's reaction to his new look. She'd be disgusted.

Wait. Ellie. Limo. Explosion. Was she even alive? What about Ben? And how did the steiner find him?

He asked the redhead, "Do you have another patient here? A girl, I mean young woman, named Ellipsis?" He wished he could say her name reverently, not in the voice of a troll. "If I was out of it for a week, she would've just turned eighteen."

She replied, "So you finally remembered your friend."

"Hey, I remembered her. I just, you know..."

"First things first," she squawked.

"So, is she here?"

"She's dead."

Jeru dropped his head back against the pillow and then curled away from the cruel, heartless bitch. Shit, fuck, Goddammit all to hell, it was his fault. Ellie had loved him, but he'd betrayed her completely. He had loved her, he realized. He still did.

His eyes burned but no tears came. Apparently the body—*his* body—was either too dehydrated or was defective inside *and* out. He didn't want to cry in front of the nurse anyway. Finally he croaked, "Did she die when the bomb exploded?"

"No, Dr. Torres was there in minutes—the bomb went off near the building where his office and surgery are. You both came through the bombing alive. The limo shielded you from the worst of it."

He uncurled and rolled back to face her. "Our driver, Ben—"

"Incinerated."

His fault too. Jeru shut his eyes. Still, he needed to hear the rest. He asked, "Then what happened?"

"Dr. Torres and his staff dragged y'all away from the blast zone, got you to his office before the police showed up, and went to work. But Ellipsis's brain transplant didn't take, and the doctor couldn't save her."

He whispered, "Did she suffer?"

"She still is—she's in hell."

His eyes popped open, and he jabbed his index finger at her. "Don't talk about Ellie that way! You didn't know her."

"And you spent, what, a total of eight conscious hours with her?"

"How do you—"

"Time enough to break her heart and ruin her life and then kill her? She died inside because of you." She covered her reddening face. Chubby hands slid up to cover her eyes and forehead. Her red mane moved. The whole hairdo slid back an inch and revealed a smoothly shaved scalp with a scar above the hairline.

"Ellie?" He extended his arm and then pulled it back, in case she might want to yank it off and beat him to death with it. Now that he no longer viewed her as Satan's Hospital Employee of the Month, he tried to take a closer look at her, to spy some element of Ellie shining through. However, she remained a faintly blurry stranger. "Hey, talk to me."

"Leave me alone." Her faux-Southern accent disappeared; now she merely squealed. "I wish you'd let me get blown up six months ago."

He said, "My God, what happened to us?"

She resettled the wig on her head and pawed at her muddy brown eyes, which continued to leak. Obviously she had water to spare. After another minute of sobbing, Ellie said in her new, reedy voice, "Dr. Torres confessed that this was the plan all along—for both of us to get identity makeovers so we'd be safe from Kliburn. And you knew it. And Doc knew it. Even poor Ben knew it." She wept again, wailing, "And I trusted all of you. Especially *you*."

He forced himself to watch her, to deal with whatever was coming. She deserved that and more, and he deserved to suffer whatever she wanted to do to him. At least his groin presented a much smaller target.

Ellie continued to rant, "Next thing I know, I'm in Two-Ton Tillie's body with more hair under my arms than on my head. Torres won't let me call Doc, so I've been waiting a whole day for you to wake up, dealing with this . . . this thing." Her sweeping hand took in herself, head to toe. "This body that smells bad, farts loud, and bumps into things 'cause it's almost a wide as the freaking doors, all of which I have to open with my hands!" She clenched them into meaty fists. "I hate it, and I hate this place. But mostly I hate you."

He nodded. "I knew you would." He tried to say it softly, gently, but his awful vocal cords would make a lullaby sound like a death threat.

" 'Be my friend,' you said. Just so you could try to fuck me."

"As I recall, you wanted to fuck *me*."

A small, dark man wearing a natty, blue four-piece suit—counting the short silk cape attached at the shoulders—walked in dragging a suitcase on wheels. He said, "If it's any consolation, sweeties, I don't want to fuck *either* of you."

Ellie grumbled, "Hello, Dr. Torres."

"Well, I see patient *numero dos* is awake and frisky." A handcuff shackled the suitcase he carried to his wrist. After walking to the bed, he set down the heavy luggage on the end of the mattress, barely missing Jeru's foot, and slid the oversized manacle over his hand as easily as removing a bracelet. Dr. Torres caught Jeru's stare and said, "Purely an affectation; it impresses the clientele." Looking from Jeru to Ellie, he popped his eyes and said, "Oh my, tough crowd."

Dr. Torres opened his case and took out some mundane physician equipment. He placed an audiovisual stethoscope against Jeru's chest, where it broadcast the sound of his heartbeat—at least *that* wasn't scrawny—and displayed and recorded healthy cardiopulmonary data. Then he checked Jeru's eyes with a lighted device that reported an array of stats, which were summed up with, "All is normal."

"Ooo," the steiner crooned, "I am good." He returned his equipment to the case.

"That's it?" Jeru said. "That's all the tests you're gonna run?"

"I did most of them before you woke up, Mr. Grumpy, but if you insist." He took a dramatic breath and paused. "Okay, close your eyes and touch your left index finger to your nose."

Moving with infinite care so he didn't screw up in front of the woman who wanted to kill him and the man who didn't want to fuck him, he swung his index finger around and jabbed his eyelid.

"Perfect," Dr. Torres exclaimed. "Everyone messes that up."

Jeru looked over at Ellie, and she nodded guiltily. He said, "But isn't there more to making sure my brain can work this body?"

The steiner tapped a finger against his lips and appeared to consider his question. "All right, dearie, get out of bed."

Jeru started to throw back the covers but remembered the last time he did that in front of Ellie. He froze.

"Oh my, Houston, maybe we do have a problem." Dr. Torres peered closer at him. "What's the matter?"

Jeru said, "The Nite-n-Daze, they sort of vanish."

Ellie said, "Jerry, remember where you are."

Dr. Torres caught on. "That's right, Toto, you're not in Oz anymore. Back in Kansas: too bad, so sad."

Jeru shook his head. He hadn't realized how quickly he'd become accustomed to what would be considered magic OTP. That is, home. He tossed back the sheets and was surprised to see that his legs were very muscular under the thin cloth. Which would make his genitals look even smaller, like a snail peeking from a shell.

He asked Dr. Torres, "What happened to this body? The bottom half looks like a track star—well, a eunuch track star—and the top belongs to a drug addict."

The man looked him over, as if for the first time. "I remember interviewing this fellow before he completed the donation paperwork. He was getting his body in tiptop shape, starting with his legs and working upward. Brain cancer caught up with him at the halfway mark."

Jeru felt his scalp, imagining residual lesions like mildew clinging to the inside of his skull. "You scrubbed him out well, didn't you? Sprayed something powerful in there, like oven cleaner?"

"Oh my, yes, I recall my head nurse commenting, 'Why, Dr. Torres, look at that shine!' "

"Okay. I know. I'm a fosh." Jeru eased his bare, callused feet to the cold floor. One thing was certain: even if he had to wear something with a damned cape attached, he wasn't going to spend another whole day in jammies.

Unsure of his balance, he started with his feet spread wide, but the legs felt more than stable. They felt ready to run a marathon. The only disappointment was that they weren't very long; in fact, he was short all over, maybe five-foot-five, the same height as Ellie and Dr. Torres.

He faced the doctor, arms wide. "Okay, now what?"

"Do this." The steiner spun in a tight circle while he tapped his toes, moved his arms in opposing, complex wave patterns, and clucked his tongue with a mambo rhythm. Slapping a blue wingtip on the floor, he held his arms open like Jeru. "Yeah!"

"I couldn't have done that when I was built like Superman."

Dr. Torres shrugged and said, "I do wish you'd at least try, *muchacho*." He turned his face to Ellie. "How about you, honey? Want to give it a whirl?"

"I'm saving all my energy, so the next time Jerry goes to sleep I can take a running, flying leap and squash him like a bug."

"Oh my."

CHAPTER TWENTY-TWO

Ellie said to Dr. Torres, "Can't you put me on ice until someone young and thin dies? Or at least cut away three-quarters of me?"

"Sorry, the young ones are required to go directly to Organ Recycling. And I don't have space in my schedule to do cosmetic surgery: suddenly everybody wants to walk a mile in someone else's feet."

"Speaking of feet," Jeru said, "I just came from a place where they wouldn't give me shoes until they tossed me out."

"Give me, give me, give me." The steiner marched to his case. "Take, take, take." He tossed out some green hospital scrubs and cheap red sneakers. "That'll have to do."

Jeru said, "Do you have a wig for me too?" He'd almost added, "Even an ugly one," but the image of Ellie launching herself on top of him had made an impact.

Dr. Torres replied, "No wig for you. In six or eight months the real stuff will have grown back in full. Well, depends on your definition of *full*. The donor did have a male-pattern-baldness issue."

"Will the scar fade at least?"

The steiner pouted. "Not entirely." He appeared to be close to tears.

"I mean," Jeru said quickly, "everything else is great." He did a few awkward, very Caucasian dance steps. Admittedly, he was getting used to the way his body moved and sensed things; he felt less and less like the puppeteer *and* the marionette. "I can move my arms and legs and remember things and see and smell and all that. Well, my vision blows, but I guess I can get laser surgery."

Dr. Torres sighed and removed some goggle-like glasses made popular ten years before by the ice-skating super-villain of *Death Spiral* and

Death Spiral 2: Another Time Around. Their popularity lasted about as long as glow-in-the-dark suntan lotion. Jeru tried them on, and Ellie hooted. Her red-with-laughter face came into perfect focus. He guessed how stupid he looked wearing the things, but he resisted sniping back. Let her make fun. She was now in his world, with a thousand chances each day to embarrass herself for his amusement. At least until she squashed him in his sleep.

"Look, children," the doctor whined, "I think a little appreciation is in order. Can you give me just a bit of credit for the scientific miracle that allows you to slouch around in bodies other than your own and complain at will?"

Ellie and Jeru apologized and mumbled their thanks like kids receiving a dictionary for Christmas instead of a Blastoff Personal Rocket Ship (*Return after five orbits or your money back*™). While the steiner's work—and results—didn't have the flashiness of Dr. Gomez's feats, but the man did save them from a disaster scene and had performed his scientific miracle as promised. Neither the RSA nor Kliburn would threaten them again.

Jeru asked, "Do we have new identities to go with our new faces?"

"Of course." The doctor still seemed petulant.

Jeru said, "Please tell me I don't have another stupid name like Bethlehem Splyvex."

Dr. Torres wrinkled his nose. "Nothing so odd. Besides, a 12/26 name wouldn't fit someone with your age profile." He reached into the breast pocket of his suit and pulled out two laminated National ID cards. "Ellipsis, you're now Cathy Eden. And you, sir, are Lou Barone." He handed over the NIDs.

The card reported the usual birth data and physical stats, which were updated regularly via an RFID chip linked to an implant the steiner would've attached behind Jeru's ribcage—what Jeru had always thought of as a real-time bathroom scale and blood-pressure cuff. Set beside these figures, his new face hovered as a hologram. This image had the sharp features he'd seen in the mirror and patchy, sandy-blond hair. It had probably been taken during the donation interview.

Tilting the card one way, Jeru saw his left profile; tilting it the other way showed the right side of his face. Likewise, he could view the top of his head and under his chin. Ellie wobbled her card similarly, her expression blank. Either she'd lost herself in fascination with the hologram or still was brooding about her appearance and her desire to kill him.

The address on Jeru's card indicated an apartment in the northwestern suburbs of Marietta, not too far from where he was born. He tapped the information and said to Dr. Torres in his troll-voice, "You've checked this place out?"

"It's a safehouse, a safe-condo really." The steiner looked from Jeru to Ellie. "I hope you don't mind bunking together for a while. There are two bedrooms," he added quickly. "Since Ellipsis—I mean Cathy—has never been OTP, I thought it would be wise for her to shadow you until she became accustomed to her new environment."

Ellie glanced at him. His expression must have reflected his doubts about the roommate situation. She curled her upper lip and said, "You'll have all the privacy you want. I don't want to have anything to do with you."

Jeru studied the card again. Lou Barone. Better than that Bethlehem name that ANGUS—or Kliburn—had arranged, but still not him. He asked, "Do we have cars? Jobs?"

"No cars, but, as you may recall, public transportation has improved in the western burbs. I registered both of you with the Georgia Employment Department. They'll contact you in a week with your new positions: minimum wage stuff—only twenty dollars an hour—but you can easily advance and build a resume."

Jeru said, "I was hoping to build some new cyber businesses, not apply laser tattoos at the mall."

Dr. Torres explained, "In the six months you were away, they tightened the Jobs Act, so now it's illegal not to earn an income unless you have an approved disability. You'll have to build those businesses in your free time. Even homemakers and students from middle school on up have to earn a taxable stipend. And it's now illegal to save more than one percent of your net income."

The doctor took the NID from Ellie's hand, flipped it over, and pointed out the information on display there. "Must be good little citizens," he went on. "Contribute to the economy by paying taxes and buying things; can't just hide out in cyberspace like people used to do. Even in the GameSphere, all the treasure you win and the profits you make are taxable. And, oh my, the virtual tax man is worse than the Bog Hag in Swamp Deathmatch III."

As the steiner's words sunk in, Jeru turned his card over. Holographic printing appeared in an instant, seemingly recessed in the plastic so that someone standing beside him wouldn't be able to read it. His new bank account, showing a current balance of two hundred dollars, and his assigned bank passcode, mobile number, and zip address were displayed via RFID technology, confirming that he was indeed Lou Barone. His access to the Net. A way to track his every move, of course, but also the gateway to virtual escape when he wasn't earning taxable income and spending ninety-nine percent of it.

Ellie said, "So can we personalize our zip address and stuff?"

Dr. Torres nodded. "These are defaults. As soon as you make new selections, the card will reflect those updates. You never have to remember them."

"But if I lose this card—"

"The RFID chip I implanted will confirm your identity, so you can get a new one for free at any NID kiosk."

"What do you do for money, here at the end of the world?"

Jeru said, "The NID doubles as a debit card."

"Wow, you OTPers have thought of everything. It's a wonder all my friends haven't moved here already."

Jeru sighed and asked, "When can we leave?"

Dr. Torres swept his hand toward the door, "Your chariot awaits, *mi amigo. Y amiga.*"

Despite their new bodies and identities, the steiner was still cautious. He'd parked his low-riding roadster from Hops Motors (*Barrow to Tierra del Fuego on One Gallon of Beer*™) behind a dumpster in the rear of the building. After Jeru changed into the green scrubs and red sneakers, they crept outside and rode away, leaving only the aroma of pale ale in their wake.

A fifteen-minute drive executed by the TrafficGrid brought them to their new digs: a condo seventeen stories up with two small bedrooms, one bathroom, and a tiny "great room" with a microwave oven set into one wall above a mini-fridge-and-freezer and an el-cheapo three terabyte laptop with an equally unimpressive seventy-two-inch screen mounted on the opposite wall, along with a pair of thrift store lounge chairs. If this was a "safehouse," it was secure because no one would bother to break in and steal anything.

Dr. Torres said, "There's a small selection of clothes in the closet of each bedroom, some basic toiletries in the shared bathroom, and we stocked the pantry and fridge, so you won't go broke shopping for necessities your first week on your own."

"Our All-n-1s?" Jeru asked.

"Should be delivered *mañana*." He clapped his hands once. "Okay, children, I'll leave you to it." He pointed to Ellie. "Cathy, don't kill Lou tonight. Sleep on it. Well—"

Ellie waved him to silence. "Don't worry. We're going to have as little to do with each other as possible. Murder is too personal. I'll just hope and pray for his demise."

"Nice. Lou, I'll tell you what I told Cathy before you awoke. If you feel ill, contact me, but I hope we never see or talk to each other again." He handed Jeru an old-fashioned business card. "Except for Dr. Gomez, I'm the only one who knows what happened to Ellipsis Stewart and Jerusalem Pix. That makes all of us vulnerable."

Jeru said, "Thanks for giving us this chance." He shook the doctor's hand.

"Cut one another some slack, sweeties. You're all each other has." He made a little bow, cape flapping, and closed the door behind him with a thump.

Ellie, who would always be Ellie to Jeru no matter how many other names she was assigned—just as he hoped he would always be Jerry to her—adjusted her red wig and looked at him, hands on her hips. She said, "*All each other has*? That's really freaking scary."

They were off to a good start.

CHAPTER TWENTY-THREE

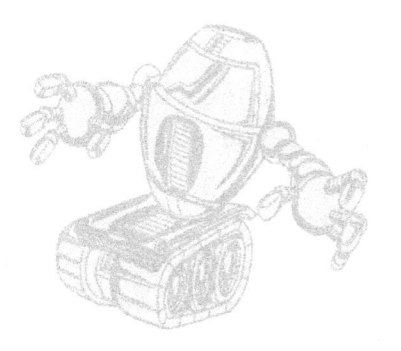

Under the bleak afternoon sky, in a parking lot with over a thousand cars, Gimbel stood at the edge of a blackened crater. More than a week earlier, Sandoval Yen had martyred himself there. Yen got points for eliminating the chauffeur, but somehow Jerusalem Pix—or Bethlehem Splyvex or whatever name he was calling himself now—got away. The fact that he now had a girl with him—Ellipsis Stewart or whatever she now went by—should've made them easier to track. But, so far, no one had recognized their faces.

All three thousand members of the church were out there looking, talking to people at work and in the shops and posting the pictures supplied by the SysOp on every website they could. Billy Bob sent all of them the story Gimbel had composed: that these attractive young people had been approached by the jihadists and needed to be pulled into the loving bosom of the church before they were seduced and taken between the wanton thighs of terrorism.

Ultra-left-wing and ultra-right-wing terrorists were like cockroaches: even if you find and kill one, you know there are a hundred sneaking away, having flipped their colleague over so his wriggling would distract you. Gimbel knew this all too well, seeing as how he'd bankrolled the nascent two-pronged terrorist movement years before, back when he thought he could control and contain them. A car bomb here, an assassination there, and pretty soon a wonderful panic had spread across America, a clamoring for old-fashioned values and a religious fervor usually only seen in those who are caught within the crosshairs of a Class 5 hurricane.

The country had needed a hero, so up he stepped with his fledgling

Real Salvation Army militia—and on national television smashed the vermin he'd secretly financed. Of course, he knew right where to look for them.

His militia and the church received grants, government funding, donations by the millions, and crayon drawings from schoolchildren. And he became a very wealthy man, had lots of naughty girlfriends, and bought his wife a great new nose, a killer ass, and a rack with the kind of suspension Hops Motors would envy. But there was that problem with cockroaches. They were breeding all along . . . and spreading. And soon he found them everywhere, with eradication all but impossible.

Meanwhile, the super-rich were fortifying their enclaves, setting up their own infrastructure, and cutting themselves off from the rest because they could afford it. His major donors began to disappear behind those insurmountable walls just when Gimbel needed their dollars the most. Worse, they wouldn't let him inside the castle keep even though he had the bucks to qualify.

Then the critics began sharpening their bowie knives and scimitars. The wealthiest one percent controlled the media, as they controlled everything else on both sides of the perimeter in every city. They could've silenced those assaults in the press—that infernal PentaHostiles label—just as they could've helped Gimbel quell the two-pronged terrorist attacks raging out of control. But they didn't. So he'd declared war on them too.

After a lovely string of successes against the wealthy across the country, all un-credited lest the RSA lose public backing and government support, Jerusalem Pix ended the winning streak, and in Gimbel's home park. It was maddening. It also heralded a wave of bad luck for his church and militia. Somehow, Gimbel thought, he'd fallen out of favor with God. Maybe the ultra-rich also pulled God's strings, but he chose to blame it all on Jerusalem. Or whichever name he was calling himself now.

Gimbel walked the circumference of the crater, chewing the inside of his cheek. The taste of blood made him walk faster, think clearer. Everyone in the church was looking for the two out of pious concern for their souls and fear that the couple would make the next Sexiest Terrorists Alive webmag. On the militia side, he'd authorized a five-million-dollar bounty and the usual guarantee of an eternity with one hundred sanctified harlots. His afterlife promise was a marketing coup the prudish terrorists couldn't top. Who'd want to hang around heaven with a bunch of no-nothing virgins when angelic sluts could invent an infinite number of games for Tab A and Slot B?

Given such incentives, why hadn't anybody found those two?

In a sign he'd been welcomed back into the fold, God told him the answer: *Maybe because they no longer looked like their pictures.* Had they somehow staggered away from Sandoval's bomb blast and made it to a safehouse . . . or a plastic surgeon? He looked at his surroundings, turning in a full circle. What if the chauffeur hadn't ended up in this place by chance? Gimbel's people had sworn on a stack of his *God's Plan, Part One* memoir that they'd talked to everyone who worked in the nearby building and no one had recognized the photos. But the church volunteers had been looking for witnesses, not lying collaborators.

A Hops Motors roadster entered the lot and drifted along the rows as the driver searched for an empty space. This being a Saturday, everyone was at work, far from home, in a desperate attempt to save their marriages. Persons Webmag (*To hell with People—we celebrate individuals*™) featured The Happiest Two Persons of the Week and, without fail, it was a couple who never saw one another except through a video screen. Four days out of seven they had sex together, albeit miles apart via webcam. These folks always complained, like everyone else, that they didn't get enough exercise, but their manual dexterity was off the charts.

Gimbel rooted for the roadster driver to find a space. He said a little prayer and bingo!—the official sound of a churchman's prayer being answered—someone backed out in the next aisle, creating a parking spot. His good deed done for the day, Gimbel strode to the office building to check the lobby directory.

He found the usual fingerprint-smudged flat screens with hundreds of names like AC Zootaphun & Associates, The Toranium Group, BoLoggy, LLC, and a collection of random consonants and vowels, as every conceivable real-word combination in every language had been copyrighted. He could tap on each name to read their mission statements, but he knew from experience (having cribbed the RSA mission statement from dozens of others) that they were all striving for excellence in customer service, maximizing value for their investors, and, oh yeah, honoring and respecting those human resource employee-types. Three or more clicks on various links might lead him to a bland statement about what product or service the company actually sold.

Buried somewhere in the directory construct, an intrepid data miner might find a plastic surgeon or even a general practitioner who dabbled in noses and tits. Gimbel knew he didn't delegate well—if there was one thing you couldn't trust, it was people—but even he recognized when it was time to call in reinforcements.

He used voice commands to dial Billy Bob. When his church secretary came on, Gimbel heard crowd noises and, with a sigh, lifted his communicator to see the video wallpaper behind Billy. As he suspected, the high-strung, paranoid man was still shaken from the church bombing of half a year ago. Billy had begun to use an app where his image was superimposed on a real-life, real-time public scene somewhere in a city in the Americas, New London, New Berlin, New Moscow, New Shanghai, or Newer South Wales, courtesy of Cheeters Anonymous, which boasted *Only one customer caught—and that was hilarious*™.

Its recently updated tagline referred to a famous incident where a husband sleeping around got a call from his wife and his hastily dressed image appeared in front of the grocery store where she happened to be standing. The video had gone mega-viral and for months people would pantomime the wife's actions: talking to her husband through her All-n-1, looking up and around for him, glancing back at the screen, and then checking her surroundings again since he should be right *there*. She could even see herself standing behind him, watching her image watch her image, which was watching her image, and so on.

"Mr. Bob," Gimbel said in what he thought of as his pulpit-patience voice, "you don't have to use that with me or other church elders. We know where you are—at your desk in the basement."

"Yes, sir." Billy fumbled with his controls, and the image behind him switched to the angel-wing white of the secretary's office.

The contrast with the vibrant public scene startled Gimbel; he had to admit that the bland, authentic background looked a good deal more suspicious than the lingerie store wallpaper the app had posted a moment before.

He said, "I need three of the new recruits to come to the address you see displayed." He explained what he wanted them to do, adding, "Get that Lun Johnson and two others. He's showing some promise, at least away from the firing range."

The Most Reverend humped the wife of one of his ministry leaders doggie-style, his laser-tattooed black ankles and feet twitching with blessed joy. His All-n-1 intoned a particular Gregorian chant, the famous Latin plea for God to smite one's oppressors: his private line, which only Billy Bob knew about.

Still on his knees behind the vixen and buried up to the hilt, he wiped any telltale musky dampness from his beard, patted down his hair, and tossed on his shirt before selecting a tight close-up and the Cheeters wallpaper. Behind him appeared a Dixie Pig BBQ joint with overstuffed patrons rocking on the front porch, groaning from one too many servings of apple brown betty.

He said, "Yes, Mr. Bob? I was just about to have—" he glanced at the time display "—dinner."

Billy's knees bounced with excitement. "Sorry to delay you, sir, but the Lun boy just called with interesting news."

Talking to righteous Billy while mounting a randy woman was a delicious turn on. She apparently felt his arousal because she began to move forward and back against him, stifling her moans with a pillow.

Billy hurriedly spoke. "You're looking wobbly, sir—maybe your blood sugar is low. I'll make it fast so you can eat something." His bouncing knees collided with the underside of his desk with the same tempo as the harlot's backward thrusts. "Lun reported that there were no plastic surgeons in the building but there was a company called Brand New U that did identity makeovers. It's run by a Dr. Daniel Torres. Sir, he's a steiner."

Gimbel pumped his fist at this revelation and shouted, "Yes!" The woman cried out the same thing, and they came as one.

Obviously alarmed, Billy asked, "Can I get you a doctor, sir?"

Gimbel assured him that shredded pork on a bun with sweet tea would cure all his ills and signed off. Kissing the shoulder of the ministry leader's wife, Gimbel's mind already was elsewhere. Time to see a man about a brain job.

CHAPTER TWENTY-FOUR

Jeru finished inventorying the pathetic collection of clothes hanging in the closet—corduroys, dress shirts, and loafers for work, and t-shirts, jeans, and sneakers for casual wear, everything in white—and counted stacks of white underwear folded in the drawers of his small bedroom. He looked around for something else to do. The condo was so cheap, there wasn't even a TV built into the bedroom wall. And last time he looked, Ellie still was hogging the one in the great room.

"Crap!" Her screeching shout echoed down the hall and into his open doorway.

Out of boredom and a little curiosity, Jeru made his way to her, still getting used to "walking in someone else's feet." Jeru's new marathoner legs seemed to want to run more than walk. He thought about the poor whole-body donor, a guy who'd worked so hard to get in shape only to be chopped down with half the race ahead of him.

Ellie shouted again, a cry that was equal parts frustration and delight. Jeru recognized her tone immediately. She was in the GameSphere, experiencing one of the most common emotions among players: *Stupid game—I love it.*

She sat in a lounge chair, her back to him, facing the itty-bitty seventy-two-incher. In her fists, she wielded two wireless CtrlSticks and probably clenched two guns onscreen. The red wig was off her head and hanging over the back of her chair like a gruesome scalp. An ominous soundtrack, typical for a tense situation, rumbled from the speakers, almost as deep as Jeru's voice. He couldn't see the scenario yet, but her sudden side-to-side shifts suggested she was in a corridor with a blind corner ahead, hoping nothing was about to jump out at her. Her hands rested on her knees as she leaned forward.

"Keep your hands up," Jeru called.

She gasped, trigger fingers locking in simultaneous spasms. He heard the flare of gunfire blast the stone floor ahead of her. "Leave me alone," she shouted.

"I can help," Jeru said. "I used to play games for a living."

Ellie said, "I don't want your—" She screamed and started shooting. Something hissed and slithered, and she cussed.

He said, "Hands wider apart, to give you a better field of fire."

"It's like I can't shoot straight. The snakes keep slithering around the bullets, and the floor's so wavy they hide in the troughs."

Aabasca's Fortress: the first game on the alphabetical list in the GameSphere, and one of the hardest. Every novice player picked it because it was first and suffered untold hours of frustration. The corporation that managed the GameSphere would never put an easy adventure at the top of the list, the sadistic bastards.

Jeru stopped behind her chair. He expected to be repulsed by the sight of her shaved-smooth head, but there was something sexy about the pale, curved skin. The fresh scar from the steiner operation made her look vulnerable, in need of protection. And watching her react to the video game caused him to smile for the first time since his latest post-surgical coma. She was clearly having a good time even while getting the bejeezus scared out of her.

The screen picture quality really sucked. Then he remembered his poor eyesight. With a sigh, he slipped on the *Death Spiral* goggles he'd shoved into one pocket. He planned to spend his first paycheck on contact lenses and some decent virtual reality gear—flat video games were too retro even for him.

Peering down at Ellie's hands, he said, "You need to have your weapons at the ready, so raise your arms and lock your elbows."

"Shut up, I know what I'm doing," she said, complying with his suggestion. Onscreen, the point-of-view image duly lifted her sleek pistols until they pointed straight ahead.

Jeru tried to keep his troll-voice soft, so it didn't sound like he was about to pounce. "Now the thing about Aabasca's Fortress is that your enemies are as likely to sneak up on you from behind as attack from the front. So here's a trick. Since you're not wearing VirtGear—the gloves, booties, and sensors—the program assumes you're looking in the same direction as where your guns are pointed."

"Jerry, you're ruining my concentration. I'm tired of you almost getting me killed."

In his element now, he kept calm. He'd spent years dealing with clients stressed out by gaming who usually became surlier by the minute. "Just try this. Save it, so you can go back to this point if I steer you wrong. Now, don't panic." He swiveled her chair ninety degrees to the right. The POV swung around too, showing her a stone wall.

"Jerry, you fosh, you're gonna—"

He stepped around to face her, took her sweaty left hand in his and aimed it at the screen. The image split in half, showing her the path up the hall to the dreaded corner and also the wall. "See, now the program is confused about which way you're looking at any one time, so it's like you've grown a second set of eyes. What you really need, though, are those eyes in the back of your head." While she watched the screen, he gently swung her right hand as far to the right as he could, so that she aimed forward and behind her. This gave her a crucified look and stretched her white blouse dangerously tight over her impressive bosom. The material crept up, revealing her pale belly. Another combination of sexy and vulnerable. She might not like her new shape, but he did. He decided he'd like her no matter her shape.

Ellie gasped at the screen. Sure enough, a purple and green serpent with glowing red eyes and obscenely long fangs was ready to strike from behind. She fired twelve rounds and finally cut it in half while another mutant snake raced around the corner to take her from the front. With a more confident single shot, she decapitated the fiend. She saved and then paused the game, lowered her arms and looked up at him as the soundtrack went silent. Initially she smirked at his glasses, but then she said, "Thanks," in a sincere, reedy voice. "That trick is cool."

"Blazing," he corrected. "Totally blazing if it's super-hot. That's the new *cool*. Unless it changed again while I was gone."

They looked each other in the eye for a long moment, and Jeru felt them reach an undeclared truce. No more death threats, no insults. They would be civil to each other. In a few years, he might even ask if she'd be a friend on his personal space and record a video testifying to his wonderfulness.

He pointed to the CtrlStick in each hand and said, "You did better with the left one. Think you're left-handed in this new body?"

Looking at her hands and weighing the controls in them, she said, "I guess so. Maybe it's Cathy's muscle memory." She handed them over to him. "Which hand is dominant for you?"

The Sticks felt awkward in both hands. Probably the only thing natural in this body was exercising the legs. Standing there, he resumed the game and held his arms as he'd instructed her. If he recalled correctly, beyond the corner was an eight-foot-tall, thirty-foot-long salamander guarding two hundred pounds of gold treasure, now taxable. Motioning forward with his right CtrlStick, he eased to the corner and peeked around it.

A slimy mouth the size of a dinner table opened wide and lunged at his face. He ducked back and retreated two steps as the hallway shook. With a roar, the lizard's head and neck whipped around the bend, coming in low to gobble him in one bite.

Shoot out its eyes, he remembered. He tried with both hands, but his aim was terrible. The screen filled with black maw, pink tongue and gleaming teeth as the soundtrack reached a blaring crescendo and a scream erupted from the speakers.

The End.

Jeru looked at his hands. "Guess that answers your question—neither."

"You were really into it, though," she said from the lounge chair. The bright smile on her heart-shaped face made her even prettier. And there was something about that bald head. "You look happy. I mean, even though you're wearing a stranger's face, I can tell you're the happiest you've been since I've known you. It's this GameSphere thing, isn't it?"

Was it the familiarity of gaming that comforted him, or the thaw in their relationship? Rather than risk damaging the truce, he said, "Yeah, I've always loved it. We sort of grew up together."

She pushed out of the chair with a grunt, pulled the white shirt down over her stomach, and grabbed her wig. "Play for a while. I need to use the bathroom. I think this body has a leaky bladder."

When Jeru sat, the body heat Ellie had left behind on the imitation leather momentarily shocked him. He wriggled against the cushions, trying to find a cool spot. She gave "totally blazing" a whole new meaning.

Before relaxing in the GameSphere, he needed to investigate some nagging questions. How were his parents? What was Geneva Bledsoe up to? What did the media report about his death?

He rolled his chair closer to the screen and exchanged the CtrlSticks for a wireless keyboard, which lay on a low table where the wallet-size, three-terabyte computer sat. He didn't trust the voice recognition software in the PC to understand his troll-voice.

Bringing up his favorite search engine, he considered which question to answer first. Maybe his death, since the other matters were more emotional. He typed in the keywords and got 3,920,741 hits. Apparently his "heroism" had been a popular news story for a brief period. The links on the first few pages contained TV and web media accounts, with information supplied by the police investigators in the Kingdom after the incident. In these videos and stories, Jeru got all the credit for stopping the bomber from harming others, though both he and Bledsoe were reportedly vaporized in the massive blast. There were no remains to turn over to his parents.

A story far down the list described Jeru's memorial service and contained videos of his mom and dad—his mother a "big-boned" woman and his dad a wiry rooster, both looking more relieved than grief-stricken—playing tug-of-war with a canister as both of them tried to hold it out for the cameras, like it was the winning Super Mega Big Lottery ticket or the prize catch-o'-the-day. Because there had been no bodily remains to cremate, the voiceover said, his parents had incinerated all his clothes. The reporter hadn't speculated, but Jeru figured they were just trying to free up closet space.

In the video, an honor guard of police and soldiers bowed their heads as a minister said a prayer. Jeru vaguely recalled the man, who had a penchant for picking his nose during Sunday school class and eating whatever he found there. As usual, Mom won the tug-of-war. She set the capsule into the chamber, and Dad hurriedly pushed the button to close the little door, his way of getting in the last word. They both beamed at the paparazzi as the canister was sucked down the vacuum tube, deep into the earth. Once at the bottom, the container would open and a built-in fan would blow out the polyester ashes into a small pocket of open space. The vacuum gear would be hauled up after the mourners departed. With a scoop of dirt tossed down over the remains by the guy with the posthole digger, the well of souls would be ready to accommodate the next Small Footprint Burial (*Live big. Rest small.*™).

Jeru wondered how many levels lay beneath that grave for his clothes and how many had been piled on top since then. A touchscreen set into the ground would tell him, if he ever got a chance to visit. Expansive cemeteries were a luxury the country couldn't afford, when retail space, office parks, and the resurrected manufacturing sector provided most of the jobs and tax revenue. In a moment of grief, he was sorry his parents had wasted their money, even on such a minor memorial. Then he remembered that they'd inherited his entire estate. Those cheap bastards! They knew he wanted to be shot into space.

He was sick of reading about the lies and charades surrounding his "fearless end." His concern about how his parents were coping vaporized, just like his mythical heroic ass. Thank God for the safehouse—at least he had a place to live. No doubt dear old Mom and Dad had turned his bedroom into the Jerusalem Pix Shrine of Courage Museum, with paid tours Monday through Saturday. See the makings of our nation's proudest hero! Witness the home movies that reveal his evolution from brat to braveheart! Marvel at his collection of bootleg porn!

Of course, most prized among that collection was his video of Geneva Bledsoe. He'd deferred gratification long enough. Leaning back in the lounger, he adjusted the damned glasses on his nose and glanced down the hall to see if Ellie was coming his way. The bathroom doorknob rattled and he heard a muffled, "Crap," before she managed to twist the knob the correct way and open the door, escaping back into her bedroom. Presumably she understood that the toilet wouldn't flush itself, but he was damned if he'd check.

The harsh sound of hangers scraping along an aluminum clothes rack drifted into the great room. Confident that she wouldn't make an appearance for a few minutes, he pulled up Geneva Bledsoe's personal space. He knew the web address by heart, having checked it several times every day for years.

Somehow it felt like the first step in cheating on Ellie, akin to surreptitiously checking out some other babe while on a date. But it wasn't like he and Ellie were ever going to get as far as even grinding and kissing again, now that she found him repugnant for betraying her.

Of course, Geneva also would have a few qualms about getting cuddly and paying up on her promise. Including the fact that he'd failed to save her brother. Then there was the complication that he no longer looked or sounded remotely like anyone she knew.

Still, hope and horniness sprang eternal. The first thing he noticed about her page was that Geneva had last updated it on the day he'd gotten blown up by her brother. Her 3-D image was newer than the last one he'd seen there—she'd changed her clothes and added more make-up for the webcam—but no updates in more than half a year was beyond disturbing. She used to obsess about constantly adding new content. Did she hear about Cairo's death and go insane? Maybe she signed up for the Rad Corps, which went into DMZs around the world, dressed in protective suits, to take readings on radioactive decay and look for treasures they could salvage in about 10,000 years. It was rumored to be the last haven for misfits, adventure-seekers, and people escaping their former lives.

Jeru returned to the search engine and entered her name. The articles he discovered about the triple homicide in the Bledsoe condo seized his heart and wrung it into red leather.

Over and over, he read media coverage of her torture and murder, the slaying of her parents, and the killing of another woman and her son on the same floor. Senseless, brutal, cold-blooded. The same quotes over and over. Why would someone do this? Why? Why? Always the same questions. Police had not apprehended the killer, or even interrogated any suspects, because the only DNA and fingerprints found were connected to the victims, and something had gone wrong with the security cameras: the lone assailant was a pixilated blur on all of the recordings.

Follow-up stories about her rehashed the thwarting of Geneva's brother and Jeru's so-called bravery. Apparently, Geneva had erased the erotic video she'd made to get his attention and send him on his quest, because the news accounts he scanned didn't mention it. The only person OTP who had known of his connection with Geneva was her brother. But what if his suicide mission had been monitored by his superiors at the RSA, maybe via a recording device Cairo carried for propaganda? The martyr's final moments, an inspiration to those who would lead the next maniacal assault. Based on Jeru's brief, tense conversation with Cairo about Geneva shortly before his death, anyone eavesdropping would blame her for ruining the attack.

Jeru sat back in the chair, no longer feeling the residual heat from Ellie in the seat. No longer feeling anything, except sadness for Geneva. She'd sent him to do a good deed, no matter the lascivious reward, but he failed. So she died horribly, along with her parents and some apparent witnesses. His fault. And the girl he did manage to save was now trapped in a stranger's body and could never go home again. And the bodyguard sent to protect them was dead. Again, all his fault.

His legs quivered with pent-up energy. Jeru knew they wanted to run. He empathized—he wanted to run like hell, too, away from all of this.

However, he did have a responsibility to Ellie. He couldn't abandon her in an unfamiliar, cruder, less accommodating world. Just the process of buying a fare card on the rapid-transit train would drive her insane. So he escaped the only way he knew how.

CHAPTER TWENTY-FIVE

The GameSphere lounge appeared onscreen, where one could select a new game or go back to the last saved point of any previously played games. Six months ago, the lounge had resembled a fraternity rec room: lots of thrift shop couches and threadbare chairs. A place to hang out, take a nap, or choose the next adventure from a menu.

Sometime since then, though, the programmers had redecorated. Lighting came from steady fluorescents instead of dim, mismatched lamps; the furniture was now worn, cracked leather instead of the stained fabric that one could easily imagine smelling of beer and intercourse; and thumb-tacked posters of avatars who currently held the high scores for the ten most popular games had replaced the vintage pin-ups that used to grace the paneled walls. Obviously more and more women were maintaining the GameSphere.

He had to admit, the avatar posters were a good idea. His own favorite avatar, a Conan-clone named Bane, would've glowered down from at least eight of those panels had he not fallen into the rabbit hole called In-Town—that is, the Kingdom.

At least the menu on the coffee table remained the same: a discolored and wrinkled paper list that resembled a Chinese takeout flyer, right down to the foo dogs, the brown residue of moo shu pork, Cantonese characters beside the English names, and the descriptions of each game, along with warnings about which adventures were "hot and spicy." Many of the programmers were émigrés who arrived in America from Beijing, Shanghai, Hong Kong, and elsewhere before the Big Blowup on 12/26.

He flicked his CtrlStick so that a crosshair settled on the battered menu. A throaty female voice asked, "Destination?" The lounge light on the screen dimmed until only the takeout menu was visible. Above it, tall letters repeated the title of each menu listing that Jeru touched with his crosshair, with accompanying graphics like a movie trailer.

Removing his glasses, he tried to read the listings, but he could only squint so much before his eyes closed completely. He settled the frames back on his nose. The cursor followed the sweep of his Stick, highlighting all the places he'd frequented six months before. Fond memories . . . mixed, in some cases, with regret and shame.

Jeru smiled ruefully. He'd come to the GameSpere to *escape* his guilt, and here he was torturing himself with memories of behaving badly. Besides escape, though, he also wanted to know one thing: did anybody out there miss him—even if it was Bane they missed, and not him exactly?

Returning his attention to the menu, he noted some new selections that looked intriguing:

Miner 2049er: Descend toward the center of the earth in a tunnel that becomes your enemy as well as your lifeline. Crushing stone, searing lava, and nightmares too ghastly to find a home in hell. Strong violence; not recommended for the claustrophobic. Beside the description were three chili peppers. Three out of four was pretty hot and spicy.

Remembering where he'd been when Geneva contacted him about her brother, he went to the last page of menu listings. Shit, they'd removed Zombie Death Rattle, his favorite four-pepper game. Some senator's kid probably got traumatized by having to crawl through a wall of rotting corpses. Damned censors.

When Geneva had sent her initial plea for help, before she'd resorted to the bath scene and erotic promises, his avatar Bane had been hip-deep in a putrid swamp playing whack-a-mole with evil skulls that kept bobbing up around him, teeth clacking. Where had his usual troupe of adventurers gone now that Zombie Death Rattle was defunct?

Nomad was always second-in-command after him. His recollection of that avatar—an unassuming dark-brown man in flowing robes and a monk's cowl—made Jeru smile. Nomad might've looked like a guru of some sort, but he was always lethal in a fight.

Jeru studied the menu again, scrolling through the pages. Where would Nomad take the team? A quick question to the GameSphere moderator would solve that mystery, but first he wanted to consider the options and make a little bet with himself. Hell's Hollow? Dragon Lair? Nomad had argued for the Wasteland of the Sphinx a couple of times, but Jeru always vetoed him, preferring standup fights to riddle-solving and survival against the elements. Having been blown up twice, shot at, and attacked by a psycho SysOp and his killer robo-vac, word games and sandstorms now sounded pretty good. After Bane vanished from the GameSphere, is that where Nomad had led their usual band of adventurers?

Wasteland of the Sphinx: Match wits with the ancient and deadly puzzler and quest for hidden riches in a world of blazing sun and wind-sculpted sand.

Real poetic, but were there enough monsters to kill? It only warranted a single pepper.

Risking his deep growl with the voice-recognition software, he said, "Find Nomad 6346."

After a long pause, perhaps to run a "What the heck did he say?" decipher sub-routine, the throaty female replied, "Wasteland of the Sphinx."

With a yawn of resignation, he tapped that item on the menu and muttered, "Subscribe."

The menu vanished, and the selected image swooped toward Jeru. Lean, bronzed men and women in light armor swung swords at a horde of jackal-like creatures that they chased through an Egyptian palace. As the preview filled the screen, complete with sound effects and music heavy on drums and flutes, it swept him into the action.

Taking on the point of view of the he-man leader, Jeru experienced a delicious sense of vertigo as the fighter suddenly plunged through a trap door in the stone floor and slid down a smooth ramp, landing at the edge of an underground lake. There he confronted a new enemy. Four massive tentacles surged from the water. Jeru raised his arms instinctively in a two-handed grip on the CtrlStick as if it were a sword as the hero hacked off one fleshy rope, but the other three seized him. Yanked off his feet, he was pulled into the lake. Air bubbles erupted from his mouth as the monster dragged him down. Through the murky gloom, he plunged toward the maw of the creature, all teeth and inky blackness. A huge yellow eye stared as the monster inspected its approaching supper.

Then the point of view detached, floated away, and looked down at the imperiled warrior as if through the eyes of God. As the music faded, the scene pulled back, back, back. Poof! He stood on the orange shag carpet in the GameSphere lounge, looking at a fish tank where an anemone waved its long arms around a yellow guppy.

Holding out his NID card to a scanner on the computer, he proved he was Lou Barone. Then he discovered that the steiner had already set him up with a GameSphere account and plenty of money to spend there. That guy really was all right.

In the six months since Jeru had been away, the subscription cost had gone up to a dollar a minute. Soon, regular people wouldn't be able to afford to play. You'd have to go through what he did and end up in the Hero Relocation Program with your brain slam-dunked into someone else's body, just so they'd set you up with some free *dinero*.

Jeru glanced down the hall once more to Ellie's bedroom. Most likely she was taking a nap. Nothing else to do around the condo, except experiment with putting different objects in the microwave.

He'd intended to reanimate Bane and surprise his old friends, but then he remembered an item at the bottom of the menu. On a hunch, he said, "Take me to the Memorial Park."

Sunlight poured down as a meadow and a terraced hillside took the place of the lounge. Only on the Net could one still see a bright yellow sun and blue sky and tender grass underfoot. Out of habit, he plucked a long green blade and put one end in his virtual mouth. From his home setup, wearing VirtGear (*Reality without the scars or guilt*™), he knew it would taste sweet. All the designers in cyberspace used the same recipe code.

Shrines dotted the endless park. Some were elaborate, with statuary and fountains and oil paintings of beloved avatars whose masters had died. Others offered simple, framed 3-D slideshows of the avatar in action, looping endlessly, with perpetually fresh flowers and tokens like champagne bottles or favorite swords planted hilt-deep in the earth.

Jeru said, "Take me to Bane 01."

In an instant he was gliding over the hillside, heading for his destination.

Shit.

Bad news and worse news. His troupe had obviously heard he'd been killed and memorialized Bane, which made it impossible to use the avatar again. If Jeru wanted to stay alive in real life, everybody needed to think he'd gone out in a blaze of glory.

Even more devastating, though, was that they hadn't kept up the shrine. The park attendants relegated it to the rear of the pasture with the other forgotten markers. His team had honored him and then moved on. Sitting in a patch of clover, a single small image showed the Conan-like Bane—flowing black hair under a closefitting steel helmet, ruggedly handsome, powerfully built beneath breastplate and leather leggings—with a bloody battleaxe in one hand and a bag of loot in the other. Luscious, naked, blond twins clung to his legs, each with a hand reaching up his thigh. In a cheap plastic vase, a clutch of chrysanthemums forever flaked away in the breeze. The only offering was a gold, filigreed cylinder lying in some weeds. Jeru picked it up, unhinged the top, and shook a small scroll into his palm.

In spidery calligraphy that made him grateful for his glasses, the team had written, "Bane/Jerusalem, you led us and fought for us. In games and while offlining. Rest in peace."

Not the tearful sentiments he expected. Hell, deserved. Who'd brought thousands of hours of gaming experience to bear? Who'd suffered terrible wounds and braved incredible odds to save their worthless hides again and again? Who'd led them to the best plunder and most lively orgies?

Now, here his memorial sat at the ass-end of the park with some puny flowers and a throw-away eulogy?

Jeru wandered away from the spot and took in the thousands of other memorials scattered around the meadow and disappearing over the hill. Owners died naturally or were killed all the time. So many. For everyone else, life went on, in and out of cyberspace.

He knew the old gang was busy. Who had time to keep up a shrine when there were evermore worlds to conquer? He'd neglected to keep up a few sites in the Memorial Park himself. Maybe it was no big deal. Maybe.

"Choose avatar," he commanded.

The park blurred and was replaced by a cavernous warehouse with seemingly endless rows of suspended-animation capsules standing upright. Avatars of every sort floated naked in eternal sleep. He had to let Bane go. Time to choose and equip a new hero.

What did he want to do in the game? When he'd chosen and outfitted Bane years before, he wanted to hack limbs and bash heads and romp with grateful maidens. Now, with a chance to start over again, he wasn't sure who to become. Someone completely different?

Who was he anyway?

He considered his experiences since waking in Ellie's house, in the first of two new bodies. It seemed he'd turned into more of a thing than a person.

Okay, he would become a true monster. He had the troll-voice already.

He said, "Categories," and reviewed the always-growing list that appeared around him in a broad semi-circle. Moving, naked images of each species, and its one or more genders, accompanied the names. Tolkien-inspired creatures; a pantheon of beasts from Greek, Roman, Native American, Hindu, Egyptian, and other ancient myths; a galaxy of critters from sci-fi and fantasy fandom; and original creations all strutted for him. He couldn't choose something too outlandish: everyone in Bane's Brigade was a human or humanoid. They wouldn't respond well to a new recruit shaped like a blob or a yellow sponge with big eyes and boxy pants.

One of the patented new creations caught his eye: a thickly muscled, leathery-brown fellow with a square head and no neck. Standing over six feet tall, it had four massive arms, two on a side. Its knees swiveled in any direction—ball-and-socket rather than hinge-jointed—and its curved phallus resembled a retractable horn. A loincloth would be sufficient for the beast, dubbed a Haythoo by its inventor.

"Weapons," he said.

The Haythoo's creator had designed a number of weapons that would be consistent with the skills the avatar possessed. A cross-index of every game with the Haythoo's armory showed that blades and range weapons like spears and bows were approved for Wasteland of the Sphinx. Can't have someone running around ancient times with laser guns. A whole set of anachronistic games were popular with kids, but Jeru had long since tired of mowing down entire Roman legions with a plasma ray. Where was the challenge?

He picked a battle axe and broadsword for his upper set of hands and crisscrossed his chest with two bandoliers of throwing knives for the bottom hands to have fun with. With each selection, his bank account balance, displayed in the lower left corner of the screen, depleted.

The haberdashery, dubbed The Hab, contained scores of chambers filled with armor from every century, street clothes, formal wear, coats, lingerie, and accessories. He belted a chain-mail kilt over the family jewels. A roomy Bedouin robe with cowl, much like Nomad's, would protect him from sunstroke, sandstorms, and frigid nights; he found one with four sleeves. His account balance was below 100 gold pieces, but all his purchases were expenses he could deduct against taxes on future winnings. Time to score some loot.

He found himself increasingly anxious to see the old gang again, even if they wouldn't know who he was and wouldn't believe him if he told them the tale, which he couldn't risk doing. Equipped and dressed, he told the system to take him to Nomad 6346. He'd have to develop his character profile on the fly.

The Hab vanished and was replaced by glaring sun, sloping and rippled dunes, and wind that whistled from the speakers. A mysterious, vaguely Arabian soundtrack began with flutes and drums but nothing blatant enough to arouse anti-Islamic sentiments.

No sign of Nomad or the others. Game designers universally agreed that it was too dangerous for a new player to materialize among a group of on-edge warriors, so one always walked into camp or eased into any battle in progress.

Footprints and wagon tracks, which were filling quickly with gusting sand, led up a broad dune. Jeru headed in that direction as the bright sun glared directly overhead. He imagined heat waves pounding him ceaselessly along with the taste of grit and alkaline air as the speakers delivered wailing from the wind and the rattle of sand against his hooded robe. Soft flute playing lured him over the ridge; the Pied Piper Effect always worked.

CHAPTER TWENTY-SIX

When Gimbel arrived at the office building, Lun Johnson, who'd finished in the bottom quartile of his class at God's Boot Camp, was outside, leaning against the glass front door, and playing a video game on his All-n-1. The boy had dressed in the official uniform of the Junior RSA—camo pants and a white t-shirt emblazoned with the slogan "Angel in Training" above a cruciform of assault rifles. He didn't look up as Gimbel approached.

"Bang!" Gimbel shouted. He watched with amusement as the plastic and silicon communicator/entertainer/best-friend-for-life flipped end over end and smashed into shards on the concrete landing. "You're dead, Lun. The terrorists just put a bullet through your head."

The boy's hands shook even after he jammed them into his camos. "S-s-sorry. I got distracted by that game, which was totally blazing, and I didn't hear you and—"

Gimbel started to put a hand on Lun's shoulder to steady the kid, but a ragged blue arc of electricity leaped between his fingertips and the boy, zapping them both. Ross couldn't get the hang of those mini-electrocutions from the DoD's cloaking spray. As Lun rubbed the welt on his shoulder, Gimbel intoned, "The best lessons in life are negative. Christ Himself said, 'It is better to know what not to do than not.' "

Lun's head bobbed up and down and then side to side, his mind no doubt chasing the double negative like a dog snapping at its tail. Before the boy short-circuited and crumpled atop the remains of his All-n-1, Gimbel whacked him with one of the three XXL white t-shirts he'd brought for the boys. Easier than stripping them down and spraying their squirming nakedness with the DoD chemical. "Put this on," he said. "It's a disguise."

The teen slid the shirt over his head, obedient to a fault. Seeing that he'd put the item on backward, his arms disappeared inside the sleeves, and the new outfit rotated 360 degrees—or his head and legs did—and then reversed by another 180. Not the crispest dollar in the tip jar, but trying to follow orders was more essential than getting them right the first time. At least until Martyr Monday. Or Tuesday or whenever the boy would have the honor of meeting the Creator and his only begotten Son while sending a busload of infidels to their eternity in hell.

Gimbel glanced at the shirtfront and allowed himself a smile. Use every opportunity to propagandize and cripple one of the many enemies threatening the homeland. At the church HQ, he had shirts depicting a cartoon ring of mullahs dancing with their arms linked, but he decided to target the ultra-right wing this time. The shirt bore the motto "Supremely White Is Supremely Right." On Lun's head, he jammed a white ball cap that proclaimed "♥ 2 H8 U." The security cameras would take it all in: a pixilated blur and the obvious terrorist-in-training. He guided Lun inside with shirts and caps for the two other boys.

When he looked around the lobby, though, he ceased to be pleased. "Where are they?"

"They, uh, told me to stand guard and went off to play BattleBoards."

Gimbel sighed. He needed to talk to the recruiters again. They kept scraping the bottom of the takeout box. At least *his* recruit stayed at his post, no matter that an elephant draped with cymbals could've snuck up on poor Lun.

He shoved the remaining clothes into a nearby trashcan, which compacted them with a mechanical belch. "Fine. It's just you and me then. I was hoping to turn this into a teaching opportunity for everyone." Patting his hips, where two holstered pistols were concealed by his extra-long polo shirt, he advanced to the elevators and, once inside, told Lun to push the button for the floor occupied by Brand New U, the steiner's company.

The boy jabbed 16 and began to adjust the cap in the hip new way—turning it inside out and backward with the bill flipped up—but Gimbel slapped his hand, giving them both another sharp jolt. Lun trembled again. He said, "The way I found it, I was reading every one of the listings and—"

"Yeah, yeah. Good work. Things might get tense up there. Might get dangerous. Think you can handle yourself?"

"Well, I failed the martial arts classes, but I did really well at covert arts and—"

Gimbel let Lun prattle. No need to tell him that he did so well at the hide-and-seek war games because no one looked for him; they were happy for the blessed silence.

The elevator doors opened on the sixteenth floor. Surrounding a sterile alcove of faux-marble flooring and cream walls were offices on three sides, each with a closed door and signs with company logos mounted beside them. Gimbel gave the finger—God forgive him—to the security cameras trained their way and headed for the door that advertised Brand New U. *Walk a mile in someone else's feet* its trademark stated, with a happy brain somersaulting from the flipped-open head of an aged, unattractive man into the empty skull of a youthful, handsome one.

To avoid a shock from the metal door handle, he gestured for Lun to open it. Also, it left both hands free so he could draw his pistols. The blunt-nosed guns, made from a graphite-ceramic composite that was feather-light, shock-free, and an anathema to metal detectors, were novelties, like exotic underwear worn only once for a new lover and then pushed to the back of the drawer. They fired non-metallic bullets and came courtesy of a firearms manufacturer in Canada that had exchanged the pair for an autographed copy of Gimbel's memoir and a plug for the company during one of his broadcasted sermons.

The Brand New U receptionist, a slender beauty with a sweep of fawn-colored hair and an obscenely luscious mouth, spread those plump lips in a professional smile that turned into an O of horror when Gimbel raised both barrels. Her right hand darted beneath the table.

He said, "Stop. Push away from the desk."

The woman shoved her chair backward on the polished, laminate floor. Her adrenaline must have kicked in, because she rocketed into the far wall.

Gimbel laughed as her arms and legs flopped like a doll's on impact. "Good," he said. "Thank you. Please take us to Dr. Torres."

Lun glanced back, obviously delighted at what Gimbel was able to do merely with his command voice. He then gaped at the guns.

"He-he's in surgery," the woman mumbled.

"Excellent! This should be fascinating to see." He motioned with one pistol. "You lead the way, my dear. Son, lock this door."

She staggered out of her chair and down a short hall. Gimbel motioned with his head for Lun to fall in behind her, while he brought up the rear. He admired the woman's hind end and then her profile as she wobbled around a left turn. They arrived at a steel door with a small glass window. A monitor over the door warned "Neurosurgery in Progress. No Smoking. No Phones. No Sudden Noises. No Flash Photography. No, Really."

Trembling, the woman pulled open the door with some effort, as if fighting a strong vacuum. It made a sucking sound when she broke its seal. They entered an airlock-like antechamber, with scrubs, booties, shower caps, wash stations, shelves, and hangers. A blue silk four-piece suit hung there, with blue and white wingtips beneath them, along with three sets of women's wear and shoes that ranged from boring to tacky.

Gimbel said, "Go on." To give her more incentive, he reached over Lun and poked the gun barrel into the back of her head.

She gasped. Collecting herself, she said, "We should sterilize."

"We're men of God," he replied. "Cleanliness is next to Godliness."

Lun nodded vigorously, no doubt pleased that he'd been lumped in as a fellow man of God. Still, the lad looked nervous about the pistols on display. Better cure him of that—avenging angels needed to be bad asses.

The receptionist's shoulders slumped in resignation. She took hold of the inner door and opened it. A blast of cold, dry air hit Gimbel. Bracing. It reminded him of last year's Rocky Mountains Fresh Pow(d)er Pastor Retreat (*Faith doesn't have to be a black diamond run*™).

A Latino-flavored voice was saying to three nurses, "This is the part of the surgery where I feel more like an electrician wiring a Baroque chandelier than a—" Hunched at the head of the table, the neurosurgeon glanced up at the interruption. His hands guided a pair of robotic tools that he'd immersed in the exposed space where the top of the patient's skull normally would've been. Three nurses monitored the forty-something man's condition on various screens, though the one farthest from the action was halfway through a deck of video solitaire. Racks of electronics and trays of surgical tools lined the walls. On a separate table sat a crockpot-like appliance on which someone had scrawled, "Skull-capper Keeper."

Gimbel greeted the assemblage with a smile and aimed one pistol so that the laser target painted a cross on the steiner's forehead.

Dr. Torres cried out and hopped back a step. His arms yanked the robots and they in turn wrenched the brain from its precarious linkages. The organ tumbled off the table, hit the top of the man's booties, and broke into sloppy pink and gray chunks.

"Oh my," Dr. Torres whined. He shook one foot and then the other as the nurses mewled fearfully behind their masks. Steeling himself, the surgeon shouted, "That's two men you've killed at once: the brain's owner and this one—he's been thawed and can't be refrozen."

Gimbel nodded. "Sort of like chicken." He aimed his other gun at the receptionist, who'd edged herself into a corner. A red cross appeared on her breastbone. "I'll give equal opportunity to the ladies unless you tell me about Ellipsis Stewart and Jerusalem Pix—or Benjamin Splyvex or whatever the hell he's calling himself. Who are they now, what do they look like, and where can I find them?"

The nurses looked at Dr. Torres. He set the robotic mechanisms next to the crockpot and shrugged. "I'm sorry, you must have the wrong steiner. I don't know who you mean."

Gimbel squeezed the trigger of the gun in his left hand, while keeping the other trained on the doctor. The pistol coughed and a starburst of red appeared over the receptionist's heart. She dropped without a sound other than a thump of sprawled limbs.

The noise, however, came from everyone else. The nurses screamed, Dr. Torres howled, Lun sobbed, and Gimbel shouted for everyone to shut up. He thrust the smoking gun at Lun, who looked like he would've been more comfortable picking the brain matter off the floor. Gimbel ordered Lun, "That one there. The one who tried to cheat by putting the four of clubs on the five of spades. Shoot her next."

The nurse yelped, "It was an accident! I thought the suit was diamonds."

Gimbel said, "Tell me the truth, Dr. Torres, or we'll cut your staff expenses even further."

Dr. Torres said, "I'd love to help you. Really!" He held out his hands. "I just don't know who you mean."

Gimbel said, "Do it, son."

Lun's hand shook as the nurse ducked and cowered. The other two dashed from behind her. "I can't," he groaned.

"Do it."

The woman cried, soaking her mask.

Lun put his other hand on the quaking gun but failed to steady his aim. "Sir, please."

"Do it, or your parents are next. And I don't mean their blue butterfly avatars."

Lun closed his tearful eyes and squeezed the trigger. A bullet punctured the nurse's shoulder. She spun around and fell over. Making frightened animal noises, she pressed a hand to her bloody wound.

"Finish her," Gimbel said. "Or else."

Lun whispered, "I'm sorry."

It took him ten more tries to deliver the woman to God's Final Judgment. Either the kid was a brilliant marksman and a masterful torturer, or he needed another few hours at the range. By the end, the other two nurses were in tears holding each other, and Dr. Torres had vomited on the scrambled brains. Lun bent over and added his own mark to the floor. The boy upchucked all over the pistol he'd dropped at his feet.

Gimbel shrugged, not really caring about breaking up the matched set of guns, and re-centered his laser sight on the doctor. "Your choice, Torres. The shooting gallery will remain open, or you can spare their lives—and yours—by confessing." With his free hand, he pointed to the side of his head. "Your mouth to God's ear."

"All right, it's true." The surgeon dropped to his knees, landing in his puke and the remnants of the brain. "I know who they are now. I know where they are."

Not only that, but Dr. Torres then showed him a wondrous surprise, like a gift from the heavens. An ace in the hole, praise the Lord.

CHAPTER TWENTY-SEVEN

As Jeru crested the sand dune, he saw red flags fluttering above an enormous tent, big enough to hold a few hundred warriors. It created a windbreak and a source of shade in which dozens of camels and horses hunkered.

Oil lamps cast flickering light around the high-walled interior. Men and women sat or reclined on colorful rugs in groups of six to ten: confederations of fighters staying close in case of trouble. Some people—humans and fantasy humanoids—milled between the parties, trading goods, forming alliances, and flirting, obviously hoping to get lucky in some private tent later.

Scanning the scores of occupants, Jeru recognized the slouching forms and favorite weaponry of several of Bane's Brigade, or whatever they called themselves now. And there in the lamplight was the broad, dark forehead and strong African features of Nomad as he traced something in the sand while the other five looked on.

As Jeru picked his way over to his six old friends, he noticed a well-endowed and lethally armed brunette in another party who once had fallen for him, or rather, for Bane. She'd had some exotic tastes—just the sort who would make it with a Haythoo for the sake of experimentation.

Nomad glanced up when Jeru came nearer. In front of the man was a floor plan drawn in the sand, which showed chambers and passageways. He had marked a large X in one sealed room and planted his dagger through it. With a casual sweep of his hand, Nomad erased the diagram while hefting his knife. "Friend," he said, his usual, neutral greeting. In the real world, he was a hostage negotiator for the police and always brought the same calming, no-drama presence to the GameSphere.

Jeru responded in his dump-truck-in-first-gear voice, "An old friend of mine recommended your group."

The other five in the party surveyed Jeru with skepticism—four men and a squat, toad-like humanoid named Sig who was a hermaphrodite, as Jeru recalled. One of the men, a wise-ass samurai who called himself Petey, asked, "Caught a cold, pardner?" There was never any point in explaining role-playing to Petey. Regardless of the avatar Petey chose, he always sounded like a cowboy. The man was a traffic-control engineer for the Grid in real life; if he hadn't been so ingenious at anticipating each game's twists and turns, Jeru would've ditched him long ago. Nomad apparently felt the same way.

"Just how I'm made," Jeru responded. He drew back his cowl with his upper arms, while the lower set pulled open the robe, revealing the crossed bandoliers of knives and his chain-mail kilt.

Nomad gave him a once-over. "You're built for battle, all right. Unfortunately, we're not looking for another fighter."

"What happened to seven being a lucky number?"

Jeru's longtime second-in-command looked away. Though otherwise purely rational, Nomad had always been superstitious about keeping their group at seven.

Petey said, "We're getting along fine with just us six."

Nomad gestured with his dagger to an unoccupied rug beside Petey. "Doesn't mean we can't be hospitable." He scratched his short, tightly curled black hair, a familiar gesture when he was stalling for time.

Jeru introduced himself as "Hellspar," a name he made up on the spot, sat down, and folded his legs and reptilian feet lotus-style on top of his thighs. Easy to do when your knees could swing in any direction.

Barlow, the man beside Petey, said, "Have you been in this world for a while?"

"Just got here, but I've gone on a bunch of campaigns." Jeru decided on a soft sell; Nomad never reacted well to being pressured.

His former lieutenant asked, "You team up with anyone we might know?"

"The old friend of mine who recommended you was called Bane."

Petey snorted, and Sig the toad rolled its crimson eyes. "Our beloved former leader," the creature muttered in its singsong voice.

Fucking ingrates! Jeru gripped his thighs with all four hands, to keep himself from reaching for his weapons. In his deepest voice, he said, "What, he wasn't any good?"

Everyone in the war party rubbed their ears. "Good at getting what he wanted," Barlow said. "He never asked for our opinions—just expected us to follow."

The quiet one beside Nomad, a Herculean strongman who had followed every order Jeru ever gave, grumbled, "Never asked me a damn thing."

"And took more than his share," Sig added. "Took the best-looking girls, too."

Petey said, "Now hold on, Sig, ol' Bane left you the pick of the boys." He slapped his knee and laughed, rattling his samurai sword in its long saber.

In his lounger, Jeru shivered from the anxiety-sweat soaking his armpits. The guys had never said anything about his leadership. They'd always acted as if they appreciated him, liked him even. He held his avatar still.

Barlow flicked a small knife across his thumbnail. "No disrespect to your pal, but if it wasn't for Nomad following behind and keeping us together, we'd have mutinied a long time ago and taken Bane apart. I guess some bomber on the outside took care of that for us."

Jeru realized the Memorial Park monument to Bane, no matter how neglected, wouldn't have existed at all if not for Nomad. He looked at his virtual friend, a man he'd gamed with for years.

Nomad said, "It takes more than one incident to be a real hero, in this world or any other."

Jeru struggled to his feet, and his former friends readied their weapons. He turned his back on them, colliding with the buxom brunette, who'd been eavesdropping. She toppled onto her butt and shouted,

"Hey!" The woman struggled to her feet and yelled after him, "I always thought Bane was a creep too. And he was a lousy lay."

Much of the big tent erupted in laughter, whistles, and applause. His humiliation complete, Jeru violated the most basic gaming etiquette by aborting the adventure. To Nomad and the others, he would simply blink out of existence. From now on, wherever Nomad's party went, he'd go elsewhere. If he went back at all. Life online didn't feel much like home anymore.

He killed the screen, dropped the Sticks to the floor, and slumped back into his chair. Sweat and a few tears wet his face.

"Hey," Ellie whispered, her voice startlingly close but soft. "I'm sorry they did that to you. I think you're a real hero."

Jeru swiveled the lounger around to face her. She sat in the second chair, a few feet behind his shoulder, her red wig back in place. He'd thought his humiliation was at one hundred percent. The fact that Ellie had snuck in and witnessed it made everything worse.

He grabbed the chair arms so he could stand and storm away, but she leaned forward and took hold of his wrists.

Because her arms were short, holding him there brought her to the edge of her seat, her heart-shaped face only inches from his. Puffy skin around her brown eyes and small, round wet spots on her shirt told him she'd not only seen everything but it had hurt her too. Certainly not as much as him—the most empathetic person in the world didn't feel a stick in the eye like the guy staggering around afterward with his face in his hands—but she *cared*. She really cared. Even after he'd betrayed her.

Ellie's lips parted, but neither of them spoke. He felt her breath on his chin. She stared at him so oddly, like she needed to hear something important . . . vital . . . maybe lifesaving. It wasn't the lusty sort of look she'd given him when they were In-Town or in the limo. This was altogether different.

He tested his leverage and found he still couldn't move. A twinge of fear caused fresh rivulets of sweat to scrape down his ribs. If she wanted to hurt him, he was in big trouble. Ellie wouldn't hit a guy with glasses, would she?

As if to discourage him from trying to move again, her fingers tightened around his wrists. She leaned so close, the tips of her bosom compressed against his chest. Her tongue darted out to moisten her lips and she swallowed. At last she whispered, "I'm so scared."

"I know. It'll get better. Easier." For the first time he noticed lovely flecks of gold and green in her irises. Maybe they were changing color after all. Or maybe he'd stopped merely looking and finally started to see her.

"You felt this way too?" she asked. "When we were in my home?"

"When I first woke up? Yeah." God, he hated his voice. He wished it could soften, wished it could comfort her. At its most delicate, it still sounded like getting caught in an avalanche. "But you were there for me, and you understood everything about In-Town. That made it easier."

"I teased you too much; I didn't understand what you were feeling."

He felt heat pulse from her. The pressure of her breasts against him increased and then diminished with each breath. What did she need him to say to make things better? He tried, "Now here you are, stuck in my world, and I've been a glans."

"No, don't. The people in the game just now, they were awful to you. Along with your parents and that Geneva girl."

"You saw me reading about them? About, uh, her?"

"I already knew about her, not from Kliburn but from the video device Doc found in your pocket when the police and paramedics brought you into her surgery."

Oh my God. He collapsed back against his lounger, which pulled her out of her chair. She could've held him fast and stayed where she was, but something compelled her to keep the distance between them very short. He was nothing much to look at anymore, but here she came, climbing onto his chair. Even though she'd seen Geneva's video. He wished he could take off the ridiculous glasses sliding down his sweaty nose.

Ellie perched above his lap, her knees pressing the outside of his thighs. She murmured, "I hated her. For months, while Doc was working on you, I tortured myself by watching her in that damned tub surrounded by candles. I wanted to be that girl, someone who'd inspire you so much you'd go out and risk everything."

"You are."

She shook her head, locks from the red wig swaying. "Maybe I was. Not anymore. I mean, look at me."

He wasn't sure when it had happened, but she'd let go of his wrists. Her hands rose up and clenched his shoulders. As if she didn't hear the right thing, said the right way, she'd die right there.

"I am looking. Really seeing you, I mean," he said, and touched her warm, damp back with his fingertips. He moved them in opposing circles on either side of her spine.

Her nails dug into the gristly meat beneath his skin. "Do you hate the way I am now?"

"No, you're lovely. And you're the same inside as you always were—lovely there too."

"Back home you said we just liked how each other looked, but not the person inside."

Jeru murmured, "I was wrong to say that. I like you. I always have."

"You do? You like me?" Her legs relaxed and she planted her bottom on his legs.

His hands stopped along with his breath as a realization shook him. "No," he said. "I love you. I love you, Ellie."

"Jerry." She wrenched the glasses from his face and tossed them aside. Before they hit the wall, she'd cupped his face in her hands. Her wet mouth crashed against his.

He wrapped his arms around her broad back and pulled her against him. So much hot, vibrant flesh. As she sucked his lips, he slid her wig aside and caressed her smooth head.

His total acceptance sent her into a frenzy, rocking her hips against him and grinding amazingly hard nipples around his chest. With one more frantic push, she rose up, her monumental breasts now in his face. He grasped handfuls of her butt and squeezed. Moaning, she leaned into him.

The lounger tipped, as did his world. Jeru crashed backward to the floor and slid off the chair. Ellie rode him all the way down.

CHAPTER TWENTY-EIGHT

The next few hours flickered in Jeru's memory like a fever dream. He and Ellie had crawled, stumbled, and rolled together into his bedroom, the closest one. The self-consciousness that overtook her came later. In the beginning, they were so frantic to taste each other everywhere, to touch everything, that he didn't know night from day, down from up.

Not even their inexperience could ruin it. As virgins, and not just with their new bodies, their pacing was all wrong. Too fast at the start. Too slow when they should've been racing toward the finish line together. Starting over again. Cramped muscles from staying too long in awkward positions. Sore, tired jaws. If she had any hair on her head, Jeru knew he would've tugged it by accident. They really didn't know what to do, where to do it, when, or how—though they'd finally got the *who* part right—and only so much practice could be gained before their bodies gave out from exhaustion. Then the mind went back on duty, and the hypercritical self-analysis began.

The worst of what had been said now replayed in his mind:

"What was I thinking?"

"I put it where?"

"But, but, just look at me. Why would anyone in their right mind want to do that to me?"

"This never happened. We'll have to pretend that. Forever."

"You probably gave me something." Ellie's final words of their fight still rang in Jeru's head as he staggered from the tangle of damp, musky sheets into the bathroom. He didn't know how long he'd napped, but the gloomy daylight outside his window blinds had turned to night. Somewhere in the condo, a door closed. Ellie must've been going through the same motions of processing everything that had happened.

Somehow, instead of lying together in bed, basking in their rutting, slurping, stroking animalness, and talking about what they wanted to try when their middle-aged, recently thawed bodies recovered, they were in separate rooms with a minefield of guilt, recrimination, and self-loathing between them. And those things were what they had to deal with just to get through dinner together.

Together. Together with Ellie. What she'd wished for and planned all along, but wishing and making plans were dangerous things. So what happens when your dreams finally come true, but you're no longer the same person who'd dreamed them?

What happens is, you go get something to eat. Jeru decided to dress for dinner, selecting pressed white corduroys and a natty white polo shirt—obviously a corporate giveaway—that advertised LusterBean: *The coffee that gleams*™.

He padded into the hall and crept to Ellie's doorway. His poor eyesight didn't allow him to see much in the nearly dark room, but he did note that it was unoccupied.

Taking a deep breath, he squared his scrawny shoulders, raised his beaky face, and prepared to deal with their latest turn for the worse. Somehow, worse kept getting worser, but they had to be touching bottom soon. So to speak. What else could go wrong?

He marched toward the great room, unnerved by the lack of light. He'd expected her to have switched on the video screen or left open the mini-fridge. Was she simply sitting in the dark, waiting for him? A thought made him stop in mid-stride. Now that she'd laid him and was not thrilled with herself or him for doing it, did she want to kill him again?

Jeru backtracked up the hall, groping for the light. With a tap of the switch, he could see into half of the room. Though his view was blurry, he knew none of the blurs resembled Ellie. Maybe she lurked in the other half, hidden from his vantage point, carving knife poised in the air.

Too many horror movies, he decided, which was what Slasher Victim #2 always decided right before the axe cleaved his head open like a pumpkin. Touching the wall as he eased down the hall, he felt ridiculous and scared to death at the same time.

Finally, he leaped out, ready to meet his fate, and confronted an Ellie-less room. Could the door he'd heard close have been Ellie going out for a walk? A stroll around the block to clear her head?

He found his glasses on the floor against the wall and slipped them on. Returning to her room, he noted the bed looked slept in, or at least laid on, but there wasn't a note there or in the bathroom. Nothing written in lipstick on the mirror like "It's your fault I jumped." Or even a simple, declarative "I hate you."

Actually, "I hate you" was easy to deal with. "I hate you, but I hate me even more" was twice as complicated and very serious. After all, she was the one who'd acted so repulsed by herself as well as him when their sweat wasn't even dry.

And while he'd slept on it, did she brood and stew and decide to—what? End it all? Try to lose herself in a world that required an NID to buy bubblegum at the corner store? Go home?

The notion struck him as he caught sight of the cordless phone by her bed. It doubled as the TV remote and that really was its prime function—the phone feature had become a throw-in accessory in case you'd left your All-n-1 in the next room or were sitting on it and too large or lazy, or both, to move. The bare-bones phone didn't have many options, but one button was labeled Redial.

He punched it and listened to a series of clicks, like the signal had to jump through extra hoops to make the connection.

A British-tinged female voice said, "Ellipsis, I'm so glad you—"

"Doc," Jeru said, "It's me."

"Who? Who is this?" Dr. Gomez demanded. "Where's Ellipsis?"

"It's Jeru. Jerusalem. I sound like a troll because of the body Dr. Torres put me in."

"Oh. Um, hello. I understand you and Ellie have had some ups and downs."

He said, "Like that's news," then caught himself. Better not rile her. He needed Doc's help as she was the last one to speak with Ellie. "We, uh, finally got together, but it wasn't what either of us thought it would be like."

"I know. She was quite explicit about what you did to her."

Jeru stared guiltily at his socks only for a moment before deciding to let off a little steam. "And was she explicit about what she did to me? You know, for a virgin—"

"Stop it this instant," she barked. "You sound just like her. Who cares what you know how to do or need to learn? You're safe out there. You can make a life together, and you should be grateful you have that life and each other."

She was right, of course. Jeru sat on Ellie's bed and fell backward across the mattress. He smelled her scent, a mix of brown sugar and honey, with a hint of the sex they'd shared hours earlier. "Doc, what can I say? She told me she was scared. I told her I love her. We wore each other out and then our brains switched on again."

"You don't understand anything. Your body would be a useless bag without your brain. Your brains were working the whole time you made love. If anything felt good, it was your brain making that decision. Everything you tried, your brain conceived of—"

"I know that," he snapped. "What I meant was, the rational part of our brains kicked in. We saw what we are, what mindless beasts we'd turned into."

She replied, "That's all bollocks, and I told Ellipsis the same. You got lost in the moment because you finally let yourselves love each other as people. You loved everything about her and she loved every aspect of you. Good God, what I wouldn't give to have that again—don't you see how lucky you are?"

Ellie's scent in the bed was driving him crazy. He rolled over to her pillows and inhaled. For an instant, she was with him again, her mouth on his, hands everywhere, legs folded around his hips. Skin to skin, from head to toe. Once immersed in that full-body sensation, he realized he wasn't thinking in terms of physical descriptions and comparisons. His sole focus was on giving her pleasure. Her first orgasm had filled him with so much joy he'd devoted his entire being to her ecstasy. He'd wanted no more from life than to love her forever.

"Oh my God," he whispered.

"A tad bit late for an epiphany, hero. Now go tell Ellipsis. She doesn't believe you're capable of such depth of feeling—and, unfortunately, she's still miffed at me so she wouldn't allow me to guide her."

"*Miffed*? I'm sure she *is* just a *tad bit* miffed at you. You should've told Ellie what was going to happen to her. You're her doctor and the friend she trusted the most."

"And you're her lover—or should've been her lover back here, if you had any sense. You bear the responsibility and the guilt as well. So make it up to our dear girl for both our sakes."

The doctor sounded like she was ready to hang up, so Jeru shouted into the phone, "She's gone."

"Where?"

"I was hoping you'd tell me."

Dr. Gomez muttered a string of curses in at least three other languages. Something clattered in the background, as if she'd whacked a tray full of instruments onto the floor. "I don't know where she could be."

"Is Kliburn listening to us right now—is that why you can't say?"

"I told you, everything in my quarters and surgery is secure."

"Well, he was able to watch us and tip off the RSA, so—"

"I discovered cameras hidden in the outer walls, far above my area. They're disabled now."

Jeru sat up. "And he's not going after you?"

"No, I have too many connections outside the house—my death couldn't be explained away so easily. I'd take down Kliburn and ANGUS and be done with it, but I lack the security codes to disable the power plant in the basement. Only Victoria knows those."

He could just imagine trying to get Ellie's mom to remember those codes in her pleasure-addled brain. An unwanted image flashed in his mind of interrogating Victoria Stewart while she lay back in one of her sex-partner lounge chairs. He asked, "How's she taking Ellie's disappearance from home?"

"So far she hasn't inquired after her daughter, so I haven't had to deal with that yet. Perhaps she thinks Ellipsis is staying with friends." She paused as if reaching a decision. When she spoke again, her voice sounded strained. Clearly, she was scared. "Ellipsis wanted to come home. I told her 'no,' that it wouldn't ever be safe. Still, she must be headed this way."

"I'll go get her."

"How?"

"I don't know, but I'll find her. I have to. Give me your number in case I get a lead." He made her repeat it several times and then said it back to her until he'd memorized the number. It was an international long-distance line: In-Town Atlanta had its own country code.

They hung up, and Jeru finally let his legs do what they'd ached for, what they were good at. He ran like the wind. Out on the street, with the murky gray sky overhead and no hint of moon or stars, ambient light from the western suburbs struck the underside of the permanent layer of insulation and bounced back, giving him plenty of brightness to see the sidewalks and streets. And steady traffic added to the glare. No Ellie of course—she had a long head start.

Which way? From navigating her family's hotel-turned-home for so long, she must've had an excellent sense of direction. However, even she wouldn't know how to get to In-Town from here. Hopefully, she hadn't stumbled on a taxi or guessed where she could find the nearest rapid-transit station. She might know the route back to Dr. Torres's recovery facility. That was his best bet. He took off in that direction at a gallop.

His corduroys were all wrong for running, and they made a racket like he was sawing wood between his legs. Plus the shoes he'd been given were so cheap he felt the impact of every footfall. But he still ran like the devil was on his ass —worse, like the RSA with Kliburn riding shotgun were accompanying Satan.

He thought he remembered spotting a shortcut during their drive to the condo. The steiner had stuck to the major avenues, but if he took a cross street and headed diagonally....

Veering off, he discovered he had the minor roads to himself. The friction of his pants echoed off the lit-up office buildings and the closed and dark shops. His steady breathing was the only other thing he heard. For a birdlike guy, this body donor had primo cardio.

Taking two more back streets, he noted he was dashing through an immigrant community. For a century. the metro area had offered an attractive jumping-off point for foreigners. Like everywhere in greater Atlanta, eateries were king in this neighborhood too. "The City Too Busy to Hate" had become "The City Too Hungry to Hate." Southern fried kabobs, Southern fried hummus, Southern fried goat, Southern fried bok choy, Southern fried haggis. You name it, they could make it taste like breaded chicken.

Far up ahead, maybe five blocks, someone in white walked past his street, heading north along the main thoroughfare toward the recovery center. With the glasses jiggling and sliding down the bridge of his sweaty nose, he couldn't be sure, but he thought he recognized Ellie's new profile. He wanted to yell out, but that might panic her. All he could do was run faster.

Two blocks from the intersection, he saw a black sports car speed northward. As he ran onto the main thoroughfare, he heard the screech of tires and Ellie's scream. He ducked back against the building and peered around its faux-brick corner.

The car had slid to the curb, only a few hundred yards from the recovery center where Jeru and Ellie had convalesced. A man with a close-cropped beard pointed a machine pistol over the car roof at Ellie. Dressed all in white, she stood frozen against a storefront, her back pressed to the blast-proof display window.

Jeru felt powerless as he watched. He had no weapon, the miles-long sprint had tired him, and he didn't understand what was going on. Was this a mugging? A kidnapping? An undercover arrest?

The bearded man said something into the car and the passenger door opened. A young man in his late teens, pudgy and short, wearing camo pants and a white tee, climbed out. After bumping his head on the doorframe, the kid rubbed his brush cut as he approached Ellie timidly. This was even stranger. Was there a father-son league for criminals now? A way to bond over Dad's work?

Ellie complied when the boy took her hand and led her back to the car. To a casual observer, it looked like a kid sweetly escorting his mom at gunpoint, a slice of Americana. As the boy stepped into the radiance from a streetlight, Jeru noticed the crossed assault rifles on his chest and something written above it. A cross of guns . . . camo pants . . .targeting Ellie: The Real Salvation Army. The vanity license plate seemed to verify his instincts: GODBLESS. And the gunman looked a lot like their leader, the celebrity evangelist Ross Gimbel.

If they knew who Ellie was now, they knew what he looked like too. Dr. Torres was the only link, so they must've gotten to the steiner. But if that were true, Gimbel and the teen would've been headed to the safehouse.

Jeru trembled. If he and Ellie hadn't fought after making love, if instead they had lain in bed, holding each other and napping, Gimbel would've burst in on them. So, thank God for disgust and self-loathing.

Not finding Jeru or Ellie in their condo, Gimbel had gone to the other place Dr. Torres must've told him about: the recovery center. If Jeru had run a little faster, had finished his conversation with Dr. Gomez a little sooner, maybe he would've beaten Ellie to that spot. But she got there first. And now he watched helplessly as the RSA got her.

Ellie and the boy climbed into the back of the car. Gimbel glanced around before getting behind the wheel. With a squeal of rubber, the car roared up the street and rounded a corner. Before the vehicle disappeared behind a row of storefronts, Jeru caught sight of Ellie's red wig in the side window. It looked like a cascade of blood.

CHAPTER TWENTY-NINE

Even if Dr. Torres were dead, Jeru thought, maybe the man's office or home—wherever the RSA had been not too long ago—held a clue that would lead to Ellie. It was a long shot, but he needed to try.

The first step was to find the office, because he didn't know where the doctor lived and didn't have an All-n-1 so he could text or call Doc and ask. He thought about the RSA chasing the limo into the parking lot where Ben and the bomber had died. Ben had said that Torres's office was in the building beside that lot. Gimbel and the RSA had probably concluded the same thing: that a doctor who could change Jeru and Ellie's identity was nearby and had rescued them from the bomb blast. They'd followed that string of logic to find Dr. Torres.

They knew where the steiner's office was, but Jeru didn't. He remembered that the tall building displayed something in one corner of its top edge, like a corporate logo. Having only glanced at it once, it didn't come to mind. He only knew from highway signs he recalled that it was somewhere in Alpharetta, and here he was, on foot in Marietta, probably twenty miles away.

Worse, now that the RSA had found Ellie and knew he'd left the condo, too, he had to get off the streets. Thinking back to the route Dr. Torres had taken from the recovery center to the safehouse, he remembered a bus stop a few streets over. Here we go again, he thought, and ran like mad in that direction.

A young punk couple stood waiting at the bus stop when he arrived. Dressed as if black were the new white, they had interesting accessories too. The woman's shoulders were pierced: a slender pole tipped with a decorative crystal ornament protruded a foot from each side, giving the impression that someone had shoved a curtain rod through her upper torso. For his part, the young man wore a mini brass catapult perched on either side of his head. Periodically, one of the spring-loaded arms would flip up and strike the side of his skull before ratcheting back into place. Each time he got smacked, he said, "Whoa, blazing."

A touch screen attached to the bus stop pole showed Jeru where the eastbound bus would go, where he needed to transfer, and the schedule for the bus that would take him into the business center of Alpharetta. He would get there around 10:00 PM. Then he'd wander around, staring at building tops until one looked familiar. Not much of a plan, but it was something.

The bus arrived on time, a recent innovation, and he watched the female punk struggle to fit her piercings through the bus door while her boyfriend got knocked silly by the catapult arms. Finally, Jeru suggested that she turn sideways so she could enter, and both of them shot him a hateful look. Apparently pain and frustration were part of the new-wave punk experience. That being the case, Jeru grabbed the back of the woman's shirt and yanked her onto her pierced butt and elbowed her boyfriend's stomach to clear a path so he could climb on board. The punks felt their bruises and called up a cheery, "Thank you!" to him.

He tapped his NID on a sensor, which debited ten dollars from his account and logged him as a passenger. The Big Brother tracking process had begun. If the RSA had moles in the state transportation department, he was in big trouble, as were the other passengers.

Not having eaten since he surfaced in this body, he consulted a snack machine at the back while the punks finally climbed on board and the bus continued on its route. The prices were outrageous—two dollars for a stick of gum, his first-born for a bottle of water—but he needed to keep up his strength. At this rate, he'd have no money before he started work. He wondered if the Jobs Act amendment specified an execution for anyone who went broke.

Two hours to midnight, he stepped off his second bus of the evening and surveyed the skyline of Alpharetta around him. Builders had erected a number of towers clustered around the north-south freeway that bisected the city. He began to walk toward the business district.

After a few hours of striding down secondary roads and trotting through alleys to avoid being stopped by the police and National Guard curfew patrols, he found himself staring at the bright blue logo of a grinning panda bear, which shined from the upper left corner of a thirty-story office building. The symbol belonged to one of the huge Chinese corporations that had bought up half of America's major businesses before 12/26 left them with a homeland in ruins. Americans had acquired this firm during the corporate feeding frenzy that ensued. However, the new owners left the well-established brand image in place, heeding the old marketing adage, "Don't screw with a good reputation someone else paid for."

Keeping the logo in sight, Jeru made his way to a hill covered in fake pine straw and synthetic azaleas. Cresting it, he realized he'd planned to scramble up the opposite side of the same hill with Ellie, while Ben held off the RSA hit man.

A few cars, trucks, and vans were in the parking lot, almost all of them clustered near the entrance. As he watched, though, the head- and taillights of most of the vehicles snapped on, and they drove off together. The center car in the procession was black and sporty.

One pickup remained in a handicap spot, and five other cars were scattered around the lot—one of those was Dr. Torres's roadster. Jeru scrambled down the hill and sprinted across the asphalt, passing the crater where Ben had shown real heroism. He spotted movement in the lobby and flattened against the building, behind a tall, spiny, plastic bush. Whoever had installed the landscaping left the price tag on the back of each shrub in Jeru's row. The laminated paper rectangle dangled from a branch beside his ear, tickling him. He snatched it off just as the front door swung open a few feet away.

Two well-armed men strolled out and headed for the truck, one saying, "—hate to be the early-morning cleaning crew in that place." The other one laughed but crossed himself.

Jeru slipped behind them and shoved the price tag into the closing door, where the lock probably would engage automatically because it was after the normal 5 AM to 10 PM working hours. He ducked back into the bushes. The fighters unslung their machine guns and placed them behind the front seat, along with holstered pistols, a couple of machete-like knives, and a pizza box.

As the men drove off together, the smell of leftover pizza taunted Jeru. He tried the door. It swung open, the tag fluttered to the concrete, and he hurried inside. Behind him, the lock clicked home.

He consulted the directory screen. On the drive to the not-very-safe-house, Dr. Torres had given Ellie and him a short history of his years of study with Dr. Gomez and the opening of Brand New U. Jeru found the business on the sixteenth floor.

When he entered the company reception area, he surveyed the ravaged desk and files, along with the overturned computer and smashed-in monitor, and braced himself for a worse spectacle in the inner offices.

He took a right at the end of a short hall and found a suite of rooms the doors for which had been kicked in. The RSA had ransacked the files and computers there as well, but he didn't see any bodies or evidence of bloody violence.

Jeru returned to the hallway and saw a metal door at the opposite end with a monitor above it. Something obscured the screen above the door. He walked closer and made out a warning about neurosurgery in progress. Dark stains, dried in a crusty reddish-brown, blocked many of the letters though. Someone had drawn a smiley face with a bloody fingertip.

Praying he wouldn't find Ellie's slaughtered remains beyond that door, he pulled it open, battling against a strong vacuum. The antechamber he edged into had been used recently. Water droplets still clung to the sides of stainless-steel washbasins, and piles of damp towels were mounded on the floor.

He eased up to the other door and peeked through the small window. Bloody corpses in hospital scrubs sprawled everywhere and a covered figure lay on an operating table shoved against the cabinets of electronics in one corner. All murdered because of their connection to him. Merely knowing him had become a death sentence.

Ordering himself not to throw up, he jerked the door open and immediately gagged on the sickly sweet stench. Grisly scenes of murder assaulted him everywhere he turned. He lurched toward a corner and stumbled over the dress shoes of a heart-shot young woman in professional clothes who clearly had died many hours before. Another woman, this one in scrubs, showed the same pallor, but she'd been blasted by a dozen or more slugs. Near her, someone had vomited atop of a solid gray lump of God-only-knew-what.

Jeru felt dizzy and heartsick as he wobbled to the other gunned-down victims: two nurses and Dr. Torres, all freshly dead. The RSA had draped a white supremacist tee over the steiner's face and a "♥ 2 H8 U" ball cap on his chest.

Jeru gave a wide berth to the gruesome frame-up in the center of the room, reluctantly making his way to the opposite end, with the covered body on the table. Slight of build, the body obviously wasn't Ellie's, but a detached, curious part of him needed to see everything, needed to bear witness to the entire massacre. He whipped the cover away and then spun around, puking half-digested bus snacks over the bloody floor.

On the table lay the teen who had helped kidnap Ellie. Jeru recalled seeing the cross-rifled "Angel in Training" RSA shirt and camo pants when the boy had escorted Ellie to Gimbel's black sports car. Now the young face was mushroom-white, as if drained of blood, and his eyes were wide open. The worst part, though, was that the top of his head was missing.

CHAPTER THIRTY

Jeru dry-heaved for another minute and then stumbled through the two rooms beyond the surgery. Machines for sterilizing instruments and additional shelves of electronics crowded the farthest room, while the one in between housed a number of cryogenic freezers for donated bodies, with space for a few more units, along with coffin-sized cold storage vessels for the aged corpses of those who'd been upgraded. Dr. Torres probably had made a nice side income from the sale of organs and tissue to labs and hospitals. A small incinerator stood in the corner, with handwritten recommendations taped there for the temperatures needed to dispose of different parts of the human body, from brains to bones, and suggested baking times.

Though the cryo-freezers were empty, bodies lay in a pair of the cold-storage units, according to the Occupied flag on each lid. A sheaf of forms affixed to the utilitarian boxes gave the names of two men, probably a couple of guys whose brains once again resided in youthful, virile bodies that could hump the night away and then shoot a mean round of golf the next morning. Still, Jeru couldn't take the chance Ellie wasn't there. He had to see, so he'd know what to do next.

Opening the hatch of one box, he received a blast of freezing, choking air. He got a quick glimpse of a male body encased in plastic before his glasses frosted over and he slammed the lid shut again. Prior to opening the other, he cleaned the lenses on his shirtfront and read the warnings about nitrogen release and risk of severe burns. Then he did the same thing as the first time except he jumped back as the door flipped up—safety first. Another man lay in that box, as advertised.

Obviously, the RSA still had Ellie, but why kill the teen? Probably, the militia had held Dr. Torres and two of the nurses as hostages until Gimbel reported that he'd captured Ellie but missed their prime target. Maybe the boy had delayed Gimbel's assault on the safehouse and was blamed for the snafu.

Jeru wanted to avert his eyes from the assorted horrors as he passed back through the operating room, but that would've meant staring at the ceiling as he tripped over the corpses. He couldn't think of anything more nightmarish than falling across one of the bodies. Perhaps the censors who'd pulled down Zombie Death Rattle knew what they were doing after all.

Edging around the perimeter, he only had to avoid the poor nurse tortured with gunshots to every limb, and to step over someone's dried puddle of vomit. The gray shape in its center intrigued Jeru even as the overall sight sickened him. It looked for all the world like a gun. Stooping down and holding his nose, he saw that it was indeed a molded pistol of some sort.

Jeru trotted into the antechamber and returned with a towel. He scooped the gun out of the jellied mess and carried it back to the washbasins. Twelve wet towels later, it appeared clean enough to handle. The readout told him four shots remained in the magazine. He'd never fired a real gun before—not that this resembled a real gun—but now he might have to shoot like an expert marksman to save Ellie. If he could find her.

What to do? Send a zip to the RSA's general mailbox (contact@rsa.god) to announce who he was and offer a swap—his life for hers? He'd never get past the spam blockers. No, he needed to find someone who knew the right people to talk to in that insane doomsday cult.

Kliburn knew. The SysOp already had ratted him out once to the RSA.

Jeru patted the odd, non-metallic gun in his waistband. He'd have to return to In-Town and have it out with the Albino Kid.

The armored railcars were crowded at six in the morning. Jeru wanted to stretch out across the three plastic seats and nap, but he was forced to sit upright, wedged against the glass. He looked past his angular, unfamiliar reflection in the blast-proof window while the Atlanta suburbs shot past in the same numbing repetition as when he'd been tailing Cairo Bledsoe, as if his nightmare were about to begin again rather than merely continue. Not wanting to stay in Dr. Torres's chamber of horrors overnight, he had slept fitfully in a culvert far from the office building. After waking for the final time at 4:30 in the already-humid springtime air, he'd hiked to the nearest bus stop to catch his first ride of the day.

The sky had lightened by the time he exited the Five Points terminal and started the last leg of his journey. Dr. Gomez had promised a visitor's pass would await him at Station 7, the same gate through which Ben had taken Ellie and him. Doc had expressed her displeasure quite vocally when he called her from Dr. Torres's office well after midnight. His news made her even more miserable. Even though she'd hated his plan, she agreed to get him back in the Stewart home. Playing the guilt card over her role in Ellie's predicament had closed the deal.

Jeru didn't tell Doc his entire scheme, as that would've wiped out any remaining goodwill. Once inside, his real challenges would begin.

At Station 7, a row of spotlights tracked his approach. Two guards stepped around the pillbox there and aimed assault rifles as Jeru halted. Inside the pillbox, someone swiveled a massive machine gun, pointing it in his direction. The guard in charge sighted along his rifle barrel and barked, "State your business. We are authorized to fire upon you if you advance closer. Or if I don't like your answer," he added.

Jeru held his hands up, squinting into the glare. In his gravelly tone, he said, "You have a pass from a Dr. Gomez for Lou Barone."

"Yes?" The man's finger remained outside the trigger guard, but he continued to aim at Jeru's chest. The other one consulted a device on his hip and murmured something to the leader.

Jeru said, "That's me. Should I reach for my ID card?"

"Only if you want to die. We'll wait for your Dr. Gomez to get here."

"Can you at least kill the lights?" The guards grinned in response, and Jeru conceded, "Okay, bad choice of words."

The leader called, "What happened to your head?"

Jeru recalled his prickly scalp and the angry red line around the circumference. He said, "It's the new look on this side. Tats and piercings got boring, so now we're doing scars."

Their prejudice about the idiocy of OTP culture no doubt confirmed, the guards seemed satisfied with his answer.

After another ten minutes, the tension abated with the spotlights shutting down and the guards lowering their weapons. Jeru blinked rapidly, waiting for his vision to clear.

He noticed a stubby silver car, identical to the one from Dr. Gomez's garage, idling near the friendly side of the gate. She stood there in her Class A physician uniform: white lab coat, practical clothes beneath, and low heels. As she conversed with the guards, she looked as sensational as he'd remembered her. Seventy-five in a few months, she'd said. Impossible to believe if he hadn't seen even more amazing things. She waved at him and continued to speak with the two outside the pillbox while the guard within still toyed with Jeru by sweeping the machine gun his way every thirty seconds.

The man in charge waved him forward and cancelled the sonic fence. While Jeru crossed over, the other guards scanned the perimeter. The moment he stood on In-Town property, the fence reactivated.

Jeru passed through a scanner beside the pillbox, causing a buzzer to squawk.

The leader instantly leveled his assault rifle a foot from Jeru's face. This time, his finger was against the trigger. Jeru raised his hands again, and the man said, "Are you carrying any metallic items?"

"Um, I bought some gum on the bus today."

"The monitor says right pocket," the soldier in the pillbox shouted.

The other soldier marched over, frisked Jeru's waistband and pockets, and came up with foil-wrapped gum and his NID. Before boarding the rapid transit, Jeru had shoved the compact plastic pistol inside his sock, hoping the chewing gum decoy would satisfy anyone looking for an excuse to search him. The pressure of the weapon was bruising his ankle; soon it would make him walk with a limp.

After returning the gum to Jeru, the leader examined the NID briefly. He said, "We'll hold your National ID card until you leave. Your pass is good for seven days."

Jeru replied, "Won't I need it in case a police officer asks for it?"

"No one will ask," the man said. "These aren't valid In-Town. Keep your visitor's pass with you at all times, and you'll be fine."

Jeru accepted the square chit and examined it. It bore his real-time picture, which turned its head when he did, looked back at him as he stared at it, and even adjusted its glasses along with him. Besides displaying his name and particulars, the chit included a warning that it would alert the authorities if not carried with him, and that he was remanded to the custody of "Dr. Lallana Gomez" for the entirety of his stay.

The lead guard welcomed him to In-Town. Jeru thanked the man and hurried to the car with Dr. Gomez. As soon as she steered toward the Stewart home, he said, "Lallana?"

The line of her mouth drew tighter.

"Lalla?"

"Leave it alone," she snapped. "*Doc* is as familiar a name as I'll permit you." She negotiated a corner with a sharp turn of the wheel. "I want you to know I refuse to take part in this scheme to neutralize Kliburn. I think you'll endanger Victoria's life."

"All the more reason you should be there, as her physician. Besides, I'll need you—with no chips in my brain, I can't open the doors." He plucked the gun from his sock and massaged the spot it had rubbed raw.

She asked, "Wherever did you get that?"

"I found it at the murder scene. Hopefully I won't need a weapon against Kliburn, but I'm glad I've got one."

Dr. Gomez grimaced again. "I fear you'll need it to persuade Victoria even more than him."

CHAPTER THIRTY-ONE

After Doc parked in the garage, Jeru followed her into the adjoining hallway and tried to reason with her again. "All I need you to do is get Ellie's mom to come to your office."

She crossed white sleeves over her chest and said, "I don't believe that will work. One doesn't summon Victoria Stewart—I must always go to her."

"If I talk to Victoria anywhere else, Kliburn will hear. Then he'll throw every obstacle he can at us: killer robo-vacs, holograms in the hallways, pains in Victoria's brain, and who knows what else."

Dr. Gomez shook her lovely head. "I'm telling you it won't work."

Jeru threw his hands up. "What is it with you? Why won't you help me save Ellie?" His voice echoed in the passageway where they faced off.

"Is that what this about," she said, eyes narrowed, "or are you merely taking revenge on Kliburn, your competition?"

"What? I'd be happy never to see the pasty-faced bastard again, but he can get the RSA's attention and set up the swap."

"So you're serious about trading your life for Ellie's?"

Jeru looked away. "I'm serious about saving Ellie's life. It'd be nice if I can save my own skin too." He leaned against one of the unmarked doors in the hall. "Listen, I'm no hero—I'm just a glans. I know that. But there are all these people who've died because of their connection to me, and the latest one could be somebody I love."

"When this is over, I hope you'll let her know that," Dr. Gomez said.

"She does know. I told her."

She replied, "In my experience, it's hearing 'I love you' *after* the sweat dries that counts. She thinks you said it just to lure her into bed."

"Hey, she came on to me—she climbed into my lap and pushed her chest in my face."

"Just so, but what she remembers is the terrible argument afterward."

Jeru stifled his retort. Doc was prodding, testing his resolve, seeing how much he cared. He drew a long, slow breath and said, "You're right. She's always deserved much better from me than I've given her. But I'll only get the chance to make it up to Ellie—and you'll only get that chance, too—if we work together," he added, unable to resist pushing her Guilt button again. "Do we have a deal?"

He put out his hand. She glanced at it but didn't shake it. Instead she said, "Stop leaning on that door."

Stepping away from it, he asked, "What's in there?" He paused, remembering some of the personal history she'd revealed. "Is that where you keep your husband's cryo-freezer?"

"Better quit while you're ahead, hero." She stalked down the hall. "Every time you open your mouth, you stand an excellent chance of pissing me off."

"It's a gift," he said, following her into the operating room. "Ask anybody."

Dr. Gomez checked a floating screen, which displayed another section of the building. Ellie's mom was in one of the rec rooms Jeru recalled from before. Panicked, he said, "Wait, this system is tied to ANGUS?"

"No, it merely makes use of the same signals emitted by her neural chips. As I said, my area is totally independent, including the power source."

"Can you tap into the speakers or send a message to her chips that'll alert her you're coming?"

"Better that I should go and get her." She double-checked another readout. "Victoria appears to be asleep."

"Probably had a long night wearing out the loveseat."

She turned to him, snapping, "That's what I meant about opening your mouth. Don't you dare judge her until you've lost someone you love."

"I have, Doc," he muttered. "Now I'm trying to get her back."

Her expression defrosted a few degrees. "Of course. Just keep your comments to yourself." She headed back toward the garage.

"Where to now?" he called.

"I'll fetch her in my cart—the one we used to transport you after the HandyBot attack."

That gave him an idea. He shouted, "Wait. Change of plans."

Dr. Gomez chatted while piloting the cart with the pickup-like bed. "So, Mr. Jacobi, are you looking forward to your move here from out West?"

"Quite so," Jeru said, trying to adopt her patrician accent with his troll-voice. He sounded like a thug posing as an English butler. She'd loaned him some of her dead husband's clothes—a butter-soft dress shirt, herringbone slacks, and hard-soled shoes, all one size too large—so he'd look like an ultra-rich citizen. Too bad he couldn't do anything about his bald, scarred head but put on a cap.

Roleplaying the part he'd improvised, he went on, "The air is just getting too thin out there, and melanoma is rampant. Who would've thought we'd fall prey to a commoner's illness?" He patted her arm. "How delightful that my physician knows you, so you could arrange this tour."

"She was at the top of our class—I trust she'll accompany you and your family?"

They carried out the charade all the way to Victoria's rec room. Then Doc excused herself so she could fetch "the mistress of the house."

While she was inside, probably dragging a limp, smiling Victoria from her lube-smeared chair, Jeru stared straight ahead. He tried to keep his expression neutral but his skin crawled as he imagined Kliburn studying him from an infinite number of vantage points. The SysOp would be searching databases of men named Jacobi in the rich Western enclaves, comparing his image with file photos, growing increasingly suspicious.

Worse, there would be no neural chips to ping, so the mystery would deepen. At last, Kliburn would check with each of the perimeter stations to see if Doc had signed for any visitors, and he'd come up with the name and face of Lou Barone. By then, Jeru hoped they'd be squirreled away in the basement power plant, ready to issue demands to him.

In the distance, he heard the cheerful ping of a HandyBot and goosebumps raced across his arms and down his back and chest. In the hallway from the opposite direction, an elevator door opened and two more of the monstrous machines emerged. They each dipped one pair of arms toward him and snapped their three-pronged tips. From behind, another two robots arrived and assumed identical battle stances.

On the other hand, if the SysOp had used drones to watch Doc depart their home and return with a visitor in tow, he might've gone right to the guard stations. Then their charade would've piqued his paranoia. And when he got piqued, he got homicidal.

"Doc?" Jeru yelled, abandoning the plummy accent. "The welcome committee is here."

The door whisked open. Dr. Gomez glanced left and right and cursed in two languages. She led a yawning Victoria Stewart, who was clad only in a jade kimono, her purple-streaked white hair a wild tangle. Jeru stepped out, and they slid Ellie's mom onto the middle seat. He let the doctor deal with Victoria's gaping kimono, which revealed smooth tan thighs and a shaved crotch, her butterfly currently at rest.

Still chiming their merry song, the robots rolled forward. Jeru sat shotgun while Doc climbed behind the wheel, with Ellie's mom between them. Dr. Gomez asked, "Now what?"

Victoria's head lolled onto Jeru's shoulder, and she rubbed against him, cooing, "Hmm."

He asked, "Will they hurt Victoria?"

"I don't think so. She's supposed to be protected by ANGUS."

"But Kliburn controls the system," he argued.

She glared at him, about to respond, when the machines behind them charged. Jeru pulled the gun from beneath his shirt and put it to Victoria's temple. She smiled wider.

Doc shouted, "What are you—"

The robots in back paused, their lance tips only inches from the rear of the cart. In front of the vehicle, the robot pair rolled toward them cautiously.

"Kliburn," Jeru growled. At last he'd found an appropriate target for his ugly voice. "I'll kill her if you move your machines another inch."

The HandyBots halted. Their pinging ceased.

"Okay," he said to Dr. Gomez. "Back up."

She glanced over her shoulder and reversed the cart. The robo-vacs blocking the way rolled backward, too, but the ones in front pursued at the same rate. Jeru put his finger on the trigger. The advancing Handy-Bots continued to follow.

Kliburn had called that bluff and won—they'd have to be satisfied with this arrangement.

Jeru swiveled the gun barrel down to Victoria's heart so he could lean across the sleeping woman and whisper in the doctor's ear, to keep Kliburn from hearing. "Are there stairs leading to the basement?"

Doc nodded slightly, her attention still on navigating the hallways in reverse while surrounded by the lethal honor guard. Jeru told her, "Go there."

He felt something smooth caress his gun hand. Victoria had pressed her palms to the outside of her silk-clad breasts and pushed them together around the pistol. His fingers twitched, and he nearly shot her.

Returning the barrel to her temple, he swiveled his head to look behind them and in front. The doctor suddenly screamed, let go of the wheel, and lifted her foot from the accelerator. Jeru grabbed the lapel of her lab coat to keep her from toppling out of the cart as it coasted to a halt.

She sobbed while holding her head and then went limp under his grip. He straddled Victoria's lap, keeping the gun on her, while he checked for a pulse in the doctor's throat. Strong, but she was out cold.

"Bastard!" Jeru swung around as the pinging started again. The attackers in the rear split off, as did the ones in front, with a Handy-Bot from each party zipping around to flank them on the left and right, where the cart offered no protection. Four pairs of lances rose until they pointed at his head.

Victoria wriggled beneath him, untied her kimono, and pulled it open. Laser-tanned breasts with large aureoles compressed and bobbed as she stroked them. Her heavy lids eased open, and she stared at him with wide, gray, unfocused eyes. "Hmm," she sighed and lifted her face to him, lips opening for a French kiss.

Jeru did the only thing that came to mind. He shot her.

CHAPTER THIRTY-TWO

Thanks to Victoria baring her chest, she had taken some of the guesswork out of Jeru's aim. The bullet tore through the meaty part of her right shoulder. No internal organs were threatened, but she howled as blood sprayed them both and peppered Doc's lab coat.

Clasping the wound, Victoria now appeared to be fully awake. She took in Jeru kneeling astride her, the gun in her face, and her naked, red-soaked torso. "Why did you shoot me?" she screamed. "Who are you?"

"Check Dr. Gomez's pockets for anything to press on it."

She drew her hand from the gory bullet hole and stared at the blood that slicked her palm. "I'm dying," she cried.

Jeru shouted at the walls and ceiling, "You hear that, Kliburn? She's dying. She needs surgery, but you've disabled her doctor. Call off your robots, or I'll shoot her again."

The HandyBots ceased their pinging and raised their metal arms to vertical, safely away from him, but they didn't retreat.

"Sorry, Victoria." He leveled the gun at her stomach. "I hear it takes a horribly long time to die from a gut shot."

"Kliburn," she screeched, "get them out of here." Tears coursed down her cheeks, and she trembled. Her wound pumped out still more blood between her fingers.

Immediately the robots turned and scooted down the hall, disappearing from view. With his free hand, Jeru dug in Dr. Gomez's pockets and dumped the contents into Victoria's naked lap. "See if something there will help," he ordered. "And then cover yourself for God's sake."

She tore open a small package with her teeth and placed a square of mustard-colored plastic against the wound. It adhered and then its edges melted and spread a few inches in every direction until it was as smooth against her skin as a splash of yellow paint. The bandage must've included a local anesthetic because Victoria relaxed her shoulder. She brushed the remaining items to the floor of the cart and drew the kimono closed over herself.

Her eyelids fluttered, so he reluctantly slapped the outside of her wounded shoulder. She yelped and then whined through fresh tears, "What do you want? Money? I know you're from OTP. Our sort of people would never do such a thing."

Resisting the urge to shoot her again, he said, "Help me pull Dr. Gomez into the back. Then you drive."

She wasn't much help with only one good arm and a bad attitude, but they managed to yank the doctor's limp form over the driver seat and lay her in the cargo bed. "Did you shoot her too?" Victoria snarled, checking the woman as if she expected to find gaping holes.

"No, your buddy Kliburn thumped her brain. I'm saving all my bullets for you."

She shrank away from him and climbed behind the wheel, right hand curled in her lap. "Where are you taking me?"

"Actually, *you're* taking *me*—to the power plant."

"Where's that?"

"You know where: in the basement," he said, raising the gun at her. "Now drive." All things considered, he would've preferred a wounded Dr. Gomez and an unconscious Victoria.

She drove one-handed without confidence, speeding up and slowing while constantly jerking the wheel with course corrections. After they stuttered down one hall and then another, she asked, "Why are we going there?"

Kliburn's smooth Southern drawl slithered out from hidden speakers. "Because, Mrs. Stewart, this man wants to shut down ANGUS and destroy me."

As Victoria gaped at Jeru, he spoke to the passing paintings, the wall sconces attempting to send forth soothing colors, and tabletop flower arrangements, only guessing where the microphones might be hidden. "I only want to make a trade, Kly."

" 'Kly'? No one ever calls me 'Kly' but Ellip—" The SysOp paused for a moment and then said, "You were Benjamin Splyvex and Jerusalem Pix before that, weren't you?"

Damn. Jeru had hoped to keep the SysOp guessing until they could get to the power plant. By knowing who Jeru was, Kliburn could anticipate his moves. "Guilty," he admitted. "And thanks to you, the RSA is holding the woman we both love."

While Kliburn sputtered, actually sounding flummoxed for once, Jeru gave Victoria the short version of what had happened to her daughter.

The woman's confused and pained expression didn't change, but her tears took on new urgency.

"Pay no attention, Mrs. Stewart," Kliburn reassured her. "He is a liar who will say anything to be persuasive. Can you trust a man who shot you?"

She shook her head and jammed on the brake. Jeru prodded her wounded shoulder with his pistol, making her bawl again.

"Drive," he ordered.

"I won't."

"If you force me to drive," he said, "I'll shoot off your kneecaps so you can't run away from me." Feeling like the cruelest monster from the GameSphere, he prodded her leg through the jade kimono.

She accelerated again, wailing, "I hate you."

"It runs in your family," he lamented. Then he had an idea—maybe he wouldn't need to shut down ANGUS to neutralize Kliburn and force him to help. He said, "I'll prove the RSA has her. Kly, dial your contact there. Is it Ross Gimbel?"

"I do not know what you mean."

"Tell him you want to arrange a swap—me for Ellie."

Kliburn replied, "As much as I would like to see her safely home—in whatever body she now resides—I have never contacted that organization, and do not know how."

"Look it up."

Silence followed while Victoria drove, looking a bit smug. Her SysOp sure showed him.

Jeru waited half a minute and then said, "Victoria, stop the cart."

She whipped around a corner and headed up another hall.

"Victoria." He made his voice even lower and more threatening.

Biting her lip, she pushed the accelerator to the floor. Jeru wrapped his free arm around the headrest and took aim at her hands.

Victoria glanced over and then squeezed her eyes shut, braking hard. They'd stopped in a hall that looked somewhat familiar. The paintings were of hunting scenes: horsemen in red coats and black-domed helmets, with packs of dogs, pursuing the fox. Where had he seen them before?

The nearest door opened. Jeru got a glimpse of darkness as black as outer space, and then Kliburn launched at him like a white comet.

Jeru only could swing the gun halfway around before the SysOp landed. They both tumbled across the seat into Victoria, colliding with her wounded arm. She screamed and fell out of the cart.

Kliburn's bearded face snarled inches from Jeru's. While they grappled, the SysOp jutted his head and snapped his teeth, barely missing Jeru's beaky nose. The SysOp's body was cold and heavy atop Jeru, who lay twisted on his side with his scrawny arms pinned together, glasses askew and gun uselessly pointing at the floor.

Victoria yelled, "Kill him. He shot me."

Kliburn rose enough to draw back a pure white fist, and he punched Jeru's ear. A starburst of pain shook Jeru's skull and brilliant flashes dazed him. An identical strike knocked off his glasses and crushed his cheekbone, blinding his right eye. The gun fell from his hand as blood from his split cheek gushed across his face. Consciousness fading, Jeru flailed and wriggled in a desperate attempt to escape.

Though his weak upper half was useless under Kliburn's weight, he managed to jerk his knee into the man's groin. Instead of grunting or pulling himself into a ball, though, the SysOp simply froze for a moment.

Jeru looked up hopefully, but life returned to Kliburn's eyes. The man pulled back his fist again for the killing shot in the center of Jeru's bloody face.

Jeru braced himself, but the blow didn't come. Instead, a blur of white speckled with red flashed above his good eye. Dr. Gomez had wrapped both her arms around Kliburn's raised one. The entwined figures tumbled to the carpeted floor, Kliburn landing on his back with the doctor on top of him. She straddled his chest and grasped his wrists, fighting to keep his deathly white hands from her throat.

In seconds it was obvious she would lose. His fingers curved into claws and made slow, steady progress toward her neck. Jeru groped for the gun. Victoria reached for it as well. Their hands met atop the gray pistol.

She yanked it free from his grip. Nearby, the doctor made a terrible choking sound, her cry dying under the SysOp's crushing grasp.

Jeru raised his face and brought down his forehead like a hammer on Victoria's wound. She screamed and slithered back to the floor, clutching her injury, the gun forgotten. Addled but managing to snatch the pistol, he swung it around as Dr. Gomez's hands fell limply from the SysOp's wrists and Kliburn shook her.

Drawing up on his elbow, Jeru squinted his one good eye and fired. The bullet punched through the back of Doc's lab coat where it draped across the man's stomach. Higher than he'd intended, but not so far off that he could've shot Dr. Gomez in the ass. Kliburn tossed her aside and sat up, showing no ill effects. Jeru shot him in the chest.

The impact knocked him back, but he rose again from the waist, like a round-bottomed punching doll that couldn't be put down. No blood flowed. Only a clear fluid that smelled like mineral oil leaked from the bullet holes.

Oh fuck.

Grinning, the SysOp sprang to his feet. Down to his final bullet, Jeru aimed upward, going for a headshot, but Victoria grabbed his arm and wrenched it down, causing him to misfire.

Jeru let her pull him flat onto the seat. This was it. Having survived so much, he was about to be slaughtered by a sex addict and her cyborg servant. Something heavy thudded against his legs, making him cry out. Why torture him? Why not just finish him off?

He kicked half-heartedly and the object slid off him and thumped on the hallway carpet.

Above him, Victoria whined, "You killed him."

Jeru snapped the barrel of the gun upward, clocking her between the eyes. She fell back and lay still. Jeru pushed himself up. He gingerly felt his face. Ruined.

Pawing at the blood that caked his right eye failed to clear his vision, but it did send daggers of pain through his cheek. He gave up and leaned over the side of the cart. Kliburn lay on his back, staring at the ceiling. Jeru prodded him with the gun barrel, half-expecting a horror movie surprise where the dead monster springs to life again. This time, the monster didn't move.

Near the front of the cart, Dr. Gomez coughed and groaned and coughed some more. She crawled on her elbows toward the fallen SysOp. "Nice shooting," she rasped and pointed to the neat hole drilled through Kliburn's crotch. "Got him in the power pack."

CHAPTER THIRTY-THREE

Dr. Gomez still sounded froggy—almost as bad as Jeru—as she handed him his glasses and doctored his wounds the best she could. Next she attended to Victoria's head injury and fashioned a sling for her right arm using the kimono belt. "You showed some restraint," she told him, "shooting her up there."

"That's before I knew she'd take Kliburn's side." He couldn't see from his right eye, a persistent ringing plagued his right ear, and there was only so much the doctor could do for a possible skull fracture with the items she normally carried in her pockets. But at least the pain had dissipated. He never claimed to be able to think clearly, but without the distraction of being in agony, his cognitive ability was back up to sub-par.

Together, they lifted Victoria into the cart bed and wrapped the folds of the robe over her naked front. It occurred to him that now all three of them had lain back there at one time or another. Doc croaked, "Since you've destroyed the one person who could set up this swap for Ellie, what's the plan now, hero?"

Kliburn's genteel drawl once again issued from hidden speakers. "You will be pleased to know I'm not dead." Jeru leaned over, prepared to see the cyborg talking, but it remained lifeless. "I still reside as a construct in ANGUS. Or ANGUS resides within me—I'm no longer sure."

Here we go again. Jeru listened for the ping of HandyBots, with the ringing in his ear creating the illusion they were already there and poised to strike. This time, though, he had no means of shooting Victoria. If they attacked again, he'd have to beat her half to death instead.

Dr. Gomez, too, seemed to be preparing for an attack. In her case though, she hunched behind the wheel, shoulders up around her ears, as if braced for another assault on her brain. If Kliburn wanted to finish them, they were no match this time. Maybe they never were.

From the cargo bed, Victoria mumbled and shifted. He glanced over the seat and met her staring gray eyes. "If you want," he growled, "you can order Kly to kill us, or you can save your daughter's life. We die, she dies. Simple as that."

She rolled onto her good side and propped her head on the uninjured arm. "Doctor, you believe him?"

Doc replied, "Yes, I do."

Victoria said to both, or neither, of them, "I never planned to be a bad mother: neglectful, indifferent, what have you. It just worked out that way, hmm?"

Jeru snorted and brandished his pistol at her. "You're lucky I'm out of bullets."

Victoria ducked her face. The tangle of purple-streaked white hair hid her expression. "Kliburn," she muttered sullenly, "contact this group like he asked you to."

The SysOp's voice sounded resigned. "As you wish."

"We want to hear it over the speakers," she added, "and we'll need to be able to speak to them. Call now."

The speakers relayed the buzz of a phone call and then, with church bells pealing in the background, a chirpy recorded female voice said, "It's early in God's favorite sanctuary, but we're already up and at 'em, working and fighting for the Lord. Someone will be with you in a moment."

The bells continued to clang and bong for thirty seconds. Just when Jeru was giving thanks for his near-deafness, a male voice said, "Thank you for holding. This is Brother Billy Bob. How may I help you?"

"Brother Billy, this is Kliburn again. I hope you are well."

"I, uh, I'm fine, God be praised. How can I help you, sir?"

"Once more, I have information about the man you seek. This time he calls himself Lou Barone."

"Oh, hallelujah! Can you tell me how we might get in touch with him?"

Kliburn said, "He is on the call with us. Mr. Barone?"

Jeru let loose with his troll-voice. "Connect Gimbel."

"Um, it's still rather early in the day for the Most Reverend."

"The message," Jeru growled, "said all of you are up already, working and fighting for the Lord."

"Well, we take different shifts, you see."

Jeru said, "You have a woman named Cathy Eden, formerly known as Ellipsis Stewart. I will give myself up to you—"

"We prefer the phrase *fellowship with us*."

"But only if you will let her go free."

"We don't hold prisoners, Mr. Barone," Billy Bob enunciated, as if for the benefit of whatever recording devices he suspected were being used. "We have wards and other guests who stay with us."

Victoria hollered, "Listen, you little fucker, I'm Ellipsis's mother, and I'll pay you people whatever you want to get my daughter back."

Billy Bob paused, but a rapid thumping sound came over the speakers, sounding a lot like bouncing knees striking the underside of a desk. He said, "Those wishing to make a donation at the Cornerstone level, joining a select group we call the Rock of Ages, may share the blessed news directly with the Most Reverend Gimbel. One moment and I'll connect you."

The church bells resumed.

Dr. Gomez said to Jeru, "You'll need someone to go with you, to get Ellipsis home."

"I'll do it," Victoria said. She looked like a woman who had emerged from a trance. Her voice retained the steely edge she'd used a moment before, and her gaze was steady and focused.

Doc turned and patted her good shoulder. "You should be home when she arrives. She'll need a loving welcome."

"Home's the only place she's seen me for most of her life." She glanced around at the paintings, sconces, and tabletop flower arrangements up and down the hallway. "I'm sick of this dump." Doc tried to protest, but the head of the household waved her silent with a few flaps of her jade kimono sleeve. "No offense, but the first friendly person she sees should be her mother, not her physician. Though she might not recognize me outdoors or in something other than a robe."

"This is Ross Gimbel," a smooth male voice said in stereo around them, "founder of the Real Salvation Army and Affiliated Glorification Churches, where all donations are tax deductible and reported not only to the government but also directly to our Lord and Savior. How may I help you?"

Jeru said, "You're looking for me."

"Mr. Barone?"

"You probably still think of me as Jerusalem Pix. I know I do. You've been gunning for me since I ruined Cairo Bledsoe's mission, but you've managed to kill only innocent bystanders."

Gimbel intoned, "This hardly seems the venue for leveling baseless, libelous accusations, good sir. Shall we meet somewhere instead?"

"Four of us: you, me, Ellipsis, and her mother. If I see anyone with a weapon, including cops or National Guardsmen who might be on your payroll, I'll disappear forever."

"How do you expect me to arrange that?" Gimbel asked.

"Create a distraction. I don't care."

"Where and when?"

Jeru had been considering some options: someplace public, with lots of witnesses and, if needed, quick access to transportation. He said, "On the plaza outside the Five Points station at noon tomorrow."

"Now," Victoria cried. "I want her back now."

Jeru said, "No. I want to give fuckface a day to consider how important this is to him. If we do it in a few hours, he'll make a snap decision and hide bad guys somewhere nearby." He fingered his crushed cheekbone, which had begun to ache again. "This way, he gets to dwell on it, to stew and think about how one pathetic little slacker has managed to cause him so much grief. And he'll decide he wants to do me himself, to pull the trigger and watch me die. He won't want to risk anything going wrong with that plan."

Gimbel said, "I don't know what you're talking about, of course, but it sounds as if you're troubled and in need of spiritual counseling. I'll be pleased to meet with you at the time and place you mentioned. I'll also bring someone to comfort Mrs. Stewart, whom she can take home with her. Incidentally, she mentioned a generous donation?"

"Just me," Jeru said. "That's all the charity you'll get."

"Well deserved, I assure you. So glad you called, Mr. Barone. Your timing was impeccable. I was just about to pay my respects to your parents, to learn if they knew your whereabouts."

The line went dead.

CHAPTER THIRTY-FOUR

Victoria smacked the back of Jeru's head. "How am I supposed to wait until tomorrow?"

"Hey, I'm in no condition to go out there yet." He pointed at her sling. "And neither are you." Gimbel's final words reverberated much worse than Victoria's blow. Touché, Most Reverend. Now he had something to stew over as well.

Doc said, "Let's get you both to my surgery."

"One stop first," Victoria said. She nodded at Kliburn's lair, from which the cyborg had attacked Jeru. Holding her jade kimono closed with her good hand, she advanced to the door. It opened for her, revealing utter darkness. Another thought-command switched on bright lights throughout the black-painted room. The hem of her robe swept regally across the threshold as she entered the SysOp's domain.

Dr. Gomez followed more tentatively. Jeru had to step over the still figure of the SysOp as he departed the cart. The perverse part of him wanted to grind his heel into the cyborg's groin, but he still possessed the little-kid fear of a creature suddenly returning from the dead. He did stomp on some snow-white fingers on his way into the room.

Though it felt as cold as deep space, the endless expanse he'd imagined proved to be an illusion. On the contrary, the room—solid black on the ceiling and floor as well as the walls—was smaller than some of the other areas he'd seen in the converted hotel. At the far end of the twenty-by-twenty-foot box sat the black office chairs he, Ellie, and Kliburn had used, along with the holographic screens that had painted the albino cyborg with so many shifting colors.

Nothing else occupied the SysOp's abode—no decorations or adornments. However, as with everywhere else in the place but Dr. Gomez's area, Jeru felt something watching him. Kliburn lived on in ANGUS, studying and waiting.

Victoria paused before the farthest wall, and a hidden door slid aside, releasing a musty, damp odor. Within, utilitarian lamps blinked on. The light revealed a concrete stairwell with a metal railing that trailed downward. "Emergency maintenance stairs," she explained. "I haven't seen them since I took the full tour, after my husband, um, after I became head of the household."

Jeru asked, "When you stopped outside, were you throwing me to Kliburn or leading me to the power plant?"

"Both," she said. "I hedged my bets."

Kliburn's silky voice echoed in the room and from the stairwell. "I really don't think this is necessary, Mrs. Stewart."

She didn't respond. Instead she grasped the railing, letting her kimono fall open, and began her descent ahead of them. Doc glanced at Jeru, eyebrows scrunched with worry, and followed.

Kliburn said, "If I have failed you in any way, Mrs. Stewart, please tell me so I can serve you better."

The simpering, drawling voice continued as Jeru entered the dank stairwell. A sign on the landing notified them that the stairwell was for "Authorized access only. Anyone entering without permission or the proper credentials will be escorted from the building." Beneath it, someone had scrawled "So there."

Below him, the two women turned a corner and continued downward, their shoes clomping on the concrete stairs. Somewhere, water dripped periodically.

Jeru took a last look behind him as another sound attracted his notice: the whirring of treads on carpet. A HandyBot rolled up to the fallen cyborg. Just before the door to the hallway closed, Jeru saw the robot extend two metal arms and lift the rigid white body onto its back.

He hustled down the stairs, calling, "Hurry." When he caught up to the others, who of course had paused out of curiosity, he explained what he'd seen. "I'll bet Kliburn's going into surgery too, so whatever you're planning to do, Victoria, let's get it done."

They trotted downward until the jarring caused Victoria to complain about her bullet wound and made Jeru's face throb.

Kliburn maintained his groveling monologue through speakers mounted at each landing. "Mistakes were made," he conceded. "There were anomalies, unknown variables, and uncharacteristic behavior, resulting in calculation rounding errors and spurious extrapolations. However, with more data, I believe—"

Victoria said, "Kliburn, I order you to shut up."

He did.

They descended another two stories. At last, they reached good old-fashioned metal double doors with a knob. And a lock.

Victoria examined the mechanism as if unsure of how it worked. Jeru drew her aside, asked her to close her robe, and gave the handle a try. It didn't budge.

Then the lights went out.

"Okay," Jeru said, "this sucks."

Beside him, something rustled. An image of rats came to mind. Big ones with red eyes and needle-sharp teeth.

He spun that way and jostled Dr. Gomez. "What are you doing?" he demanded.

"Inventorying my pockets." A light flashed on from a slender communicator in her hand, much less boxy than an All-n-1. "Now be quiet and let me think; I'm trying to remember a prank from med school."

Victoria began to whimper. She said, "I was much happier in a state of constant orgasm."

"Aren't we all?" he and Dr. Gomez replied simultaneously. Then Doc said, "You still have that chewing gum, hero?"

He patted his pocket. "I do."

"Give me the foil and get the gum good and pliant. I want to try something I haven't done in fifty years."

"What's that?"

"Make an explosive."

"Oh, good. That'll let *all of us* go out with a bang—not just Victoria."

"If you're going to talk, at least chew."

Jeru masticated as ordered, holding out the wrapper to her. Dr. Gomez tore open packages, dropped things as she combined them, and muttered to herself in an Asian dialect.

Her fingers formed a cup below his lower lip. "Spit," the doctor ordered.

He deposited the gum in her palm and awaited further instructions. It occurred to him to reach for Victoria to give comfort, but he feared where she'd direct his hand.

Dr. Gomez had Jeru aim the light at the doorknob while she patted an oval of putty, made from his gum and the other concoctions, over the bulbous part of it. She took the communicator from him and set it on a step high enough up so that the light shined on the door. "We need to go under the stairwell for protection."

They wedged into the dark, triangular space behind the concrete staircase, which looked like the perfect home for a lethal spider.

Doc shook what appeared to be an aerosol can. "I hope there's enough range on this." Edging partly away from the protection of the stairs, she sprayed a long stream at the doorknob until the container emptied with a wet dribble. Nothing dramatic occurred.

"What now?" Jeru asked.

"Ideally, this has frozen the mixture, and its chemical state is now unstable."

"Then what's supposed to happen?"

"If it hasn't exploded yet, then one needs to strike it. From a distance, preferably." She tapped the can in her grip and leaned out again. "Here goes."

The hollow cannister struck the solid door a few inches below the knob, bounced twice on the floor, and rolled away. Cursing, Dr. Gomez sat against Jeru and removed her hard-soled shoes. She threw one, again merely striking the door, and then she hurled the other.

A fireball lit up the stairwell, accompanied by a clap of thunder. In the sudden brightness, Jeru saw Dr. Gomez tumble backward into the concrete wall and slump over before darkness descended. If nothing else, she'd managed to kill her communicator with the light source, if not herself.

The only thing he could see now were dancing purple and white spots. He choked on the decades of dust blown into the air. His ears rang in stereo this time. If he survived this, he promised himself, no more explosions. Not even virtual ones.

Cold air gusted into their hiding place. Peeking around the staircase, Jeru saw through the blasted-open doors a large expanse with tiny amber, green, and red lights, some blinking and others glowing steadily. "Doc?" he said.

Victoria coughed from the dust and spit on his leg.

Jeru crawled forward, patting in front of him until he touched a warm, gritty hand, palm down. He checked her pulse for the second time in as many hours. Taking a page from the *Physician's Guide to Diagnoses in the Dark*, he followed the path from her arm to shoulder to head and dirt-caked hair, and back down to her other arm. She was lying face down. He shoved his hands under her armpits, his fingers splaying just above her breasts, and he lifted the doctor into a sitting position against the wall.

"Unhand me, hero," she groaned. "Unless you're willing to propose marriage."

"Sorry, there's someone ahead of you, but I'll let you know if it doesn't work out." With her permission, he found her hands again and lifted her to her bare feet. They rocked to and fro in a slow dance until she steadied. Then he extracted Victoria from the narrow space.

They advanced from darkness into mere gloom. Jeru wiped his glasses free of grime on his shirtfront, found a set of switches by the door, and turned on the lights. Large air conditioning units kept the power plant cold enough to suit Kliburn and any surviving polar bears. Racks and cabinets full of electronics were arranged in domino-like rows throughout the cavernous space. Victoria led them to the center of the room, where huge junction boxes had been overlaid with glass-fronted displays and controls.

An elevator ping sounded from a far wall.

Jeru grumbled at Victoria, "Why didn't we use that instead of going through everything we just did?"

She lifted her dusty chin and scoffed. "That's the *service* lift. Taking the stairs was more dignified." Her kimono gaped wide, giving him another unwanted full-frontal.

Above twin metal panels, a light glowed, and the elevator doors slid aside. Kliburn stalked out, naked this time, chalk-white with a silver box now affixed to his groin like a high-tech codpiece. He walked with a lumbering, unsteady gait, as if the hastily attached power supply didn't provide all the juice he needed for smooth human movement. Spotting Jeru and the women, he swiveled and advanced on them.

Victoria shouted, "I order you to stop."

The cyborg continued its march toward them. "I'm sorry," the SysOp said through speakers affixed to a lab bench, "this fellow is autonomous, operating on a program I just loaded. He's beyond my control now. Have a nice day."

Jeru looked around for a big red arrow with an accompanying sign that stated, "Throw this switch to shut down the power plant." He didn't see anything like that.

Victoria gestured at a nearby control panel. "I need to give the system the proper codes." She bounced the heel of her hand off her dirt-smudged forehead. "I had them memorized at one time."

With the albino menace now only twenty feet away, Kliburn suggested in his oh-so-reasonable tone, "This would be a good time to negotiate terms of an agreement. I will agree to cease and desist if you will return to the main floors. We'll keep our friend down here in perpetuity to enforce both sides of our pact."

Dr. Gomez waved at the cyborg and tried to draw it away, but it remained focused on Jeru and Victoria. While Ellie's mom recited possible passwords to no avail, Jeru circled the opposite way from Doc, hoping to lure it. The animatron swiveled its head to look at Jeru, but then resumed its path toward Victoria, who continued to call out possible codes.

Kliburn's voice suddenly sounded panicked. "What? The power is ebbing—I feel my mind fading away . . . Fading . . ." After a pause, he said in a flat, robotic tone, "Hello, ladies and gentlemen. My programmers have taught me a song. Would you like me to sing it for you? 'Daisy, Daisy, give me your answer true.'" Then he reverted to his normal drawl, "Sorry, I just couldn't resist."

Still circling and feinting at the cyborg, Jeru called, "Got another bomb, Doc?"

"No."

"Any other plan?"

"Grab him."

She and Jeru lunged at the cyborg's cold, hard legs. It continued forward, dragging them across the concrete floor, while Victoria babbled nonsense passwords, speaking in tongues. The creature stopped and batted Jeru's stubbly head, whacking his skull with the force of a hammer.

Jeru let go. Fresh blood ran down his scalp, and he fought against blacking out. The cyborg lunged on its other side and grabbed the back of Dr. Gomez's lab coat and a hank of her hair. As she screamed, Jeru kicked his marathoner legs against the outside of its knee.

The cyborg's leg buckled. It released Doc, turned, and threw itself onto Jeru. Knocking the breath out of him, it clamped icy fingers around his throat. The creature with the SysOp's youthful, bearded face looked down at him without expression and squeezed.

Kliburn's voice overlaid Victoria's. "Mrs. Stewart, did you just say 'Rumpelstiltskin'?" he asked with evident glee. "I do believe you've grown desperate, mistress. Why don't you come upstairs for a long massage, a coconut oil body treatment, and a selection of new toys? *Hmm*?"

She kept trying, now reciting strings of letters and numbers as the cyborg continued to choke the life out of Jeru.

The overhead lamps quit, the air conditioners shut down with a clatter, and the colored lights all winked out. Emergency power switched on, shining spotlights across the basement.

"Mrs. Stewart," Kliburn said with alarm as Victoria spoke with increasing confidence, "perhaps we can—"

Victoria bellowed another combination. The battery backup lights went off. Kliburn instantly died with them.

"Got you," Victoria shouted in the dark. "Arrogant prick."

In spite of the blackout, the cyborg didn't relinquish its stranglehold.

Desperate sounds gurgled from Jeru's throat as he tried to call for help. Not even a knee to the thing's groin worked this time. His hands pulled uselessly at its wrists. In steady, deadly increments, the fingers continued to crush his neck. His legs and arms began to spasm as consciousness ebbed.

Blue lightning flashed: maybe a hint of the tunnel that was supposed to lead him to the afterlife. The pressure around his neck held steady. And continued to hold steady. It did not increase.

Someone grabbed his foot. Doc said, "Can you hear me?"

He could only kick in response.

"Let's get you free, hero." For the first time, the moniker sounded sincere, like she finally believed he was brave and self-sacrificing. Something metallic clattered to the concrete and came to rest against his side, warm and flat-sided like a metal box. She said, "All it took was a sharp twist to unman him. A good thing for you fellows to bear in mind."

CHAPTER THIRTY-FIVE

Jeru sat on the examination table in Dr. Gomez's treatment room while she took care of Victoria in surgery. As promised, the doctor's suite was the only area in the building that remained powered. The other rooms and the annexes were dark, as were the hallways, and no air moved through the vents.

During the ride back to Dr. Gomez's, with the cart headlights on, Jeru couldn't quite believe that Kliburn was dead. All the doors had sprung open when Victoria killed the electricity and canceled the backup batteries, creating an eerie scene of regularly spaced gaps in the walls. In his imagination, the SysOp kept springing out at them again and again from the black.

Thoughts about Gimbel holding Ellie, the threat that the PentaHostiles leader had made against his parents, and the two battles with Kliburn all swirled in his head. At least the hurricane of anxiety kept him from dwelling on the terrible damage to his body.

The door to the operating theater slid open, and Doc walked in, shrugging into a new surgical tunic. "Okay, Mr. Chivalrous, you said, 'Ladies first,' and now the lady is recuperating from that odd ceramic bullet you shot into her scapula. Your turn."

He felt the right side of his face, which had begun to throb again. "I can't meet Gimbel looking like this." Thanks to the cyborg nearly crushing his windpipe, his voice sounded worse than ever.

"I know," she said with exaggerated patience. "That's why you have to undergo surgery."

"No, I mean I can't go as Lou Barone. Even if Gimbel doesn't bring his troops, he'll have some trick planned, and I'm damned sure Kliburn sent him all kinds of photos and video of what I look like now. I need to catch him by surprise before he does that to me."

She looked him over. "Are you contemplating a disguise? Putting on a wig and fake mustache and ruining some more of my husband's clothes?"

"Nothing so obvious—he'll be looking for that."

"What then?"

He'd been rehearsing his request on and off since his return to In-Town. Steeling himself for her reaction—probably an attack more vicious than Kliburn's—he said, "I need to go as your husband."

"Victoria insisted that she go with you. You can pretend to be *her* husband."

"No, I'm not being clear. I mean, I need to go in your husband's body."

Dr. Gomez stared at him. Outrage, fury, and every other hostile emotion twisted her expression. She remained frozen in place, though, until she only showed profound sadness. Then tears cut glistening lines down her face.

Jeru murmured, "He's never coming back, Doc, but he can still save a life. Maybe two or more. Isn't that what doctors do?"

She rasped, "Do you realize what you're asking?"

He nodded. "I'm asking you to give up hope. But in return, you'll give hope to Ellie and me." He shifted under her searing gaze. "You have to decide if the tradeoff is worth it."

"He's all I have left from my years here," she said as more tears fell. "You've stolen everything else from me and now you want to take him as well?"

"I'm sorry. In Lou Barone's body—especially as injured as I am—we don't have a chance. There's no regular disguise good enough to fool Gimbel." He adjusted his glasses, forced himself to meet her glare, and stared back with his one good eye. "I know there are huge risks, and maybe I'll die in surgery, but I'm willing to chance everything. Ellie's that important to me. Is she that important to you, Doc?"

"Goddamn you."

Jeru touched his battered face again. "I think He's doing His best."

She leaned against a nearby cabinet, arms folded, head hanging. "Only twenty-four hours remain before you have to meet with Gimbel. This kind of operation normally requires a week of recuperation before you even open your eyes."

Jeru shrugged. "Then you better fast-track it."

Without another look at him, she turned and stalked into the operating room. The door remained open: the only indication she hadn't rejected him. He slid off the table and followed her. "One more thing," he called. "I'll need a gun."

"Don't tempt me."

That would be one good thing about assuming her husband's body: she'd no longer want to kill him.

A blunt metal tip pressed the inside of Jeru's elbow and a shot of high-pressure air dimpled his skin. Something hot seared his veins in that arm and rocketed into his chest, causing his heart to beat as fast as if he were sprinting for the finish line. His runner's muscles had vanished, however, replaced by solid but unimpressive legs. Lying there naked under a sheet in the dimly lit surgery, he checked himself out, discovering his body was in shape without being bulky. His genitals appeared to be more than acceptable again: not the award-winner Ellie and her mom had picked out, but a damn sight more promising than Lou's pitiful package. All in all, a better-than-average guy whose pulse was pounding like crazy. Dr. Gomez must've injected him with adrenaline—part of the "fast track" to recovery, so his body would be ready for action soon.

Action. Maybe fatal on his part. Worse, maybe he'd get Ellie killed too. Jeru stared at the operating room ceiling, which he'd seen far too often during his time In-Town.

His vision was sharp again, which he noted the instant Dr. Gomez moved into his line of sight. She gazed down at him tenderly, unlike any look she'd ever given him. "Welcome back," she murmured. Even her voice had lost the irritation and sarcasm she usually directed his way. She brought her face closer, dark hair falling around it, and moistened her mouth like she was going to eat him up.

In his new voice, this one a tenor—masculine enough but nothing to make a woman swoon—he replied, "Thank you."

Doc swooned. Eyelids fluttering, she brought her warm hands up to cup his cheeks. Her hair draped his forehead and neck, her sweet breath warm on his face.

Millimeters from what was sure to be one of the greatest kisses in recorded history, he sputtered, "It's me."

"Mm-hmmm," she purred.

Soft, wet lips covered his. They moved up and down and in a gentle counterclockwise circle. Then harder, faster, as if her heartbeat were matching his. Her right hand slid under the sheet, past his arms, and down his torso; five eager fingers on a mission. Before her tongue could find his, he said into her open mouth, "Om Jawuzawum."

"What's that?" she whispered, now pushing her breasts against his arm. Her hand found its target and enfolded him.

Grabbing her wrist, he only made her stroking more emphatic.

Her lips danced against his, just light enough for him to form words. He repeated, "I'm Jerusalem."

Doc froze, fingers rigid, mouth halted in mid-kiss. Then she leaped back from the table as if yanked by a hook around her waist. "Oh good God," she cried. "I'm so sorry." She covered her blushing face. Then she shoved her skillful right hand into her lab coat pocket and made do with her left one as a screen. From behind it, she groaned, "That was most unprofessional."

"It's okay, Doc, give yourself a break. You must've dreamed of doing that a lot. Not to me, I mean, but to him."

She swept back her hair, composing herself, but her eyes stayed closed. "Please, just be quiet a moment. His voice—your voice—is making me weak. I can't look at you without seeing Rafael. I can smell you—him—from all the way over here. It's like warm cookies. I don't think I can bear this."

Jeru watched her standing there, fists clenched, eyes firmly shut, fighting for self-control. The awfulness of her situation struck him. The way he talked, his movements, the scent of him—*everything*—would tell her that her husband was alive and well. And yet he wasn't. The man named Rafael was dead. Someone else's thoughts and memories and attitudes and feelings inhabited the space behind those eyes she'd gazed into so lovingly. He inflicted torture on poor Lallana Gomez with every breath he took.

Empathy was a strange thing. He never used to care about how other people felt—he only cared about the way they made him feel. Is this what love did to you? It wasn't just Ellie he felt deeply about. He wanted Doc to be happy. Hell, he even wanted Victoria to be happy. All these people had been strangers a short time ago, but now he longed to see them enjoying life. Odder than that, he wanted to help them any way he could.

Within reason, he thought, still tasting Doc's urgent kiss and willing his erection to subside. It was taking forever. Rafael must've been upgraded at some point in his life. And, no doubt, Lallana Gomez's butterfly had been flapping like crazy a moment ago. Ooo Lalla, indeed.

She blinked away tears, swallowed a few times, and looked at him anew. "I have your . . . his . . . um, your clothes in the next room. I'll just go fetch them." As she lurched away, she braced herself against equipment and furniture to stay upright. The door leading to the rest of her suite opened. She gripped the frame and maintained a hand on the wall, staggering along like a sailor in rough seas.

With his heart returning to normal and his manhood at half-mast, he eased onto an elbow and then sat up, letting the sheet fall to his waist. A nearby glass-fronted cabinet gave him a good full-body view. His head was bald from the surgery, of course, but didn't show the scars that Dr. Torres—may he rest in peace—had left behind on Lou Barone's scalp. Inspecting his face, he noted the well-formed jaw, dimpled chin, and heavy brows, which complemented tan skin and a naturally roguish smile. God only knew how old the body really was—mid-seventies like Doc?—but it appeared to be mid-thirties. He could come to love this body—if he lived long enough.

Dr. Gomez remained hidden in one of her rooms. Holding the table for balance, he swept the sheet aside and slid onto bare feet. A little wobbly at first, he turned slowly and inspected his naked reflection. His initial touch-impressions had been accurate: he was now a fit, limber man, an inch or two over six feet, much taller than Lou.

Heels clacked behind him. "Oh God," Dr. Gomez yelped. She dropped his clothes in the doorway and fled back down the hall.

If he did survive, manage to rescue Ellie, and get her back home, things were going to remain very awkward with the doctor. Too bad Lallana and Victoria couldn't get together: between Doc's manual dexterity and Victoria's toys, they'd show each other a blazing time.

Such thoughts didn't make it easy to pull on his clothes. Worse, they were Sssagers, so they began to vibrate the instant they contacted his aroused skin.

The door leading to the forward treatment room opened. Jeru turned to find Victoria gaping at him. "Rafael," she sighed.

"I'm Jerusalem." He started to keep count of the times he would have to say this.

"Oh, yes, of course." She'd clipped up her purple-streaked hair and wore a short-sleeved top and loose slacks. The rich had good fashion sense: mustn't look too ostentatious when saving your daughter from kidnappers.

He asked, "How's your shoulder?"

Moving her arm in a circle, she said, "Much better." She walked up and gave him a once-over. "Thank you for asking. You were always so considerate."

"That was Rafael," he reminded her. "I'm still learning how not to be a glans." She frowned in reply, so he explained OTP slang, just as he had with her daughter two bodies and what felt like a century ago.

She smiled. "It's hard to get used to, hmm? Not the slang, but this." She gestured at him, from head to glans. "A man gets sick. He goes to sleep. He wakes up awhile later, but he's entirely different, even though he looks and sounds exactly the same." She licked red-painted lips. "He even still smells like oatmeal with brown sugar."

Jeru sniffed his forearm. Smelled like skin to him, a little musky maybe, and warm against his nose. Victoria remained very close to him. He said, "How, uh, how well did you know Rafael?"

"He was my physician, in concert with Lallana, so of course he knew every part of me, inside and out." She glanced past him and then confided, "He was gentler than she is, very soothing. Always made me feel completely relaxed. I think the world of Lallana, but she's a trifle . . . abrupt. Very business-like. One desires a friendlier hand with certain things, hmm?"

Lallana had the friendliest hand he'd encountered, but the conversation was moving into weird enough territory without him playing True Confessions too. He asked her for the time, and she said with a hopeful look, "We still have an hour before we're supposed to be there. Sixty long minutes."

"That's all?" In a panic, he reached up to tug at his hair, but could only claw his bald scalp. "Dammit, we haven't even talked about a plan."

"Don't fret. That's just like you, I mean him." She put her hands on his shoulders and kneaded them. "Always so tense about things."

"A little massage therapy, Victoria?" Dr. Gomez walked in from the hall.

Victoria dropped her hands and stepped back. From the way the women glowered at each other, Jeru foresaw a bloody battle over him—or, rather, over Rafael, a dead man. Funny, Doc had defended Victoria before, when he'd make his smarmy remarks about her humping the furniture, but she'd obviously had Victoria the Widow in mind. When contemplating Victoria the Seductress, perhaps Dr. Gomez considered the endless sessions of partner-less sex a fitting punishment for the "mistress" of the house. And maybe Lallana had kept her dead husband around so she could bring him back to life one day and then murder the unfaithful rogue.

Jeru shattered the brittle silence by cornering Dr. Gomez. "You revived me with just an hour before show time? We need to get there ahead of him, figure out some backup strategies, discuss signals—"

"Listen," she spat, the sarcasm and irritation back in spades, "you should consider yourself fortunate that you're alive at all. I broke every medical rule to expedite your recovery, and I bent a few laws of nature." She gestured at him, head to glans. "The fact that you're strutting around and flirting in my husband's body is only because my love for Ellipsis narrowly outweighs my contempt for you."

"Really?" A sharp knee to his balls would've been more welcomed. The Sssagers worked their magic, soothing him with delicate, warm vibrations. That was the problem with empathy—you opened yourself up to emotional harm when those you cared about turned on you. Maybe he wasn't cut out for offline relationships with real people.

She turned away, studying her shoe tops. "Perhaps I overstated my rancor a bit. As I told you before, you have a habit of saying precisely the wrong thing, the wrong way, at the wrong time."

Victoria interjected, "That's the big difference between him and Rafael. Rafe always knew just the right thing to say. And do."

Dr. Gomez drew a small, boxy pistol from her lab coat pocket. After a moment of hesitation, as she stared at Victoria, she flipped the gun in her hand, caught it by the barrel, and handed it butt-first to Jeru. "It's a B12—stands for Baker's Dozen, *Thirteen confirmed kills or the next one's on us*. It's programmed to shoot people only—it'll hit the center of the heart if you aim anywhere close to your intended target." She misread his incredulity, saying, "I'm sorry, hero, but that's the best I could do on short notice. I was busy saving both your lives."

"Don't worry, I think it'll do." Jeru slid the gun into his waistband, where it felt cold and oily against his skin, and pulled his shirt over it. "Thank you," he added and took her hands. "I should be the one to apologize. You've done everything I've asked, even when it broke your heart. If I wasn't in love with Ellie, I'd want to be worthy of your love someday."

Victoria sighed, hands clasped to her heart, eyes misty. "Oh, Rafe's in there after all."

Doc shook him off. Apparently trying to counteract the blush on her cheeks with a harsh tone, she snapped, "You are so full of shit, you need a spare body to put it all in."

"I'm sure you still have Lou Barone lying around."

"Go!" Dr. Gomez said, pushing on his back. "Come back with Ellie or don't come back at all."

He said, "Yeah, that's pretty much how this is going to go down."

Doc gave him another shove. "Aren't you being somewhat glib about this?"

"Doc, you've just given me the smartest gun in the world and a whole new body—it's my ace in the hole."

"Well just make sure you don't get flushed."

The three of them walked down the hall and past the unmarked room where Dr. Gomez had probably incinerated her husband's damaged brain and put Lou in cryo-storage. In the garage, Doc said, "By the way, I checked the Atlanta OTP media sites and couldn't find any news stories about your parents—they appear to be safe. Gimbel was bluffing, just to shake you up."

"Well, he did a terrific job. Let's hope that's the only thing he's good at."

"Yes, touch wood." From Doc's expression, he could tell that was a slim hope. She sat in the driver seat of the stubby silver car and told the onboard computer, "Accept guest driver."

The car replied in a Jersey accent "Hey, why don't ya introduce us?"

Victoria replaced Doc behind the wheel. The car whistled and said, "Yeah, baby, have I got some accessories for you. You ever been simonized?"

Doc thumped the roof. "Knock it off."

Jeru asked, "Should I get behind the wheel too?"

"No chips in the head, remember?" Dr. Gomez knocked on his skull much the way she'd pounded the roof. "How do you think it knew about Victoria's, um, proclivities?"

Victoria said, "I would appreciate my employee and my guest not talking about me like I'm elsewhere, hmm? Shall I remind you that killers are holding my daughter hostage?"

Dr. Gomez pulled Jeru away. In the distance he could hear Victoria quizzing the car about its "accessories" with a frankness that reddened his ears. The weave of his Sssagers loosened to cool him down.

Doc said, "She's very tense. Do you still want her to go instead of me?"

"It was her choice, not mine. I'd rather have you there." He tried the roguish smile that felt so natural on this face.

He'd never seen a woman melt before. She melted. Weak-kneed, hand to breast, parted lips, the works. If he did it again, she might faint. Doc sighed, "I'm sorry I was waspish earlier." She pulled him close, gave him a full-body hug, and rested her face against his chest. "I guess I'm tense as well."

Jeru eased his chin onto the top of her head. "Me too—it means we all care about each other."

She peered up at him suspiciously. "You're showing more and more sensitivity. Makes me think I jiggled your brain a couple of times during the transfer."

"I'm trying to change, Doc, but I'll go back to being a crude, selfish glans if you want."

She pushed him away, but not far and with apparent reluctance. "You better leave now. Stay alert, Jerusalem."

Doc had never said his name before—it touched him deeply, but he corrected her: " 'Jerry,' that's what Ellie calls me. I want all my friends to call me that, Lallana."

"*Lalla*," she whispered. "Come back safe with Ellie."

Jeru leaned in and gave her the Rafael smile and a quick kiss on the cheek. Then he climbed into the passenger seat beside Victoria. "Okay," he said, "here's the plan."

CHAPTER THIRTY-SIX

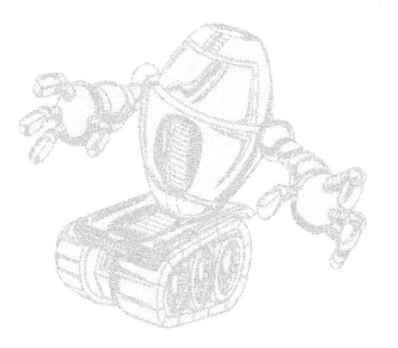

"Okay," Gimbel said, "here's the plan." Over a hundred RSA militiamen and -women leaned forward in their auditorium seats, staring up at him onstage as if they were about to receive the Word. He did have the Living Word for his Crusaders, and that word was "Kick ass." Well, it was two Words, but he didn't want to quibble.

It had taken him an entire day and night of calls, videoconferences, middlemen, bribes, donations, and threats of reprisal, but finally it had come together. He knew his efforts would be worth it: to look into Jerusalem Pix's—now Lou Barone's—eyes and watch the light in them fade as the bullet tore through him, and then to extract those eyes for his collection, while wondering what unspeakable horrors they were seeing in hell.

As he described his brilliant plan to his troops, sheer genius coupled with an ace in the hole, he imagined it playing out all over again. A big proponent of "believe to achieve" and visualizing the accomplishment of goals, he'd pictured the glorious results so often it was as if they'd already happened. In a few short hours, he'd merely be taking part in the reenactment. Maybe he'd keep Lou Barone's entire ugly head as a companion he could taunt at leisure.

Oh Lord, he wanted it badly, even more than winning the PraiseGod award at the annual Evangelists and Religious Celebrities banquet. For five years running, he'd lost out to pompous, self-righteous assholes who thought that being a spiritual leader meant reading and interpreting the Bible. Well not this time, pal. He'd spent months picturing their fat, sorry butts at the back table, beside the kitchen, with only horse-faced choir ladies to comfort them, while he got the big prize, the standing O, and the hot chicks who promised standing Os, sitting Os, and Os in every other position.

The engrossing image of himself naked and suspended above a rotating circular bed of writhing, baby-oil-drenched lovelies was interrupted by the Q&A period that always concluded their planning meetings in the auditorium. One of the RSA squad leaders raised his hand and asked, "So how do we know these terrorists are going to follow this scheme your spies overheard? Those infidels are devious."

Gimbel replied, "They seem very dedicated to losing their lives today. But that's why you'll be on hand, in case they overreach." He knew damned well the terrorists would follow the scheme, because he'd paid them a bundle to do it, as in the old days.

The heat was on terrorists of all stripes since the War on Terror Part VI had recently racked up some primetime successes. As a result, the ultra-right wouldn't come out and play like they used to. So began the calls, videoconferences, and whatnot to the ultra-left. Posing as an anonymous donor, Gimbel had tried everyone, starting with the most violent groups like the Community Association of Death and Slaughter-Avondale Estates Chapter, Fatwah Anonymous, and Show Me the Virgins. Not a lick of interest. Even the more-political-than-militant organizations that were often looking for something to do on a weekday morning, such as the Islamic Brotherhood of Misgivings and Jews for Jihad, refused to offer up some martyrs regardless of the donation amount. He'd resorted to asking the youth group Goodnight, Crescent Moon, but no dice. Finally, he was left with a loose association of misfits and rebels called For ALlah And For Everyone eLse—or, as they called themselves, FALAFEL—a group he knew nothing about but who would take his donation on their website, www.falafel.ter.

In Gimbel's estimation, a FALAFEL terrorist action planned near the Five Points plaza for a few minutes before noon would lure away the Guardsmen and police, and Jerusalem would show himself. Smart boy, demanding that: lots of those troopers were in fact on the RSA payroll.

"Excuse me, sir," another fighter said. "But aren't we supposed to be wiping out the terrorists?"

"Indeed, but my mission today takes precedence." He spread his arms wide in his Jesus Gesticulation™. "Your slain comrades Cairo Bledsoe and Sandoval Yen haunt me night and day, calling out for vengeance against the man who turned their noble martyrdom into pitiful suicides. In a matter of hours, we'll have that man in our custody. Or what's left of him."

That earned a smattering of applause. Certainly not the most enthusiastic room he'd ever worked. He walked to the edge of the stage. "Any more questions?"

A hand in the back went up. "Sir, you mentioned an ace in the hole. Can you tell us what that is?"

Gimbel grinned at the assemblage and acted as if he were considering the request for a moment. Finally he said, "Very well." He exited stage-right, where Billy Bob waited with the "ace," and returned clasping the wrist of the most beautiful blonde the Good Lord had ever created.

She wore a black micro-mini-dress he'd picked out especially for the swap with Jerusalem at noon. The red-blooded American males—and some of the females—in the crowd went nuts, like war-weary soldiers at a USO show. He twirled her around, staggering her a bit. Either she was still getting used to the ultra-high heels from TipToes (*Yes, they go all the way up*™) or was continuing to recover from the brain transfer he'd forced the steiner to perform. Torres, that unethical little pissant, had kept her body instead of sending it immediately to the Organ Recycling Center.

Ellipsis Stewart's eyes were glazed and for whatever reason kept changing color, but they did so out of sync. Currently, the left one flashed from aquamarine to purple, while the right one stayed locked in an orange marmalade hue.

Her body was beyond perfection, because even a perfectionist wouldn't have conceived of the exquisite details this creature possessed. Her only flaws were the scarring around her shaved scalp and the wig of wavy, curled gold that covered the scar but only somewhat matched the luscious hair he'd seen in the videos provided by Kliburn.

Amid the wolf-whistles, applause, "ace in *that* hole" jokes, and offers of marriage called up from the audience, she took an awkward step and tripped, pitching toward the front edge of the stage while those miraculous breasts tried to escape through the top of her dress.

At once, more than two dozen grasping, groping hands were there to ensure she didn't fall, or to cop a feel if she did. Gimbel wrapped his arms around the remarkable wasp waist and pulled her back to safety.

In a demonstration of enormous self-restraint, Gimbel stepped away from the Holy Grail of Sex. He said, "It will break your hearts, as it's already broken mine, to know we are giving up this worthy Christian to the enemy." The expected deluge of catcalls and boos rained down. He yelled into the storm of protest, "But our 'ace in the hole' is not that we're going to dazzle our enemy with this stunning creature. Rather, it's what behind this extraordinarily beautiful face."

He paused as the auditorium fell silent once more, expectant. Gimbel considered the decision he'd made at Brand New U to be his most brilliant stroke of genius. God couldn't take all of the credit for this one.

"Through the miracle of science," he intoned, "standing before you is the body of a goddess, yes, but with the patriotic, RSA-trained mind of your comrade in arms: London Johnson. Take a bow—or rather, a curtsy—Lun."

CHAPTER THIRTY-SEVEN

Jeru and Victoria left through Station 16, far away from any In-Town gate where the RSA would bother to post a lookout. She parked miles from the Five Points plaza, and they walked from there. Jeru took the lead according to his plan; soon, his much-longer strides carried him way ahead of her. He arrived at the plaza with twenty minutes to spare, according to the watch Victoria loaned him, a delicate accessory so feminine he self-consciously kept it in his pocket when he wasn't checking the time.

Scanning the broad arcade, his hopes sank. He'd expected a typical Monday crowd, where he could spot any possible threats. Instead, hundreds of people roamed the faux cobblestones. Worse, nearly all wore fantasy or sci-fi costumes and most of them were armed to the teeth, or to the gills in several cases. Swords, axes, maces, flails, spiked clubs, crossbows, and guns of endless varieties adorned hands, scabbards, slings, and holsters.

Oh shit. It was HydraCon.

The largest convention of cosplayers, gamers, hobbyists, aficionados, reenactors, and sci-fi/fantasy fans in America had once again come to Atlanta. Ninety thousand typically flocked to the weeklong orgy of selling, trading, videogaming, workshopping, networking, gawking, feasting, drinking, and boffing between fantastical species. There would be limitless pairings, triplings, quadruplings, and so on, up to a limit of twenty, at which time the Fire Marshall would join in. Most of the hotels selected for HydraCon apparently were a block or two north, given the primary direction of the crowd. Unfortunately, plenty of the costumed conventioneers wandered right where Jeru had intended to outwit Gimbel and, if necessary, the entire RSA.

Jostled on one side by a squid on a BattleBoard and on the other by a bullet-breasted Amazon with a long sword across her back and a bag of popcorn in each hand, Jeru wanted to shout at everyone to just go away. Here he was, in the greatest disguise in the universe, but at *this* costume party he wouldn't even qualify for a judging, let alone win an award. Worse, because he hadn't hidden behind something fake like a mask, encased himself in plastic armor, or used layers of face paint, he stood out more than the squid-boy would at church.

Gimbel could be anywhere close by: the Killer Slime Mold oozing out of the Five Points station, the nine-foot-tall giraffopotamus pretending to munch one of the artificial trees on the plaza, or the cyclopedian funnel cake vendor spattered with hot oil and dusted with powdered sugar. The homicidal maniac could've forced Ellie to don a costume too. In fact, slaves and manacled harem-girls appeared to be very popular this year, based on the scores of humanoids being led around in chains. Maybe HydraCon had merged with BDSMCon (*Whips of all nations flail together*™).

Okay, Jeru decided, better switch to Plan B: improvise. He ambled over to a convention employee—dressed like a Haythoo of all things—and took one of the rolled filmies offered in its four hands. Leaning against a fake tree, he un-scrolled the always-updating source of event news and pretended to read while he scanned the crowd.

He caught sight of Victoria entering the plaza. She stopped short, gaping at the bizarre scene, and then she lit up like a kid at her first Halloween party. They'd agreed to stay at least twenty feet apart, as Gimbel surely would know what she looked like, courtesy of Kliburn. Now such caution appeared to be pointless because they stood out as the only pair not in costume.

The parade of conventioneers continued around him. Strolling across the arcade, cops and National Guardsmen eyed the warrior princesses, superheroines, and intergalactic temptresses with a three-breast minimum. Apparently, Gimbel had ignored Jeru's demand to clear the plaza of security forces.

In a moment of paranoid insanity, he considered heading back to the Stewart place so he could resurrect Kliburn and try to set up the exchange for Ellie under different terms. After all, Gimbel had broken his word, the HydraCon crowd made him nervous as hell, and his instincts said the RSA had put a huge bull's eye on the entire plaza. If the Penta-Hostiles were looking to expedite Judgment Day for as many people as possible, this was the perfect place.

A tremendous bang to the east made everyone duck involuntarily. Black smoke drifted from a tall building in that direction. Though helmets and rubber masks stifled many screams, panicked shouts still raced through the crowd. Police officers and troops consulted their communicators and then sprinted toward the burning office tower. They drew their guns as they ran.

The distraction he'd demanded? Jeru sneaked a peek at the woman's watch in his pocket: two minutes before noon. Okay, the swap was on. Just relax. There was no reason to suddenly start sweating like this; the spring day wasn't any hotter than usual.

Victoria glanced over at him, and he rolled his shoulders, the agreed-upon signal for "Just relax and quit looking at me." He stayed behind his filmy but studied the crowd more intently. The revelers, assured that the threat was a quarter mile away to the east—someone else's terror and heartache—resumed ogling one another and ever-questing for reasonably priced snacks and beverages from the vendors on hand.

Sirens wailed around the plaza. The TrafficGrid halted all vehicles and moved them to the curb so emergency first-responders could race to the bombing. In addition to the usual collection of police, fire, and medical teams, camo-colored armored personnel carriers from the Georgia National Guard with bumper stickers declaring "Chattanooga, GA: Get used to it," and black, low-riding anti-terrorism units whizzed past. Anyone within earshot recognized the discordant tones of the latter group's siren—like a piano falling down an endless staircase—meant to warn citizens to stay away.

Soon Gimbel would give Victoria some sign he was there, either with Ellie or with the trap he intended to spring. Jeru followed the progress of a statuesque woman in a fluorescent-green body stocking who walked toward Victoria's part of the plaza. Several such models strolled the arcade, hired by the vendor of Fantasi glasses (*Don't leave it to your imagination*™), which would display, in random rotation, all manner of lingerie, ornamentation, fetish gear, and nude body types on anyone wearing that shade of green. The couple's kit included two body stockings for one low, low price.

The woman in green sauntered past Victoria, allowing Jeru to look that way without arousing suspicion. Damn! Gimbel had already made his move. He was engaging her in conversation dressed as a Mooma, the seven-foot-tall Bigfoot-like creature from the Forests on Fire video game series. A sash of purple, identical in color to the streaks in Victoria's hair, marked him as the chief. Nearby stood Gimbel's RSA militia, disguised to complement their leader: a band of Moomas, squat and slimy Wuzzles, and reptilian Saureens. One of the supporting cast of Moomas held the arm—or appendage—of a rotund, yellow ladybug, which no doubt encased poor Ellie.

Jeru strolled in a long, curving trajectory toward the Fire party, throwing the filmy in a recycling compactor along the way. He paused to scan the crowd again, to see if anyone was tracking his progress. A flitting glance at the Five Points station turned into a double-take . . . and then became a crystalline moment outside of time.

Gimbel passed through the exit in a tailored, two-button navy suit, white dress shirt with high Edwardian collar, and a yellow tie patterned with crowns of thorns. Despite the oversized FarSighters that hid his eyes as well as his identity from casual observers, his open mouth betrayed his bewilderment as he took in the glut of characters and weaponry. Stumbling alongside him on outrageously spiked heels, Ellie shined in all her original splendor.

Impossible, but there she was. In her black micro-mini-dress, she stole his breath. Only her hair didn't match his memories. Then he reminded himself that to get from the Cathy Eden body back into hers, she would've had to undergo the same expedited surgery he did. The horror show in Brand New U was clear now: her brain transfer had been done by Dr. Torres and his staff at gunpoint, and was followed by the massacre he'd discovered. Her glossy, golden wig no doubt covered a scar ringing her head. The thought didn't detract one bit from her radiance.

My God, just look at her. She made teetering on ridiculous shoes a glamorous, erotic feat. Even if he'd never seen her before now, he would do anything for her if she asked. Many others in the vicinity seemed to share his thought. Males, females, hermaphrodites, and neuters turned to feast their one, two, or more eyes on her.

If he walked up to Gimbel, shot him, and whisked Ellie away—Plan A—the crowd she captivated would come to her rescue and hack him to bits. The only way to kill the RSA leader and save his love would be to create a distraction. But what could distract this galaxy of creatures from the most beautiful woman in the universe?

Looking around for inspiration, he noticed that not everyone had fallen under Ellie's spell. If anybody deserved to stare at her now, that privilege should've gone to her mother, but Victoria and the lead Mooma continued to stand close, eyes locked. She craned her neck, and he gazed down from on high. Their lips moved in conversation, probably independent of their fevered brains. Not until one of the Fire party said, "Whoa, look at that," did the Mooma snap out of his trance and follow the direction of a pointing talon.

Eventually, Victoria glanced that way too. Her complexion turned as white as her hair. "Ellipsis," she cried and ran toward Ellie and Gimbel, with the lead Mooma and his party trailing. She'd promised not to do that. Plan B was going to get a workout.

In the distance, the shriek of sirens began again, but for some reason they were coming closer. The pop and rattle of fireworks accompanied those noises. Apparently the RSA leader had arranged for stuff to happen all over the downtown area.

Gimbel leaned close to Ellie and snarled a few words, startling her. Sounding uncertain, she yelled, "Mom?"

Jeru fell in behind the Fire party, thinking this could all work out fine. When Ellie fingered Gimbel as her kidnapper, Victoria would scream for his head and the chief Mooma and his crew would gladly provide it to her. Jeru would follow them to safety. Then, after a moment of confusion—with him no doubt saying, "I'm Jerusalem," for the third time that day—a joyous reunion would commence. Totally blazing. None of his plans could compare with such a simple, elegant solution.

Conventioneers on the east edge of the plaza gathered and pointed. Screaming, running, slithering, and hopping soon followed. An interstellar, pan-historical menagerie streamed away from that end of the mall, and swept up others in the stampede.

Behind them, twenty men and women wearing street clothes and ball caps emblazoned with FALAFEL of all things brandished assault rifles, machine guns, and shoulder-fired rocket launchers. The terrorists comprised a variety of ethnicities from around the world, a veritable United Nations of hatred, but they hesitated as they surveyed the panoply of species and sexes fleeing before them. From behind came gunfire as their rear guard battled the oncoming police and soldiers.

At the same moment, Jeru flanked the side of the Fire party, ready to draw on Gimbel. The man shielded Ellie from Victoria and her entourage and shouted into his All-n-1, "Red team, go, go, go! Goddammit, the jihadists are out of control and coming this way."

From the parking garage across Peachtree Street, dozens of RSA militiamen in rifle-cross tees and camo pants stormed toward the plaza, taking aim at the FALAFELs. However, the StaySafe sonic fence had been activated at the intersection and along the sidewalk as the TrafficGrid continued to divert vehicles from the rolling terrorist action and keep additional cars from venturing into the street. The RSA fighters collided with the invisible fence and each other like an old-time freeway pileup.

The terrorists swung around and laid down a blistering field of fire across Peachtree. Bullets and rockets, fired at supersonic velocities, passed through the StaySafe barrier and literally shredded the RSA. The dead remained vertical, propped upright by the invisible fence and from behind by their fellow warriors. Those at the head of the charge became disintegrating human shields for those who'd moments before sulked about being in back. As the surviving fighters spread out along the curb, leaving what was left of their comrades to crumple at last, FALAFEL merely widened the death zone. The rout was total. Killed and wounded militiamen and -women lay atop each other like the Confederate dead in the Battle of Atlanta.

All across the plaza, conventioneers were fleeing as fast as their costumes would allow. Police, troops, and anti-terrorist specialists to the east had taken cover to assess the situation. They wouldn't risk drone missile strikes and other heavy ordinance among so many civilians.

Reveling in their easy victory over the RSA, the cheering terrorists turned and fired into the fleeing, costumed crowd.

And something happened to those people who had commuted all the way from the burbs, or flown in from out of town, just to have a good time for once in their complicated, uneasy lives. The men and women who had spent months crafting the perfect costumes and accessories, and paid good money to participate in the spectacle of HydraCon, collectively snapped. They remembered they too had weapons, and they got pissed.

Rallying cries went up in a hundred invented languages. The lemmings turned and became a bloodthirsty mob.

Naturally many in the first wave fell victim to gunfire, but the conventioneers closed the gap quickly, in overwhelming numbers. Unconstrained by StaySafe fences, command and control drills, or common sense, they attacked along multiple fronts across the plaza. They swung and jabbed and hurled whatever they held. Not every blade was sharp enough to puncture flesh or whack off limbs, but even heavy plastic weapons were capable of delivering a crippling blow when wielded with sufficient force, in the righteous fury that only an enraged consumer could summon.

When the melee began, the chief Mooma swept Victoria into his hairy arms and seven feet of fake brown fur carried her from the battlefield. His party turned from Ellie and Gimbel and joined the fight. They handled themselves well, accounting for three dead or incapacitated terrorists while only suffering one casualty.

The hand-to-hand combat ended with the last of the FALAFELs losing his head to the woman in the green body stocking who'd picked up a sword and started hacking. Though a novice with the blade, she looked marvelous doing it, even to those not wearing Fantasi glasses.

By that time, the area around Gimbel and Ellie had cleared out. The RSA leader—ducking down like everyone else not in the fight—had watched the slaughter of his militia with growing horror and pointed his FarSighters right at Jeru several times during the subsequent tumult, as if seeking a sympathetic listener to tell his troubles to. For his part, Jeru kept deciding to shoot Gimbel but then he would choose to wait until the timing was "better." What he really wanted to do was snatch Ellie and get her away before the maniac snapped out of his stupor.

Something was wrong with Ellie, though. She'd noticed him several times as well, but showed no sign of recognition. Ellie should've known Dr. Gomez's husband instantly—a tip-off that her rescue was at hand. Instead, her strangely out-of-sync irises, one now pewter and the other still stuck in orange, paused on his face and then moved away without acknowledging that the resurrected Rafael stood fifteen feet from her.

Maybe she'd experienced partial or complete memory loss during the surgery. Looking on the bright side, if she didn't know him she also wouldn't remember how badly he'd screwed up their relationship. He could start the romance all over again, knowing everything about her personality and preferences while behaving much better this time. A clean slate, a fresh start.

Behind Jeru, cheers went up, mixed with crying and shouts for a medic. One man called for his Class 9 healer while others cussed and kicked the dead and dying terrorists who'd started it. Police and soldiers swarmed that end of the mall. Separating the good guys from the bad was an easy task from a security perspective. For the EMTs, though, working on a casually dressed FALAFEL with stab wounds and blunt-force trauma was a hell of a lot easier than extricating a gunshot victim from their spiky latex exoskeleton.

The authorities continued to suspend TrafficGrid operations so they could cross Peachtree with some EMTs to pick through the gore of butchered RSA militiamen. Gimbel watched them for a moment without expression and then said to Ellie, "Come on, let's go. He didn't come, or he's too scared to show himself."

"I'm right here." Jeru drew his pistol and advanced on him.

"Gun!" Gimbel shouted.

In a flash, Jeru pictured the mall behind him, now crawling with high-strung cops and soldiers holding weapons galore and looking for surviving terrorists—armed men in civilian clothes, just like him—who were trying to escape. He'd picked exactly the wrong time to make his move.

CHAPTER THIRTY-EIGHT

Fresh screams went up from the crowd. Behind Jeru, military boots and hard-soled shoes pounded the fake cobblestones. He reached Gimbel and Ellie at a run and feinted to his right. When Gimbel took a step that way, Jeru spun to his left, grazing Ellie as he got behind them. He jabbed his gun into the back of the RSA leader's skull.

"I'll blow his head off," he shouted at the advancing troops. To his ears, his threat sounded eerily similar to Cairo Bledsoe's before the backpack bomb exploded. He'd been a hero back then, Jeru reflected; police officers and soldiers had shown up at his phony funeral to pay their respects. Now they viewed him as just another nutjob with a gun. The fact that he was kidnapping a kidnapper wouldn't mean a thing to the uniformed men and women who aimed their weapons his way.

Before they could flank him, Jeru pulled Gimbel back toward the Five Points station. "Stay here, Ellie," Jeru said. "You're safe now."

"No, I won't leave you." Her husky voice was exactly as he remembered it: full of warmth and compassion. She'd sounded that way at least a couple of times, when she wasn't pissed at him. In a move that stunned him with its bravery and selflessness, she shielded his left side as he jerked Gimbel along on his right. He struggled to focus on his dire situation instead of gaping at her, so close to him now, so courageous.

"Another body switch, Jerusalem?" Gimbel growled. "How devious."

"I thought you'd like it." He shoved the barrel harder against Gimbel's head, earning a satisfying "oof" as he marched the villain backward. Jeru cut his eyes again to Ellie. "Don't you recognize me?"

She hesitated and looked at Gimbel, of all people, for help. Finally, she apologized. "I'm a little dazed, I guess, and I'm scared to death and don't know what to do and—"

"I'm in Rafael's body. You know, Dr. Gomez's husband."

"Oh, right." She whacked her temple with the heel of her hand, knocking her wig askew.

Jeru checked behind him. Shit, they had troops coming out of the station now. Surrounded.

Beyond the soldiers, the conventioneers posed a second front as they ringed the area. Because the police were holding them until each one gave his, her, their, or its statement, the cosplayers had nowhere else to go. Hundreds of humanoid and utterly alien faces—a whole GameSphere of creatures—stared at him. They all looked like they wanted to take a whack if the professionals didn't shoot him first.

The officer in charge, a captain in the Atlanta police force, shouted, "Drop your gun, buddy. Drop it now."

Gimbel muttered, "Don't worry, Jerusalem, you won't go into custody. You're about to die."

"Ellie," Jeru said, "tell the troops who I am. Explain what this is all about."

She didn't reply and, in fact, wouldn't meet his eyes. Instead, she reached into Gimbel's suit jacket and withdrew a molded gray gun, identical to the one Jeru had used to halt Kliburn.

"Totally blazing," he said. "Two against one."

The captain warned, "Your head is in our crosshairs. Throw your gun down, or you'll be killed."

"I'm dropping it," he called back. He let the pistol fall to the ground and raised his hands. "This guy's a monster," he said to Ellie. "Shoot him."

Ellie glanced at Gimbel, her gun aimed between them. She said, "I'm sorry, Jerusalem."

Jerusalem instead of *Jerry*. And she didn't recognize Rafael's face. And she kept looking at her kidnapper. If it wasn't Ellie then . . . The image of the young commando missing the top of his head flashed into Jeru's mind.

Oh fuck.

She turned the gray gun on him, but it really didn't matter. He'd just died inside. This twist could only mean that Ellie was gone. No doubt the RSA—probably Gimbel himself—had killed her as soon as they knew the steiner's surgery had been successful. Why bother with a hostage once they'd put their own fighter inside her original body? Was there a more effective lure? Was there any better trap? It certainly had worked. Gimbel's ace trumped his own.

Gimbel sidestepped out of the line of fire. He said to Ellie, "Shoot him."

She hesitated, still not meeting Jerusalem's gaze.

Behind them, someone asked, "Who do we shoot, Captain?"

The officer replied, "Damned if I know. Hold your fire."

One of the conventioneers yelled, "Shoot 'em all and let God sort 'em out."

Gimbel crouched and came up with Jeru's gun. "Two against one," he said with a grin. "Totally blazing."

"Nice trick, glans," Jeru said.

"I thought you'd like it." Gimbel lifted the FarSighters to his forehead so he could examine the B12 pistol. He nodded appreciatively. "The Good Lord provides."

Jeru took his final breath. "See you in hell," he said.

"I think not." Gimbel sighted along the barrel and quoted, " 'Vengeance is mine,' sayeth—"

The young man residing inside Ellie's body turned and shot Gimbel in the face.

Spewing blood and gray matter, the RSA leader tumbled sideways, his FarSighters flipping end over end. He hit the ground, amber eyes wide and blank, mouth frozen in a bloody O. His feet twitched as if being held to a flame.

Ellie's mom crashed through the line of soldiers. The chief Mooma followed her at a fast shamble. "My baby," Victoria cried. "Don't shoot my baby."

Jeru and Ellie—the young man, really—stared down at Gimbel's death rattle. "He made me do a terrible thing," Ellie's voice said. The gun clattered between her spiked heels. "And I can't ever make that right, but maybe saving you helps a little."

Not quite believing what had happened, Jeru looked Ellie over and asked, "Did he do anything bad to you . . . I mean, to Ellie?"

"He looked like he was going to and he almost did a bunch of times and I think the only reason he didn't was because he knew I'm in here . . . so I sort of protected her. Weird, huh?"

The National Guardsmen, police, and anti-terrorist unit closed in and formed a tight circle around the crime scene.

Jeru said, "I think we can get you out of this mess. What's your name?"

"London. My friends call me Lun." She—he—shook Jeru's hand as solemnly as Ellie had done after he awoke in her home for the first time.

Victoria spun Lun around with a fierce hug. "My baby, my baby. Oh God, are you all right?"

"I'm fine, um, Mom." Lun patted Victoria's back and stepped from her embrace.

The captain barked at Jeru and the others, "All of you, hands in the air and step away from the guns and that body."

"Victoria," Jeru said, as they complied, "you need to tell these people what happened. They'll believe you about the kidnapping."

"There's something else," Lun said. "The girl, Ellipsis . . . she's alive."

The only reason Jeru didn't faint with relief was because they'd probably shoot him on the way down. He did give himself permission to cry unabashedly.

Lun nodded at his tears and continued, "It's true. She's still in that other body, and they're holding her in a van parked in the garage over there, and—" He pointed one of Ellie's upraised hands in the direction of the carnage "—if the Most Rev . . . uh, if he doesn't come back, the driver's supposed to kill her and if he sees me alone, or her—I mean *Mom*—or the police, he's supposed to do the same." Ellie's eyes blinked at them. "You know, you haven't interrupted me once."

The Mooma said with a distinct Scottish burr, "What you're saying is important, lassie. Tell me about the van—my war party and I will see to it."

Victoria's look of confusion turned to love and admiration as she beamed at the Mooma. Her hairy hero.

Jeru gestured with his head to the armed personnel surrounding them. "We're all going to have to answer a lot of questions first."

Lun glanced at the slender watch on Ellie's upturned wrist. "Better hurry. There's also a time limit."

"Then we need to explain things very clearly the first time," Jeru said. "Afterward, I'm going with the Mooma." He smiled through his tears at the wonderful strangeness of saying that.

The seven-foot-tall creature said, "My name is Angus." He waved one of the huge, hairy paws he kept in the air.

"Of course it is," Jeru said. "On a day like this, it couldn't be anything else."

The officer in charge—Captain Ingram—along with the ranking Guardsman and the anti-terrorist lead had worked through the jurisdictional disputes without any of them firing a weapon at the others, so the onsite interrogations got underway quickly.

Victoria, Jeru, and Lun each gave the same simple story about Gimbel kidnapping Ellie to draw out Jeru, and the agreed-upon, ill-fated swap. For his part, Angus the Mooma played the role of innocent bystander, involved only because he'd hoped to commit interspecies miscegenation with Victoria. Therefore, he was the only one who told the complete truth.

Lun explained the other hostage situation in complicated, run-on sentences, leaving out the fact that he and the girl in question shared something in common. A statement like, "Her brain goes in this body," certainly would've added to the interrogators' interview time, to say nothing of the paperwork.

Captain Ingram said, "So if these men see anyone in uniform, the girl dies?"

"Those are his orders. He's definitely got a gun and the van is bulletproof and he'll kill her even if it means he'll die, too, because it's really a suicide cult more than a church and—"

"All right, sweetie, I got it." Ingram patted Ellie's arm and approached Angus, saying, "We're commandeering your costumes."

"Aye, and I'd love to give them to you, Captain, but it took me weeks to learn how to walk properly on the stilts built into this hairy beastie. How tall do you think I really am, anyway?"

It was a similar story for everyone else the authorities asked: by the time a conventioneer could strip out of the costume and a cop could don it and figure out how to move around and where to conceal his firearms, cuffs, and so on—let alone shoot accurately with a tentacle or talon in many cases—the girl would be dead. Just to reach that conclusion left her with only a few precious minutes remaining.

Jeru said to Ingram, "Deputize me and Angus and his war party. Stay hidden behind us and feel free to open fire if we do anything you don't like."

"No way. We'll send in our snipers."

Jeru, Victoria, and the others had to watch helplessly as the Atlanta SWAT officers swooped into the parking garage. He took Ellie/Lun's hand and held Victoria's with his other. After being the reluctant hero for so long, complaining and worrying the whole time, he was surprised at how much it hurt him to stand back and let others finally rescue the woman he loved.

The SWAT guys made quick work of it. Two rapid rifle cracks and then silence. Jeru watched Ingram speaking through a slim headset, the man's face loose with relief. The captain met Jeru's gaze and gave him a thumbs-up.

Across the street, the officers led a balding, sweating man toward the plaza, hands cuffed behind him. Lun/Ellie murmured to Jeru, "That's Billy Bob, the church secretary, and he was driving the van and he was supposed to shoot her but I guess he saw the others get shot and he gave up and I always liked him the best of everybody so I'm glad he's not dead."

Jeru gaped at the man being put in the back of a police cruiser. "That harmless-looking guy was Gimbel's fail safe, his last resort in case everything else went wrong?"

Lun shrugged. "The Most Reverend was always complaining about good help being hard to find and usually he was looking at me when he said it but maybe he was talking about everybody in the church."

"Or maybe he thought his ace trumped any surprise I had, so what could go wrong?" Jeru glanced over to where Gimbel's body was being loaded onto a gurney. "Famous last words."

"I stopped his actual famous last words," Lun said, "and now I'm trapped in this girl's body and there's no more God's Boot Camp for me 'cause there's no more God's Boot Camp for anybody and—"

Despite the tingle he continued to feel hearing Ellie's voice, Jeru tuned out the boy's prattling as he caught sight of the real Ellipsis Stewart emerging from the garage. In the Cathy Eden body, she walked on unsteady legs between two officers, the sound of her screechy voice carrying across Peachtree Street and the Five Points plaza.

She caught sight of him, broke off in mid-sentence, and then called, "Dr. Rafe?"

He gave her the 1000-watt roguish smile and shouted, "I'm Jerusalem." Third time's a charm.

She whooped and hurried ahead of her escorts, her tears and the joy in her eyes conveying that she understood the sacrifices he had made to save her. "I knew you'd come," she said. Her arms slid around him, and she held him fiercely.

Jeru tilted her face up, kissing her softly at first and then with urgency. Her red wig shifted beneath his hands as they roamed over the prickly hairs emerging from her scalp. Breaking their kiss, he turned to Victoria. "This is Ellie," he said.

Mrs. Stewart took hold of Angus' furry mitt, confusion etching her usually smooth features. "Hmm?"

"Mom," Ellie screeched, "It's me."

Victoria gave Ellie a quick up and down. "Child, what have you been eating?"

Before Jeru could try to smooth the reunion, Captain Ingram stepped up. "All right, this is getting stranger by the minute. The driver in the van—"

Ellie said, "His name is Billy. Billy Bob. He's not a bad man. He hardly ever pointed his gun at me."

"Maybe not, but he's a nutcase. He's raving about body swapping and SysOps and I don't know what all."

"It's all true," Victoria said. "We need to get my daughter out of that—" she pointed at Ellie "—and back where she belongs." Her finger arced toward Lun. "Now!"

As Captain Ingram rubbed his haggard face, Jeru muttered, "This is going to be a long day."

CHAPTER THIRTY-NINE

Jeru was wrong. It was a long three days, with everyone sequestered in one of the HydraCon hotels. Conventioneers' deaths in the "Battle of Five Points," as the media dubbed it, had created some convenient, albeit tragic, vacancies.

Dr. Gomez joined them to provide additional corroboration and technical expertise. Lalla also made daily room calls to check up on Lun in Ellie's body and Ellie in Cathy's body. Doc insisted on physical examinations for Jeru/Rafael as well. Since he mostly hung out in Ellie/Cathy's room, he made sure Ellie stayed during the whole procedure, giving Doc only enough time with his body to satisfy her needs as his physician. Lalla's frustrations seemed to increase daily and exponentially. For her sake, he only used his roguish smile on Ellie.

Obvious thoughts of making love with both women occurred to him, but his fantasies had enough to keep up with whenever he saw Lun and Ellie together at mealtimes. He developed a major case of whiplash looking between sexpot Ellie with the young man trapped inside and the real Ellie in a body he'd come to love as well.

During his second evening in Ellie's room, he waited until their heart rates settled down before asking if she'd considered the possibility of inviting Lun to bed with them. "I wouldn't mind," he said. "I'll try anything once. With Lun, you could think of it as masturbation."

She barely let him get the last word out before exiling him to his room for the rest of the night.

Based on her response, he decided not to suggest a four-way that included Dr. Gomez. Besides, he needed to consider another possibility even more intimate in nature: the surprise in the back of the RSA van.

Billy Bob had explained Gimbel's escape plan in case there were witnesses to his murder of Jeru, forcing him to adopt a foolproof disguise to avoid law enforcement. Gimbel had made an appointment to see the only other steiner in the Southern US, a woman who worked in Richmond, Virginia. Gimbel had even negotiated a discounted fee, because the operation was BYOB: bring your other body. It turned out Dr. Torres had also saved—and Gimbel had stolen—Jeru's suped-up body in a cryogenic freezer, which plugged into the AC adapter in the van to stay cold. That final ace up Gimbel's sleeve, as far as Jeru was concerned, changed the whole game.

On their third evening in the hotel, Captain Ingram assembled Jeru and the others in a luxurious suite vacated by a Colorado oil shale baron and his mistress, who were among the first to be slaughtered by FALAFEL, dying together in a unicorn costume, mid-gallop. Jeru and Ellie sat on one king-size bed holding hands. On the other bed, Victoria and Angus lounged with an arm around each other's waist. Angus—all of five-foot-six, with hair the same shade as Victoria's minus the purple streaks—was an old-money Scotsman who had coped with his wife's death by taking up video games and live-action role-playing.

Seated at an oval table in the suite, Lun slouched in Ellie's body, knees spread wide, still not comfortable with his female form. At least he'd started to wear pants—everyone had gotten tired of reminding him that his panties were showing. On one side of him, Dr. Gomez played holographic, 3-D Berserk (*Tetris on crack*™) using the console built into the tabletop; her games ended quickly as she seemed unable to stop ogling her dead husband's body.

Captain Ingram paced from the table to the beds as he spoke. "After talking to the state and federal attorneys general, the FBI, Homeland Security, and a psychiatrist—that was for me, because of this nutty case—here's the way this is going to play out. Billy Bob has cooperated fully with the authorities, and, according to an agreement with the church lawyer, he'll be given immunity from prosecution provided he testifies and continues to make himself available as we need him."

Ingram addressed Lun at the table. "Your case is a little more complicated. I'd release you into the custody of your parents, but there's a hitch." He patted Lun/Ellie's shoulder, either in a show of sympathy or to look down her blouse. Probably both. "I'm sorry to tell you this," he went on, "but your parents have split, and we can't get either one of them to take you voluntarily. They both said you're old enough to make it on your own, and when I told them about your, uh, unusual situation, they both balked at the thought of raising a teenaged girl."

Betrayed by his pastor and his parents, Lun stared at the mismatched sneakers he'd strapped onto Ellie's delicate feet. He rolled and unrolled a golden curl from his wig around one index finger.

Across the room, Ellie/Cathy said, "Those jerks. We're easier to raise than boys, right, Mom?"

Victoria shrugged. "You and your brother both offered unique challenges, hmm? At least Istanbul stayed in his own body."

Ellie was about to protest, but Captain Ingram stepped in. "Please, we're talking about Lun."

Jeru cleared his throat. "I think I might have a solution. My original—well, *improved*—body is in the police evidence warehouse, hopefully with the freezer still plugged in. If you can get it released, Captain, I'd love to move back into it and finally grow hair long enough to comb." He rubbed his prickly scalp. "That frees up this body and starts a chain reaction. Lun could move in here so he can enjoy being a man again, and Ellie could return to her former self."

"After my upgrade," she insisted, bouncing with excitement.

Dr. Gomez shut down her game. After considering Jeru's idea for a minute, she said, "I think it would work, Captain. I can fly in some colleagues if Mrs. Stewart will agree to pay the expenses for the whole enterprise."

Victoria replied, "It's only money, hmm? What's that compared to love?" She hugged Angus. Jeru wondered if she made him wear the Mooma costume sometimes. He did notice it outside their room the day before, with dry-cleaning instructions pinned to the fur.

Captain Ingram said, "What happens to the Cathy Eden body?"

Dr. Gomez said, "Same as Lou Barone's. We send them to Organ Recycling."

"Or," Ellie said, "offer it to one of the conventioneers paralyzed during the Battle of Five Points. It's a good enough body, but I want to go home—after my upgrade."

Jeru could just imagine the surgery: bodies lined up on the tables, Dr. Gomez and the others juggling brains between them—hopefully with ownership labels attached—and then the confusion about which shaved lid went on which skull.

Captain Ingram asked Lun, "What do you think? You started out as a teenage boy, then you became a teenage girl, and now you would go into a full-grown man's body."

"I've had to grow up pretty fast over the last few months, and I'm sure not doing well in this body—no offense, Ellie—and, well, there is one advantage to getting Rafael's body." Ducking Ellie's head, ears reddening under the golden wig, Lun stole a peek at Dr. Gomez.

Lalla stroked Lun/Ellie's hand. "I've been counseling him about this situation he was forced into. He's a sweet and sensitive person. You might think it a bit sudden, but we've become very close over the last three days."

"Doc," Ellie said, "you haven't ... I mean ... with my body?"

"Good heavens, no. I'd resigned myself to waiting for another solution to present itself. If Lun moves into Rafael's body, I'm prepared to love him for who he is, and not as if my deceased husband has returned to me."

Jeru pointed to Lun and said, "I recommend her expedited recovery program."

"I just don't know, Lallana," Victoria said. "Taking up with an eighteen-year-old, a mere boy." She gave her Scotsman a squeeze. "You should find someone more age appropriate and worldly, hmm?"

"Aye," Angus added, "I've built a castle with a loch on Prince Edward

Island. There are plenty of fellows in search of a lovely, accomplished woman up there."

Dr. Gomez replied, "All men are boys. At least this one isn't set in his ways yet. If any attitude or behavior adjustments are necessary, I'll mold him like I molded Rafael's body."

Jeru said, "And you did a helluva job with that." He nudged Ellie, who'd been enjoying those benefits. "Right?"

"Oh, oink," she sneered, but glanced at his lap even as she said it.

Victoria merely shrugged and hugged Angus again. They were due to leave for that castle on PEI in a few weeks, after she sold her In-Town home. The island off the east coast of Canada didn't have the amenities of In-Town, and the castle only had a dozen servants—not a Handybot among them—but she'd confessed to Ellie and Jeru, "Roughing it is sexy."

Jeru hoped his body-swap proposal didn't delay Dr. Gomez's plans to move to Birmingham, Alabama, within the month. She planned to open a clinic named for her favorite Southern delicacy, Brains and Eggs, specializing in cerebral transfers, advanced fertility treatments, and In-Town-quality cosmetic surgery for the masses.

Perhaps Lun could assist her in the business; maybe he would even go to medical school. That was what Ellie hoped to do. She and Jeru had discussed finding a new In-Town home so she could pursue her college and MD degrees while he explored an idea born of his experience with Kliburn's holograms: true virtual reality. The wealthiest one percent had all the best toys—what he could show the In-Towners, though, was how to have fun with them.

Captain Ingram stepped away from the room to make a few quick calls and reported back to them, "I think I can get Jerusalem's body released. I'll never get used to how this sounds, but here goes: everyone can get a new body or their old body back."

Ellie insisted, "Or their original one with an *upgrade*." She looked around the room. "Have you all forgotten that my body over there turned eighteen almost two weeks ago? I want my butterfly, dammit."

Responding to the captain's question about this, Doc and Victoria provided graphic details and testimonials. Angus nodded happily, Jeru rolled his eyes, and Lun looked scared.

Ingram shook his head and said, "I gotta tell you, after this case closes, I won't mind going back to boring ol' suicide bombers and spree killings."

CHAPTER FORTY

Ellie planted her hands on Jeru's damp, thickly muscled chest and pushed herself upright, still astride him. Her eyes changed from copper to teal, and her freshly shaved head gleamed in the lamplight of their In-Town condo bedroom. Temporary quarters until they purchased a house. Sweat trickled down from her neck. He pushed her breasts together and trapped it.

Jeru flicked his thumbs across her nipples, making her shudder. Grinning—his own smile, not Rafael's—he did it again, loving the feel of her, loving that he could give her pleasure. Loving her.

"So, what do you think?" she asked, once she'd caught her breath. Too bad: feeling her chest heave was half the fun.

"I'm still not sure we did the right thing, going back into our original—"

"Upgraded."

"Yes, *upgraded* bodies. We first made love inside Lou and Cathy. Maybe we didn't truly fall for each other until that night." He shifted beneath her, feeling ready to go again. Lou never had it so good, and neither had Cathy. "If the craziness of the past few weeks has taught me anything, it's that we did better together as regular, OTP sort of people."

Ellie said, "That's crap." She wiped her chest with the bed sheet, knocking his hands off her bosom. "Going through all that horror is what made us learn to trust each other and fall in love. Our first time was in Lou and Cathy only because you were too dumb to romance me properly when you had all those chances earlier. Not that I could've done this to you." She rocked her pelvis against him, squeezing with the tempo of a drum solo and giving him a rippling massage from inside her and outside with those remarkable muscle upgrades. "So, what do you think?"

What he thought was, thank God for the premature ejaculation prohibitor Lalla had installed way back. But what he said was, "I think maybe you're right about how we fell in love."

"What's this?" She leaned forward until her chest grazed his own. Her mouth stayed just out of kissing range. "No snappy comeback? No wisecrack that'll land your ass on the couch?"

"Doc gave me some wonderful parting advice: 'Better to be silent and be thought a fool, than to speak and remove all doubt.' I'm trying to follow it whenever possible."

"That's very wise of you." She reached up and stroked the top of his shaved head. "Those smart chips I asked her to install during the transfer are working."

He reached for the top of his head automatically. Doc's joke about the hinges came back to him. Taking her fingers, he said, "You're kidding, right?"

"Maybe I am, maybe I'm not. You'll never know."

"Why are you teasing me?"

She said, "Because *you're* teasing *me*. You won't answer my question."

"I keep answering it."

"Maybe those chips don't work after all, you fosh. Now quit stalling. What do you think—of my butterfly?"

"Oh, that. It's okay."

" 'Okay'?" She seized his nipples and twisted them in opposite directions.

"Hey, quit it." He grabbed hers to retaliate but only tweaked them gently. "Don't you know the current slang? 'Okay' is the new 'totally blazing.' "

She leaned back, giving him a suspicious look, and then nodded. "The new slang. Got it."

Not wanting to ruin the mood, he said, "You ever hear of 'the butterfly effect'? You know, where the butterfly flaps its wings and halfway around the world a hurricane blows."

"Yeah, so?"

"You give me a Class 5 every time."

Ellie grinned down at him and bounced a couple of times, her eyes smoky. "Now that's what I call a good save," she said. As a reward, she gave him a series of long and short squeezes and flaps, a secret code he was eager to learn, even if it took the next hundred and fifty years. She asked, "Want to do it again? Take advantage of those upgrades you never got a chance to use?"

"Why not?" He could tell she didn't buy his nonchalance.

In short order, she proved how phony he was acting, and he showed her how much he really cared.

Making love with Ellie was like moving together toward light speed. The faster their climaxes approached, the slower the minutes seemed to pass, but when they finished, an entire hour had gone by. And he always felt younger than when they started.

This time, Jeru ended up on top. He gave her a long, loving kiss, which made him hard yet again. It was possible he wouldn't do anything else for the rest of his life. His old self wouldn't have minded, but now there was so much he wanted to experience with Ellie. Still, third time was the charm, right?

"So," he asked, grinding against her, "what do you think? How was *I*?"

She stroked the back of his head and pulled him close for another deep kiss. Speaking into his mouth and straight down to his heart, she said, "Okay."

Acknowledgements

My deepest gratitude first, foremost, and forever goes to my wife, critique partner, and co-publisher Kim Conrey for encouraging me to blow the virtual dust off this manuscript and finally put it out in the world, figuring I've done enough good for others that at least some of them will forgive me or do the polite Southern thing and pretend it never happened.

Thanks too to the critique groups who endured portions of the novel over the years and gave me great feedback whenever I dared to show them a bit of it. I'm reminding them here that it's too late to make the book better: put the red pen away.

Finally, I'd like to thank my readers who, if you made it this far, experienced what Monty Python dubbed "something completely different." It was good to get this out of my system, and I hope it provided a few laughs, chuckles, and snorts between the times when you were scandalized, dismayed, or otherwise offended.

About the Author

GJ Weinstein is the unimaginative pseudonym of an Atlanta area author who has delighted and inspired thousands of readers with his serious—some would say melodramatic—works of fiction and has helped innumerable writers on their publication journey through his efforts on behalf of an historic nonprofit that requested to have its name withheld here lest it be connected with this rather suspect piece of work.

Printed in the USA
CPSIA information can be obtained
at www.ICGtesting.com
LVHW040443130124
768900LV00013B/37